Praise for the Roy Grace Series

'One of the most fiendishly clever crime fiction plotters' *Daily Mail*

'Achingly well plotted, with suspense that has no let-up' *Booklist*

'This is the first in a new crime series which promises to be both fascinating and destined for the bestsellers' *Independent on Sunday*

'Peter James's superior thriller . . . gripping . . . nail-biting . . . a satisfyingly complex puzzle' *The Times*

'A terrific tale of greed, seduction and betrayal' *Daily Telegraph*

'Peter James is a very gifted writer and he kept me guessing with his relentless pacing and suspense. I would be reading what I thought was a lead in to the climax, only to notice I was only halfway through the book. This book is a gem' *Crimespree*

'At a time when more than ever we feel beholden to be seen with pretentious novels which, in the privacy of our own homes, we find hard to pick up, what a relief to finally find a book which it is well nigh literally impossible to put down' **Julie Burchill**

'With memorable characters and nail-biting tension, *Looking Good Dead* is a terrifying "it could happen to you" thriller' **Kathy Reichs**

'I couldn't put it down . . . even better than the first' *Independent*

'Full of gripping twists and turns' *Guardian*

'Will have you glued to your deckchair' *Observer*

'Hugely well paced, marvng ending' *Classic FM*

NOT DEAD ENOUGH

Peter James was educated at Charterhouse and then at film school. He lived in North America for a number of years, working as a screenwriter and film producer before returning to England. His novels, including the number one bestseller *Possession*, have been translated into thirty languages and three have been filmed. All his novels reflect his deep interest in the world of the police, with whom he does in-depth research, as well as science, medicine and the paranormal. He has produced numerous films, including *The Merchant of Venice*, starring Al Pacino, Jeremy Irons and Joseph Fiennes. He also co-created the hit Channel 4 series *Bedsitcom*, which was nominated for a Rose d'Or. He is currently, as co-producer, developing his Roy Grace novels for television with ITV Productions.

Peter James won the Krimi-Blitz 2005 Crime Writer of the Year award in Germany, and *Dead Simple* won both the 2006 Prix Polar International award and the 2007 Prix Cœur Noir award in France. *Looking Good Dead* was shortlisted for the 2007 Richard and Judy Crime Thriller of the Year award, and has been shortlisted for both France's SNCF and Le Grand Prix de Littérature award. *Not Dead Enough* was shortlisted for the Theakstons Old Peculier Crime Thriller of the Year award and the ITV3 Crime Thriller of the Year award. He divides his time between his homes in Notting Hill in London and near Brighton in Sussex.

www.peterjames.com

Also by Peter James

DEAD LETTER DROP

ATOM BOMB ANGEL

BILLIONAIRE

POSSESSION

DREAMER

SWEET HEART

TWILIGHT

PROPHECY

ALCHEMIST

HOST

THE TRUTH

DENIAL

FAITH

Children's novel

GETTING WIRED!

The Roy Grace series

DEAD SIMPLE

LOOKING GOOD DEAD

DEAD MAN'S FOOTSTEPS

DEAD TOMORROW

NOT DEAD ENOUGH

PETER JAMES

PAN BOOKS

First published 2007 by Macmillan

First published in paperback 2007 by Pan Books

This edition published 2012 by Pan Books
an imprint of Pan Macmillan, a division of Macmillan Publishers Limited
Pan Macmillan, 20 New Wharf Road, London N1 9RR
Basingstoke and Oxford
Associated companies throughout the world
www.panmacmillan.com

ISBN 978-1-4472-2650-5

Typeset by Intype Libra Ltd
Printed and bound by CPI Group (UK) Ltd, Croydon, CR0 4YY

Visit **www.panmacmillan.com** to read more about all our books
and to buy them. You will also find features, author interviews and
news of any author events, and you can sign up for e-newsletters
so that you're always first to hear about our new releases.

TO BERTIE, SOOTY AND PHOEBE

ACKNOWLEDGEMENTS

The world of Sussex Police is central to my Roy Grace series of novels, and I am indebted to the many officers and support staff there who make me so welcome and give me so much help. At the top of the list is Chief Constable Joe Edwards for his very kind sanction. Totally indispensable is my wise, good friend, retired Chief Superintendent Dave Gaylor, who has been my mentor within Sussex Police for many years, as well as my inspiration for the character of Roy Grace. He is my chief researcher, a font of creative ideas, and has the patience of a saint, helping me in so many ways on this novel, as on the previous ones. It would have been a considerably lesser book without him.

To single out a few other names in particular – and please forgive omissions – Chief Superintendent Kevin Moore has been incredibly supportive, and High Tech Crime Investigator Ray Packham of the High Tech Crime Unit and his wife, Jen, have been brilliantly helpful and inventive with their ideas. I've had a quite exceptional amount of help in understanding the current state of Brighton's lowlife – and the policing of it – from Constable Paul Grzegorzek of the Local Support Team. And also Sergeant Julian Clapp, who sent more than a few shivers through me when walking me through the custody process, and Inspector Mark Powles of the Sussex Police Force Identification Unit.

I want to thank Detective Inspector Roy Apps, Detective Inspector Paul Furnell, PC Matt Webster, Inspector Andy Parr, Sergeant Mark Baker, Chief Superintendent Peter Coll;

Acknowledgements

Sergeant Phil Taylor, Head of the High Tech Crime Unit, and John Shaw, formerly of the High Tech Crime Unit, now at Control Risks Group; Julie Page of the PNC; Detective Sergeant Keith Hallet of the Sussex Police Holmes Unit; Brian Cook, Scientific Support Branch Manager; Detective Inspector William Warner; Senior Scenes of Crime Investigator Stuart Leonard; Senior Analyst Suzy Straughan; DS Jason Tingley; Family Liaison Officers DC Amanda Stroud and DS Louise Pye; and a very special mention to Senior Support Officer Tony Case of the HQ Criminal Investigation Department, who has been incredibly generous with his time, help and enthusiasm.

Huge thanks are also due to my fantastic Munich team of helpers: Kriminalhauptkommissar Walter Dufter, Ludwig Waldinger and Detlef 'Ted' Puchelt of Bayerisches Landeskriminalamt, Franz-Joseph Wilfling, Kriminaloberrat at Kriminalpolizeidirektion 1 München; Andy and Sabine from Krimifestival München; Anette Lippert for all her hard work with the Munich geography for me; and, of course, the Greatest Living German Actor, Hans Jürgen Stockeri, for his enduring patience in driving me to every landmark in Munich at least ten times in search of locations for scenes.

I've had great help from Essex Coroner Dr Peter Dean, consultant pathologist Dr Nigel Kirkham and Home Office Pathologist Dr Vesna Djurovic. And from Dr Robert Dorion, Director of Forensic Dentistry at the Laboratoire de Sciences Judiciaires et de Médecine Légale, Montreal, and author of the definitive 'Bitemark Evidence'. And I owe a massive thanks to my wonderful friends at Brighton and Hove Mortuary, Elsie Sweetman, Victor Sinden and Sean Didcott, for their endless patience with me and their immense kindness and thoughtfulness.

Thanks also to Brian Ellis, Dr Andrew Davey, Dr Jonathan Pash, Tom Farrer, Pathology Technician, and Robert Frankis –

Acknowledgements

one of the few people to have caught me out on cars . . . And thanks to Peter Bailey for his encyclopedic knowledge of Brighton modern and past, and the railway network. And I really owe a very special thank you to Post Adoption Counsellor Chrissie Franklin, who helped me energetically and enthusiastically in so many ways in very difficult terrain.

Thanks as ever to Chris Webb, who keeps my computer working and my back-ups safe, and a massive thanks to my unofficial editors, Imogen Lloyd-Webber, Anna-Lisa Lindeblad and Sue Ansell, who read the manuscript in varying stages and provided me with invaluable input. And thanks also to the hard work of the team at Midas Public Relations, Tony Mulliken, Margot Veale and Amelia Rowland.

I count my blessings to be represented by my fabulous book agent, Carole Blake – and I'm honoured that I help to keep her in a few of her three gazillion pairs of designer shoes! – and my film agent, Julian Friedmann. And I consider it a very great privilege to be published by Macmillan. To single out a few names, thank you Richard Charkin, David North, Geoff Duffield, Anna Stockbridge, Vivienne Nelson, Marie Slocombe, Michelle Taylor, Caitriona Row, Claire Byrne, Ali Muirden, Richard Evans, Chloe Brighton, Liz Cowen, my copyeditor Lesley Levene, and last, but most important of all, Stef Bierwerth – you just keep on getting more and more wonderful! And across the Channel I have to say again a massive *Danke!* to the team at my German publishers, Scherz, for their incredible support. Especially Peter Lohmann, Julia Schade, Andrea Engen, Cordelia Borchardt, Bruno Back, Indra Heinz and the quite awesome Andrea Diederichs, the Greatest Living German Editor!

Thank you as ever to my faithful hounds Bertie, Sooty and Phoebe for reminding me that there is a life beyond my study door.

Acknowledgements

And the penultimate but biggest thank you to my darling Helen – for believing that I could do it and never letting me consider there was any other option.

And lastly, once more, a very special thank you to all you readers of my books. Thank you for all your mail and all your kind words. They mean so much to me.

Peter James
Sussex, England
scary@pavilion.co.uk
www.peterjames.com

NOT DEAD ENOUGH

1

Darkness took a long time to arrive, but it was worth the wait. And besides, time was not a problem for him. Time, he had come to realize, was one of the things you have plenty of in life when you have little else. He was time-rich. Near on a time billionaire.

Shortly before midnight, the woman he was following turned off the dual carriageway and drove into the lonely glow of a BP filling-station forecourt. He halted his stolen van in the unlit slip road, fixating on her brake lights. They seemed to be getting brighter as he watched them. Glowing red for danger, red for luck, red for sex! *Seventy-one percent of murder victims were killed by someone they knew.* The statistic was whizzing round and round inside his head, like a pinball looking for a slot. He collected statistics, squirrelled them carefully away, like nuts, to sustain him through that long hibernation of the mind that he knew, one day, would come to him.

The question was, *How many of those 71 percent knew they were about to be murdered?*

Do you, lady?

Headlights of vehicles flashed past, the slipstream of a lorry rocking the little blue Renault, making some of the plumbing implements behind him rattle. There were just two other cars standing by the pumps, a Toyota people-carrier that was about to drive off and a large Jaguar. Its owner, a plump man in an ill-fitting tuxedo, was heading back from the pay window, cramming his wallet into his jacket. A BP tanker was parked up, the driver in a boiler suit uncoiling a long hose, getting ready to refuel the filling-station tanks.

So far as he could ascertain in a careful sweep, there was just one CCTV camera scanning the forecourt. A problem, but he could deal with it.

She really could not have picked a better place to stop! He blew her a silent kiss.

2

In the warm summer-night air, Katie Bishop tossed her untidy flame-red hair away from her face and yawned, feeling tired. Actually, beyond tired. Exhausted – but very, very nicely exhausted, thank you! She studied the petrol pump as if it was some extraterrestrial creature put on Planet Earth to intimidate her, which was how she felt about most petrol pumps. Her husband always had problems figuring out the instructions on the dishwasher and the washing machine, claiming they were written in some alien language called 'Woman'. Well, so far as she was concerned, petrol pumps came with an equally alien language, the instructions on them were written in 'Bloke'.

She struggled, as usual, to get the filler cap off her BMW, then stared at the words *Premium* and *Super*, trying to remember which one the car took, although it seemed to her she could never get it right. If she put in premium, Brian criticized her for putting in petrol that was too low-grade; if she filled up with super, he got annoyed with her for wasting money. But at this moment, nothing was going in at all. She held the nozzle in one hand, squeezing the trigger hard, and waved with the other, trying to attract the attention of the dozy night attendant behind the counter.

Brian irritated her increasingly. She was tired of the way he fussed about all kinds of stupid little things – like the position of his toothpaste on the bathroom shelf, and making sure all the chairs around the kitchen table were exactly the same distance apart. Talking inches, not feet.

And he was becoming increasingly kinky, regularly bringing home carrier bags from sex shops filled with weird stuff that he insisted they try out. And that was really causing her problems.

She was so wrapped up in her thoughts, she didn't even notice the pump jigging away until it stopped with an abrupt *kerlunk*. Breathing in the smell of petrol fumes, which she had always quite liked, she hung the nozzle of the pump back up, clicked the key fob to lock the car – Brian had warned her cars often got stolen on petrol station forecourts – and went to the booth to pay.

As she came out, she carefully folded her credit card receipt and tucked it into her purse. She unlocked the car, climbed in, then locked it from the inside, pulled on her seat belt and started the engine. The *Il Divo* CD started playing again. She thought for a moment about lowering the BMW's roof, then decided against. It was past midnight; she would be vulnerable driving into Brighton at this hour with an open top. Better to stay enclosed and secure.

It was not until she had driven off the forecourt and was a good hundred yards down the dark slip road that she noticed something smelled different in the car. A scent that she knew well. *Comme des Garçons*. Then she saw something move in her mirror.

And she realized someone was inside her car.

Fear caught the inside of her throat like a fish hook; her hands froze on the wheel. She jammed her foot down hard on the brake pedal, screeching the car to a halt, scrabbling with her hand on the gear lever to find reverse, to back up to the safety of the forecourt. Then she felt the cold, sharp metal digging into her neck.

'Just keep driving, Katie,' he said. 'You really haven't been a very good girl, have you?'

Straining to see him in her rear-view mirror, she saw a sliver of light shear off the blade of the knife, like a spark.

And in that rear-view mirror he saw, reflected, the terror in her eyes.

3

Marlon did what he always did, which was to swim around and around his glass bowl, circumnavigating his world with the tireless determination of an explorer heading into yet another uncharted continent. His jaws opened and closed, mostly on water, just occasionally gulping down one of the microscopic pellets which, Roy Grace presumed from the amount they cost, were the goldfish equivalent of dinner at Gordon Ramsay's.

Grace lay slouched in his recliner armchair in the living room of his home, which had been decorated by his long-vanished wife, Sandy, in black and white Zen minimalism, and which until recently had been filled with memorabilia of her. Now there were just a few funky 1950s pieces they had bought together – the one taking pride of place was a juke box they'd had restored – and just one photograph of her, in a silver frame, taken twelve years ago on holiday in Capri, her pretty, tanned face grinning her cheeky grin. She was standing against craggy rocks, with her long blonde hair flailing in the wind, bathed in sunlight, like the goddess she had been to him.

He gulped down some Glenfiddich on the rocks, his eyes rooted to the television screen, watching an old movie on DVD. It was one of the ten thousand his mate Glenn Branson *just so totally* could not believe that he had never seen.

And recently it hadn't been a question of Branson's one-upmanship getting the better of his competitive nature.

Grace was on a mission to learn, to educate himself, to fill that vast cultural black hole inside his head. He had slowly come to the realization, during the past month, that his brain was a repository for pages and pages of police training manuals, rugby, football, motor-racing and cricketing facts, and not much else. And that needed to change. Quickly.

Because at long last he was dating – going out with – in lust with – totally smitten by – maybe even in love with – someone again. And he could not believe his luck. But she was a lot better educated than he was. It seemed at times that she'd read every book that had ever been written, seen every movie, been to every opera and was intellectually acquainted with the work of every artist of note, living or dead. And as if that wasn't enough, she was halfway through an Open University course in philosophy.

Which explained the pile of philosophy books on the coffee table beside his chair. Most of them he had recently bought from City Books in Western Road, and the rest from a trawl of just about every other bookshop in the whole of Brighton and Hove.

Two supposedly accessible titles, *The Consolations of Philosophy* and *Zeno and the Tortoise*, were on the top of the pile. Books for the layman, which he could just about understand. Well, parts of them, anyhow. They gave him enough at least to bluff his way through discussions with Cleo about some of the stuff she was on about. And, quite surprisingly, he was finding himself genuinely interested. Socrates, in particular, he could connect with. A loner, ultimately sentenced to death for his thoughts and his teachings, who once said, 'The unexamined life is not worth living.'

And last week she had taken him to Glyndebourne, to

see Mozart's *Marriage of Figaro*. Some parts of the opera had dragged for him, but there had been moments of such intense beauty, in both the music and the spectacle, that he was moved almost to tears.

He was gripped by this black and white movie he was watching now, set in immediate post-war Vienna. In the current scene, Orson Welles, playing a black-marketeer called Harry Lime, was riding with Joseph Cotten in a gondola on a Ferris wheel in an amusement park. Cotten was chastising his old friend, Harry, for becoming corrupt. Welles retaliated, saying, 'In Italy for thirty years under the Borgias they had warfare, terror, murder, bloodshed – but they produced Michelangelo, Leonardo da Vinci and the Renaissance. In Switzerland, they had brotherly love; they had five hundred years of democracy and peace, and what did that produce? The cuckoo clock.'

Grace took another long swig of his whisky. Welles was playing a sympathetic character, but Grace had no sympathy for him. The man was a villain, and in the twenty years of his career to date, Grace had never met a villain who didn't try to justify what he had done. In their warped minds, it was the world that was skewed wrong, not them.

He yawned, then rattled the ice cubes in his empty glass, thinking about tomorrow, Friday, and dinner with Cleo. He hadn't seen her since last Friday – she had been away for the weekend, for a big family reunion in Surrey. It was her parents' thirty-fifth wedding anniversary, and he had felt a small pang of discomfort that she hadn't invited him to go with her – as if she were keeping her distance, signalling that although they were dating, and making love, they weren't actually an *item*. Then on Monday she'd gone away on a training course. Although they'd spoken every day, and texted and emailed each other, he was missing her like crazy.

And tomorrow he had a meeting with his unpredictable boss, the alternately sweet and sour Alison Vosper, Assistant Chief Constable of Sussex Police. Dog-tired suddenly, he was in the process of debating whether to pour himself another whisky and watch the rest of the movie or save it for his next night in when the doorbell rang.

Who the hell was visiting him at midnight?

The bell rang again. Followed by a sharp rapping sound. Then more rapping.

Puzzled and wary, he froze the DVD, stood up, a little unsteadily, and walked out into the hall. More rapping, insistent. Then the bell rang again.

Grace lived in a quiet, almost suburban neighbourhood, a street of semi-detached houses that went down to the Hove seafront. It was off the beaten track for the druggies and the general nocturnal flotsam of Brighton and Hove, but all the same, his guard was up.

Over the years he had crossed swords with – and pissed off – plenty of miscreants in this city because of his career. Most were just plain lowlife, but some were powerful players. Any number of people could find good reason to settle a score with him. Yet he'd never bothered to install a spy hole or a safety chain on his front door.

So, relying on his wits, somewhat addled by too much whisky, he yanked the door wide open. And found himself staring at the man he loved most in the world, Detective Sergeant Glenn Branson, six foot two inches tall, black, and bald as a meteorite. But instead of his usual cheery grin, the DS stood all crumpled up and was blubbing his eyes out.

4

The blade pressed harder against her neck. Cutting in. Hurting more and more with every bump in the road surface.

'Don't even think about whatever it is you are thinking about doing,' he said, in a voice that was calm and filled with good humour.

Blood trickled down her neck; or maybe it was perspiration, or both. She didn't know. She was trying, desperately trying, through her terror, to think calmly. She opened her mouth to speak, watching the oncoming headlights, gripping the wheel of her BMW with slippery hands, but the blade just cut in deeper still.

They were cresting a hill, the lights of Brighton and Hove to her left.

'Move into the left-hand lane. Take the second exit at the roundabout.'

Katie obediently turned off, into the wide, two-lane Dyke Road Avenue. The orange glow of street lighting. Large houses on either side. She knew where they were heading and she knew she had to do something before they got there. And suddenly, her heart flipped with joy. On the other side of the road was a starburst of blue flashing lights. A police car! Pulling up in front of another car.

Her left hand moved from the wheel on to the flasher stalk. She pulled it towards her, hard. And the wipers screeched across the dry windscreen.

Shit.

'Why have you put the wipers on, Katie? It isn't raining.'
She heard his voice from the back seat.

Oh shit, oh shit, oh shit. Wrong fucking stalk!

And now they were past the police car. She saw the
lights, like some vanishing oasis, in her mirrors. And she
saw the silhouette of his bearded face, shadowed by his
baseball cap and further obscured by dark glasses although
it was night. The face of a stranger but at the same time a
face – and a voice – that were uncomfortably familiar.

'Left turn coming up, Katie. You should slow down. You
know where we are, I hope.'

The sensor on the dash would automatically trigger the
switch on the gates. In a few seconds they would start to
open. In a few seconds she would turn into them, and then
they would close behind her, and she would be in darkness,
in private, out of sight of everyone but the man behind her.

No. She had to stop that from happening.

She could swerve the car, smash into a lamp post. Or
smash into the headlights of a car that was coming towards
them now. She tensed even more. Looked at the speedometer. Trying to work it out. If she braked hard, or smashed
into something, he would be flung forward, the knife would
be flung forward. That was the smart thing to do. Not *smart*.
It was the only option.

Oh, Jesus, help me.

Something colder than ice churned in her stomach. Her
mouth felt arid. Then, suddenly, her mobile phone, on the
seat beside her, began to ring. The stupid tune her step-
daughter, Carly, who was just thirteen, had programmed in
and left her stuck with. The bloody 'Chicken Song', which
embarrassed the hell out of her every time it rang.

'Don't even think about answering it, Katie,' he said.

She didn't. Instead, meekly, she turned left, through the

wrought-iron gates that had obligingly swung open, and up the short, dark tarmac driveway that was lined by huge, immaculately tended rhododendron bushes that Brian had bought, for an insane price, from an architectural garden centre. For privacy, he had said.

Yep. Right. Privacy.

The front of the house loomed in her headlights. When she had left, just a few hours earlier, it had been her home. Now, at this moment, it felt like something quite different. It felt like some alien, hostile edifice that was screaming at her to leave.

But the gates were closing behind her.

5

Roy Grace stared at Glenn Branson for some moments in shock. Usually sharply dressed, tonight the Detective Sergeant was wearing a blue beanie, a hooded grey track-suit top over a sweatshirt, baggy trousers and trainers, and had several days' growth of stubble on his face. Instead of the normal tang of his latest, macho cologne-of-the-month, he reeked of stale sweat. He looked more like a mugger than a cop.

Before Grace had a chance to say anything, the DS threw his arms around him, clutching him tightly, pressing his wet cheek against his friend's face. 'Roy, she's thrown me out! Oh, God, man, she's thrown me out!'

Somehow, Grace manhandled him into the house, into the living room and on to the sofa. Sitting beside him and putting an arm around his massive shoulders, he said lamely, 'Ari?'

'She's thrown me out.'

'*Thrown you out?* What do you mean?'

Glenn Branson leaned forward, elbows on the glass coffee table, and buried his face in his hands. 'I can't take this. Roy, you've got to help me. I can't take this.'

'Let me get you something. Whisky? Glass of wine? Coffee?'

'I want Ari. I want Sammy. I want Remi.' Then he lapsed into more deep, gulping sobs.

For a moment, Grace stared at his goldfish. He watched Marlon drifting, taking a rare break from his globetrotting, mouth opening and shutting vacantly. He found his own mouth opening and shutting also. Then he got up, went out of the room, cracked open a bottle of Courvoisier that had been gathering dust in the cupboard under the stairs for years, poured some into a tumbler and thrust it into Glenn's meaty hands. 'Drink some of that,' he said.

The DS cradled the glass, peering into it in silence for some moments, as if searching for some message he was supposed to find written on the surface. Finally he took a small sip, followed immediately by a large gulp, then set the glass down, keeping his eyes gloomily fixed on it.

'Talk to me,' Grace said, staring at the motionless black and white image of Orson Welles and Joseph Cotten on the screen. 'Tell me – tell me what's happened?'

Branson looked up and stared at the screen too. Then he mumbled, 'It's about loyalty, yeah? Friendship. Love. Betrayal.'

'What do you mean?'

'That movie,' he rambled. '*The Third Man.* Carol Reed directed. The music. The zither. Gets me every time. Orson Welles peaked early, couldn't ever repeat his early success, that was his tragedy. Poor bastard. Made some of the greatest movies of all times. But what do most people remember him for? The fat man who did the sherry commercials.'

'I'm not totally on your bus,' Grace said.

'Domecq, I think it was. Domecq sherry. Maybe. Who cares?' Glenn picked up his glass and drained it. 'I'm driving. Screw that.'

Grace waited patiently; there was no way he was letting Glenn drive anywhere. He'd never seen his friend in a state like this.

Glenn held the glass up, almost without realizing.

'You want some more?'

Staring back down at the table, the DS replied, 'Whatever.'

Grace poured him four fingers. Just over two months ago, Glenn had been shot during a raid which Grace had organized – and which Grace had felt guilty as hell about ever since. The .38 bullet that hit the DS had, miraculously, done relatively little damage. Half an inch to the right and it would have been a very different story.

Entering his abdomen low down beneath his ribcage, the low-velocity, round-nose bullet managed to just miss the spinal cord, the aorta, the inferior vena cava and ureters. It nicked part of his loops of bowel, which had needed to be surgically resected, and caused soft-tissue damage, mostly to his fat and muscle, which had also required surgery. He had been allowed home, after ten days in hospital, for a lengthy convalescence.

At some point during every single day or night in the following two months, Grace had replayed the events of that raid. Over and over and over. Despite all the planning and precautions, it had gone badly wrong. None of his superiors had criticized him over it, but in his heart Grace felt guilty because a man under his command had been shot. And the fact that Branson was his best friend made it worse for him.

What made it even worse still was that earlier, in the same operation, another of his officers, an extremely bright young DC called Emma-Jane Boutwood, had been badly injured by a van she was trying to stop, and was still in hospital.

One quotation from a philosopher he had come across recently had given him some solace, and had taken up permanent residence in his mind. It was from Søren

Kierkegaard, who wrote, 'Life must be lived forward, but it can only be understood backwards.'

'Ari,' Glenn said suddenly. 'Jesus. I don't get it.'

Grace knew that his friend had been having marital problems. It went with the territory. Police officers worked insane, irregular hours. Unless you were married to someone also in the force, who would understand, you were likely to have problems. Virtually every copper did, at some point. Maybe Sandy did too, and she never discussed it. Maybe that was why she had vanished. Had she simply had enough one day, upped sticks and left? It was just one of the many possibilities of what had happened to her that July night. On his thirtieth birthday.

Nine years ago, last Wednesday.

The Detective Sergeant drank some more brandy and then coughed violently. When he had finished he looked at Grace with large, baleful eyes. 'What am I going to do?'

'Tell me what's happened?'

'Ari's had enough, like, that's what's happened.'

'Enough of what?'

'Me. Our life. I don't know. I just don't know,' he said, staring ahead. 'She's been doing all these self-improvement courses. I told you she keeps buying me these books, *Men Are from Mars, Women Are from Venus*, yeah? *Why Women Can't Read Maps and Men Can't Find Stuff in Fridges*, or some crap like that. Right? Well, she's been getting angrier and angrier that I keep coming home late and she misses her courses cos she's stuck with the kids. Right?'

Grace got up and poured himself another whisky, then found himself, suddenly, craving a cigarette. 'But I thought she'd encouraged you to join the police in the first place?'

'Yeah. And that's now one of the things pissing her off, the hours. You go figure a woman's mind out.'

'You're smart, ambitious, making great progress. Does she understand that? Does she know what a high opinion your superiors have of you?'

'I don't think she gives a shit about any of that stuff.'

'Get a grip, man! Glenn, you were working as a security guard in the daytime, and three nights a week as a bouncer. Where the hell were you heading? You told me that when your son was born you had some kind of an epiphany. That you didn't want him having to tell his mates at school that his dad was a nightclub bouncer. That you wanted a career he would be proud of. Right?'

Branson stared lamely into his glass, which was suddenly empty again. 'Yeah.'

'I don't understand—'

'Join the club.'

Seeing that the drink was at least calming the man down, Grace took Branson's glass, poured in a couple more fingers and returned it to his hands. He was thinking about his own experience as a beat copper, when he had done his share of *domestics*. All police hated getting called to domestic 'situations'. It mostly meant turning up to a house where a couple were fighting hammer and tongs, usually one – or both – drunk, and the next thing you knew you were getting punched in the face or whacked with a chair for your troubles. But the training for these had given Grace some rudimentary knowledge of domestic law.

'Have you ever been violent to Ari?'

'You're joking. Never. *Never*. No way,' Glenn said emphatically.

Grace believed him; he did not think it was in Branson's nature to be violent to anyone he loved. Inside that hulk was the sweetest, kindest, most gentle man. 'You have a mortgage?'

'Yeah, me and Ari jointly.'

Branson put down his glass and started crying again. After some minutes, faltering, he said, 'Jesus. I'm wishing that bullet hadn't missed everything. I wish it had taken my fucking heart out.'

'Don't say that.'

'It's true. It's how I feel. I can't fucking win. She was mad at me when I was working twenty-four/seven cos I was never home, now she's fed up cos I've been at home for the past seven weeks. Says I'm getting under her feet.'

Grace thought for a moment. 'It's your house. It's your home as much as Ari's. She might be pissed off with you, but she can't actually throw you out. You have rights.'

'Yeah, and you've met Ari.'

Grace had. She was a very attractive, very strong-willed lady in her late twenties who had always made it abundantly clear who was boss in the Branson household. Glenn might have worn the trousers, but his face poked out through the fly buttons.

*

It was almost five in the morning when Grace pulled some sheets and a blanket out of the airing cupboard and made up the spare bed for his friend. The whisky bottle and the brandy bottle were both nearly empty, and there were several crumpled cigarette butts in the ashtray. He had almost stopped smoking completely – after recently being shown, in the mortuary, the blackened lungs of a man who had been a heavy smoker – but long drinking sessions like this clobbered his willpower.

It seemed it was only minutes later that his mobile phone was ringing. Then he looked at the digital clock beside his bed and saw, to his shock, that it was ten past nine.

Knowing almost certainly the call was from work, he let it ring a few times, trying to wake up properly so he didn't sound groggy, his head feeling like it had a cheese-wire sawing through it. He was the duty Senior Investigating Officer for this week and really should have been in the office by eight thirty, to be prepared for any major incident that might occur. Finally he pressed the answer button.

'Roy Grace,' he said.

It was a very serious-sounding young civilian dispatcher from the Control Room called Jim Walters, whom Grace had spoken to a few times but did not know. 'Detective Superintendent, I've a request from a Brighton Central detective sergeant for you to attend a suspicious death at a house in Dyke Road Avenue, Hove.'

'What details can you give me?' Grace asked, now fully alert and reaching for his BlackBerry.

As soon as he had hung up, he pulled on his dressing gown, filled his toothbrush mug with water, took two paracetamols from the bathroom cabinet, downed them, then popped another two from their foil, padded into the spare room, which reeked of alcohol and body odour, and shook Glenn Branson awake. 'Wakey-wakey, it's your therapist from hell!'

One of Branson's eyes opened, part-way, like a whelk in the safety of its shell. 'Whatthefucksupman?' Then he put his hands to his head. 'Shit, how much did I drink last night? My head is like—'

Grace held up the mug and the capsules. 'Brought you breakfast in bed. You now have two minutes to shower, get dressed, swallow these and grab a bite from the kitchen. We're going to work.'

'Forget it. I'm on sick leave. Got another week!'

'Not any more. Your therapist's orders. No more sickies! You need to get back to work now, today, *this instant*. We're going to see a dead body.'

Slowly, as if every movement was painful, Branson swung himself out of bed. Grace could see the round, discoloured mark on his six-pack, some inches above his belly button, where the bullet had entered. It seemed so tiny. Less than half an inch across. Terrifyingly tiny.

The DS took the pills, washing them down with the water, then stood up and tottered around in his boxer shorts for some moments, looking very disoriented, scratching his balls. 'Shit, man, I got nothing here, just these stinky clothes. I can't go see a body dressed in these.'

'The body won't mind,' Grace assured him.

6

Skunk's phone was ringing and vibrating. *Preeep-preeep-bnnnzzzz-preeep-preeep-bnnnzzzz*. It was flashing, slithering around on the sink-top, where he had left it, like some large, crazed, wounded beetle.

After thirty seconds it succeeded in waking him. He sat up sharply and, as he did most mornings, hit his head on the low Luton roof of his clapped-out camper van.

'Shit.'

The phone fell off the sink-top and thudded on to the narrow strip of carpeted floor, where it continued its fuck-awful noise. He'd taken it last night from a car he'd stolen, and the owner had not been thoughtful enough to leave the instruction manual with it, or the pin code. Skunk had been so wired he hadn't been able to figure how to put it on silent, and hadn't risked switching it off because he might need a pin code to switch it back on. He had calls to make before its owner realized it was missing and had it disconnected. Including one to his brother, Mick, who was living in Sydney, Australia, with his wife and kids. But Mick hadn't been pleased to hear from him, told him it was four in the morning and hung up on him.

After one more round of shrieking and buzzing, the thing fell silent: spent. It was a cool phone, with a gleaming stainless-steel case, one of the latest-generation Motorolas. Retail price in the shops without any special deal would be around three hundred pounds. With luck, and probably after a bit of an argument, he'd get twenty-five quid for it later this morning.

He was shaking, he realized. And that black, undefined gloom was seeping through his veins, spreading to every cell in his body, as he lay on top of the sheets in his singlet and underpants, sweating one moment, then shivering. It was the same every morning, waking to the sensation that the world was a hostile cave that was about to collapse on him, entombing him. Forever.

A scorpion walked across his eyes.

'FUCKSHITGETOFF!' He sat up, whacked his head again and cried out in pain. It wasn't a scorpion; it wasn't anything. Just his mind jerking around with him. The way it was telling him now that maggots were eating his body. Thousands of them crawling over his skin, so tight together they were like a costume. 'GERROFFFF!' He squirmed, shook them off, swore at them again, even louder, then realized, like the scorpion, there was nothing there. Just his mind. Telling him something. Same way it did every day. Telling him he needed some brown – or some white. Oh, Jesus, anything.

Telling him he needed to get out of this stench of feet, rank clothes and sour milk. Had to get up, go to his office. Bethany liked that, the way he called it his *office*. She thought that was funny. She had a strange laugh, which kind of twisted her tiny mouth in on itself, so that the ring through her upper lip disappeared for a moment. And he could never tell whether she was laughing with him or at him.

But she cared for him. That much he could sense. He'd never known that feeling before. He'd seen characters talk about caring for each other in soaps on television, but had never known what it meant until he'd met her – picked her up – in the Escape-2 one Friday night some weeks – or maybe months – back.

Cared for him, in the sense that she looked in from time to time as if he was her favourite doll. She brought food, cleaned the place up, washed his clothes, dressed the sores he sometimes got and had clumsy sex with him before hurrying off again, into the day or the night.

He fumbled on the shelf behind his twice-bashed head, stretched out his thin arm, with a rope tattoo coiled all the way along it, and found the cigarette pack and the plastic lighter, and the tinfoil ashtray, lying beside the blade of his flick-knife, which he always kept open, at the ready.

The ashtray spilled several butts and a trail of ash as he swung it across and down on to the floor. Then he shook out a Camel, lit it, lay back against the lumpy pillow with the cigarette still in his mouth, dragged, inhaled deeply, then blew the smoke out slowly through his nostrils. Sweet, such an incredible, sweet taste! For a moment the gloom faded. He felt his heart beating stronger. Energy. He was coming alive.

It sounded busy out there in his *office*. A siren came and went. A bus rumbled past, roughing up the air all around it. Someone hooted impatiently. A motorbike blatted. He reached out for the remote, found it, stabbed it a few times until he hit the right button, and the television came on. That black girl, Trisha, he quite fancied, was interviewing a sobbing woman whose husband had just told her he was gay. The light below the screen said ten thirty-six.

Early. No one would be up. None of his *associates* would be in the *office* yet.

Another siren went past. The cigarette started him coughing. He crawled off his bed, made his way carefully over the sleeping body of a Scouse git, whose name he couldn't remember, who had come back here with his mate some time during the night, smoked some stuff and drunk a bottle of vodka one of them had nicked from an off-licence. Hopefully they'd fuck off when they woke up and discovered there was no food, drugs or booze left here.

He pulled open the fridge door and removed the only thing in it, a half-full bottle of warm Coca-Cola – the fridge hadn't worked for as long as he'd had this van. There was a faint hiss as he unscrewed the top; the liquid tasted good. Magic.

Then he leaned over the kitchen sink, piled with plates that needed washing and cartons that needed chucking – when Bethany next came – and parted the orange speckled curtains. Bright sunlight hit him in the face like a hostile laser beam. He could feel it burning the backs of his retinas. Torching them.

The light woke up Al, his hamster. Even though one paw was in a splint, it did a sort of jump-hop into its treadmill and began running. Skunk peered in through the bars to check the creature had enough water and food pellets. It looked fine. Later he'd empty the droppings out of the cage. It was about the only housework he ever did.

Then he jerked the curtains back together. Drank some more Coke, picked the ashtray up off the floor and took a last drag on the cigarette, right down to the filter, then stubbed it out. He coughed again, that long racking cough he'd had for days. Maybe even weeks. Then, feeling giddy suddenly, holding on carefully to the sink, and then the edge of the wide dining-area seat, he made his way back to his bunk bed. Lay down. Let the sounds of the day swirl all around him. They were his sounds, his rhythms, the pulse and voices of his city. The place where he had been born and where, no doubt, would one day die.

This city that didn't need him. This city of shops with stuff he could never afford, of arts and cultural stuff that were beyond him, of boats, of golf, of estate agents, lawyers, travel shops, day trippers, conference delegates, police. He saw everything as potential pickings for his survival. It didn't matter to him who the people were, it never had. *Them* and *me*.

Them had possessions. Possessions meant cash.

And cash meant surviving another twenty-four hours.

Twenty quid from the phone would go on a bag of brown or white – heroin or crack, whatever was available. The other fiver, if he got it, would go towards food, drink, fags. And he would supplement that with whatever he could steal today.

7

It was promising to be that rarest of things, a sublime English summer's day. Even high up on the Downs, there was not a hint of a breeze. At ten forty-five in the morning, the sun had already burned most of the dew off the swanky greens and fairways of the North Brighton Golf Club, leaving the ground dry and hard and the air heady with the scent of freshly mown grass, and money. The heat was so intense you could almost scrape it off your skin.

Expensive metal gleamed in the car park, and the only sounds, other than the intermittent *parp-parp-parp* of a rogue car alarm, were the hum of insects, the snick of titanium against dimpled polymer, the whirr of electric trolleys, the rapidly silenced ring tones of mobile phones and the occasional stifled cuss of a golfer who had hit a totally crap shot.

The views from up here made you feel you were almost standing on top of the world. To the south was the whole vista of the City of Brighton and Hove, the rooftops, the cluster of high-rises around the Brighton end of the seafront, the single chimney stack of Shoreham power station and the normally grey water of the English Channel beyond, looking as blue as the Med today.

Further to the south-west, you could make out the silhouette of the genteel seaside town of Worthing, fading away, like many of its elderly residents, into the long-distance haze. To the north stretched a view virtually unbroken, apart from a few pylons, of green Downland grass and fields of wheat. Some were freshly harvested, with square or cylindrical bales laid out like pieces in a vast board game; others were being criss-crossed at this moment by combine harvesters, looking as small as Dinky toys from here.

But most of the members out on the golf course this morning had seen all these views so often, they barely noticed them any more. The players comprised a mixture of the elite of Brighton and Hove's professionals and business people (and those who liked to imagine they were a part of the elite), a fair showing of ladies for whom golf had become the fulcrum of their world and a large number of retired people, mostly rather lost-looking men who seemed to all but live here.

Bishop, on the ninth, perspiring like everyone else, focused his mind on the gleaming white Titleist he had just planted on the tee. He flexed his knees, swung his hips and tightened his grip on the handle of his driver, preparing for his practice swing. He only ever allowed himself one practice, it was a discipline; he believed in following disciplines. Tuning out the drone of a bumblebee, he glared at a ladybird which suddenly alighted on the ground right in front of him. As if settling in for the duration, it retracted its wings, closing its back-flaps after them.

There was something about ladybirds his mother had once told him that he was trying to recall. Some superstition about them bringing luck, or money, not that he was into superstition – no more than anyone else, at any rate. Conscious of his three partners waiting to drive off after him, and that the players behind them were already on the green, he knelt, picked the orange and black creature up gently with his gloved hand and tossed it to safety. Then he resumed his stance and his focus, ignored his shadow falling directly in front of him, ignored the bumblebee that was still hovering around somewhere and took his practice swing. *Thwackkkk*. 'Yup!' he exclaimed to himself.

Despite the fact that he had arrived at the clubhouse dog-tired this morning, he had been playing a blinder. Three under par on the first eight holes and neither his partner, nor his two opponents, could quite believe their eyes. OK, he was a reasonable-standard club player, with a handicap that had remained resolutely at eighteen for many years, but it seemed to them this morning he had swallowed some kind of a happy pill that had transformed both his normally intensely serious mood, and his golf. Instead of walking around with them moody and silent, immersed in his own inner world, he had cracked a couple of jokes and even slapped them on the back. It was as if some private demon that he normally carried in his soul had been banished. For this morning, at least.

All he needed to do was to stay out of trouble on this hole, to finish the first nine in great shape. There was a long cluster of trees over to the right, filled with dense under-growth capable of swallowing a ball without trace. Plenty of open terrain to the left. Always safest to aim a little left on this hole. But today he felt so confident he was just going to shoot dead straight for the green. He stepped up to the ball, swung his Big Bertha and did it again. With the sweetest possible *snick*, the ball soared forward, dead straight, arcing through the cloudless, cobalt sky, and finally rolled to a halt just yards short of the green.

His close friend Glenn Mishon, whose mane of long brown hair made him look more like an ageing rock star than Brighton's most successful estate agent, grinned at him, shaking his head. 'Whatever you're on, matey, I want some!' he said.

Brian stepped aside, slotting his club back into his bag, and watched his partner line up for his shot. One of their opponents, a diminutive Irish dentist wearing plus fours and a tam-o'-shanter, was taking a swig from a leather hip flask – which he kept offering round, even though it was only ten fifty in the morning. The other, Ian Steel, a good player whom he had known for some years, wore expensive-looking Bermuda shorts and a Hilton Head Island embossed polo shirt.

None of their drives was a patch on his own.

Grabbing his trolley, he strode ahead, keeping his distance from the others, determined to maintain his concentration and not be distracted by small talk. If he could finish the first nine with just a chip and a single putt he would be an incredible four under. He *could* do it! He was that damn close to the green!

A tad over six foot tall, Bishop was a fit forty-one-year-old, with a lean, coldly handsome face beneath neat, slicked-back brown hair. People often remarked on his resemblance to the actor Clive Owen, which was fine by him. He rather liked that; it fed his not inconsiderable ego. Always correctly – if flashily – dressed for every occasion, this morning he was attired in a blue, open-throat Armani polo shirt, tartan trousers, impeccably polished two-tone golfing shoes and wrap-around Dolce & Gabbana sunglasses.

Ordinarily he would not have been able to spare the time to play golf on a weekday, but since recently being elected to the committee of this prestigious club – and with ambitions to become captain – it had been important for him to be seen participating in all the club's events. The captaincy itself did not really mean a lot to him. It was the perceived kudos of the title he was after. The North

Brighton was a good place for making local contacts and several of the investors in his business were members here. Equally – or perhaps even more importantly – it was about keeping Katie happy, by helping to further her local social ambitions – something she pushed for relentlessly.

It was as if Katie kept lists inside her head that she had obtained from some kind of *social mountaineering* hand-book. Items that needed ticking off one after another. *Join golf club*, tick, *get on committee*, tick, *join Rotary*, tick, *become president of Rotary branch*, tick, *get on NSPCC committee*, tick, *Rocking Horse Appeal*, tick. And recently she had started a new list, planning a good decade ahead, telling him they should be cultivating the people who could one day get him elected High Sheriff or Lord Lieutenant of East or West Sussex.

He stopped a courteous distance behind the first of the four balls on the fairway, noticing with some smugness just how far in front of the others his own ball was. Now that he was closer he could see just how good his drive had been. It was lagged up less than ten feet from the green.

'Great shot,' said the Irishman, proffering the flask.

He waved it away. 'Thanks, Matt. Too early for me.'

'You know what Frank Sinatra said?' the Irishman responded.

Distracted suddenly by the sight of the club secretary, a dapper former army officer, standing outside the club-house with two men, and pointing in their direction, Bishop said, 'No – what?'

'He said, "I feel sorry for people who don't drink, because when they wake up in the morning, that's as good as their day's going to get."'

'Never been a Sinatra fan,' Bishop commented, keeping

a weather eye on the three men who were very definitely striding over towards them. 'Frivolous schmaltz.'

'You don't have to be a Sinatra fan to enjoy drinking!'

Ignoring the hip flask, which the Irishman now offered him for the second time, he concentrated on the big decision of which club to take. The elegant way to go was his pitching wedge, then, hopefully, just a short putt. But years of hard experience at this game had taught him that when you were up, you should play the percentages. And on this arid August surface, a well-judged putt, even though he was off the green, would be a much safer bet. The immaculate green looked as if it had been shaved by a barber with a cutthroat razor rather than mown. It was like the baize of a billiards table. And all the greens were lethally fast this morning.

He watched the club secretary, in a blue blazer and grey flannels, stop on the far side of the green and point towards him. The two men flanking him, one a tall, bald black man in a sharp brown suit, the other an equally tall but very thin white man in an ill-fitting blue suit, nodded. They stood motionless, watching. He wondered who they were.

The Irishman bunkered with a loud curse. Ian Steel went next, hitting a perfectly judged nine iron, his ball rolling to a halt inches from the pin. Bishop's partner, Glenn Mishon, struck his ball too high and it dropped a good twenty feet short of the green.

Bishop toyed with his putter, then decided he should put on a classier performance for the secretary, dropped it back in his bag and took out his pitching wedge.

He lined himself up, his tall gaunt shadow falling across the ball, took a practice swing, stepped forward and played his shot. The club head struck the ground too early, taking a huge divot out, and he watched in dismay as his ball sliced, at an almost perfect right angle to where he was standing, into a bunker.

Shit.

In a shower of sand, he punched the ball out of the bunker, but it landed a good thirty feet from the pin. He managed a great putt that rolled the ball to less than three feet from the hole, and sank it for one over par.

They marked each other's scorecards; he was still a creditable two under par for the front nine. But inwardly he cursed. If he had taken the safer option he could have finished a shattering four under.

Then, as he tugged his trolley around the edge of the green the tall, bald black man stepped into his path.

'Mr Bishop?' The voice was firm, deep and confident.

He halted, irritated. 'Yes?'

The next thing he saw was a police warrant card.

'I'm Detective Sergeant Branson of the Sussex CID. This is my colleague, DC Nicholl. Would it be possible to have a word with you?'

As if a massive shadow had fallen across the sky, he asked, 'What about?'

'I'm sorry, sir,' the officer said, with what seemed a genuinely apologetic expression. 'I'd rather not say – out here.'

Bishop glanced at his three fellow players. Stepping closer to Detective Sergeant Branson, keeping his voice low in the hope he could not be overheard, he said, 'This is really not a good time – I'm halfway through a golf tournament. Could it wait until I've finished?'

'I'm sorry, sir,' Branson insisted. 'It's very important.'

The club secretary gave him a short, unreadable glance and then appeared to find something of intense interest to him in the relatively shaggy grass in which he was standing.

'What is this about?' Bishop asked.

'We need to speak to you about your wife, sir. I'm afraid we have some rather bad news for you. I'd appreciate it if you could step into the clubhouse with us for a few minutes.'

'My wife?'

The DS pointed towards the clubhouse. 'We really need to speak in private, sir.'

8

Sophie Harrington did a quick mental count of the dead bodies. There were seven on this page. She flipped back. Eleven, four pages ago. Add those to four in a car bomb on page one, three blown away by a burst of Uzi fire on page nine, six on a private jet on page nineteen, fifty-two in a fire-bombed crack den in Willesden on page twenty-eight. And now these seven, drug runners on a hijacked yacht in the Caribbean. Eighty-three so far, and she was only on page forty-one of a 136-page screenplay.

Talk about a pile of poo!

Yet, according to the producer who had emailed it two days ago, Anthony Hopkins, Matt Damon and Laura Linney were attached, Keira Knightley was reading it, and the director Simon West, who had made *Lara Croft*, which she had thought was OK, and *Con Air*, which she had really liked, was, apparently, gagging to make it.

Yeah, sure.

The tube train was pulling into a station. The spaced Rastafarian opposite her, earphones plugged in, continued to knock his raggedly clad knees together in time with his jigging head. Beside him sat an elderly, wispy-haired man, asleep, his mouth gaping open. And beside him a young, pretty Asian girl reading a magazine with intense concentration.

At the far end of the carriage, sitting beneath a swinging grab-handle and an advertisement for an employment agency, was a creepy-looking shell-suited jerk in a hoodie and dark glasses, long-haired with a beard, face buried in one of those free newspapers they give out in the rush hour at tube station entrances, occasionally sucking the back of his right hand.

It had been Sophie's habit, for some time now, to check out all the passengers for what she imagined the profile of a suicide bomber to be. It had become one more of her survival checks and balances, like looking both ways before crossing a road, that were part of the automatic routine of her life. And at this moment her routine was in slight disarray.

She was late because she'd had to run an errand before coming into town. It was ten thirty and ordinarily she would have been in the office an hour ago. She saw the words *Green Park* sliding past; the advertisements on the wall turn from a blur into images and clear print. The doors hissed open. She turned back to the script, the second of two which she had intended to finish reading last night before she had been interrupted – but wow, what an interruption! God – even just thinking about it was making her dangerously horny!

She flipped the page, trying to concentrate, in the hot, stuffy carriage, in the few minutes she had left before the next stop, Piccadilly, her destination. When she got to the office she would have to type a script report.

The story so far . . . Squillionaire daddy, distraught after beautiful twenty-year-old daughter – and only child – dies from a heroin overdose, hires former mercenary turned hit man. Hit man is given unlimited budget to track down and kill every person in the chain, from the man who planted the poppy seed to the dealer who sold the fatal fix to his daughter.

The logline: *Death Wish* meets *Traffic*.

And now they were pulling into Piccadilly. Sophie crammed the script, with its classy bright red cover, into her rucksack, between her laptop, a copy of the chick-lit book, *Alphabet Weekends*, which she was halfway through, and a copy of the August edition of *Harpers & Queen*. It wasn't her kind of magazine, but her beloved – her *fella*, as she discreetly referred to him to everyone but her two closest friends – was some years older than her, and a lot more sophisticated, so she tried to keep up to speed with the latest in fashion, in food, in pretty well everything, so that she could be the smart, hip girl-about-town that suited his planet-sized ego.

A few minutes later she was striding in the clammy heat down the shady side of Wardour Street. Someone had once told her Wardour Street was the only street in the world that was shady on both sides – a reference to its being the home of both the music and the film industries. Not entirely untrue, she always felt.

Twenty-seven years old, long brown hair swinging around her neck and an attractive face with a pert snub nose, she wasn't beautiful in any classic adman's sense, but there was something very sexy about her. She was dressed in a lightweight khaki jacket over a cream T-shirt, baggy grungy jeans and trainers, and was looking forward, as always, to her day in the office. Although today she felt a pang of longing for her fella, not sure quite when she would see him next, and an even deeper pang of jealousy that tonight he would be at his home, sleeping in a bed with his wife.

She knew the relationship wasn't going anywhere, just could not see him giving up all that he had for her – even though he had ended a previous marriage, one from which he had two children. But that did not stop her adoring him. She just couldn't bloody help that.

She totally adored him. Every inch of him. Everything about him. Even the clandestine nature of their relationship. She loved the way he looked furtively around when they entered a restaurant, months before they had actually started sleeping together, in case he spotted someone who knew him. The texts. The emails. The way he smelled. His humour. The way he had started, recently, to arrive unexpectedly in the middle of the night. Like last night. Always coming to her little flat in Brighton, which she thought was strange as he had a flat in London, where he lived alone during the week.

Oh shit, she thought, reaching the door to the office. *Oh shit, oh shit, oh shit.*

She stopped and tapped out a text:

> *Missing you! Totally adore you! Feeling*
> *dangerously horny! XXXX*

She unlocked the door and was halfway up the narrow staircase when there were two sharp beeps on her phone. She stopped and looked at the incoming text.

To her disappointment it was from her best friend, Holly:

> *RU free 4 party 2morrow nite?*

No, she thought. I don't want to go to a party tomorrow night. Nor any night. I just want—

What the hell do I want?

On the door in front of her was a logo: a symbol of lightning made in the image of celluloid. Beneath it the words, in shadowed letters, BLINDING LIGHT PRODUCTIONS.

Then she entered the small, hip office suite. It was all

Perspex furniture – Ghost chairs and tables, aquamarine carpets, and posters on the walls of movies the partners in the company had at some time been involved with. *The Merchant of Venice*, with the faces of Al Pacino and Jeremy Irons. An early Charlize Theron movie that had gone straight to video. A vampire movie with Dougray Scott and Saffron Burrows.

There was a small reception area with her desk and an orange sofa, leading through to an open-plan office where sat Adam, Head of Business and Legal Affairs, shaven-headed, freckled, hunched in front of his computer, dressed in one of the most horrible shirts she had ever seen – at least since the one he wore yesterday – and Cristian, the Finance Director, staring at a coloured graph on his screen in deep concentration. He was dressed in one of his seemingly bottomless collection of fabulously expensive-looking silk shirts, this one in cream, and rather snazzy suede loafers. The black frame of his collapsed fold-up bike sat next to him.

'Morning, guys!' she said.

For a response, she received a brief wave of the hand from each.

Sophie was the company's Head of Development. She was also the secretary, the tea-maker and, because the Polish cleaning lady was away having a baby, the office cleaner. And receptionist. And everything else.

'I've just read a really crap script,' she said. '*Hand of Death*. It's dross.'

Neither of them took any notice.

'Coffee, anyone? Tea?'

Now that did elicit an instant response. The usual for both of them. She went into the kitchenette, filled the kettle and plugged it in, checked the biscuit tin – which contained just a few crumbs, as usual. No matter how many times a day she filled it, the gannets emptied it. Tearing open a packet of chocolate digestives, she looked at her phone. No response.

She dialled his mobile.

Moments later he answered and her heart did a back-flip. It was so great just to hear his voice!

'Hi, it's me,' she said.

'Can't talk. Call you back.' Colder than stone.

The phone went dead.

It was as if she had just spoken to a total stranger. Not the man she had shared a bed with, and a whole lot more, just a few hours ago. She stared at her phone in shock, feeling a deep, undefined sense of dread.

*

Across the street from Sophie's office was a Starbucks. The shell-suited jerk in the hoodie and dark glasses who had been sitting at the far end of the tube train carriage was standing at the counter, the freebie newspaper rolled up under his arm, ordering a skinny latte. A large one. He was in no hurry. He put his right hand to his mouth and sucked on it to try to relieve the mild, tingling pain like a nettle sting.

As if on cue, a Louis Armstrong song began to play. Maybe it was playing inside his head, maybe inside this café. He wasn't sure. But it didn't matter, he heard it, Louis was playing it just for him. His own private, favourite tune. His mantra. 'We Have All the Time in the World'.

He hummed it as he collected his latte, picked up two biscotti, paid for them in cash and carried them over to a window seat. *We have all the time in the world,* he hummed again, to himself. And he did. Hell, the man who was near on a *time billionaire* had the whole damn day to kill, praise the Lord!

And he had a perfect view of the entrance to her office from here.

A black Ferrari drove along the road. A recent model, an F430 Spider. He stared at it unexcitedly as it halted in front of him, its path blocked by a taxi disgorging a passenger. Modern cars had never done it for him. Not in that way they did for so many people. Not in that *must-have* way. But he knew his way around them, all right. He knew all the models of just about every make of car on the planet, and carried most of their specifications and prices in his head. Another advantage of having plenty of time. Staring through the wheel spokes, he noticed this car had the Brembo brake upgrade, with 380mm ceramic discs with eight-pot callipers in front and four-pots at the rear. The weight saving was 20.5kg over steel.

The Ferrari passed from his line of vision. Sophie was up on the second floor, but he wasn't sure which window. Didn't matter; she was only ever going to go in and come out of this one door here, which he could see.

The song was still playing.

He hummed to himself happily.

9

The club secretary's office at the North Brighton Golf Club
had a military feel which reflected the secretary's own background, as a retired army major who had managed to
survive active service in the Falklands and Bosnia with his
important bits – and most important of all, his golf handicap – intact.

There was a polished mahogany desk, piled with several
orderly stacks of papers, as well as two small flags, one a
Union Jack, the other sporting the green, blue and white
logo of the club. On the walls were a number of framed
photographs, some in sepia, of golfers and golf holes, and a
collection of antique putters, crossed like duelling swords.

Bishop sat alone on a large leather sofa, staring up at
Detective Sergeant Glenn Branson and Detective Constable
Nick Nicholl in chairs facing him. Bishop, still wearing his
golfing clothes and studded shoes, was sweating profusely,
from the heat and from what he was hearing.

'Mr Bishop,' the tall, black Detective Sergeant said, 'I'm
sorry to have to tell you this, but your cleaning lady –' he
flipped back a couple of pages in his notepad – 'Mrs
Ayala, arrived at your house in Dyke Road Avenue, Hove,
at eight thirty this morning to discover that your wife,
Mrs Katherine Bishop –' He paused expectantly, as if for
confirmation that this was indeed her name.

Bishop stared blankly.

'Um – Mrs Bishop did not appear to be breathing. An
ambulance attended at eight fifty-two and the paramedics

reported there were no responses to any of their checks for signs of life. A police surgeon attended at nine thirty and certified your wife dead, I'm afraid to say, sir.'

Bishop opened his mouth, his face quivering; his eyes seemed momentarily to have become disconnected and rolled around, as if not seeing anything, not locking on anything. A faint croak escaped from his throat: 'No. Please tell me this isn't true. Please.' Then he slumped forward, cradling his face in his hands. 'No. No. I don't believe this! Please tell me it's not true!'

There was a long silence, punctuated only by his sobs.

'Please!' he said. 'It's not true, is it? Not Katie? Not my darling – my darling Katie . . .'

The two police officers sat, motionless, in deep discomfort. Glenn Branson, his head pounding from his mighty hangover, was privately cursing for allowing himself to be bullied back to work early by Roy Grace, and being dumped into this situation. It had become normal for family liaison officers, trained in bereavement counselling, to break this kind of news, but it wasn't the way his senior officer always operated. In a suspicious death, like this, Grace wanted either to do it himself or to have one of his close team members break the news and immediately observe the reactions. There would be time enough for the FLOs to do their job later.

Since waking up this morning at Roy's house, Glenn's day had been a nightmare. First he'd had to attend the scene of death. An attractive red-headed woman, in her thirties, naked in a bed, manacled with two neckties, a Second World War gas mask beside her, and a thin bruise line around her neck that could have been caused by a ligature. Probable cause of death was strangulation, but it was too early to tell. A sex game gone wrong, or murder? Only the

Home Office pathologist, who would be arriving at the scene about now, would be able to establish the cause of death for certain.

The sodding bastard Grace, whom he totally idolized – but sometimes was not sure why – had ordered him to go home and change, and then break the news to the husband. He could have refused, he was still off sick; and he probably would have refused if it had been any other police officer. But not Grace. And in some ways, at the time, he had been quite grateful for the distraction from his woes.

So he had gone home, accompanied by DC Nick Nicholl, who kept blathering on about his newborn baby and the joys of fatherhood, and found to his relief that Ari was out. So now, shaved, suited and booted, he found himself in this establishment golf clubhouse, breaking the news and watching Bishop's reactions like a hawk, trying to divorce emotion from the job he was here to do. Which was to assess the man.

It was a fact that around 70 percent of all murder victims in the UK were killed by someone they knew. And in this case, the husband was the first port of call.

'Can I go to the house and see her? My darling. My—'

'I'm afraid not to the house, sir, that's not possible until forensics have finished. Your wife will be taken to the mortuary – probably later this morning. You will be able to see her there. And we will need you to identify her body, I'm afraid, sir.'

Branson and Nicholl watched in silence as Bishop sat, cradling his face in his hands, rocking backward and forward on the sofa.

'Why can't I go to the house? To my home? *Our* home!' he suddenly blurted.

Branson looked at Nicholl, who was conveniently

staring out of the wide window at four golfers putting out the ninth. What the hell was the tactful way of saying this? Staring back hard at Bishop, watching his face, in particular his eyes, he said, 'We can't go into detail, but we are treating your house as a crime scene.'

'Crime scene?' Bishop looked bewildered.

'I'm afraid so, sir,' Branson said.

'What – what kind of a crime scene do you mean?'

Branson thought for some moments, really focusing his mind. There just wasn't any easy way to say this. 'There are some suspicious circumstances about your wife's death, sir.'

'Suspicious? What do you mean? What? In what way?'

'I'm afraid I can't say. We will have to wait for the pathologist's report.'

'Pathologist?' Bishop shook his head slowly. 'She's my wife. Katie. My wife. You can't tell me how she died? I'm – I'm her husband.' His face dropped back into his hands. 'She's been murdered? Is that what you are saying?'

'We can't go into detail, sir, not at this moment.'

'Yes, you can. You can go into detail. I'm her husband. I have a right to know.'

Branson stared back at him levelly. 'You will know, sir, as soon as we do. What we would appreciate is for you to come to our headquarters in order that we can talk to you about what has happened.'

Bishop raised his hands. 'I – I'm in the middle of a golf tournament. I . . .'

This time Branson made eye contact with his colleague and each clocked the other's raised eyebrows. It was an odd priority. But in fairness, when in shock people often said strange things. It wasn't necessarily worth reading anything into it. Besides, Branson was partially preoccupied with trying to remember how long it was since he had last swallowed any paracetamols. Whether it was safe to take a couple more now. Deciding it was OK, he surreptitiously dug his hand into his pocket, popped a couple of capsules from their foil wrapper and slung them into his mouth. Attempting to swallow them with just saliva, it felt as if they had lodged halfway down his throat.

'I've explained the situation to your friends, sir. They are carrying on.' He tried swallowing again.

Bishop shook his head. 'I've screwed up their chances. They'll be disqualified.'

'I'm sorry about that, sir.' He wanted to add, *Shit happens*. But tactfully, he left it at that.

10

Blinding Light were in pre-production on a horror movie they were going to be shooting in Malibu and Los Angeles. It was about a group of young, rich kids in a house party in Malibu who get eaten by hostile micro-organisms from outer space. In her original script report, Sophie Harrington had written, '*Alien* meets *The OC*.'

Ever since watching *The Wizard of Oz* as a child, she had wanted, in some way, however small her role, to be involved with movies. Now she was in her dream job, working with a bunch of guys who between them had made dozens of movies, some of which she had seen, either on a cinema screen or on video or DVD, and some, in development, which she was sure were destined for, if not Oscars, at least some degree of commercial success.

She handed a mug of coffee, milky, with two sugars to Adam and a mug of jasmine tea, neat, to Cristian, then sat down at her desk with her own mug of builder's tea (milk, two sugars), logged on and watched a whole bunch of emails invade her inbox.

All of them needed dealing with but – shit – there was only one priority. She pulled her mobile phone to her ear and dialled his number again.

It went straight to voicemail.

'Call me,' she said. 'As soon as you can. I'm really worried.'

An hour later, she tried again. Still voicemail.

There were even more emails now. Her tea sat on her

desk in reception, untouched. The script she had been reading on the tube was at the same page as when she had got off. So far this morning, she had achieved nothing. She had failed to get a lunch reservation at the Caprice for tomorrow for another one of her bosses, Luke Martin, and she had forgotten to tell Adam that his meeting this afternoon, with film accountant Harry Hicks, had been cancelled. In short, her whole day was a total mess.

Then her phone rang and it suddenly got a whole lot worse.

11

The woman had not yet started to smell, which indicated she hadn't been dead for very long. The air conditioning in the Bishops' bedroom helped, doing an effective job of keeping the corrosive August heat at bay.

The blowflies hadn't arrived yet either, but they wouldn't be long. Blowflies – or bluebottles, as they were more attractively named – could smell death from five miles away. About the same distance as newspaper reporters, of which species there was already one outside the gates, questioning the constable guarding the entrance and, from the reporter's body language, not getting much from him.

Roy Grace, garbed in a hooded white sterile paper suit, rubber gloves and overshoes, watched him for some moments from the front window of the room. Kevin Spinella, a sharp-faced man in his early twenties, dressed in a grey suit with a badly knotted tie, notebook in hand and chewing gum. Grace had met him before. He worked for the local paper, the *Argus*, and seemed to be developing an uncanny ability to reach a crime scene hours before any formal police statement was issued. And from the speed – and accuracy – with which serious crimes had been hitting the national media recently, Grace reckoned someone in the police – or the Control Centre – had to be leaking information to him. But that was the least of his problems.

He walked across the room, keeping to the taped line across the carpet laid down by the SOCO team, making one call after another on his mobile phone. He was organizing office and desk space in the Major Incident Suite for the team of detectives, typists and indexers he was putting together, as well as arranging a meeting with an intelligence officer to plan the intelligence strategy for his policy book for this investigation. Every minute was precious at the moment, in the *golden hour*. What you did in that first hour of arriving at the scene of a suspicious death could greatly affect your likelihood of a successful arrest.

And in this chilly room, pungent with the smell of classy perfume, the thought presenting itself to him between each of his calls was, *Is this death an accident? A night of kinky sex gone wrong?*

Or murder?

In almost every murder, the chances were that the perpetrator was in a much more ragged frame of mind than yourself. Roy Grace had met his share of killers over the years and not many were able to keep cool, calm and collected, not at any rate in the immediate aftermath. Most would be in what was termed a *red mist*. Their adrenaline out of control, their thinking confused, their actions – and whatever plan they might have had – all muzzed up by the fact that they simply had not reckoned on the chain reaction of chemicals inside their brains.

He had seen a television documentary recently about human evolution failing to keep pace with the way humans had evolved socially. When confronted by the income tax inspector, people needed to stay cool and calm. Instead, instinctive primitive fight-or-flight reactions kicked in – those same reactions as if you had been confronted out on the savannah by a sabre-toothed tiger. You would be hit by a massive adrenaline surge that made you all shaky and clammy.

Given time, that surge would eventually calm down. So your best chance of a result was to grab your villains while they were still in that heightened phase.

The bedroom ran the entire width of the house – a house he knew, without any envy, that he could never afford. And even if he could, which would only happen if he won the Lottery – unlikely, since most weeks he forgot to buy a ticket – he would not have bought this particular house. Maybe one of those mellow Georgian manors, with a lake and a few hundred rolling acres. Something with a bit of style, a bit of class. Yep. *Squire Grace*. He could see that. Somewhere in the wildest recesses of his mind.

But not this vulgar, faux-Tudor pile behind a forbidding whitewashed wall and electric wrought-iron gates, in Brighton and Hove's most ostentatious residential street, Dyke Road Avenue. No way. The only good thing about it, so far as he could see at this moment, was a rather beautifully restored white 3.8 Jaguar Mk II under a dustsheet in the garage, which showed that the Bishops had at least some taste, in his view.

The other two of the Bishops' cars in the driveway didn't impress him so much. One was a dark blue cabriolet BMW 3-series and the other a black Smart. Behind them, crammed into the circular, gravelled area in front of the house, was the square hulk of the mobile Major Incident Room vehicle, a marked police car and several other cars of members of the SOCO team. And shortly they would be joined by the yellow Saab convertible belonging to one of the Home Office pathologists, Nadiuska De Sancha, who was on her way.

On the far side of the room, to the left – and right – of the bed, the view from the windows was out over rooftops towards the sea, a mile or so away, and down on to a garden

of terraced lawns, in the centre of which, and more promi-
nent than the swimming pool beyond, was an ornamental
fountain topped with a replica of the Mannequin Pis, the
small, cherubic stone boy urinating away, and no doubt
floodlit in some garish colours at night, Grace thought, as
he made yet another call.

This one was to an old sweat of a detective, Norman
Potting – not a popular man among the team, but one Grace
had learned, from a previous successful investigation, was
a workhorse he could trust. Seconding Potting to the case,
he instructed him to coordinate the task of obtaining all
CCTV footage from surveillance cameras within a two-mile
radius of the murder scene, and on all routes in and out of
Brighton. Next, he organized a uniformed house-to-house
inquiry team for the immediate neighbourhood.

Then he turned his attention, once more, to the grim
sight on the canopied, king-sized, two-poster bed. The
motionless woman, arms splayed out, each strapped by a
man's necktie to one of the two posts, revealing freshly
shaven armpits. Apart from a thin, gold necklace, with a
tiny orange ladybird secured in a clasp, a gold wedding
band and an engagement ring with a massive rock of a diamond, she was naked, her attractive face framed by a tangle
of long, red hair, and a black rim around her eyes, probably
caused by the Second World War gas mask that lay beside
her, he surmised, thinking the words that had become a
mantra to him at murder investigations over the years.

What is the body at the scene telling you?

Her toes were short and stubby, with chipped pink
varnish. Her clothes were strewn on the floor, as if she had
undressed in a hurry. An ancient teddy bear lay in their
midst. Apart from an alabaster-white bikini line around her
pubic area, she was tanned all over, from either the current

hot English summer or an overseas holiday, or both. Just above the necklace, there was a crimson line around her neck, more than likely a ligature mark, indicating the probable cause of death, although Grace had learned, long ago, never to jump to conclusions.

And staring at the dead woman, he was struggling not to keep thinking about his missing wife, Sandy.

Could this be what happened to you, my darling?

At least the hysterical cleaning lady had been removed from the house. God alone knew how much she had already contaminated the crime scene, by ripping off the gas mask and running around like a headless chicken.

After he'd managed to calm her down, she'd provided him with some information. She knew that the dead woman's husband, Brian Bishop, spent most of the week in London. And that this morning he was playing in a golf tournament at his club, the North Brighton – a club far too expensive for most police officers to afford, not that Grace was a golfer anyway.

The SOCO team had arrived a while ago and were hard at work. One officer was on his hands and knees on the carpet, searching for fibres; one was dusting the walls and every surface for fingerprints; and their forensic scene manager, Joe Tindall, was carrying out a room-to-room survey.

Tindall, who had recently been promoted from Scene of Crime Officer to Scientific Support Officer, which gave him responsibility for the management of several different crime scenes simultaneously if the need arose, appeared now out of the en-suite bathroom. He had recently left his wife for a much younger girl and had had a complete makeover. Grace never ceased to be amazed at the man's transformation.

Only a few months ago, Tindall had resembled a mad scientist, with a paunch, wiry hair and bottle-lensed glasses. He now sported a completely shaven head, a six-pack, a quarter-inch-wide vertical strip of beard running from the centre of his lower lip down to the centre of his chin, and hip rectangular glasses with blue-tinted lenses. Grace, who was going out with a woman again for the first time in many years, had recently tried to sharpen up his own image. But, a tad enviously, he realized he was nowhere close to the cooler-than-thou Tindall.

Every few moments the dead woman was suddenly, vividly, illuminated for a millisecond by the flash of a camera. The photographer, an irrepressibly cheerful silver-haired man in his late forties called Derek Gavin, used to have a portrait studio in Hove, before the world of home digital photography had dented his profits enough to make him pack it in. He joked, darkly, that he preferred crime-scene work, because he never had to worry about making corpses sit still or smile.

The best news of the morning, so far, was that Grace's favourite Home Office pathologist had been assigned to this case. Spanish-born, of Russian aristocratic descent, Nadiuska De Sancha was fun, irreverent at times, but brilliant at her work.

He stepped carefully around the body of the woman, and there were moments when he felt the marks of the ligature around his own neck, then inside his gut. Everything inside him tightened. What goddamn sadist had done this? His eyes dropped to the tiny stain on the white sheet just below her vagina. Where semen had leaked out?

Christ.

Sandy.

It was always a problem for him, whenever a young

woman died. He wished desperately that someone else had been on duty today.

There was a phone on one of the gilded, reproduction Louis XIV bedside tables. Grace nearly picked it up, old habits dying hard. Under new *Best Practice* guidelines, police officers had recently been reminded that the best way to secure potential evidence from phones was for them to be recovered and forensically examined by an expert, rather than the old method of dialling 1471. He called out to a scene of crime officer in the next room and reminded him to ensure all the phones were collected up.

Then he did what he always liked to do at a potential crime scene, which was to wander around the area, immersed in his thoughts. His eye was caught, momentarily, by a striking modern painting on the wall. He peered at the artist's name, Helen Steele, wondering if she was famous, and realizing again how little he knew about the art world. Then he went into the vast, en-suite bathroom and opened the glass door of a shower big enough to live in. He clocked the soap, the gels hanging on hooks, the shampoos. The mirrored cabinet door was open and he checked out the pills. Thinking all the time about the cleaning lady's words.

Missa Bishop no here wik time. No here lass night. I know no here lass night, I have to make supper Missy Bishop. She jus salad. When Missa Bishop here, he like meat or fish. I make big food.

So if Brian Bishop wasn't here last night, having kinky sex with his wife, who was?

And if he killed her – why?

An accident?

The ligature mark shouted a very distinctive 'No.'

As did his instinct.

12

ARTHUR JAMES

Like many of the products of the early post-war building boom, Sussex House, a sleek, rectangular, two-storey building, was not ageing particularly well. The original architect had clearly been influenced by the Art Deco period and the place looked from some angles like the superstructure of a small, tired cruise liner.

Originally constructed in the early 1950s as a hospital for contagious diseases, at that time it had occupied a commanding, isolated position on a hill on the outskirts of Brighton, just beyond the suburb of Hollingbury, and the architect could no doubt have seen his vision in its full, stand-alone glory. But the ensuing years had not been kind. As the urban sprawl encroached, the area around the building became designated as an industrial estate. For reasons no one today was clear about, the hospital closed down and the building was bought by a firm that manufactured cash registers. Some years later it was sold to a freezer company, which subsequently sold it to American Express, which in turn, in the mid-1990s, sold it to the Sussex Police Authority.

Refurbished and modernized, it was opened in a blaze of publicity as the flagship, high-tech headquarters for Sussex CID, positioning the county's force at the very cutting edge of modern British policing. More recently it had been decided to move the custody centre and cell block out there also, so these were built on and annexed to the building. Now, despite the fact that Sussex House was bursting at the seams, some of the uniformed divisions were also being moved here. And with just ninety parking spaces for a workforce that had expanded to 430 people, not everyone found the place lived up to its original promise.

The Witness Interview Suite was a rather grand name for two small boxrooms, Glenn Branson thought. The smaller, which contained nothing but a monitor and a couple of chairs, was used for observation. The larger, in which he was now seated with DC Nick Nicholl and the very distressed Brian Bishop, had been decorated in a manner designed to put witnesses, and potential suspects, at their ease – despite two wall-mounted cameras pointing straight down at them.

It was brightly lit, with a hard, grey carpet and cream walls, a large south-facing window giving partial views of Brighton and Hove across the slab-like roof of an ASDA supermarket, three bucket-shaped chairs upholstered in cherry-red fabric, and a rather characterless coffee table with black legs and a fake pine top, which looked like it might have been the last item to go in a Conran shop sale.

The room smelled new, as if the carpet had just been laid minutes before and the paint on the walls was still drying, yet it had smelled like this for as long as Branson could remember. He had only been in here a few minutes and was perspiring already, as were DC Nicholl and Brian Bishop. That was the problem with this building: the air conditioning was crap and half the windows did not open.

Announcing the date and time, Branson activated the wall switch for the recording apparatus. He explained that this was standard procedure to Bishop, who responded with an acquiescent nod.

The man appeared totally wretched. Dressed in an expensive-looking tan jacket with silver buttons, pulled on untidily over his blue, open-throat Armani polo shirt, sun-glasses sticking out of his top pocket, he sat all hunched up, broken. Away from the golf course, his tartan trousers and two-tone golfing shoes seemed a little ridiculous.

Branson couldn't help feeling sorry for him. And try as he might, the DS could not get the image of Clive Owen in the movie *Croupier* out of his mind. In other circumstances he might have asked Bishop if they were related. And although it had no bearing on the task he was here to carry out, he could also not help wondering why golf clubs, which always seemed to him to have ludicrously formal and out-dated dress codes, such as wearing ties in clubhouses, allowed their members to go out on the course looking like they were starring in a pantomime.

'May I ask when you last saw your wife, Mr Bishop?'

He clocked the hesitation before the man answered.

'Sunday evening, about eight o'clock.' Bishop's voice was suave, but deadpan, and totally classless, as if he had worked on it to lose whatever accent he might once have had. Impossible to tell whether he came from a privileged background or was self-made. The man's dark red Bentley, which was still parked at his golf club, was the kind of flash motor Branson associated more with footballers than class.

The door opened and Eleanor Hodgson, Roy Grace's prim, nervy, fifty-something Management Support Assist-ant, came in with a round tray containing three mugs of coffee and a cup of water. Bishop drained the water before she had left the room.

'You hadn't seen your wife since Sunday?' Branson said, with an element of surprise in his voice.

'No. I spend the weeks in London, at my flat. I go up to town Sunday evenings and normally come back Friday night.' Bishop peered at his coffee and then stirred it carefully, with laboured precision, with the plastic stick Eleanor Hodgson had provided.

'So you would only see each other at weekends?'

'Depends if we had anything on in London. Katie would come up sometimes, for a dinner, or shopping. Or whatever.'

'Whatever?'

'Theatre. Friends. Clients. She – liked coming up – but . . .'

There was a long silence.

Branson waited for him to go on, glancing at Nicholl but getting nothing from the younger detective. 'But?' he prompted.

'She had her social life down here. Bridge, golf, her charity work.'

'Which charity?'

'She's involved – was – with several. The NSPCC mainly. One or two others. A local battered-wives charity. Katie was a giver. A good person.' Brian Bishop closed his eyes and buried his face in his hands. 'Shit. Oh, Christ. What's happened? Please tell me?'

'Do you have children, sir?' Nick Nicholl asked suddenly.

'Not together. I have two by my first marriage. My son, Max, is fifteen. And my daughter, Carly – she's thirteen. Max is with a friend in the south of France. Carly's staying with cousins in Canada.'

'Is there anyone we need to contact for you?' Nicholl continued.

Looking bewildered, Bishop shook his head.

'We will be assigning you a family liaison officer to help you with everything. I'm afraid you won't be able to return to your home for a few days. Is there anyone you could stay with?'

'I have my flat in London.'

'We're going to need to talk to you again. It would be more convenient if you could stay down in the Brighton and Hove area for the next few days. Perhaps with some friends, or in a hotel?'

'What about my clothes? I need my stuff – my things – wash kit . . .'

'If you tell the family liaison officer what you need it will be brought to you.'

'Please tell me what's happened?'

'How long have you been married, Mr Bishop?'

'Five years – we had our anniversary in April.'

'Would you describe your marriage as happy?'

Bishop leaned back and shook his head. 'What the hell is this? Why are you interrogating me?'

'We're not interrogating you, sir. Just asking you a few background questions. Trying to understand a little more about you and your family. This can often really help in an investigation – it's standard procedure, sir.'

'I think I've told you enough. I want to see my – my darling. I want to see Katie. Please.'

The door opened and Bishop saw a man dressed in a crumpled blue suit, white shirt and blue and white striped tie come in. He was about five foot ten tall, pleasant-looking, with alert blue eyes, fair hair cropped short to little more than a fuzz, badly shaven, and a nose that had seen better days. He held out a strong, weathered hand, with well-trimmed nails, towards Bishop. 'Detective Superintendent Grace,' he said. 'I'm the Senior Investigating Officer for this – situation. I'm extremely sorry, Mr Bishop.'

Bishop gave him a clammy grip back with long, bony

fingers, one of which sported a crested signet ring. 'Please tell me what's happened.'

Roy Grace glanced at Branson, then at Nicholl. He had been watching for the past few minutes from the observation room, but was not about to reveal this. 'Were you playing golf this morning, sir?'

Bishop's eyes flicked, briefly, to the left. 'Yes. Yes, I was.'

'Can I ask when you last played?'

Bishop looked thrown by the question. Grace, watching like a hawk, saw his eyes flick right, then left, then very definitely left again. 'Last Sunday.'

Now Grace would be able to get a handle on whether Bishop was lying or telling the truth. Watching eyes was an effective technique he had learned from his interest in neuro-linguistic programming. All people have two sides to their brains, one part that contains memory, the other that works the imagination – the creative side – and lying. The *construct* side. The sides on which these were located varied with each individual. To establish that, you asked a control question to which the person was unlikely to respond with a lie, such as the seemingly innocent question he had just asked Bishop. So in future, when he asked the man a question, if his eyes went to the left, he would be telling the truth, but if they went to the right, to the construct side, it would be an indicator that he was lying.

'Where did you sleep last night, Mr Bishop?'

His eyes staring resolutely ahead, giving nothing away intentionally, or unintentionally, Bishop said, 'In my flat in London.'

'Could anyone vouch for that?'

Looking agitated, Bishop's eyes shot to the left. To memory. 'The concierge, Oliver, I suppose.'

'When did you see him?'

'Yesterday evening, about seven o'clock – when I came back from the office. And then again this morning.'

'What time were you on the tee at the golf club this morning?'

'Just after nine.'

'And you drove down from London?'

'Yes.'

'What time would that have been?'

'About half-six. Oliver helped me load my stuff into the car – my golf sticks.'

Grace thought for a moment. 'Can anyone vouch for where you were between seven o'clock yesterday and half past six this morning?'

Bishop's eyes shot back to the left, to memory mode, which indicated he was telling the truth. 'I had dinner with my financial adviser at a restaurant in Piccadilly.'

'And did your concierge see you leave and come back?'

'No. He's not usually around much after seven – until the morning.'

'What time did your dinner finish?'

'About half past ten. What is this, a witch hunt?'

'No, sir. I'm sorry if I'm sounding a bit pedantic, but if we can eliminate you it will help us focus our inquiries. Would you mind telling me what happened after your dinner?'

'I went to my flat and crashed out.'

Grace nodded.

Bishop, staring hard at him, then at Branson and Nick Nicholl in turn, frowned. 'What? You think I drove to Brighton at midnight?'

'It does seem a little unlikely, sir,' Grace assured him. 'Can you give us the phone numbers of your concierge and your financial adviser? And the name of the restaurant?'

Bishop obliged. Branson wrote them down.

'Could I also have the number of your mobile phone, sir? And we need some recent photographs of your wife,' Grace requested.

'Yes, of course.'

Then Grace said, 'Would you mind answering a very personal question, Mr Bishop? You are not under any obligation but it would help us.'

The man shrugged helplessly.

'Did you and your wife indulge in any unusual sexual practices?'

Bishop stood up abruptly. 'What the hell is this? My wife has been murdered! I want to know what's happened, Detective – Super – Super whatever you said your name was.'

'Detective Superintendent Grace.'

'Why can't you answer a simple question, Detective Superintendent Grace? Is it too much for anyone to answer one simple question?' Getting increasingly hysterical, Bishop continued, his voice rising, 'Is it? You're telling me my wife died – are you now telling me I killed her? Is that what you're trying to say?'

The man's eyes were all over the place. Grace would need to let him settle. He stared down at him. Stared at the man's ridiculous trousers, and at the shoes which reminded him of spats worn by 1930s gangsters. Grief affected everyone in a different way. He'd had enough damn experience of that in his career, and in his private life.

The fact that the man lived in a vulgar house and drove a flash car did not make him a killer. It did not even make him a less than totally honourable citizen. He had to dump all prejudices out of his mind. It was perfectly possible for a man to live in a house worth north of a couple of million and still be a thoroughly decent, law-abiding human being. Even if he did have a bedside cabinet full of sex toys and a book on sexual fetishes in his office, that didn't necessarily mean he had jammed a gas mask over his wife's face, then strangled her.

But it didn't necessarily mean he hadn't, either.

'I'm afraid the questions are necessary, sir. We wouldn't ask them if they weren't. I realize it's very difficult for you and you want to know what's happened. I can assure you we'll explain everything in due course. Please just bear with us for the time being. I really do understand how you must be feeling.'

'You do? Really, Detective Superintendent? Do you have any idea what it is like to be told your wife is dead?'

Grace nearly replied, *Yes, actually, I do*, but he kept calm. Mentally he noted that Bishop had not demanded to see a solicitor, which was often a good indicator of guilt. And yet something did not feel right. He just couldn't put a finger on it.

He left the room, went back to his office and called Linda Buckley, one of the two family liaison officers who were being assigned to look after Bishop. She was an extremely competent WPC with whom he had worked several times in the past.

'I want you to keep a close eye on Bishop. Report back to me any odd behaviour. If necessary, I'll get a surveillance team on to him,' he briefed her.

13

Clyde Weevels, tall and serpentine, with little spikes of black hair and a tongue that rarely stopped wetting his lips, stood behind the counter, surveying his – at this moment empty – domain. His little retail emporium in Broadwick Street, just off Wardour Street in Soho, bore the same anonymous legend as a dozen other places like it sprinkled around the side – and not-so-side – streets of Soho: *Private Shop*.

In the drably lit interior, there were racks of dildos, lubricating oils and jellies, flavoured condoms, bondage kits, inflatable sex dolls, thongs, G-strings, whips, manacles, racks of porno magazines, softcore DVDs, hardcore DVDs, and even harder stuff in the backroom for clients he knew well. There was everything in here for a great night in, for straights, gays, bis and for plain old saddo loners – which was what he was, not that he was ever going to admit that to himself, or to anyone else, no way, José. Just waiting for the right relationship to come along.

Except it wasn't going to come along in this place.

She was out there somewhere, in one of those lonely-hearts columns, on one of those websites. Waiting for him. Gagging for him. Gagging for a tall, lean, great-dancer-dude who was also a mean kick boxer. Which he was practising now. Behind the counter, behind the bank of CCTV monitors that were the window on his shop and the outside world, he was practising. *Roundhouse kick. Front kick. Side kick.*

And he had a ten-inch dick.

And he could get you anything you wanted. You name it – I mean, like, you *name* it. What kind of porno you want? Toys? Drugs? Yeah.

Camera Four was the one he liked to watch most. It showed the street, outside the door. He liked watching the way they came into the shop, especially the men in suits. They sort of nonchalantly sidled past, as if they were en route to someplace else, then rocked back on their heels and shot in through the door, as if pulled by an invisible magnet that had just been switched on.

Like the pinstriped git in a pink tie who walked in now. They all gave him a sort of *this-isn't-really-me* glance, followed by the kind of inane semi-grin you see in stroke victims, then they'd start fondling a dildo, or a pair of lace knickers, or a set of handcuffs, like sex had not yet been invented.

Another man was coming in. Lunch hour. Yeah. He was a bit different. A shell-suited jerk in a hoodie and dark glasses. Clyde lifted his eyes from the monitor and watched as he entered the shop. His type were the classic shoplifters, the hood shielding their face from the cameras. And this one was behaving really weirdly. He just stopped in his tracks, staring out through the opaque glass in the door for some moments, sucking his hand.

Then the man walked over to the counter and said, without making eye contact, 'Do you sell gas masks?'

'Rubber and leather,' Clyde replied, pointing a finger towards the back of the store. A whole selection of masks and hoods hung there, between a range of doctor, nurse, air hostess and Playboy bunny uniforms, and a jokey *Hung Like a Stallion* pouch.

But instead of walking towards them, the man strode back towards the door and stared out again.

*

Across the road, the young woman called Sophie Harrington, whom he had followed from her office, was standing at the counter of an Italian deli, with a magazine under her arm, waiting for her ciabatta to be removed from the microwave, talking animatedly on her mobile phone.

He looked forward to trying the gas mask out on her.

14

'Gets me every time, this place,' Glenn Branson said, looking up from the silent gloom of his thoughts at the even gloomier view ahead. Roy Grace, indicating left, slowed his ageing maroon Alfa Romeo saloon and turned off the Lewes Road gyratory system, past a sign, in gold letters on a black ground, saying BRIGHTON AND HOVE CITY MORTUARY. 'You ought to donate your rubbish music collection to it.'

'Very funny.'

As if out of respect for the place, Branson leaned forward and turned down the volume of the Katie Melua CD that was playing.

'And anyhow,' Grace said defensively, 'I *like* Katie Melua.'

Branson shrugged. Then he shrugged again.

'What?' Grace said.

'You should let me buy your music for you.'

'I'm very happy with my music.'

'You were very happy with your clothes, until I showed you what a sad old git you looked in them. You were happy with your haircut too. Now you've started listening to me, you look ten years younger – and you've got a woman, right? She's well fit, she is!'

Ahead, through wrought-iron gates attached to brick pillars, was a long, single-storey, bungalow-like structure with grey pebbledash rendering on the walls that seemed to suck all the warmth out of the air, even on this blistering summer's day. There was a covered drive-in one side, deep enough to take an ambulance – or more often, the coroner's dark green van. On the other side, several cars were parked alongside a wall, including the yellow Saab, with its roof down, belonging to Nadiuska De Sancha and, of much more significance to Roy Grace, a small blue MG sports car, which meant that Cleo Morey was on duty today.

And despite all the horror that lay ahead, he felt a sense of elation. Wholly inappropriate, he knew, but he just could not help it.

For years he had hated coming to this place. It was one of the rites of passage of becoming a police officer that you had to attend a post-mortem early in your training. But now the mortuary had a whole different significance to him. Turning to Branson, smiling, he retorted, 'What the caterpillar calls the end of the world, the master calls the butterfly.'

'What?' Branson responded flatly.

'Chuang Tse,' he said brightly, trying to share his joy with his companion, trying to cheer the poor man up.

'Who?'

'A Chinese philosopher. Died in 275 BC.' He didn't reveal who had taught him this.

'And he's in the mortuary, is he?'

'You're a bloody philistine, aren't you?' Grace pulled the car up into a space and switched the engine off.

Perking just a little, again, Branson retorted, 'Oh yeah? And since when did you get into philosophy, old-timer?'

References to Grace's age always stung. He had just celebrated – if that was the right word – his thirty-ninth birthday, and did not like the idea that next year was going to be the big four-zero.

'Very funny.'

'Ever see that movie *The Last Emperor*?'

'Don't remember it.'

'Yeah, well, you wouldn't,' Glenn said sarcastically. 'It only won nine Oscars. Well brilliant. You should get it out on DVD – except you're probably too busy catching up on past episodes of *Desperate Housewives*. And,' he added, nodding towards the mortuary, 'are you still – you know – she still yanking your chain?'

'None of your damn business!'

Although in reality it was Branson's business, it was everyone's business, because at this moment it was causing Grace's focus to be elsewhere, in totally the wrong place from where it should have been. Fighting his urge to get out of the car and into the mortuary, to see Cleo, and changing the subject rapidly back to the business of the day, he said, 'So – what do you think? Did he kill her?'

'He didn't ask for a lawyer,' Branson replied.

'You're learning,' Grace said, genuinely pleased.

It was a fact that the majority of criminals, when apprehended, submitted quietly. The ones that protested loudly often turned out to be innocent – of that particular crime, at any rate.

'But did he kill his wife? I dunno, I can't call it,' Branson added.

'Me neither.'

'What did his eyes tell you?'

'I need to get him in a calmer situation. What was his reaction when you told him the news?'

'He was devastated. It looked real enough.'

'Successful businessman, right?' They were in the shade here, alongside a flint wall, by a tall laurel bush. Air wafted in through the open sun-roof and windows. A tiny spider suddenly abseiled down its own thread from the interior mirror.

'Yeah. Software systems of some kind,' Branson said.

'You know the best character trait to become a successful businessman?'

'Whatever it is, I wasn't born with it.'

'It's being a sociopath. Having no conscience, as ordinary people know it.'

Branson pressed the button, lowering his window further. 'A sociopath is a psychopath, right?' He cupped the spider in the massive palm of his hand and gently dropped it out of the window.

'Same characteristics, one significant difference: sociopaths can keep themselves under control, psychopaths can't.'

'So,' Branson said, 'Bishop is a successful businessman, ergo he must be a sociopath, ergo he killed his wife. Bingo! Case closed. Let's go and arrest him?'

Grace grinned. 'Some drug dealers are tall, black, with shaven heads. You are tall, black, with a shaven head. Ergo you must be a drug dealer.'

Branson frowned then nodded. 'Of course. Get you anything you want.'

Grace held out his hand. 'Good. Let me have a couple of those little babies I gave you this morning – if you've got any left.'

Branson handed him two paracetamols. Grace popped them from their foil wrapper and washed them down with a swig of mineral water from a bottle in the glove locker. Then he climbed out of the car and walked swiftly, purposefully, over to the small blue front door with its frosted glass panel and pressed the bell.

Branson stood by his side, crowding him, and for a moment Grace wished the DS could just sod off for a few minutes and give him some privacy. After almost a week since seeing Cleo, he had a deep longing just to have a few private minutes with her. To know that she still felt the same about him as she had last week.

Moments later she opened the door, and Grace did exactly what he always did each time he saw her. He went into a kind of internal meltdown of joy.

In the *new-speak* devised by one of the political-correctness politburo that Grace detested, Cleo Morey's official title had recently been changed to Senior Anatomical Pathology Technician. In the old-fashioned language that ordinary folk spoke and understood, she was the Chief Mortician.

Not that anyone who didn't know her, who saw her walking down a street, would have guessed that in a gazillion years.

Five feet ten inches tall, in her late twenties, with long blonde hair, and brimming with confidence, she was, by any definition – and it was probably the wrong one for this particular place she worked in – drop-dead gorgeous. Standing in the tiny lobby of the mortuary, her hair scraped up, draped in a green surgical gown, with a heavy-duty apron over the top and white wellington boots, she looked more like some stunning actress playing a role than the real thing.

Despite the fact that the inquisitive, suspicious Glenn Branson was standing right beside him, Grace couldn't help himself. Their eyes locked, for more than just a fleeting moment. Those stunning, amazing, wide, round, sky-blue eyes stared straight into his soul, found his heart and cradled it.

He wished Glenn Branson would vaporize. Instead the bastard continued standing beside him, looking at each of them in turn, grinning like an imbecile.

'Hi!' Grace said, a little tamely.

'Detective Superintendent, Detective Sergeant Branson, how very nice to see you both!'

Grace desperately wanted to put his arms around her and kiss her. Instead, restraining himself, clicking back into professional mode, he just smiled back. Then, barely even noticing the sickly sweet reek of Trigene disinfectant that permeated the place, he followed her into the familiar small office that doubled as the reception room. It was an utterly impersonal room, yet he liked it because it was her space.

There was a fan humming on the floor, pink Artexed walls, a pink carpet, an L-shaped row of visitor chairs and a small metal desk on which sat three telephones, a stack of small brown envelopes printed with the words PERSONAL EFFECTS and a large green and red ledger bearing the legend MORTUARY REGISTER in gold block lettering.

A light box was fixed to one wall, as well as a row of framed PUBLIC HEALTH AND HYGIENE certificates, and a larger one from the BRITISH INSTITUTE OF EMBALMERS, with Cleo Morey's name inscribed beneath. On another wall was a CCTV, which showed, in a continuous jerky sequence, views of the front, the back, then each side of the building, followed by a close-up on the entrance.

'Cup of tea, gentlemen, or do you want to go straight in?'

'Is Nadiuska ready to start?'

Cleo's clear, bright eyes engaged with his for just a fraction longer than was necessary for the question. Smiling eyes. Incredibly warm eyes. 'She's just nipped out for a sandwich. Be starting in about ten minutes.'

Grace felt a dull ache in his stomach, remembering they hadn't had anything to eat all morning. It was twenty past two. 'I'd love a cup of tea. Do you have any biscuits?'

Pulling a tin out from under her desk, she prised off the

lid. 'Digestives. Kit-Kats. Marshmallows? Dark or plain chocolate Leibniz? Fig rolls?' She offered the tin to him and Branson, who shook his head. 'What kind of tea? English breakfast, Earl Grey, Darjeeling, China, camomile, pepper-mint, green leaf?'

He grinned. 'I always forget. It's a proper little Starbucks you run here.'

But it elicited no hint of a smile from Glenn Branson, who was sitting with his face buried in his hands, sunk back into depression suddenly. Cleo blew Grace a silent kiss. He took out a Kit-Kat and tore off the wrapper.

Finally, to Grace's relief, Branson said suddenly, 'I'll go and get suited.'

He went out of the room and they were alone together. Cleo shut the door, threw her arms around Roy Grace and kissed him deeply. For a long time.

When their lips parted, still holding him tightly, she asked, 'So how are you?'

'I missed you,' he said.

'Did you?'

'Yes.'

'How much?'

He held out his hands, about two feet apart.

Feigning indignation, she said, 'Is that all?'

'Did you miss me?'

'I missed you, a lot. A lot, a lot.'

'Good! How was the course?'

'You don't want to know.'

'Try me?' He kissed her again.

'Tell you over dinner tonight.'

He loved that. Loved the way she took the initiative. Loved the impression she gave that she *needed* him.

He had never felt that with a woman before. Ever. He'd

been married to Sandy for so many years, and they had loved each other deeply, but he'd never felt that she *needed* him. Not like this.

There was just one problem. He'd planned to create dinner at home tonight. Well, to buy stuff in from a deli, at any rate – he was useless at cooking. But Glenn Branson had put the kibosh on that. He could hardly have a romantic evening at home with Glenn moping around, blubbing his eyes out every ten seconds. But there was no way he could tell his friend to get lost for the night.

'Where would you like to go?' he said.

'Bed. With a Chinese takeaway. Sound like a plan?'

'A very good plan. But it will have to be at your place.'

'So? You have a problem with that?'

'No. Just a problem with my place. Tell you later.'

She kissed him again. 'Don't go away.' She went out of the room and came back moments later, holding a green gown, blue overshoes, a face mask and white latex gloves, which she handed to him. 'These are all the rage.'

'I thought we'd save the dressing up for later,' he said.

'No, we *undress* later – or maybe after a week you've forgotten?' She kissed him again. 'What's up with your friend Glenn? Looks like a sick puppy.'

'He is. Domestic situation.'

'So go and cheer him up.'

'I'm trying.'

Then his mobile phone rang. Irritated by the distraction, he answered it. 'Roy Grace.'

It was the family liaison officer, Linda Buckley. 'Roy,' she said, 'I'm at the Hotel du Vin, where I checked Bishop into a room an hour ago. He's disappeared.'

15

Sophie's mother was Italian. She had always taught her daughter that food was the best cure for shock. And at this moment, standing at the counter of the Italian deli, unaware of the man in the hoodie and dark glasses watching her from behind the opaque window of the Private Shop across the road, Sophie was clutching her mobile phone to her ear, in deep shock.

She was a creature of habit, but her habits changed with her mood. For several months, day after day, she had taken an Itsu box of sushi back to her office for lunch, but then she had read an article about people getting worms from raw fish. Since then she had been hooked on a mozzarella, tomato and Parma ham ciabatta from this deli. A lot less healthy than sushi, but yummy. She'd had one for lunch almost every day for the past month – maybe even longer. And today, more than ever, she needed the comfort of familiarity.

'Tell me,' she said. 'My darling, what's happened? Please tell me?'

He was babbling, incoherent. 'Golf . . . Dead . . . Won't let me into the house . . . Police. Dead. Oh, Jesus Christ, dead.'

Suddenly the short, bald Italian behind the counter was thrusting the steaming sandwich, wrapped in paper, towards her.

She took it and, still holding her phone to her ear, stepped out into the street.

'They think I did it. I mean . . . Oh, God. Oh, God.'

'Darling, can I do something? Do you want me to come down?'

There was a long silence. 'They were asking me – grilling me,' Bishop blurted out. 'They think I did it. They think I killed her. They kept asking me where I was last night.'

'Well, that's easy,' she said. 'You were with me.'

'No. Thank you, but that's not smart. We don't need to lie.'

'Lie?' she replied, startled.

'Christ,' he said. 'I feel so confused.'

'What do you mean, *We don't need to lie*? Darling?'

A police car was roaring down the street, siren screeching. He said something, but his voice was drowned out. When the car had passed she said, 'Sorry, I couldn't hear. What did you say?'

'I told them the truth. I had dinner with Phil Taylor, my financial adviser, then I went to bed.' There was a long silence, then she heard him sobbing.

'Darling, I think you missed something out. What you did after dinner with your financial adviser guy?'

'No,' he said, sounding a little surprised.

'Hello! I know you are in shock. But you came down to my flat. Just after midnight. You spent the night with me – and you shot off about five in the morning, because you had to get your golf kit from your house.'

'You're very sweet,' he said. 'But I don't want you to have to start lying.'

She froze in her tracks. A lorry rumbled past, followed by a taxi. 'Lying? What do you mean? It's the truth.'

'Darling, I don't need to invent an alibi. It's better to tell the truth.'

'I'm sorry,' she said, suddenly feeling confused. 'I'm not with you at all. It is the truth. You came over, we slept together, then you went off. Surely that's the best thing, to tell the truth?'

'Yes. Absolutely. It is.'

'So?'

'So?' he echoed.

'So you came to my flat some time after midnight, we made love – pretty wildly – and you left just after five.'

'Except that I didn't,' he said.

'Didn't what?'

'I didn't come to your flat.'

She lifted the phone away from her ear, stared at it, then held it clamped to her ear again, wondering for a moment if she was going mad. Or if he was.

'I – I don't understand?'

'I have to go,' he said.

16

A small card, with a seductive photograph of an attractive-looking Oriental girl, was printed with the words 'Pre-op transsexual' and a phone number. Next to it was another card depicting a big-haired woman in leather, brandishing a whip. A stench of urine rose from a damp patch on the floor that Bishop had avoided standing in. It was the first time he had been in a public phone booth in years and this one didn't exactly make him feel nostalgic. And apart from the smell, it felt like a sauna.

A chunk of the receiver had been smashed off, several of the glass panes were cracked and there was a chain with some fragments of paper attached, presumably belonging to the phone directory. A lorry had halted outside, its engine sounding like a thousand men hammering inside a tin shed. He looked at his watch. Two thirty-one p.m. It already felt like the longest day of his life.

What the hell was he going to say to his children? To Max and Carly. Would they actually care that they had lost their stepmother? That she had been murdered? They had been so poisoned against him and Katie by his ex-wife that they would probably not feel that much. And how, logistically, was he going to break the news? Over the phone? By flying to France to tell Max and Canada to tell Carly? They were going to have to come back early – the funeral – oh, Jesus. Or would they? Did they need to? Would they want to? Suddenly he realized how little he knew them himself.

Christ, there was so much to think about.

What had happened? Oh, my God, what had happened? My darling Katie, what happened to you?

Who did this to you? Who? Why?

Why wouldn't the damn police tell him anything? That up-his-own-backside tall black cop. And that Detective Inspector or Superintendent or whatever he was, Grace, staring at him as if he was the only suspect, as if he *knew* he had killed her.

His head spinning, he stepped out into the searing sunlight of Prince Albert Street, opposite the town hall, totally confused by the conversation he had just had, and wondering what he was going to do next. He had read a book in which it talked about just how much a mobile phone could give away about where you were, who you called and, for anyone who needed to know, what you said. Which was why, when he slipped out of the kitchen entrance of the Hotel du Vin, he had switched off his mobile and made for a public phone kiosk.

But the response he had got from Sophie was so utterly bizarre. *Well, that's easy, you were with me . . . You came down to my flat, we slept together . . .*

Except they hadn't. He had parted with Phil Taylor outside the restaurant and the doorman had hailed him a cab, which he had taken back to his flat in Notting Hill, then collapsed, tired, straight into bed, wanting a decent night's sleep before his golf game. He hadn't gone anywhere, he was certain.

Was his memory playing tricks? Shock?

Was that it?

Then, like a massive, unseen wave, grief flooded up inside him and drew him down, into a void of darkness, as if there had been a sudden, instant, total eclipse of the sun and all the sounds of the city around him.

17

The post-mortem room at the mortuary was like nowhere else on earth that Roy Grace could imagine. It was a crucible in which human beings were deconstructed, back almost, it seemed sometimes, to their base elements. No matter how clean it might be, the smell of death hung in the air, clung to your skin and your clothes, and repeated on you wherever you were for hours after you had left.

Everything felt very grey in here, as if death leached away the colour from the surroundings, as well as from the cadavers themselves. The windows were an opaque grey, sealing the room off from prying eyes, the wall tiles were grey, as was the speckled tiled floor with the drain gully running all the way round. On occasions when he had been in here alone, with time to reflect, it even felt as if the light itself was an ethereal grey, tinged by the souls of the hundreds of victims of sudden or unexplained death who suffered the ultimate indignity here within these walls every year.

The room was dominated by two steel post-mortem tables, one fixed to the floor and the other, on which Katie Bishop lay – her face already paler than when he had seen her earlier – on castors. There was a blue hydraulic hoist and a row of steel-fronted fridges with floor-to-ceiling doors. Along one wall were sinks and a coiled yellow hose. Along another was a wide work surface, a metal cutting board and a macabre 'trophy' cabinet, a display case filled with grisly items – mostly pacemakers and replacement hip joints – removed from bodies. Next to it was a wall chart itemizing the name of each deceased, with columns for the weights of their brain, lungs, heart, liver, kidneys and spleen. All that was written on it so far was: KATHERINE BISHOP. As if she was the lucky winner of a competition, Grace thought grimly.

Like an operating theatre, the room contained nothing that served any decorative purpose, nothing superfluous or frivolous, nothing to relieve the grimness of the work that took place in it. But at least in an operating theatre, people were driven by hope. In this room there was no hope, just clinical curiosity. A job that had to be done. The soulless machinery of the law at work.

The moment you died, you ceased to belong to your spouse, your partner, your parents, your siblings. You lost all your rights and became the custodial property of your local coroner, until he, or she, was satisfied that it was really *you* that was dead and that it was clear what had killed you. It didn't matter that your loved one didn't want your body eviscerated. It didn't matter that your family might have to wait weeks, sometimes months before burying or cremating you. You were no longer *you*. You were a biology specimen. A mass of decomposing fluids, proteins, cells, fibres and tissues, any microscopic fragment of which might or might not have a story to tell about your death.

Despite his revulsion, Grace was fascinated. He always had to watch their seemingly tireless professionalism, and he was in awe of the painstaking care which these Home Office pathologists took. It wasn't just the cause of death that would be established for certain on this slab; there were countless other clues the body might yield, such as the approximate time of death, the stomach contents, whether there had been a fight, sexual assault, rape. And with luck, perhaps in a scratch or in semen, the current holy grail of clues, the murderer's DNA. Often, today, the post-mortem was really the place where a crime got solved.

Which was why Grace, as Senior Investigating Officer, had to be present, accompanied by another officer – Glenn Branson – in case for any reason he had to leave. Derek Gavin from the SOCO team was also there, recording every stage on camera, as well as the coroner's officer, a grey-haired former policewoman in her mid-forties, so quiet and unobtrusive she almost blended into the background. Also present were Cleo Morey and her colleague Darren, the Assistant Anatomical Pathology Technician, a sharp, good-looking young man of twenty, with spiky black hair, who had started life appropriately enough, Grace thought, as a butcher's apprentice.

Nadiuska De Sancha, the pathologist, and the two technicians wore heavy-duty green aprons over green pyjamas, rubber gloves and white gumboots. The rest of the people in the room were in protective green gowns and overshoes. Katie Bishop's body was wrapped in white plastic sheeting, with a plastic bag secured by elastic bands over her hands and feet, to protect any evidence that might be trapped under her nails. At the moment, the pathologist was unwrapping the sheeting, scrutinizing it for any hairs, fibres, skin cells or any other matter, however small, that might turn out to have belonged to her assailant, which she might have missed when examining Katie's body in her bedroom.

Then she turned away to dictate into her machine. Twenty years or so older than Cleo, Nadiuska was, in her own way, an equally striking-looking woman. Handsome and dignified, she had high cheekbones, clear green eyes that could be deadly serious one moment and sparkling with humour the next, beneath fiery red hair, at this moment pinned up neatly. She had an aristocratic bearing, befitting someone who was, reputedly, the daughter of a Russian duke, and wore a pair of small, heavy-rimmed glasses of the kind favoured by media intellectuals. She put the dictating machine back down near the sink and returned to the corpse, slowly unbagging Katie's right hand.

When Katie's body was, finally, completely naked, and she had taken and logged scrapings from under all the nails, Nadiuska turned her attention to the marks on the dead woman's neck. After some minutes of examining them with a magnifying glass, she then studied her eyes before addressing Grace.

'Roy, this is a superficial knife wound, with a ligature mark over the same place. Take a close look at the sclera – the whites of the eyes. You'll see the haemorrhaging.' She spoke in a voice just slightly tinged with a guttural mid-European inflection.

The Detective Superintendent, in his rustling green gown and clumsy overshoes, took a step closer to Katie Bishop and peered through the magnifying glass, first at her right eye, then at her left. Nadiuska was right. In the whites of each eye he could clearly see several bloodshot spots, each the size of a pinprick. As soon as he had seen enough he retreated a couple of paces.

Derek Gavin stepped forward and photographed each eye with a macro-lens.

'The pressure on the veins in the neck was enough to compress them, but not the arteries,' Nadiuska explained, more loudly now, as if for the benefit of both Roy and everyone else in the room. 'The haemorrhaging is a good indication of strangulation or asphyxiation. What is strange is that there are no marks on her body – you would have thought if she had resisted her assailant there would be scratches or bruises, wouldn't you? It would be normal.'

She was right. Grace had been thinking the same thing. 'So it could be someone she knew? A sex game gone wrong?' he asked.

'With the knife wound?' Glenn Branson chipped in dubiously.

'I agree,' Nadiuska said. 'That doesn't fit, necessarily.'

'Good point,' Grace conceded, startled at how he could have missed something so obvious – and putting it down to his tired brain.

Then the pathologist finally started the dissection. With a scalpel in one gloved hand, she lifted Katie's tangled hair up and made an incision all the way around the back of the scalp, then peeled it forward, hair still attached, so that it hung down, inside out, over the dead woman's face like a hideous, featureless mask. Then Darren, the assistant technician, walked across with the rotary band saw.

Grace braced himself, and caught the look in Glenn Branson's eyes. This was one of the moments he most disliked – this and the cutting open of the stomach, which invariably released a smell that could send you retching. Darren clicked the start button and the machine whined, its sharp teeth spinning. Then that grinding sound that hit the pit of his stomach, and every nerve in his body, as the teeth tore into the top edge of Katie's skull bone.

It was so bad, so particularly bad at this moment with his queasy stomach and pounding hangover, that Grace wanted to retreat into a corner and jam his fingers in his ears. But of course he couldn't. He had to stick it out, as the young mortuary technician steadily worked the saw all the way round, bone fragments flying like sawdust, until finally he had finished. Then he lifted the skull cap clear, like a teapot lid, exposing the glistening brain beneath.

People always referred to it as *grey matter*. But to Grace, who had seen plenty, they were never actually grey – more a creamy brown colour. They turned grey later. Nadiuska stepped forward and he watched her studying the brain for some moments. Then Darren handed her a thin-bladed boning knife, a Sabatier that could have come from a kitchen cabinet. She dug inside the skull cavity, cutting the sinews and the optical nerves, then lifted the brain clear, like a trophy, and handed it to Cleo.

She carried it over to the scales, weighed it and chalked up the amount on the wall-mounted list: 1.6 kg.

Nadiuska glanced at it. 'Normal for her height, weight and age,' she said.

Darren now placed a metal tray over Katie's ankles, its legs standing on the table either side of her legs. Taking a long-bladed butcher's knife, the pathologist prodded the brain in a number of places with her fingers, peering at it closely. Then, with the knife, she cut a thin slice off one end, as if she were carving a Sunday joint.

At that moment Grace's mobile rang.

He stepped away to answer it. 'Roy Grace,' he said.

It was Linda Buckley again. 'Hello, Roy,' she said. 'Brian Bishop's just come back. I've phoned and called off the alert for him.'

'Where the hell was he?'

'He said he just went out for some air.'

Walking out of the room, into the corridor, Grace said, 'Like hell he did. Get on to the CCTV team – see what they've picked up around that hotel in the last few hours.'

'I will do, right away. When will you be ready for me to bring him down for the viewing?'

'Be a while yet. A good three or four hours – I'll call you.'

As he hung up, his phone immediately rang again. He didn't recognize the number – a long string of digits starting with 49 that suggested it was from somewhere overseas. He answered it.

'Roy!' said a voice he instantly knew. It was his old friend and colleague Dick Pope. Once Dick and his wife, Leslie, had been his best friends. But Dick had been transferred to Hastings and since they had moved over there, Grace hadn't seen so much of them.

'Dick! Good to hear from you – where are you?'

There was a sudden hesitation in his friend's voice. 'Roy, we're in Munich. We're on a motoring holiday. Checking out the Bavarian beer!'

'Sounds good to me!' Grace said, uneasy at the hesitation, as if there was something his friend was holding back from saying.

'Roy – look – this may be nothing. I don't want to cause you any – you know, upset or anything. But Leslie and I think we may have seen Sandy.'

18

Skunk's phone was ringing again. He woke, shivering and sweating at the same time. Jesus, it was hot in here. His clothes – the ragged T-shirt and undershorts he was sleeping in – and his bedding were sodden. Water was guttering off him.

Breeep-breeep-breeeep.

From somewhere in the fetid darkness down towards the rear of the camper, the Scouse voice shouted out, 'Fokking thing. Turn the fokking thing off, for Chrissake, 'fore I throw it out the fokking window.'

It wasn't the phone he had stolen last night, he realized suddenly. It was his pay-as-you-go phone. His *business* phone! Where in hell was it?

He stood up hurriedly and shouted back, 'You don't like it, get the fuck out of my van!'

Then he looked on the floor, found his shell-suit bottoms, dug his hands in the pocket and pulled the small green mobile out. 'Yeah?' he answered.

The next moment he was looking around for a pen and a scrap of paper. He had both in his top, wherever the hell that was. Then he realized he had been sleeping on it, using it as a sort of pillow. He pulled out a thin, crappy ballpoint with a cracked stem, and a torn, damp sheet of lined paper, and put it down on the work surface. With a hand shaking so much he could barely write, he managed to take down the details in a spiky scrawl, and then hung up.

A good one. Money. Moolah! Mucho!

And his bowels felt OK today. None of the agonizing gripes followed by diarrhoea that had been plaguing him for days – not yet, at any rate. His mouth was parched; he was desperate for some water. Feeling light-headed and giddy, he made his way to the sink, then, steadying himself on the work surface, he turned on the tap. But it was already on, the contents of the water tank all run out. *Shite*.

'Who left the fucking tap on all night? Hey? Who?' he yelled.

'Chill out, man!' a voice replied.

'I'll fucking chill you out!' He pulled open the curtains again, blinking at the sudden intrusion of the blinding, early-afternoon sunlight. Outside he saw a woman in the park, holding the hand of a toddler on a tricycle. A mangy-looking dog was running around, sniffing the scorched grass where a circus big-top had been until a couple of days ago. Then he looked along the camper. A third crashed-out body he hadn't noticed before, stirred. Nothing he could do about any of them now, just hope the fuck they'd be gone when he came back. They usually were.

Then he heard an almost rhythmic *squeak-squeak-squeak*, and saw Al, his hamster, with his busted paw all bound up in a splint by the vet, still spinning the shiny chromium treadmill, his whiskers twitching away. 'Man, don't you *ever* get tired?' he said, putting his face up close to the bars of the cage – but not too close – Al had bitten him once. Actually, twice.

He had first found the creature abandoned in its cage, which had been tossed by some callous bastard into a roadside skip. He had seen its paw was busted and tried to lift it out, and been bitten for his troubles. Then another time he had tried to stroke it through the bars and it had bitten him again. Yet other days he could open the cage door and it would scamper into the palm of his hand, and sit there happily, for an hour or more, only shitting on it occasionally.

He pulled on the grey Adidas shell-suit bottoms and hooded top, which he had stolen from the ASDA superstore at the Marina, and the brand-new blue and white Asics trainers he had tried on and run out with from a shop in Kemp Town, and grabbed a Waitrose carrier bag containing his tools, into which he dropped the mobile phone from the car he had stolen yesterday. He opened the door of the camper, shouted, 'I want you all fucking gone when I come back,' and stepped out into the searing, cloudless heat of The Level, the long, narrow strip of parkland in the centre of Brighton and Hove. The city that he jokingly – but not that jokingly – called his *office*.

Written on the damp sheet of paper he carried, safely folded and tucked into his zipped breast pocket, were an order, a delivery address and an agreed payment. A no-brainer. Suddenly, despite the shakes, life was looking up. He could make enough money today to last him an entire week.

He could even afford to play hardball in negotiations on the sale of the mobile phone.

19

*My father is crying today. I've never seen him cry before.
I've seen him drunk and angry, which is how he is most
of the time, drunk and angry, slapping my mother or
me, or punching one of us in the face, or maybe both of
us depending on his mood. Sometimes he kicks the dog
because it's my dog and he doesn't like dogs. The only
person he doesn't punch or slap or kick is Annie, my
sister, who is ten. He does other things to her instead.
We hear her crying out when he is in her room. And
crying, sometimes, after he has left her room.*

*But today he is crying. My father. All twenty-two of
his pigeons are dead. Including two that he has had for
fifteen years. And his four Birmingham Rollers that
could fly upside-down and do other kinds of aerobatics.*

*I gave them one large shot of insulin each from his
diabetic kit. Those pigeons were his life. It is strange
that he could love these noisy, smelly birds so much,
yet hate us all. I never understood how they could have
given us children to him and my mother in the first
place. Sometimes there are as many as eight of us here.
The others come and go. Just my sister and I are the
constant ones. We suffer along with our mother.*

*But today, for once, he is suffering. He is hurting
really badly.*

20

Sophie's ciabatta sat on her desk, going cold and making its paper wrapper soggy. She had no appetite. The copy of *Harpers & Queen* lay on her desk unopened.

She liked to ogle the dreamy clothes on the almost insanely beautiful models, the pictures of stunning resorts she sometimes dreamed that Brian might whisk her off to, and she loved to trawl through the diary photographs of the rich and famous, some of whom she recognized from film premieres she had attended for her company, or from a distance when she had walked along the Croisette or crashed parties at the Cannes Film Festival. It was a lifestyle so far from her own modest, rural upbringing.

She had never particularly sought glamour when she came to London to do a secretarial course – and she certainly had not found it when she'd got her first job with a firm of bailiffs, carrying out work seizing goods from the homes of people who had run into debt. She found the company cruel and much of its work heartbreaking. When she had decided to make a change, and began trawling the ads in the *Evening Standard* newspaper, she had never imagined that she would land up in quite such a different world as she was in now.

But at this moment her world had, suddenly, gone completely out of kilter. She was trying to get her head around the totally bizarre conversation she had had with Brian on her mobile a short while ago, outside the café, when he'd told her his wife was dead and had denied that he had come over to her last night – or rather, early this morning – and made love to her.

The office phone rang.

'Blinding Light Productions,' she answered, half hoping it was Brian, her voice devoid of its usual enthusiasm.

But it was someone wanting to speak to the Head of Business and Legal Affairs, Adam Davies. She put them through. Then she returned to her thoughts.

OK, Brian was strange. In the six months since she had met him, when they had sat next to each other at a conference on tax incentives for investors in film financing, which she had been asked to attend by her bosses, she still felt she only knew just a very small part of him. He was an intensely private person and she found it hard to get him to talk about himself. She didn't really understand what he did, or, more importantly, what it was he wanted from life – and from her.

He was kind and generous, and great company. And, she had only very recently discovered, the most amazing lover! Yet there was a part of him that he kept in a compartment from which she was excluded.

A part of him that could deny, absolutely, that he had come to her flat in the early hours of today.

She was desperate to know what had happened to his wife. The poor, darling man must be distraught. Deranged with grief. *Denial*. Was the answer as simple as that?

She wanted to hold him, to comfort him, to let him pour it all out to her. In her mind a plan was forming. It was vague – she was so shaken up she could not think it through properly – but it was better than just sitting here, not knowing, helpless.

Both the owners of the company, Tony Watts and James Samson, were away on their summer holidays. The office was quiet, no one would be that bothered if she left early today. At three o'clock she told Cristian and Adam that she wasn't feeling that good, and they both suggested she went home.

Thanking them, she left the building, took the tube to Victoria, and made straight for the platform for Brighton.

As she boarded the train and settled into a seat in the stiflingly hot compartment, she was unaware of the shell-suited man, in the hoodie and dark glasses, who was entering the carriage directly behind hers. He gripped the red plastic bag containing his purchase from the Private Shop, and was quietly mouthing to himself the words of an old Louis Armstrong song, 'We Have All the Time in the World', which were being fed into his ears by his iPod.

21

When Roy Grace hung up he walked back into the post-mortem room in a daze. Cleo made eye contact, as if she had picked up a vibe that something was wrong. He signalled back lamely that all was fine.

His stomach felt as if wet cement was revolving inside it. He could barely focus his eyes on the scene unfolding in front of him, as Nadiuska De Sancha dissected Katie Bishop's neck with a scalpel, layer of tissue by layer, looking for signs of internal bruising.

He did not want to be here right now. He wanted to be in a room on his own, sitting somewhere quiet, where he could think.

About Sandy.

Munich.

Was it possible?

Sandy, his wife, had disappeared off the face of the earth just over nine years ago, on the day of his thirtieth birthday. He could remember it vividly, as if it was yesterday.

Birthdays had always been very special days for them both. She had woken him with a tray on which was a tiny cake with a single candle, a glass of champagne and a very rude birthday card. He'd opened the presents she had given him, then they had made love.

He'd left the house later than usual, at nine fifteen, promising to be home early, to go out for a celebratory meal with Dick and Leslie Pope. But when he had arrived home almost two hours later than he had planned, because of problems with a murder case he had been investigating, there was no sign of Sandy.

At first he'd thought she was angry with him for being so late and was making a protest. The house was tidy, her car and handbag were gone, and there was nothing to suggest a struggle.

For years he had searched everywhere. Tried every possible avenue, distributed her photograph, through Interpol, around the world. And he had been to mediums – still went to them every time he heard of a credible new one. But nothing. Not one of them had picked up anything to do with her. It was as if she had been teleported off the planet. Not one sign, not a single sighting by anyone.

Until this phone call now.

From Dick Pope. Saying he and Leslie had been on a boating lake in a beer garden in Munich. The Seehaus in the Englischer Garten. They had been out in a rowing boat, and both of them could have sworn they saw Sandy, sitting among the crowds at a table, singing away as a Bavarian band played.

Dick said they had rowed straight over to the edge of the lake, shouting to her. He'd scrambled out of the boat and run towards her, but she had gone. Melted away into the crowd. He said that he couldn't be sure, of course. That neither he nor Leslie could be completely sure.

After all, it was nine years since they had seen Sandy. And Munich, in summer, like anywhere else, had countless dozens of attractive women with long, blonde hair. But, Dick had assured him, both he and Leslie thought the resemblance was uncanny. And the woman had stared at them, with what looked like clear recognition. So why had she left her table and fled?

Leaving three-quarters of a large glass of beer behind.

And the people sitting near her claimed never to have seen her before.

Sandy liked a glass of beer on a hot day. One of the million, billion, trillion, gazillion things Roy Grace had loved about her was her appetites in life. For food, wine, beer. And sex. Unlike so many women he had dated before her, Sandy was different. She went for everything. He had always put that down to the fact that she was not 100 percent British. Her grandmother, a great character, whom he had met – and really liked – many times before she had died, had been German. A Jewish refugee who had got out in 1938. Their family home had been in a small village in the countryside near Munich.

Jesus. The thought struck him now for the first time.

Could Sandy have gone back to her roots?

She had often talked about going to visit. She had even tried to persuade her grandmother to go with her, and show her where they had lived, but for the elderly lady the memories were too painful. One day, Grace had promised Sandy, they would go there together.

A sharp *crunch*, followed by a *snap*, brought him back to the present moment.

Katie Bishop's breasts were inverted, beneath peeled-back flaps of skin, the ribs, muscles and organs of her midriff now exposed. The heart, lungs, kidneys and liver were all glistening. With her heart no longer pumping, only a trickle of blood slid, sluggishly, into the concave metal table on which she lay.

Nadiuska, holding what looked like a pair of gardening shears, began cutting through the dead woman's ribs. Each grisly, bone-crunching *snap* brought Grace, and all the other observers in this room, to a strange kind of focused silence. It didn't matter how many post-mortems you had attended, nothing prepared you for this sound, this awful reality. This was someone who had once been a living, breathing, loving human being reduced to the status of meat on a butcher's hook.

And for the very first time in his career, it was more than Grace could take. With all kinds of confusion about Sandy swirling in his mind, he stepped back, as far away from the table as he could get without actually leaving the room.

He tried to focus his thoughts. This woman had been killed by someone, almost certainly murdered. She deserved more than a distracted cop, fixated on a possible sighting of his long-gone wife. For the moment he had to try and push the phone call from Dick Pope to the back of his mind and concentrate on the business here.

He thought about her husband, Brian. The way he had behaved in the witness interview room. Something had not felt right. And then he realized what, in his tired, addled state, he had totally forgotten to do.

Something that he had recently learned that would tell him, very convincingly, whether Brian Bishop had been telling the truth or not.

22

Sophie stepped off the train at Brighton station and walked along the platform. Using her season ticket at the barrier, she came out on to the polished concourse floor. High above her a lone pigeon flew beneath the vast glass roof. A tannoy announcement echoed around the building, a tired male voice reeling off a list of places some train was going to be stopping at.

Perspiring heavily in the clammy, airless heat, she was parched. She stopped at the news kiosk to buy a can of Coke, which she snapped open and drained in two draughts. She desperately, just desperately, wanted to see Brian.

Then, right in front of her nose, she saw the black scrawled letters on the white *Argus* news billboard: *WOMAN FOUND DEAD IN MILLIONAIRE'S HOME*.

She dropped the empty can in a bin and snatched up a copy of the newspaper from a pile on the stand.

Beneath the headline, with the same words, was a colour photograph of an imposing, mock-Tudor house, the driveway and street outside sealed with crime scene tape and cluttered with vehicles, including two marked police cars, several vans and the large square slab of a Major Incident vehicle. Much smaller, offset, was a black and white photograph showing Brian Bishop in a bow tie and an attractive woman with an elegant tangle of hair.

The copy beneath read:

The body of a woman was found at the Dyke Road Avenue mansion of wealthy businessman Brian Bishop, 41, and his wife, Katie, 35, early this morning. A Home Office pathologist was called to the house and a body was subsequently removed from the premises.

Sussex Police have launched an inquiry, headed by Detective Superintendent Roy Grace of Sussex CID.

Brighton-born Bishop, the Managing Director of International Rostering Solutions PLC, one of this year's *Sunday Times* 100 fastest-growing UK companies, was unavailable for comment. His wife is on the committee of Brighton-based children's charity the Rocking Horse Appeal and has raised money for many local causes.

A post-mortem was due to be carried out this afternoon.

Feeling sick in the pit of her stomach, Sophie stared at the page. She had never seen Katie Bishop's picture before, had no idea what she looked like. God, the woman was beautiful. Way more attractive than she was – and could ever be. She looked so classy, so happy, so—

She dropped the newspaper back on the pile, in even more turmoil now. It had always been hard to get Brian to talk about his wife. And at the same time, although one part of her had had a burning curiosity to know everything about the woman, another part had tried to deny she existed. She had never had an affair with a married man before, never wanted to have one – she had always tried to live her life by a simple moral code. *Don't do anything that you wouldn't want someone to do to you.*

All that had fallen over when she'd met Brian. He had,

quite simply, blown her off her feet. Mesmerized her. Although it had started as an innocent friendship. And now, for the first time, she was looking at her rival. And Katie wasn't the woman she had expected. Not that she had really known what to expect, Brian had never talked about her much. In her mind she had imagined some sour-faced biddy with her hair in a bun. Some ghastly old goat who had lured Brian into a loveless marriage. Not this quite stunning, confident and happy-looking beauty.

And suddenly she felt totally lost. And wondering what on earth she thought she was doing here. Half-heartedly, she pulled her mobile phone from her handbag – the cheap lemon-coloured canvas bag that she had bought at the start of summer because it was fashionable, but which was now looking embarrassingly grubby. Just like she was, she realized, catching sight of herself, and her grungy work clothes, in a photo-booth mirror.

She would need to go home and change, and freshen up. Brian liked her to look good. She remembered how disapproving he had seemed on one occasion when she'd been kept working late at the office and had turned up to meet him in a smart restaurant without having changed.

After some moments of hesitation, she called his number, held the phone to her ear, concentrating fiercely, still unaware of the man in the hoodie who was standing just a few feet from her, apparently browsing through a series of paperback books on a spinner at the kiosk.

As another tannoy announcement boomed and echoed around her, she glanced up at the massive, four-faced clock with its Roman numerals.

Four fifty-one.

'Hi,' Brian said, his voice startling her, answering before she had even heard it ring.

'You poor thing,' she said. 'I'm so sorry.'

'Yes.' His voice was flat, porous. It seemed to absorb her own, like blotting paper.

There was a long, awkward silence. Finally, she broke it. 'Where are you?'

'I'm in a hotel. The bloody police won't let me into my house. They won't let me into my home. They won't tell me what's happened – can you believe it? They say it's a crime scene and I can't go in. I— Oh, Jesus, Sophie, what am I going to do?' He started crying.

'I'm in Brighton,' she said quietly. 'I came down early from work.'

'Why?'

'I – I thought – I thought that maybe – I don't know – I'm sorry – I thought maybe I could do something. You know. To help.' Her voice tailed off. She stared up at the ornate clock. At a pigeon that suddenly alighted on the top of it.

'I can't see you,' he said. 'It's not possible.'

She felt foolish now for even suggesting it. What the hell had been going through her mind?

'No,' she said, the sudden harshness of his voice hurting her. 'I understand. I just wanted to say, if there was anything I could do—'

'There isn't anything. It's sweet of you to call. I – I have to go and identify her body. I haven't even told the children yet. I . . .'

He fell silent. She waited patiently, trying to understand the kinds of emotions he must be going through, and realizing how very little she really knew about him, and quite what an outsider she was in his life.

Then, in a choking voice, he said, 'I'll call you later, OK?'

'Any time. Absolutely any time, OK?' she reassured him.

'Thanks,' he said. 'I'm sorry – I – I'm sorry.'

After their conversation, Sophie called Holly, desperate to talk to someone. But all she got was Holly's latest voicemail greeting, which was even more irritatingly jolly than her previous one. She left a message.

Then she wandered aimlessly around the station concourse for some minutes, before walking out into the bright sunlight. She didn't feel like going to her flat – she didn't really know what she wanted to do. A steady stream of sunburned people were heading up the street towards the station, many of them in T-shirts, singlets or gaudy shirts and shorts, lugging beach bags, looking like trippers who had spent the day here and were now heading home. A lanky man, in jeans cut off at the knees, swung a massive radio blaring out rap, his face and arms the colour of a broiled lobster. The city felt in holiday mood. It was about as far from her own mood as Jupiter.

Suddenly her phone rang again. For an instant, her spirits rose, hoping it was Brian. Then she saw Holly's name on the display. She hit the answer button. 'Hi.'

Holly's voice was mostly drowned out by a continuous, banshee howl. She was in the hairdresser's, she informed her friend, under the drier. After a couple of minutes trying to explain what had happened, Sophie gave up and suggested they speak later. Holly promised to call her back as soon as she was out of the salon.

The man in the hoodie was following her at a safe distance, holding his red plastic bag and sucking the back of his free hand. It was nice to be back down here at the seaside, out of the filthy air of London. He hoped Sophie would head down to the beach; it would be pleasant to sit there, maybe eat an ice cream. It would be a good way of passing the time, of spending a few of those millions of hours he had sitting on deposit in his bank.

As he walked, he thought about the purchase he had made at lunchtime today and jiggled it in his bag. In the zippered pockets of his top, in addition to his wallet and his mobile phone, he carried a roll of duct tape, a knife, chloroform, a vial of the knockout, so-called *date rape* drug, Rohypnol. And a few other bits and pieces – you could never tell when they might come in handy . . .

Tonight would be a very good night. Again.

23

Cleo's skills really came into their own when, shortly after five p.m., Nadiuska De Sancha finally finished the post-mortem on Katie Bishop.

Using a large soup ladle, Cleo removed the blood that had drained into Katie's midriff, spoonful by spoonful, pouring it into the gully below. The blood would run into a holding tank beneath the building, where chemicals would slowly break it down, before it passed into the city's main drainage system.

After that, as Nadiuska leaned on the work surface, dictating her summary, then in turn filling in the Autopsy sheet, the Histology sheet and the Cause of Death sheet, Darren handed Cleo a plain white plastic bag containing all the vital organs that had been removed from the cadaver and weighed on the scales. Grace watched, with the same morbid fascination he had each time, as Cleo inserted the bag into Katie's midriff, as if she were stuffing giblets into a chicken.

He watched with the shadow of the phone call about Sandy hanging heavily over him. Thinking. He needed to call Dick Pope back, quiz him more, about exactly when he had seen Sandy, which table she had been at, whether he had talked to the staff, whether she had been alone or with anyone.

Munich. The city had always had a resonance for him, partly because of Sandy's family connections, and partly because it was a city that was constantly, in one way or another, in the world's consciousness. The Oktoberfest, the World Cup football stadium, it was the home of BMW, and, he seemed to remember, Adolf Hitler had lived there, before Berlin. All he wanted to do at this moment was jump on a plane and fly there. And he could just imagine how well that would go down with his boss, Alison Vosper, who was looking for *any* opportunity, however small, to twist the knife she had already stuck into him, and get rid of him.

Darren then went out of the room and returned with a black garbage bag containing shredded council tax correspondence from Brighton and Hove City Council, removed a handful, and started to pack the paper into the dead woman's empty skull cavity. Meanwhile, using a heavy-duty sailcloth needle and thread, Cleo began carefully but industrially to sew up the woman's midriff.

When she had finished, she hosed Katie down to remove all the blood streaks, and then began the most sensitive part of the procedure. With the greatest care, she was putting on make-up, adding some colouring to the woman's cheeks, tidying her hair, making her look as if she was just having a little nap.

At the same time, Darren began the process of cleaning up the post-mortem room around Katie Bishop's trolley. He squirted lemon-scented disinfectant on to the floor, scrubbing that in, then bleach, then Trigene disinfectant and finally Autoclave.

An hour later, laid out beneath a purple shroud, with her arms crossed and a small bunch of fresh pink and white roses in her hand, Darren wheeled Katie Bishop into the viewing room, a small, narrow area with a long window, and just enough space for loved ones to stand around the corpse. It felt a little like a chapel, with dinky blue curtains, and instead of an altar, there was a small vase of plastic flowers.

*

Grace and Branson stood outside the room, observing through the glass window, as Brian Bishop was led in by WPC Linda Buckley, an alert, pleasant-looking woman in her mid-thirties, with short blonde hair, dressed in a sober dark blue two-piece and white blouse.

They watched him stare at the dead woman's face, then rummage under the shroud, pull out her hand, kiss it, then grip it tightly. Tears streamed down Bishop's face. Then he fell to his knees, totally overcome with grief.

It was at moments like this, and Grace had experienced far too many in his long career, that he wished he was anything but a police officer. One of his mates from school had gone into banking and was now a building society branch manager in Worthing, enjoying a good salary and a relaxed life. Another operated fishing trips from Brighton Marina, without an apparent care in the world.

Grace watched, unable to switch his emotions off, unable to stop himself feeling the man's grief in every cell of his own body. It was all he could do to stop crying himself.

'Shit, he's hurting,' Glenn said quietly to him.

Grace shrugged, the cop inside him speaking, rather than his heart. 'Maybe.'

'Jesus, you're a hard bastard.'

'Didn't used to be,' Grace said. 'Wasn't until I let you drive me. Needed to be a hard bastard to survive that.'

'Very funny.'

'So did you pass your Advanced Police Driving test?'

'I failed, right?'

'Really?'

'Yeah. For driving too slowly. Can you believe that?'

'Me, believe that?'

'Jesus, you hack me off. You're always the same. Every time I ask you a question you answer with a question. Can't you ever stop being a bloody detective?'

Grace smiled.

'It's not funny. Yeah? I asked you a simple question, can you believe I got failed for driving too slowly?'

'Nah.' And he really could not! Grace remembered the last time Glenn had driven him, when his friend had been practising his high-speed driving for his test. When Grace had climbed out of the car with all his limbs intact – more by luck than by anything to do with driving skills – he had decided he would prefer to have his gall bladder removed without an anaesthetic than be driven in earnest by Glenn Branson again.

'For real, man,' Branson said.

'Good to know there are still some sane people in the world.'

'Know your problem, Detective Superintendent Roy Grace?'

'Which particular problem?'

'The one you have about my driving?'

'Tell me.'

'No faith.'

'In you or in God?'

'God stopped that bullet from doing serious harm to me.'

'You really believe that, don't you?'

'You have a better theory?'

Grace fell silent, thinking. He always found it easier to park his God questions safely away and to think about them only when it suited him. He wasn't an atheist, not even really an agnostic. He did believe in something – or at least he *wanted* to believe in something – but he could never define exactly what. He always fell short of being able to openly accept the concept of God. And then immediately after that he would feel guilty. But ever since Sandy had disappeared, and all his prayers had gone unanswered, much of his faith had eroded.

Shit happened.

As a policeman, a big part of his duty was to establish the truth. *The facts.* Like all his fellow officers, his beliefs were his own affair. He watched Brian Bishop, on the other side of the window. The man was totally grief-stricken.

Or putting on a great act.

He would soon know which.

Except, wrong though it was, because it was personal, Sandy had priority in his mind right now.

24

PETER JAMES

Skunk was tempted to call his dealer's mobile on the phone he had stolen, because credit on his own one had just run out, but he decided it wasn't worth risking the man's wrath. Or worse, getting ditched as a customer, tight bastard though his dealer was. The man would not be impressed to have his number on the call list of a hot mobile – particularly one he would be selling on.

So he stepped into a payphone in front of a grimy Regency terrace on The Level and let the door swing shut against the din of the Friday afternoon traffic. It felt like an oven door closing on him, the heat was almost unbearable. He dialled, holding the door open with his foot. After two rings, the phone was answered with a curt, 'Yeah?'

'Wayne Rooney,' Skunk said, giving him the password they had agreed last time. It changed each time they met.

The man spoke in an east London accent. 'Yeah, all right then, your usual? Brown you want? Ten-pound bag or twenty?'

'Twenty.'

'What you got? Cash?'

'A Motorola Razor. T-Mobile.'

'Up to my neck in 'em. Can only give you ten for that.'

'Fuck you, man, I'm looking for thirty.'

'Can't help you then, mate. Sorry. Bye.'

In sudden panic, Skunk shouted urgently, 'Hey, no, no. Don't hang up.'

There was a brief silence. Then the man's voice again.

'I'm busy. Haven't got time to waste. Street price is going up and there's a shortage. Going to be short for two weeks.'

Skunk logged that comment. 'I could take twenty.'

'Ten's best I can do.'

There were other dealers, but the last one he'd used had been busted and was now off the streets, in jail somewhere. Another, he was sure, had given him some crap stuff. There were a couple of buyers he could take the phone to, get a better price, but he was feeling increasingly strung out; he needed something now, needed to get his head together. He had a job to do today which was going to make him way more money than this. He would be able to buy some more later in the day.

'Yeah, OK. Where do I meet you?'

The dealer, whom he knew only as Joe, gave him instructions.

Skunk stepped outside, feeling the sun searing down on his head, and dodged through the jammed lanes of traffic on Marlborough Place, just in front of a pub where he sometimes bought Ecstasy in the men's toilet at night. He might even have the cash to buy some this evening, if all went well.

Then he turned right into North Road, a long, busy, one-way street that ran uphill, steeply. The lower end was skanky, but halfway up, just past a Starbucks, the trendiest part of Brighton started.

The North Laine district was a warren of narrow streets that sprawled across most of the hill running down east from the station. If you turned any corner you'd find yourself staring at a line of antique marble fireplaces out on the pavement, or racks of funky clothes, or a row of Victorian terraced cottages, originally built for railway workers in the nineteenth century and now trendy townhouses, or the sandblasted façade of an old factory now converted into chic urban loft dwellings.

As he walked a short distance up the hill, Skunk was finding the exertion hard. There used to be a time when he could run like the wind, when he could have snatched a bag, or goods from a shop, with confidence, but now he could only do something physical for a short time without getting exhausted, apart from during the hours immediately following a hit, or when he was on uppers. No one took any notice of him, apart from two plain-clothes policemen seated at a table in the packed Starbucks, with a clear view out through the window of the goings-on in the street.

Both of them, scruffily dressed, could have passed as students, eking out their coffees for as long as possible. One, shorter and burly, with a shaven head and goatee beard, wore a black T-shirt and ripped jeans; the other, taller, with lanky hair, in a baggy shirt hanging loose over military fatigues. They knew most of Brighton's lowlife by sight, and Skunk's mug-shot had been up on a wall in Brighton Central, along with forty or so other regular offenders, for as long as both of them had been in the force.

To most of the populace of Brighton and Hove, Skunk was all but invisible. Dressed the same way he had been dressing since his early teens, in his crumpled nylon hoodie over a ragged orange T-shirt, tracksuit bottoms and trainers, hands in his pockets, body slouched forward, he blended into the city like a chameleon. It was the uniform of his gang, the WBC – Well Big Crew – a rival gang to the long-established TMC – Team Massive Crew. They weren't as vicious as the TMC, whose initiation rites were rumoured to involve either beating up a copper, raping a woman or stabbing an innocent stranger, but WBC liked to give off a menacing image. They hung around shopping areas, their hoods up, stealing anything that was readily to hand, mugging anyone who was stupid enough to get isolated, and they spent the money mostly on alcohol and drugs. He was too old for the gang now, they were mostly teenagers, but he still wore the clothes, liking the feeling of belonging to something.

Skunk's head was shaven – by Bethany each time she came by – and there was a narrow, uneven stripe of hair running from below the centre of his lower lip to the base of his chin. Bethany liked it, told him it made him look mysterious, particularly with his purple sunglasses.

But he didn't look in mirrors that much. He used to stare at himself for hours, as a small boy, trying not to be ugly, trying to convince himself that he wasn't *as* ugly as his mother and his brother told him. Now he didn't care any more. He'd done fine with the girls. Sometimes his face scared him now, it was so dry, blistered, emaciated. It looked like it had been shoehorned over the skull bones beneath.

His body was rotting – you didn't need to be a rocket scientist to figure that one out. It wasn't the drugs, it was the impurities crooked suppliers mixed with them that destroyed you. Most days his head swam as if he had flu, as if he was living in a permanent heat haze one moment and winter fog the next. His memory was crap; he wasn't able to concentrate long enough to watch any film or TV show all the way through. Ulcers kept breaking out on his body. He couldn't hold food down. He lost track of the time. Some days he couldn't even remember how old he was.

Twenty-four, he thought; or thereabouts. He'd meant to ask his brother, when he phoned him in Australia last night, but that hadn't worked out.

It was his brother, three years older and a foot taller, who had first called him Skunk, and he'd quite liked it.

Skunks were mean, feral creatures. They slunk about, they had their defences. You didn't mess with a skunk.

Cars had been his thing in his teens. He discovered, without really thinking about it, that he could steal cars, easily. And when word got out that he could nick any car anyone wanted, he suddenly found he had friends. He'd been arrested twice, the first time put on probation and banned from driving, even though he was too young to have a licence, and the second time, aggravated by an assault, he'd been sent to a young offenders' institute for a year.

And now this afternoon, on that damp sheet of paper folded in his pocket, was an order for another car. A new-shape Audi A4 convertible, automatic, low mileage, metallic blue, silver or black.

He stopped to take a breath, and dark, undefined fear suddenly rolled through him, drawing all the heat of the day away from him, leaving him feeling as if he had suddenly walked into a deep-freeze. His skin crawled again, the way it had done earlier, as if a million termites were swarming over it.

He saw the phone booth. Needed that booth. Needed that hit to get his focus, his equilibrium. He stepped into it, and the effort of pulling the heavy door left him gasping for breath. *Shit.* He leaned against the wall of the booth, in the airless heat, feeling dizzy, his legs buckling under him. He grabbed the phone, steadying himself with one hand, dug a coin from his pocket and put it in the slot, then dialled Joe's number.

'It's Wayne Rooney,' he said, talking quietly as if someone might overhear him. 'I'm here.'

'Give me your number. I'm going to call you back.'

Skunk waited, getting nervous. After several minutes, it

finally rang. A new set of instructions. Shit, Joe was getting more paranoid every day. Or had watched too many Bond movies.

He left the booth, walked about fifty yards up the street, then stopped and stared in the window of a shop that cut foam rubber to order, as he had been instructed.

The two police officers sipped their cold coffees. The shorter, burly one, whose name was Paul Packer, gripped his cup by looping his middle finger through the handle. Eight years ago, the top of his right-hand index finger had been bitten off below the first knuckle, in a scuffle, by Skunk.

This was the third deal they had witnessed in the past hour. And they knew that the same thing would be going on in half a dozen other hot spots around Brighton at this very moment. Every hour of the day and night. Trying to stop the drugs trade in a city like this was like trying to stop a glacier by throwing pebbles at it.

To feed a ten-pound-a-day drug habit, a user would commit three to five thousand pound's worth of acquisitive crime a month. Not many users were on ten pounds a day – most were on twenty, fifty, one hundred and more. Some could be as high as three or four hundred a day. And a lot of middlemen took rake-offs on the way. There were rich pickings all along the chain. You busted a bunch of people, took them off the streets, and a few days later a whole load of new faces, with a fresh supply, would appear. Scousers. Bulgarians. Russians. All with one thing in common. They made a fat living off sad little bastards like Skunk.

But Paul Packer and his colleague, Trevor Sallis, had not paid fifty pounds out of police funds to an informer to help them find Skunk in order to bust him for drugs. He was too small a player there to bother with. It was an altogether different player, in a very different field, they were hoping he would lead them to.

After some moments, a short, fat kid of about twelve, with a round, freckled face and a brush cut, wearing a grubby *South Park* T-shirt, shorts and unlaced basketball shoes, and sweating profusely, sidled up to Skunk.

'Wayne Rooney?' the kid said, in a garbled, squeaky voice.

'Yeah.'

The kid popped a small cellophane-wrapped package from his mouth and handed it to Skunk, who in turn put it straight into his mouth and handed the kid the Motorola. Seconds later the kid was sprinting away, up the hill. And Skunk was heading back towards his camper.

And Paul Packer and Trevor Sallis were out of the Starbucks door and following him down the hill.

25

NOT DEAD ENOUGH

The Major Incident Suite at Sussex House occupied much of the first floor of the building. It was accessed by a door with a swipe pad at the end of a large, mostly open-plan area housing the force's senior CID officers and their support staff.

Roy Grace felt there was always a completely different atmosphere in this part of the CID headquarters from elsewhere in the building – and indeed any of the other police buildings in and around Brighton and Hove. The corridors and offices of most police stations had a tired, institutional look and feel, but here everything always seemed new.

Too new, too modern, too clean, too damn tidy. Too – *soulless*. It could have been the offices of a chartered accountancy practice, or the admin area of a bank or insurance company.

Diagrams on white cards, which also looked brand new, were pinned to large, red-felt display boards at regular intervals along these walls. They charted all the procedural information that every detective should know by heart; but often at the start of an investigation Grace would take the time to read them again.

He had always been well aware of how easy it was to become complacent and forget things. And he had read an article recently which reinforced that view. According to the paper, most of the world's worst air disasters during the past fifty years were due to pilot error. But in many cases it wasn't an inexperienced junior, it was the senior pilot of the airline who had slipped up. The article went so far as to say that if you were sitting on an aeroplane and discovered your pilot was going to be the senior captain of the airline, then get off that plane at once!

Complacency. It was the same with medicine. Not long back, a consultant orthopaedic surgeon in Sussex had amputated the wrong leg of a male patient. Just a simple error. Caused, almost certainly, by complacency.

Which was why, at a few minutes to six p.m., Grace stopped in the hot, stuffy corridor at the entrance of the Major Incident Suite, his shirt clinging to his chest from the savage afternoon heat, the sighting of Sandy in Munich clinging to his mind. He nodded to Branson and pointed at the first diagram on the wall, just past the door of the HOLMES system manager's office, which was headed COMMON POSSIBLE MOTIVES.

'What does *maintain active lifestyle* actually mean?' Branson asked, reading off the diagram.

In an oval in the centre was a single word: *motive*. Arranged around it, at the end of spokes, were the words *jealousy, racism, anger/fright, robbery, power/control, desire, gain, payment, homophobia, hate, revenge, psychotic, sexual* and *maintain active lifestyle*.

'Killing to inherit someone's money,' Grace answered.

Glenn Branson yawned. 'There's one missing.' Then he frowned. 'Actually, two,' he said gloomily.

'Tell me?'

'*Kicks*. And *kudos*.'

'Kicks?'

'Yeah. Those kids who set fire to an old bag lady in a bus shelter last year. Poured petrol over her while she was sleeping. They didn't hate her, it was just something to do, right? Kicks.'

Grace nodded. His mind really wasn't in gear. He was still thinking about Sandy. Munich. Christ, how was he going to get through this? All he wanted to do right now was to take a plane to Munich.

'And kudos, right?' Glenn said. 'You join a gang, it's one way to get street cred, right?'

Grace moved on to the next board. It was headed DEVELOPING FORENSIC OVERVIEW. He glanced down the list, the words a meaningless blur at this moment. *Assess potential information, intelligence, witnesses. Reassess. Develop and implement forensic strategy.* Then, out of the corner of his eye, he saw a dapper, energetic-looking man in his early fifties, wearing smart fawn suit trousers, a beige shirt and a brown tie, striding up to them. Tony Case, the Senior Support Officer for this building.

'Hi, Roy,' he said cheerily. 'I've got MIR One all set up for you, and the tape's ready for you to rock and roll.' Then he turned to the Detective Sergeant and shook his hand vigorously. 'Glenn,' he said. 'Welcome back! I thought you weren't going to be working for a while yet.'

'I wasn't.'

'Have to be careful when you drink now, do you? So it doesn't come squirting out the holes in your belly?'

'Yeah, something like that,' responded Glenn, missing the joke, either deliberately or because his mind was elsewhere – Grace couldn't tell which.

'I'll be around for a while,' Case said breezily. 'Anything you need, let me know.' He tapped the mobile phone jammed in his shirt's breast pocket.

'A fresh-water dispenser? Going to need it with this heat,' Grace said.

'Already done that.'

'Good man.' He looked at his watch. Just over twenty

minutes to the six-thirty pre-briefing he had called. There should be enough time. He led Glenn Branson along, past the SOCO evidence rooms and the Outside Inquiry Team rooms, then doglegged right towards the Witness Interview Suite, where they had been earlier this afternoon.

They went into the small, narrow viewing room, adjoining the main interview room. Two mismatched chairs were pulled up against a work surface, running the width of the room, on which sat the squat metal housing of the video recording machinery, and a colour monitor giving a permanent, dreary colour picture of the coffee table and three red chairs in the empty Witness Interview Room on the other side of the wall.

Grace wrinkled his nose. It smelled as if someone had been eating a curry in here, probably from the deli counter of the ASDA supermarket across the road. He peered in the wastepaper bin and saw the evidence, a pile of cartons. It always took him a while after leaving a post-mortem before he was comfortable at the thought of food, and at this moment, having just seen the remnants of what appeared to be a shrimp rogan josh among the contents of Katie Bishop's stomach, the sickly reek of the curry in here was definitely not doing it for him.

Grace ducked down, picked up the bin and plonked it outside the door. The smell didn't clear, but at least it made him feel a little better. Then he sat in front of the monitor, refamiliarized himself with the controls of the video machine and hit the *play* button.

Thinking. Thinking all the time. *Sandy loved curries. Chicken korma. That was her favourite.*

Brian Bishop's interview from earlier began to play on the screen. Grace fast-forwarded, watching the dark-haired man in his tan designer jacket with its flashy silver buttons and his two-tone brown and white golfing shoes.

'Look like spats, those shoes,' Branson said, sitting down next to him. 'You know, like those 1930s gangsters films. Ever see *Some Like It Hot*?' His voice was flat, lacking its usual energy, but he seemed to be making a superhuman effort to be cheerful.

Grace realized this must be a difficult time of day for him. Early evening. Normally, if he were home, he'd be helping get his two children ready for bed. 'That the one with Marilyn Monroe?'

'Yeah, and Tony Curtis, Jack Lemmon, George Raft. Well brilliant. That scene, right, when they wheel the cake in and the man steps out from inside it with a machine gun and blows everyone away, and George Raft says, "There was summin' in that cake that didn't agree wid him!"'

'A modern spin on the Trojan Horse,' Grace said.

'You mean it was a remake?' Branson said, puzzled. '*The Trojan Horse*? Don't remember it.'

Grace shook his head. 'Not a movie, Glenn. What the Greeks did, in Troy!'

'What did they do?'

Grace stared hard at his friend. 'Did you get all your bloody education from watching movies? Didn't you ever learn any history?'

Branson shrugged defensively. 'Enough.'

Grace slowed the tape. On the screen Glenn Branson said, '*May I ask when you last saw your wife, Mr Bishop?*'

Grace paused the tape. 'Now, I want you to concentrate on Bishop's eyes. I want you to count his blinks. I want the number of blinks per minute. You got a second hand on that NASA control tower on your wrist?'

Branson peered down at his watch as if thrown by the

question. It was a fashionably large Casio chronometer, one of the kind that had so many dials and buttons Grace wondered if his friend had any idea what half of them did. 'Somewhere,' he said.

'OK, start timing now.'

Glenn messed it up a couple of times. Then, on the screen, Roy Grace entered the room and began questioning Bishop.

'*Where did you sleep last night, Mr Bishop?*'

'*In my flat in London.*'

'*Could anyone vouch for that?*'

'Twenty-four!' Glenn Branson announced, his eyes switching from his watch, to the screen, then back again.

'Sure?'

'Yes.'

'Good. Do it again.'

On the screen Grace asked Bishop, '*What time were you on the tee at the golf club this morning?*'

'*Just after nine.*'

'*And you drove down from London?*'

'*Yes.*'

'*What time would that have been?*'

'*About half-six.*'

'Twenty-four again!'

Grace froze the tape. 'Interesting,' he said.

'What exactly?' Branson asked.

'It's an experiment. I'm trying out something I read the other day in a psychology newsletter I subscribe to. The writer said they'd established in a lab at a university – I think it was Edinburgh – that people blink more times a minute when they are telling the truth than when they are lying.'

'For real?'

'They blink 23.6 times a minute when they are telling

the truth and 18.5 times a minute when they are lying. It's a fact that liars sit very still – they have to think harder than people telling the truth – and when we think harder we are stiller.' He ran the tape on.

Brian Bishop seemed to be getting increasingly agitated, finally standing up and gesticulating.

'A constant twenty-four,' Branson said.

'And his body language tallies,' Grace said. 'He looks like a man who is telling the truth.'

But, he knew only too well, it was only an indicator. He had misread someone's body language before and been badly caught out.

26

The press called August the *silly season*. With Parliament in its summer recess and half the world on holiday, it tended to be a quiet news month. Papers often made major items out of minor stories which, at other times, might never have even reached their pages at all; and they liked nothing better than a serious crime, the grimmer and more horrific the better. The only people who didn't seem to go on holiday, in the same way that they didn't stick to conventional office hours, were criminals.

And himself, Roy Grace contemplated.

His last proper holiday had been over nine years ago, when he and Sandy had flown to Spain and stayed in a rented flat near Malaga. The flat had been cramped and, instead of the advertised sea view, it overlooked a multistorey car park. And it rained for most of the week.

Unlike this current August heatwave here in Brighton, which brought even more holidaymakers and trippers flooding into the city than usual. The beaches were packed, as were all the bars and cafés. Brighton and Hove had a hundred thousand vertical drinking spaces, and Grace reckoned every single one of them was probably taken at this moment. It was a paradise for the street criminals. More like *open season* than *silly season* for them.

And he was well aware that, with the lack of news to go around, a murder inquiry such as the one he now had on his hands was going to be subject to even closer press scrutiny than normal. A rich woman found dead, a swanky house, possibly some kinky sex involved, a flash, good-looking husband. A slam-dunk for every editor looking to fill column inches.

From the getgo, he needed to plan the handling of the press and media with extra caution, and to try, as he always did, to make the coverage work for, rather than against, his investigation. Tomorrow morning he would be holding the first of what would become a regular series of press conferences. Before then, he had two briefing meetings with the team he was assembling, to get prepared.

And somehow, despite all that was going on, he had to find a space to get on a plane to Munich. Had to.

Absolutely had to.

So many thoughts swirled through his head about Sandy. *Sitting in a beer garden.* With a lover? With memory loss? Or was it just mistaken identity? If it had been anyone else who'd told him he would probably have dismissed it. But Dick Pope was a good detective, a thorough man, with a fine memory for faces.

A few minutes before six thirty, accompanied by Glenn Branson, Grace left the Witness Interview Suite viewing room, grabbed them both a coffee from the vending machine in the tiny kitchen area, and walked along the corridor to MIR One, which his investigation had been allocated by Tony Case. He passed a large red-felt board headed OPERATION LISBON, beneath which was a photograph of a Chinese-looking man with a wispy beard, surrounded by several different photographs of the rocks at the bottom of the tall cliffs of local beauty spot Beachy Head, each with a red circle drawn around them.

Beachy Head, a dramatic and beautiful white chalk headland, had the unwelcome reputation as England's most popular suicide spot. It offered jumpers a sheer, and grimly tantalizing, 570-foot plunge on to the shore of the English Channel. The list of people who had stepped, dived, rolled or driven over its grassy edge and survived was short.

This unfortunate, unidentified man had been found dead in May. At first he had been assumed to be just another jumper, until the post-mortem indicated that he'd probably had some assistance, on account of the fact he had been dead for some considerable while before he took his plunge. It was an ongoing investigation, but getting scaled down all the time as each successive line of inquiry hit a blank.

Every major incident was allocated a name thrown up at random by the Sussex Police computer. If any of the names had any bearing on the case to which they related, it was entirely coincidental. And they rarely did.

Unlike the workstations in the rest of Sussex House – and in all the other police stations in the county – there was no sign of anything personal on the desks here in MIR One. No pictures of families, or footballers, no fixture lists, no jokey cartoons. Everything in this room, apart from the furniture and the business hardware, related to the investigation. There wasn't much banter either, just fierce concentration. The warble of phones, the *clack* of keyboards, the shuffle of paper ejecting from laser printers. The silence of concentration.

He surveyed his initial team with mixed feelings as he walked across the room. There were several familiar faces he was happy to see. Detective Sergeant Bella Moy, an attractive woman of thirty-five with hennaed brown hair, had, as ever, an open box of Maltesers, to which she was addicted, in front of her. Nick Nicholl, short-haired, tall as a beanpole, in an open-throat short-sleeved shirt, had the pasty-faced, worn-out look of the father of a six-week-old baby. The indexer, a young, plump woman with long brown hair called Susan Gradley, who was extremely hard-working and efficient. And the long-serving Norman Potting, whom he would need to keep an eye on.

Detective Sergeant Potting was fifty-three. Beneath a thinning comb-over he had a narrow, rather rubbery face criss-crossed with broken veins, protruding lips and tobacco-stained teeth. He was dressed in a crumpled fawn linen suit and a frayed yellow short-sleeved shirt, on which he appeared to be wearing most of his lunch. Unusually, he was sporting a serious suntan, which, Grace had to admit, did improve his looks. Because he was totally politically incorrect, and most women on the force found him offensive, Potting tended to get shunted around the county, filling in gaps when a division was desperately short of manpower.

The team member Grace was least happy about of all was DC Alfonso Zafferone. A sullen, arrogant man in his late twenties, with Latino good looks and gelled, mussed-about hair, he was slickly dressed in a black suit, black shirt and cream tie. The last time he had worked with him, Zafferone had proved to be sharp, but had had a serious attitude problem. It was partly due to lack of choice, because it was the holiday season, but equally from a desire to teach the runt a lesson in manners that Grace had pulled him on to his team.

As he greeted each person in turn, Grace thought about Katie Bishop on the bed in her house in Dyke Road Avenue this morning. He thought about her on the post-mortem slab this afternoon. He could feel her, as if he carried her spirit in his heart. The weight of responsibility. This lot here in this room, and the others who would be joining his team in the conference room shortly, had a huge responsibility.

Which was why he had to push all thoughts of Sandy into a separate compartment of his mind, and lock them in there, for the time being. Somehow.

Over the course of the following hours and days he would get to know more about Katie Bishop than anybody else on earth. More than her husband, her parents, her siblings, her best friends. They might think they *knew* her, but they would only have ever known what she let them know. Inevitably something would have been held back. Every human being did that.

And inevitably, for Roy Grace, it would become personal. It always did.

But he had no way of knowing, at this moment, quite how personal the case was going to become.

27

Skunk was feeling a whole lot stronger. The world was suddenly a much better place. The heroin was doing its stuff – he felt all kind of warm and fuzzy, everything was good, his body awash with endorphins. This was how life should feel; this was how he wanted to stay feeling forever.

Bethany had turned up, with a chicken and some potato salad and a tub of crème caramel she had taken from her mother's fridge, and all the shit-heads had left his camper, and he'd boned her from behind, the way she liked it – and the way he liked it too, with her massive ass pushing into his stomach.

And now she was driving him along the seafront in her mother's little Peugeot, and he lounged in the passenger seat, tilted back, staring out through his purple lenses at his *office*. Clocking each of the parked cars in turn. Every kind of car you could think of. All dusty and sun-baked. Their owners on the beach. He was looking for one that matched the make and model that were written on the damp, crumpled sheet of lined notepaper on his lap, his *shopping list*, which he had to keep looking back at because his memory was crap.

'Have to get home soon. My mum needs the car. She's going out to bridge tonight,' Bethany said.

Every fucking make of car in the world was parked along the seafront this evening. Every fucking make except the one he was looking for. A new-shape Audi A4 convertible, automatic, low mileage, metallic blue, silver or black.

'Head up to Shirley Drive,' he said.

The clock on the dash read six fifteen p.m.

'I really have to get home by seven. She needs the car – she'll kill me if I'm late,' Bethany replied.

Skunk looked at her for a moment appreciatively. She had short black hair and thick arms. Her breasts bulged out of the top of a baggy T-shirt and her plump brown thighs were scantily covered by a blue denim mini-skirt. He kept one hand up under the elastic of her knickers, nestling in her soft, damp pubes, two fingers probing deep inside her.

'Turn right,' he instructed.

'You're making me horny again!'

He pushed his fingers even further up.

She gasped. 'Skunk, stop it!'

He was feeling horny again too. She turned right at traffic lights, past a statue of Queen Victoria, then suddenly he shouted out, 'Stop!'

'What?'

'There! There! There!' He grabbed the wheel, forcing her over to the kerb, ignoring the squeal of brakes and the blast of the horn of the car behind them.

As she pulled the car up, Skunk extracted his fingers, then his hand. 'Fucking brilliant! See ya!'

He opened the car door, stumbled out and was gone without even a backward glance.

There, halted at the traffic lights on the opposite side of the road was a dark metallic blue Audi A4 convertible. Skunk pulled a biro out of his pocket, wrote down the licence plate on his sheet of paper, then tugged his mobile phone out of his trouser pocket and dialled a number.

'GU 06 LGJ,' he read out. 'Can you have them for me in an hour?'

He was so pleased he didn't even see the Peugeot

driving off, the wave of Bethany's hand, nor hear her brief toot of the horn.

Brilliant! he thought. *Yeah!*

Nor did he see the small grey Ford, sitting at the kerb a couple of hundred yards behind him. It was one of a five-car surveillance team that had been tailing him for the past half-hour, since he had left his camper.

28

Brian Bishop sat on the edge of the large bed, his chin cupped in his hands, staring at the television in his hotel room. A cup of tea on a tray beside him had long gone cold, while the two biscuits in their cellophane wrapper remained untouched. He had turned the air conditioning off because it was too cold and now, still wearing his golfing clothes beneath his jacket, he was dripping with perspiration.

Outside, despite the double-glazing, he could hear the wail of a siren, the faint chunter of a lorry engine, the intermittent *parp-parp-parp* of a car alarm. A world out there that he felt totally disconnected from as he stared at his house – his *home* – on bloody Sky News. It felt totally surreal. As if he had suddenly become a stranger in his own life. And not just a stranger. A pariah.

He'd felt something like this before, during his separation and then divorce from Zoë when his children, Carly and Max, had taken her side, after she had done a successful job of poisoning them against him, and refused to speak to him for nearly two years.

A mediagenic newscaster with perfect hair and great teeth was standing outside his house, in front of a strip of blue and white POLICE – CRIME SCENE – DO NOT CROSS tape, brandishing a microphone. 'A post-mortem was carried out this afternoon. We will be returning to this story in our seven o'clock news. I'm David Wiltshire, Sky News.'

Brian was feeling totally and utterly bewildered.

His mobile phone started ringing. Not recognizing the number, he let it ring on. Almost every call this afternoon had been from the press or media, who had picked up his mobile number off his company's website, he presumed. Interestingly, other than Sophie, only two friends had phoned him, his mate Glenn Mishon and Ian Steel; his business partner, Simon Walton, had also called. Simon had sounded genuinely concerned for him, asked him if there was anything he could do, and told him not to worry about the business, he would take care of everything for as long as Brian needed.

Brian had spoken several times to Katie's parents, who were in Alicante, in Spain, where Katie's father was setting up yet another of his – almost certainly doomed – business ventures. They were flying back in the morning.

He wondered whether he should call his lawyer, but why? He didn't have anything to be guilty about. He just did not know what to do, so he sat there, motionless and mesmerized, staring at the screen, vaguely taking in the cluster of police vehicles jamming his driveway and parked out on the street. A steady stream of cars crawled by, their drivers and passengers rubber-necking, every one of them. He had work to do. Calls to make, emails to answer and send. So damn much, but at this moment he was incapable of functioning.

Restless, he stood up, paced around the room for some moments, then he walked through into the gleaming, clean bathroom, stared at the towels, lifted the lavatory seat, wanting to pee. Nothing happened. Stared at his face in the mirror above the basin. Then his eye was caught by a row of toiletries. Small, imitation-marble plastic bottles of shampoo, conditioner, shower gel and body lotion. He moved them until they were evenly spaced out, but then he didn't like their position on the shelf, and he moved them several inches to the right, carefully ensuring they were evenly spaced.

That made him feel a little better.

At ten o'clock this morning, he'd been feeling good, contented, enjoying this incredible summer weather. Playing one of the best rounds of golf of his life, on one of the most beautiful days of the year. Now, a mere eight and a half hours later, his life was in ruins. Katie was dead.

His darling, darling, darling Katie.

And the police quite clearly believed he was involved. Jesus.

He'd just spent most of the afternoon with two policewomen who said they were acting as his family liaison officers. Nice ladies, they'd been very supportive, but he was worn out with their questions and needed this break.

And then sweet Sophie – what was all that about? What the hell did she mean that they'd spent the night together? They hadn't. No way. Absolutely no which way.

Sure, he fancied her. But an affair? No way. His ex-wife, Zoë, had had an affair. He'd discovered that she had been cheating on him for three years, and the pain when he'd found out had been almost unbearable. He could never do that to anyone. And recently he'd felt things were not right between himself and Katie, and he'd been making a big effort with their relationship, or so he felt.

He enjoyed flirting with Sophie. He enjoyed her company. Hell, it was flattering to have a girl in her mid-twenties crazy about you. But that was as far as it went. Although, he realized, maybe he'd encouraged her too far. Quite why he'd ever invited her to lunch, after sitting next to her at the conference on tax relief on film investments he had been invited to, he didn't know. All the danger flags had been up, but he'd gone right ahead. They'd seen each other again, several times. Exchanged emails sometimes two or three times a day – and hers, recently, had been getting more suggestive. And in truth he had thought about her a couple of times, during the – increasingly rare, these days – act of making love to Katie.

But he'd never slept with her. Damn it, he'd never even kissed her on the lips.

Had he?

Was he doing things and not remembering them? There *were* people who did things without realizing it. Stress could cause people mental problems, make the brain function in weird ways, and he'd been under plenty of stress lately, worrying about both his business and Katie.

His company, International Rostering Solutions, which he had founded nine years ago, was doing well – but almost too well. He needed to be in his office earlier every morning, just to clear all his emails from the previous day – as many as two hundred – but then the new lot would deluge in. And now that they had more offices opening up around the world – most recently in New York, Los Angeles, Tokyo, Sydney, Dubai and Kuala Lumpur – communications were twenty-four/seven. He had taken on a lot more staff, of course, but he had never been good at delegating. So increasingly he found himself working in the office until well into the evening, and then going home and continuing to work after supper – and, to Katie's displeasure, over the weekends as well.

In addition, he sensed that all was not right in their marriage. Despite her charity and Rotary interests, Katie was resenting the increasing amount of time she was left alone. He had tried to tell her that he would not be working at this pace forever – within a couple of years they might float the business or sell out, with enough money never to have to work again. Then she reminded him he had said that two years ago. And a further two years before then.

She had told him very recently, and quite angrily, that he would always be a workaholic, because he didn't really have any interests outside his business. Lamely, he had argued back that his *baby*, the 1962 Jaguar he had lovingly restored, was an interest. Until she had responded, scathingly, that she couldn't recall the last time he had taken it out of the garage. And, he was forced to admit to himself, nor could he.

He remembered, during the break-up of his marriage to Zoë, when he had found himself barely able to cope, his doctor had suggested he check into a psychiatric clinic for a couple of weeks. He'd rejected that, and somehow got through everything. But he had that same low and some-times muddled feeling now that he'd had then. And he was picking up from Katie some of those same kinds of vibes he'd experienced with Zoë, before he'd discovered she was having an affair. Maybe it was just in his mind.

Maybe his mind just wasn't working that well right now.

29

The camera panned slowly, and a little jerkily, around the Bishops' bedroom at 97 Dyke Road Avenue. It stopped for some moments on the naked body of Katie Bishop, lying spread-eagled, her wrists tied to the rather fancy wooden bedposts, ligature mark on her neck, gas mask lying beside her.

'The gas mask was on her face when she was found,' Roy Grace said to his team, which had now increased to twenty, assembled in the conference room of the Major Incident Suite and watching the SOCO video of the crime scene.

The room could hold, at a pinch, twenty-five people seated on the hard, red chairs around the rectangular table, and another thirty, if necessary, standing. One of its uses was for major crime briefings for press conferences, and it was for this reason that there stood, at the far end opposite the video screen, a curved, two-tone blue board, six feet high and ten feet wide, boldly carrying the Sussex Police website address, plus the Crimestoppers legend and phone number. All press and media statements were given by officers against this backdrop.

'Who removed it, Roy?' Detective Inspector Kim Murphy asked, in an amiable but very direct voice.

Grace had worked with Kim before, on bringing a Brighton landlord to trial for conspiracy to murder, with a recently successful conclusion, and it had been a good experience. He had requested her for this inquiry as his deputy SIO. She was a sparky, ferociously intelligent DI in her mid-thirties and he liked her a lot. She was also very attractive, with neat, shoulder-length fair hair streaked with highlights, a wide, open face and an almost constant, beguiling smile, which masked, very effectively – to many a villain's surprise and regret – a surprisingly tough, don't-mess-with-me, streetwise character. Despite her senior rank, there was something of a tomboy about her. It was accentuated this evening by the sporty, quite butch beige linen jacket with epaulettes that she wore over a white T-shirt and trousers. Most days she turned up to work on a Harley-Davidson, which she maintained herself.

'The cleaning lady,' he said. 'And God only knows what other evidence she trampled over.'

He was struggling this evening. Really struggling. He was supposed to be the Senior Investigating Officer on a murder inquiry, with all the responsibilities that entailed. But however much he tried to concentrate, part of him was in another place, another city, another investigation altogether. *Sandy*. And, he just realized, he'd completely forgotten to call Cleo, to tell her what time he thought he might be through tonight. He would try to sneak a text to her during this briefing.

He was feeling confused about his relationship with Cleo suddenly. What if Sandy really was in Munich? What would happen if he met her?

There were just too many imponderables. Here at this moment, seated at the workstation in the real world of MIR One, expectant faces were staring at him. Was it his imagination or were they looking at him strangely?

Pull yourself together!

'The time is six thirty, Friday 4 August,' he read out from his briefing notes. He had removed his suit jacket, pulled his tie to half-mast and popped open his top two shirt buttons against the sweltering heat.

'This is our first briefing of Operation Chameleon,' he went on. 'The investigation into the murder of a thirty-five-year-old female person identified as Mrs Katherine Margaret Bishop – known as Katie – of 97 Dyke Road Avenue, Hove, East Sussex, conducted on day one following the discovery of her body at eight thirty this morning. I will now summarize the incident.'

For some minutes, Grace reviewed the events leading up to the discovery of Katie's body. When he got to the gas mask, true to form, Norman Potting interrupted him.

'Maybe he had chronic wind, Roy. Gave her the gas mask out of kindness.' Potting looked around with a grin. But no one smiled.

Inwardly, Grace groaned. 'Thank you, Norman,' he said. 'We've got a lot to get through. We can do without the humour.'

Potting continued to look around, grinning irrepressibly at his audience, unfazed by their blank faces.

'We can also do without the gas mask being leaked any-where,' Grace added. 'I want absolute silence on that. Understood, everyone?'

It was common practice to withhold key pieces of information discovered at a crime scene from the public. This way, if anyone rang in and mentioned a gas mask, the investigating team would know immediately that the caller was almost certainly for real.

Grace began reviewing the tasks for each person. Katie Bishop's family tree needed to be established, the names of all the people she associated with, plus backgrounds on them. This was being worked on by the FLOs, and he had assigned supervision of the task to Bella Moy earlier in the day.

Bella read from a printout of notes in front of her. 'I don't have much so far,' she said. 'Katie Bishop was born Katherine Margaret Denton, the only child of parents living in Brighton. She married Brian Bishop five years ago – her third marriage, his second. No children.'

'Any idea why not?' Grace asked.

'No.' Bella seemed a little surprised by the question. 'Bishop has two by his first marriage.'

Grace made a note on his pad. 'OK.'

'She spends her weeks mostly in Brighton – usually goes up to London for one night. Brian Bishop has a flat in London, where he stays Monday to Fridays.'

'His knocking shop?' ventured Norman Potting.

Grace didn't respond. But Potting had a point. No children after five years of marriage, and substantially separate lives, did not indicate a particularly close relationship. Although he and Sandy had been married nine years, and they hadn't had children – but there were reasons for that. Medical ones. He made another note.

Alfonso Zafferone, chewing gum, with his usual insolent expression, had been detailed to work with the HOLMES analyst to plot the sequence of events, list the suspects – in this case, one so far, her husband. A full time-line needed to be run on Brian Bishop to establish if he could have been present within the period that Katie was murdered. Were there any similar murders in this county, or in others, recently? Anything involving a gas mask? Zafferone leaned back in his chair; he had shoulders so massive he must have worked on them, Grace thought. And like all the men in the room, he had removed his jacket.

Flashy rhinestone cufflinks and gold armbands glinted on the sleeves of his sharp, black shirt.

Another action Grace had assigned to Norman Potting was to obtain plans of the Bishops' house, an aerial photograph of the property and surrounding area, and to ensure all routes by which someone could have got to the house were carefully searched. He also wanted from Potting, and then separately from the forensic scene manager, a detailed assessment of the crime scene, including reports from the house-to-house search of the neighbourhood, which had been started early that afternoon.

Potting reported that two computers in the house had already been taken to the High Tech Crime Unit for analysis; the house landline records for the past twelve months had been requisitioned from British Telecom, as had the mobile phone records for both the Bishops.

'I had the mobile phone that was found in her car checked by the Telecoms Unit, Roy,' Potting said. 'There was one message timed at eleven ten yesterday morning, a male voice.' Potting looked down at his notepad. 'It said, *See you later.*'

'That was all?' Grace asked.

'They tried a call-back but the number was withheld.'

'We need to find out who that was.'

'I've been on to the phone company,' Potting replied. 'But I'm not going to be able to get the records until after the start of office hours on Monday.'

Fridays, Saturdays and Sundays were the worst days for starting a murder inquiry, Grace thought. Labs were shut and so were admin offices. Just at the very moment you needed information quickly, you could lose two or three vital days, waiting. 'Get me a tape of it. We'll ask Brian Bishop if he recognizes the voice. It might be his.'

'No, I checked that already,' Potting said. 'The gardener turned up, so I played it to him.'

'He on your suspect list?'

'He's about eighty and a bit frail. I'd put him a long way down it.'

That did elicit a smile from everyone.

'By my calculations,' Grace said, 'that places him at the bottom of a list of two.'

He paused to drink some coffee, then some water. 'Right, resourcing. At the moment all divisions are relatively quiet. I want you each to work out what assistance you need drafted in to supplement our own people. In the absence of any other major news stories, we're likely to have the pleasure of the full attention of the press, so I want us to look good and get a fast result. We want a full dog-and-pony show.' And it wasn't just about pleasing the public, Grace knew but did not say. It was about, again, demonstrating his credibility to his acerbic boss, the Assistant Chief Constable Alison Vosper, who was longing for him to make another slip-up.

Any day soon, the man she had drafted in from the Met, and had promoted to the same rank as himself, the slime-ball Detective Superintendent Cassian Pewe – her new *golden boy* – would finish his period of convalescence after a car accident and be taking up office here at Sussex House. With the unspoken goal of eating Roy Grace's lunch and having him transferred sideways to the back of beyond.

It was when Grace turned to forensics that he could sense everyone concentrate just a little bit harder. Ignoring Nadiuska De Sancha's pages of elaborate, technical details, he cut to the chase. 'Katie Bishop died from strangulation from a ligature around her neck, either thin cord or wire. Tissue from her neck has been sent to the laboratory for further analysis, which may reveal the murder weapon,' he announced. He took another mouthful of coffee. 'A significant quantity of semen was found in her vagina, indicating sexual intercourse had taken place at some point close to death.'

'She was a dead good shag,' Norman Potting muttered.

Bella Moy turned to face Potting. 'You are so gross!'

Bristling with anger, Grace said, 'Norman, that's enough from you. I want a word after this meeting. None of us are in any mood for your bad-taste jokes. Understand?'

Potting dropped his eyes like a chided schoolboy. 'No offence meant, Roy.'

Shooting him daggers, Grace continued, 'The semen has been sent to the laboratory for fast-track analysis.'

'When do you expect to have the results back?' Nick Nicholl asked.

'Monday by the very earliest.'

'We'll need a swab from Brian Bishop,' Zafferone said.

'We got that this afternoon,' Grace said, smug at being ahead of the DC on this.

He looked down at Glenn Branson for confirmation. The DS gave him a gloomy nod and Grace felt a sudden tug in his heart. Poor Glenn seemed close to tears. Maybe it had been a mistake pulling him back to work early. To be going through the trauma of a marriage bust-up, on top of not feeling physically at his best, and with a hangover that still had not gone away to boot, was not a great place to be. But too late for that now.

Potting raised a hand. 'Er, Roy – the presence of semen – can we assume there is a sexual element to the victim's death – that she'd been raped?'

'Norman,' he said sharply, 'assumptions are the mother and father of all fuck-ups. OK?' Grace drank some water, then went on. 'Two family liaison officers have been appointed,' he said. 'WPC Linda Buckley and WPC Maggie Campbell—'

He was interrupted by the loud ring tone of Nick Nicholl's mobile phone. Giving Roy Grace an apologetic look, the young DC stood up, bent almost double, as if somehow reducing his height would reduce the volume of his phone, and stepped a few paces away from his work-station.

'DC Nicholl,' he said.

Taking advantage of the interruption, Zafferone peered at Potting's face. 'Been away, Norman, have you?'

'Thailand,' Potting answered. He smiled at the ladies, as if imagining they would be impressed by such an exotic traveller.

'Brought yourself back a nice suntan, didn't yer?'

'Brought myself back more than that,' Potting said, beaming now. He held up his hand, then raised his third finger, which sported a plain gold wedding band.

'Bloody hell,' Zafferone said. 'A *wife*?'

Bella popped a half-melted Malteser into her mouth. She spoke with a voice that Grace liked a lot. It was soft but always very direct. Despite looking, beneath her tangle of hair, like she was sometimes in another world, Bella was very sharp indeed. She never missed anything. 'So that's your fourth wife now, isn't it?'

'That's right,' he said, still beaming, as if it were an achievement to be proud of.

'Thought you weren't going to get married again, Norman,' Grace said.

'Well, you know what they say, Roy. It's a woman's prerogative to change a man's mind.'

Bella smiled at him with more compassion than

humour, as if he were some curious but slightly grotesque exhibit in a zoo.

'So where did you meet her?' Zafferone asked. 'In a bar? A club? A massage parlour?'

Looking coy suddenly, Potting replied, 'Actually, through an agency.'

And for a moment, Grace saw a rare flash of humility in the man's face. A shadow of sadness. Of loneliness.

'OK,' Nick Nicholl said, sitting back down at the work-station and putting his phone back in his pocket. 'We have something of interest.' He put his notepad on the surface in front of him.

Everyone looked at him with intensity.

'Gatwick airport's on security alert. ANPR cameras have been installed on the approach bridges either side of the M23. A Bentley Continental car, registered to Brian Bishop, was picked up by one at eleven forty-seven last night. He was on the south-bound carriageway, heading towards Brighton. There was a technical problem with the north-bound camera, so there is no record of him returning to London – if he did.'

ANPR was the automatic number plate recognition system increasingly used by the police and security services to scan vehicles entering a particular area.

Glenn Branson looked at Grace. 'Seems like he failed your blink test, Roy. He told us a porky. He said he was tucked up in bed in London at that time.'

But Grace wasn't upset about this. Suddenly his spirits lifted. If they could force a confession out of Brian Bishop, tonight perhaps, then with luck the investigation would be over almost before it had begun. And he could go straight to Munich – perhaps as early as tomorrow. Another option would be to leave Kim Murphy running the inquiry, but that wasn't the way he operated. He liked to be fully hands on, in charge of everything, overseeing every detail. It was when you had someone working with you, at almost your level, that mistakes happened. Important things could easily fall between the cracks.

'Let's go and have a word with the FLOs,' he said. 'See if we can find out more about his car. See if we can jog Bishop's memory for him.'

30

At a quarter past seven, the sun was finally starting to quit the Sussex coast. The Time Billionaire sat at a table at a crowded outdoor café, sipping his third Coke Zero and occasionally scraping out more remains of pecan ice cream from the glass in front of him, to help pass the time. Spending some of his time dollars, his time pounds, his time euros. Might as well spend it, you couldn't take it with you.

He brought his right hand up to his mouth and sucked for some moments. That stinging pain was still there and, he wasn't sure if it was his imagination, the row of tiny red marks, surrounded by faint bruising the colour of a nicotine stain, seemed to be looking steadily more livid.

A steel band was playing a short distance away. 'Island in the Sun'.

He'd been going to go to an island in the sun once. Everything had been all set and then the *thing* had happened. Life had pissed on him from a great height. Well, not life exactly, no, no, no.

Just one of its inhabitants.

The air tasted salty. It smelled of rope, rust, boat varnish and, every few minutes, a sudden faint but distinct reek of urine. Some time after the sun had gone, the moon would rise tonight. Men had pissed on that too.

The receipt for his bill, already paid, lay pinned under the ashtray, flapping like a dying butterfly in the light sea breeze. He was always prepared, always ready for his next move. Could never predict what that would be. Unlike the sun.

He wondered where that ochre disc of dumb, broiling gases was heading next and tried to calculate some of the world time zones in his head. Right now, thirteen and a half thousand miles away, it would be a crimson ball, slowly creeping up towards the horizon in Sydney. It would still be blisteringly bright, high in the afternoon sky in Rio de Janeiro. No matter where it was, it never had any sense of its power. Of the power it gave to people. Not like the way he could feel the power in himself.

The power of life and death.

Perspective. Everything was about perspective. One man's darkness was another man's daylight. How come so many people did not realize that?

Did that dumb girl, sitting on the beach just yards in front of him, staring across the bodies laid out on the beach, at the flat, shifting mass of ocean? Staring at the slack sails of dinghies and windsurfers? At the distant grey smudge of tankers and container ships sitting, motionless, high up on the horizon, like toys on a shelf? At late, stupid bathers splashing about in the filthy lavatory they imagined to be pure, clean seawater?

Did Sophie Harrington know it was the last time she would see any of this?

The last time she would smell tarred rope, boat paint or the urine of strangers?

The whole damn beach was a sewer of bare flesh. Bodies in skimpy clothing. White, red, brown, black. Flaunting themselves. Some of the women topless, bitch whores. He watched one waddling around, straggly ginger hair down to her shoulders, tits down to her stomach, stomach down to her pelvis, swigging a bottle of beer or lager – too far away to tell which – fat arse sticking out of a skein of electric blue nylon, thighs dimpled with cellulite. Wondered what she'd look like in his gas mask with her straggly ginger pubes jammed against his face. Wondered what it would smell like down there. Oysters?

Then he switched his attention back to the stupid girl who'd been sitting on the beach for the past two hours. She was standing up now, stepping over the pebbles, holding her shoes in her hands, wincing with every step she took. Why, he wondered, didn't she just put her shoes on? Was she really *that* dim-witted?

He would ask her that question later, when he was alone in her bedroom with her, and she had the gas mask on her face, and her voice would come at him all mumbled and indistinct.

Not that he cared about the answer.

All he cared about was what he had written in the blank section for notes at the back of his blue Letts schoolboy's diary, when he was twelve years old. That diary was one of the few possessions he still had from his childhood. It was in a small metal box where he kept the things that were of sentimental value to him. The box was in a lock-up garage, quite near here, which he rented by the month. He had learned as a small child the importance of finding a space in this world, however small, that is your own. Where you can keep your things. Sit and have your thoughts.

It was in a private space he had found, when he was twelve years old, that the words he wrote in his diary first came to him.

If you want to really hurt someone, don't kill them, that only hurts for a short time. It's much better to kill the thing they love. Because that will hurt them forever.

He repeated those words over and over like a mantra, as

he followed Sophie Harrington, as ever keeping a safe distance. She stopped and put her shoes on, then made her way along the seafront promenade, past the shops in the red-brick-faced Arches on Brighton seafront, one a gallery of local artists, past a seafood restaurant, the steel band, an old Second World War mine that had been washed up and was now mounted on a plinth, and a shop that sold beach hats, buckets and spades and rotating windmills on sticks.

He followed her through the carefree, sunburnt masses, up the ramp towards busy Kings Road, where she turned left, heading west, past the Royal Albion hotel, the Old Ship, the Odeon Kingswest, the Thistle Hotel, the Grand, the Metropole.

He was getting more aroused by the minute.

The breeze tugged at the sides of his hood and for one anxious moment it nearly blew back. He snatched it down hard over his forehead, then pulled his mobile phone from his pocket. He had an important business call to make.

He waited for a police car, siren wailing, to go past before dialling, continuing to stride along, fifty yards behind her. He wondered whether she would walk the whole way to her flat, or take a bus, or a taxi. He really did not mind. He knew where she lived. He had his own key.

And he had all the time in the world.

Then, with a sudden stab of panic, he realized he had left the plastic carrier bag containing the gas mask back in the café.

31

Linda Buckley had positioned herself intelligently in a leather armchair in the large, smart and comfortable foyer of the Hotel du Vin, Grace thought, as he entered the building with Glenn Branson. She was close enough to hear anyone asking for Brian Bishop at the reception desk and had a good view of people entering and leaving the hotel.

The family liaison officer reluctantly put down the book she was reading, *The Plimsoll Sensation*, a history of the Plimsoll Line by Nicolette Jones, which she had heard serialized on the radio, and stood up.

'Hi, Linda,' Grace said. 'Good book?'

'Fascinating!' she replied. 'Stephen, my husband, was in the Merchant Navy, so I know a bit about ships.'

'Is our guest in his room?'

'Yes. I spoke to him about half an hour ago, to see how he was doing. Maggie's gone off to make some phone calls. We're giving him a break – it's been fairly intensive this afternoon, particularly up at the mortuary, when he identified his wife.'

Grace looked around the busy area. All the stools at the stainless-steel bar, on the far side of the room, were taken, as were all the sofas and chairs. A group of men in dinner jackets and women in evening dresses were clustered together, as if about to head off to a ball. He didn't spot any journalists.

'No press yet?'

'So far, so good,' she said. 'I checked him in under a false name – Mr Steven Brown.'

Grace smiled. 'Good girl!'

'It might buy us a day,' she said. 'But they'll be here soon.'

And with luck, Brian Bishop will be in a custody cell by then, he thought to himself.

Grace headed towards the stairs, then stopped. Branson was staring dreamily at four very attractive girls in their late teens, who were drinking cocktails on a huge leather sofa. He waved a hand to distract his colleague. Glenn walked over to him pensively.

'I was just thinking . . .' the Detective Sergeant said.

'About long legs?'

'Long legs?'

From his baffled look, Roy realized his friend hadn't been looking at the girls at all; he hadn't even clocked them. He had just been staring into space. He put an avuncular arm around Branson's waist. Lean, and rock hard from weight training, it felt like a sturdy young tree inside his jacket, not a human midriff. 'You're going to be OK, mate,' he said.

'I feel like I'm in someone else's life – know what I mean, man?' Branson said, as they climbed the first flight of stairs. 'Like I've stepped out of my life and into someone else's by mistake.'

Bishop's room was on the second floor. Grace rapped on the door. There was no answer. He rapped again, louder. Then, leaving Branson waiting in the corridor, he went downstairs and came up with the duty manager, a smartly suited man in his early thirties, who opened the room with a pass key.

It was empty. Stifling hot and empty. Closely followed by

Branson, Grace strode across and opened the bathroom door. It looked pristine, untouched, apart from the fact that the lavatory seat had been raised.

'This is the right room?' Grace asked.

'Mr Steven Brown's room, absolutely, sir,' the duty manager said.

The only clues that anyone had been in here during the past few hours were a deep indent in the purple bedcover, close to the foot of the bed, and a silver tray containing a stone-cold cup of tea, a teapot, a jug of milk and two biscuits in an unopened pack, in the centre of the bed.

32

As she walked along the teeming, wide, promenade pavement of Kings Road, Sophie was trying to remember what she had in the fridge or the freezer to make some supper. Or what tins were in her store-cupboard. Not that she had much appetite, but she knew she must eat something. A cyclist pedalled past on the track in his crash helmet and Lycra. Two youths clattered by on skateboards.

In a novel some while ago she had read a phrase that had stuck in her mind: *Bad things happen on beautiful days.*

9/11 had happened on a beautiful day. It was one of the things that had most struck her about all the images, that the impact of those planes striking the towers might not have had quite the strength of emotional resonance if the sky had been grey and drizzly. You kind of expected shit to happen on grey days.

Today had been a double-shit or maybe even a triple-shit day. First the news of Brian's wife's death, then his coldness to her when she had phoned to try to comfort him. And now the realization that all her weekend plans were down the khazi.

She stopped, walked through a gap in the row of deckchairs and rested her elbows on the turquoise metal railings overlooking the beach. Directly below her, several children were lobbing brightly coloured balls in a gravel play area that had once been a boating pond. Parents chatted a few yards away, keeping a watchful eye. She wanted to be a parent too, wanted to see her own children playing with their friends. She had always reckoned she would be a good mother. Her own parents had been good to her.

They were nice, decent people, still in love with each other after thirty years of marriage; they still held hands whenever they walked together. They had a small business, importing handmade lace doilies, napkins and tablecloths from France and from China, and selling them at craft fairs. They ran the business from their little cottage on their smallholding near Orford in Suffolk, using a barn as a warehouse. She could take the train up to see them tomorrow. They were always happy for her to come home for a weekend, but she wasn't sure she wanted that kind of weekend.

She wasn't sure at all what she wanted at this moment. Surprisingly, she just knew, for the first time since she had met him, that it wasn't Brian. He was right not to see her today. And there was no way she could sit in the wings like a vulture, waiting for the funeral and a decent period of mourning. Yes, she liked him. Really liked him, actually. In fact, *adored* him. He excited her – in part, OK, it was the flattery of having this older, immensely attractive and successful man doting on her – but he was also an incredible lover, if a little bit kinky. Absolutely the best ever in her, admittedly limited, experience.

One thing she could just not get her head around was his denial that they had slept together last night. Was he worried that his phone was bugged? Was he in denial because of his grief? She guessed she was learning, as she grew older, that men were very strange creatures sometimes. Maybe always.

Sophie looked up, beyond the play area at the beach. It seemed filled with couples. Lovers kissing, nuzzling, walking arm in arm, hand in hand, laughing, relaxing, looking forward to the weekend. There were still plenty of boats out. Half past seven; it would be light for a while yet. Light evenings for a few more weeks, before the steady drawing in of the winter darkness.

Suddenly, for no reason, she shivered.

She walked on, past the remains of the West Pier. For so long she had thought it a hideous eyesore, but now she was starting to quite like it. It no longer looked like a building that had collapsed. Instead, to her the fire-blackened skeleton resembled the ribcage of a monster that had risen from the deep. One day people would gasp in shock as the whole of the sea in front of Brighton filled with these creatures, she thought for a moment.

Weird, the notions that sometimes came into her head. Maybe it was from reading too many horror scripts. Maybe it was her conscience punishing her for the bad thing she was doing. Sleeping with a married man. Yes, absolutely, totally and utterly, it was wrong.

When she'd confided to her best friend, Holly's first reaction had been one of excitement. Conspiratorial glee. The best secret in the world. But then, as always happened with Holly – a practical person who liked to think things through – all the negatives came out.

Somewhere, in between buying a ripe avocado, some organic tomatoes and a tub of ready-made Atlantic prawn cocktail, and reaching her front door, she had made her mind up, very definitely, that she would end her relationship with Brian Bishop.

She would just have to wait for a more tactful time. Meanwhile, she remembered the text she'd had this morning from Holly, telling her about a party tomorrow night. That would be the sensible thing. Go to the party and hang out with some people her own age.

Her flat was on the third floor of a rather tired Victorian terrace, just north of the busy shopping street of Church Road. The lock on the front door had worked so loose in its rotting surround that anyone could have opened it with just a sharp push to shear the screws out of the wood. Her land-lord, a friendly, diminutive Iranian, was forever promising to get it fixed, the same way he kept promising to have the drip in the loo cistern fixed, and never did.

She opened the door and was greeted by the smell of damp carpets, a faint aroma of Chinese takeaway and a strong whiff of dope. From the other side of the door lead-ing into the ground-floor flat came a frenetic pounding, rhythmic, bass beat. The post lay spread out on the thread-bare hall carpet, untouched from where it had fallen this morning. She knelt and checked it. The usual decimated rainforest-worth of pizza menus, summer sale offers, fliers for concerts, home insurance and a whole ton of other junk, with a few personal letters and bills interspersed.

Naturally tidy, Sophie scooped it up into two piles, one comprising rubbish mail, one the proper post, and put them both on the shelf. Then she eased herself past two bicycles, which were blocking most of the passageway, and up the balding treads of the staircases. On the first-floor landing, she heard the sound of Mrs Harsent's television. Raucous studio laughter. Mrs Harsent was a sweet old lady of eighty-five who, fortunately for her, with the noisy students she had underneath, was deaf as a post.

Sophie loved her top-floor flat, which although small was light and airy, and had been nicely modernized by the landlord with beige fitted carpets, creamy white walls and smart cream linen curtains and blinds. She had decorated it with framed posters of some of the films from Blinding Light Productions and with large, moody black and white sketches of the faces of some of her favourite stars. There was one of Johnny Depp, one of George Clooney, one of Brad Pitt, and her favourite, Heath Ledger, which had pride of place on the wall facing her bed.

She switched on her television, channel-hopped, and found *American Idol*, a show she really liked. With the volume up loud, partly to drown out the sound of Mrs Harsent's television and partly so she could hear it in her kitchenette, she took a bottle of New Zealand Sauvignon from her fridge, opened it and poured herself a glass. Then she cut open the avocado, removed the stone and dropped it in her waste bin, before squeezing some lemon over the avocado.

Half an hour later, having had a refreshing bath, she sat propped on her bed, wearing just a baggy white T-shirt, with her avocado and prawn salad, and her third glass of wine on the tray on her lap, watching a geeky-looking man in huge glasses reach sixty-four thousand pounds on *Who Wants to be a Millionaire?*, which she had recorded earlier in the week. And finally, with the sky gradually darkening outside her window, her day was starting to improve.

She did not hear the key turning in the lock of her front door.

33

Roy Grace stood in the empty hotel room and dialled Brian Bishop's mobile phone number. It went straight to voice-mail. 'Mr Bishop,' he said. 'This is Detective Superintendent Grace. Please call as soon as you get this message.' He left his number. Then he rang Linda Buckley down in the lobby. 'Did our friend have any luggage?'

'Yes, Roy. An overnight bag and a briefcase – a laptop bag.'

Grace and Branson checked all the drawers and cupboards. There was nothing. Whatever he had brought here, Bishop had taken away with him. Grace turned to the duty manager. 'Where's the nearest fire escape?'

The man, who wore a name tag which said ROLAND WRIGHT – DUTY MANAGER, led them along a corridor to the fire escape door. Grace opened it and stared down the metal steps into a courtyard filled mostly with wheelie bins. A strong aroma of cooking rose up. He closed the door, thinking hard. Why the hell had Bishop left again? And where had he gone to?

'Mr Wright,' he said, 'I need to check if our guest, Steven Brown, made or received any phone calls while he was here.'

'No problem – we can go down to my office.'

Ten minutes later, Grace and Branson sat down in the lobby of the hotel with Linda Buckley. 'OK,' Grace said. 'Brian Bishop received a phone call at five twenty.' He checked his own watch. 'Approximately two and a half hours ago. But we have no information who it was from. He made no outgoing calls from the hotel phone. Maybe he used his mobile – but we won't know that until we get his records – which will be Monday at the earliest, from past experience with the phone companies. He's slunk out, with his luggage, probably down the fire escape, deliberately avoiding you. Why?'

'Not exactly the actions of an innocent man,' Glenn Branson said.

Grace, deep in thought, acknowledged the somewhat obvious comment with a faint nod. 'He has two bags with him. So did he walk somewhere or take a taxi?'

'Depends where he was going,' Branson said.

Grace stared at his colleague with the kind of look he normally reserved for imbeciles. 'So where was he going, Glenn?'

'Home?' Linda Buckley said, trying to be helpful.

'Linda, I want you to get on to the local taxi companies. Call all of them. See if anyone picked up a man matching Bishop's description in the vicinity of this hotel some time around five twenty, five thirty this afternoon. See if anyone called a cab to come here. Glenn, check the staff. Ask if anyone saw Bishop get into a taxi.'

Then he dialled Nick Nicholl. 'What are you doing?'

The young DC sounded in something of a state. 'I'm – er – changing my son's nappy.'

How fucking great is that? Grace thought but restrained himself from saying. 'I hate to drag you from your domestic bliss,' he said.

'It would be a relief, Roy, believe me.'

'Let's not run it by your wife,' Grace said. 'I need you to get down to Brighton station. Brian Bishop's done another

disappearing act on us. I want you to check the CCTVs there
– see if he turns up on the concourse or any platforms.'

'Right away!' Nick Nicholl could not have sounded more
cheerful if he had just won the Lottery.

*

Ten minutes later, terrified out of his wits, Roy Grace sat
belted into the passenger seat of the unmarked police Ford
Mondeo.

Having recently failed his Advanced Police Driving
course – which would have enabled him to take part in
high-speed chases – Glenn was now preparing to take it
again. And although his head was full of the words of
wisdom his driving instructor had imparted, Grace did not
think that they had permeated his brain. As the speedometer needle reached the 100-mph mark on the approach
to a gentle left-hander, on the road out of Brighton towards
the North Brighton Golf Club, Grace was thinking ruefully,
*What am I doing, letting this maniac drive me again? This
tired, hung-over, deeply depressed maniac who has no life
and is suicidal?*

Flies spattered on the windscreen, like red-blooded
snowdrops. Oncoming cars, each of which he was convinced would wipe them out in an explosion of metal and
pulped human flesh, somehow flashed past. Hedgerows
unspooled on each side at the speed of light. Vaguely, out
of the furthest reach of his retina, he discerned people
brandishing golf clubs.

And finally, in defiance of all the laws of physics that
Grace knew and understood, they somehow arrived in the
car park of the North Brighton, intact.

And among the cars still sitting there was Brian Bishop's
dark red Bentley.

Grace climbed out of the Mondeo, which reeked of burning oil and was pinging like a badly tuned piano, and called the mobile of Detective Inspector William Warner at Gatwick airport.

Bill Warner answered on the second ring. He had gone home for the night, but assured Grace he would put an alert out for sightings of Brian Bishop at the airport immediately.

Next Grace rang the police station at Eastbourne, as it was responsible for patrolling Beachy Head, and Brian Bishop could now be considered a possible suicide risk. Then he called Cleo Morey, to apologize for having to blow out their date tonight, which he had been looking forward to all week. She understood, and asked him over for a late drink when he was finished instead, if he wasn't exhausted.

Finally he got one of the assistants in the office to ring each of his team, in turn, telling them that because of Brian Bishop's disappearance, he needed them all back at the conference room at eleven p.m. Following that, he rang CG99, the call sign for the duty inspector in charge of the division, in order to update him and get extra resources. He advised that the scene guard at the Bishops' home in Dyke Road Avenue should be vigilant, in case Bishop attempted to break in.

As he returned to the Mondeo, he figured his next plan of action was to call the list of friends that Brian Bishop had been playing golf with that morning, to see if any had been contacted by him. But just as he was thinking about that, his phone rang.

It was the controller from one of the local taxi companies. She told him a driver of theirs had picked up Brian Bishop from a street close to the Hotel du Vin an hour and a half ago.

34

Chris Tarrant cradled his chin in his hand. The audience fell silent. Harsh television studio lights flared off the unfashionably large glasses of the studious, geeky-looking man in the chair. The stakes had risen rapidly. The man was going to spend the money he won – if he won – on a bungalow for his disabled wife, and was popping beads of sweat on his high forehead.

Chris Tarrant repeated the question. 'John, you have sixty-four thousand pounds.' He paused and held the cheque in the air for all to see. Then he put it down again. 'For one hundred and twenty-five thousand pounds, where is the resort of Monastir? Is it a) Tunisia, b) Kenya, c) Egypt or d) Morocco?'

The camera cut to the contestant's wife, sitting in her wheelchair among the studio audience, looking as if someone was about to hit her with a cricket bat.

'Well,' the man said. 'I don't think it's Kenya.'

On her bed watching the television, Sophie took a sip of her Sauvignon. 'It's not Morocco,' she said out aloud. Her knowledge of geography wasn't that great, but she had been on holiday to Marrakech once, for a week, and had learned a fair amount about the country before going. Monastir rang no bells there.

Her window was wide open. The evening air was still warm and sticky, but at least there was a steady breeze. She'd left the bedroom door and the windows in the sitting room and kitchen open to create a through-draught. A faint, irritating *boom-boom-boom-boom* of dance music shook the quiet of the night out in the street. Maybe her neighbours below, maybe somewhere else.

'You still have two lifelines,' Chris Tarrant said.

'I think I'm going to phone a friend.'

Was it her imagination, or did she just see a shadow move past the bedroom door? She waited for a moment, only one ear on the television now, watching the doorway, a faint prickle of anxiety crawling up her back. The man had decided to phone a friend called Ron. She heard the ring tone.

Nothing there. Just her imagination. She put her glass down, picked up her fork, skewered a prawn and a chunk of avocado and put them in her mouth.

'Hi, Ron! It's Chris Tarrant here!'

'Hi, Chris. How you doing?'

Just as she swallowed, she saw the shadow again. Definitely not her imagination this time. A figure was moving towards the door. She heard a rustle of clothes or plastic. Outside a motorcycle blattered down the street.

'Who's there?' she called out, her voice a tight, anxious squeak.

Silence.

'Ron, I've got your mate John here. He's just won sixty-four thousand pounds and he's now going for one hundred and twenty-five thousand. How's your geography?'

'Yeah, well, all right.'

'OK, Ron, you have thirty seconds, starting from now.

'For one hundred and twenty-five thousand pounds, where is the resort of Monastir? Is it—'

Sophie's gullet tightened. She grabbed the remote and muted the show. Her eyes sprang to the doorway again, then to her handbag containing her mobile phone, well out of reach on her dressing table.

The shadow was moving. Jigging. Someone out there, motionless, but not able to stand without swaying a fraction.

She gripped her tray for an instant. It was the only weapon she had, apart from her small fork. 'Who's there?' she said. 'Who is that?'

Then he came into the room and all her fear evaporated.

'It's *you*!' she said. 'Jesus Christ, you gave me a fright!'

'I wasn't sure whether you'd be pleased to see me.'

'Of course I am. I – I'm really pleased,' she said. 'I so wanted to talk to you, to see you. How are you? I – I didn't think—'

'I've brought you a present.'

35

When he was a child growing up here, Brighton and Hove
had been two separate towns, each of them shabby in their
own very different way. They were joined at the hip by a
virtual border so erratic and illogical it might have been
created by a drunken goat. Or more likely, in Grace's view,
by a committee of sober town planners, which would have
contained, collectively, less wisdom than the goat.

Now the two towns were enshrined together, forever, as
the City of Brighton and Hove. Having spent most of the last
half-century screwing up Brighton's traffic system and ruin-
ing the fabled Regency elegance of its seafront, the moronic
planners were now turning their ineptness on Hove. Every
time he drove along the seafront, and passed the hideous
edifices of the Thistle Hotel, the Kingswest, with its ghastly
gold-foil roof, and the Brighton Centre, which had all the
architectural grace of a maximum-security prison, he had
to resist a desire to drive to the Town Hall, seize a couple of
planning officers and shake their fillings out.

Not that Roy Grace was against modern architecture –
far from it. There were many modern buildings that he
admired, the most recent one being the so-called Gherkin,
in London. What he hated was seeing his home city, which
he so loved, being permanently blighted by whatever
mediocrity went on behind the walls of that planning
department.

To the casual visitor, Brighton became Hove at the only
part of the border that was actually marked, by a rather fine

statue on the promenade of a winged angel holding an orb in one hand and an olive branch in the other: the Peace Statue. Grace, in the passenger seat of the Ford Mondeo, stared at it over to his left, out of the window, silhouetted against the steadily darkening sky.

On the opposite side of the road, two lines of traffic streamed into Brighton. With the windows down, he could hear every car. The *blam-blam* of show-off exhausts, the *boom-boom-boom* of in-car woofers, the stuttering rasp of *tuc-tuc* tricycle taxis. Hell was Friday night in central Brighton. Over the coming hours, the city would explode into life, and the police would be out in force, mostly down West Street – Brighton's answer to the Las Vegas strip – doing their best, as they did every Friday night, to stop the place turning into a drug-fuelled war zone.

From memories of his own time as a beat copper here, he did not envy the uniform crews out tonight one bit.

The light changed to green. Branson put the car in gear and moved forward in the slow stream of traffic. Regency Square was passing by on their right. Grace peered past Branson's bulk at the fine square of cream-painted eighteenth-century façades, with gardens in the middle, marred by signs for an underground car park and various letting agencies. Then Norfolk Square, a cheap-rent area. Students. Transients. Hookers. And the impoverished elderly. On Grace's left now was coming up a part of this city he loved the most, the Hove Lawns, a large expanse of neatly mown grass behind the seafront promenade, with its green shelters and, a short distance further on, its beach huts.

In daytime you could spot the old codgers out in force. Men in blue blazers, suede brogues, cravats, taking their constitutionals, some steadied by their walking sticks or

Zimmer frames. Blue-rinse dowagers with chalky faces and ruby lips, exercising their Pekinese, holding their leads in white-gloved hands. Stooped figures in white flannels, moving in slow motion around the bowling greens. And nearby, ignoring them as if they were all already long dead, were the clusters of iPodded kids who now owned the promenade on the far side of the railings, with their roller blades and skateboards, and games of volleyball, and their sheer, raw youth.

He wondered, sometimes, if he would make old bones. And what it would be like. To be retired, hobbling along, confused by the past, bewildered by the present and with the future mostly irrelevant. Or being pushed along in a wheelchair, with a blanket over his knees, another one over his mind.

Sandy and he used to joke about it sometimes. *Promise me you'll never drool, Grace, no matter how gaga you get?* she used to say. But it had been a comfortable joke, the kind of banter engaged in by two people content together, happy at the prospect of growing old as long as they are able to make that journey together. Another reason he just could not fathom her disappearance.

Munich.

He had to go. Somehow, he had to go there, and quickly. He desperately wanted to get on a plane tomorrow, but he couldn't. He had responsibilities to this case, and the first twenty-four hours were crucial. And with Alison Vosper breathing down his neck . . . Perhaps, if things went well tomorrow, he could go over there on Sunday. Over and back in one day. He might be able to get away with that.

There was just one more problem: what was he going to say to Cleo?

Glenn Branson was holding his mobile phone to his ear,

despite the fact that he was driving. Suddenly, glumly, he switched it off and placed it back in his top pocket. 'Ari's not picking up,' he said, raising his voice above the music that was playing on the car's stereo. 'I just want to say goodnight to the kids. What do you think I should do?'

The Detective Sergeant had selected a local pop station, Surf, on Grace's car radio, shunning his own music collection. A God-awful rap song from some group Grace had never heard of was belting out, far more loudly than was comfortable for him. 'You could turn the bloody music down for starters!'

Branson turned it down. 'Do you think I should go round there – after we're done, I mean?'

'Jesus,' Grace said. 'I'm the last person on the planet to ask about marital advice. Look at the fuck-up of my life.'

'Well, it's different. I mean, like, I could go home, yeah?'

'It's your legal right.'

'I don't want a scene in front of the kids.'

'I think you should give her space. Leave it a couple of days, see if she calls.'

'You sure you're OK about me crashing with you? I'm not cramping your style or anything? You're cool about it?'

'Totally,' Grace said, through gritted teeth.

Branson, picking up on the absence of enthusiasm in his voice, said, 'I could check into a hotel or something, if you'd rather?'

'You're my mate,' Grace said. 'Mates look after each other.'

Branson turned right into a wide, elegant street, lined on both sides with once-grand Regency terraced houses. He slowed down, then pulled over in front of the triple-fronted portals of the Lansdowne Place Hotel and killed the engine, mercifully, thought Grace, silencing the music. Then he switched off the lights.

Not long back, the place had been a tired old two-star dump, inhabited by a handful of geriatric resident guests and a spattering of drab trippers on budget seaside package tours. Now it had been transformed into one of the city's latest hip hotels.

They climbed out of the car and went inside, to a riot of purple velour, chrome and gilded kitsch, and walked up to the front desk. A female receptionist, tall and statuesque in a black tunic and a Bettie Page black fringe, greeted them with an efficient smile. Her gold lapel badge read GRETA.

Grace showed her his police warrant card. 'Detective Superintendent Grace of the Sussex CID. My colleague and I would like to have a word with a guest who checked in a short while ago – Mr Brian Bishop.'

Her smile assumed the motions of a deflating balloon, as she looked down at her computer screen and tapped on her keyboard. 'Mr Brian Bishop?'

'Yes.'

'One moment, gentlemen.' She picked up a phone and pressed a couple of buttons. After half a minute or so, she replaced the receiver. 'I'm sorry, he doesn't seem to be picking up.'

'We are concerned about this person. Could we go up to his room?'

Looking totally thrown now, she said, 'I need to speak to the manager.'

'That's fine,' Grace replied.

And five minutes later, for the second time in the past hour, he found himself entering an empty hotel bedroom.

36

Skunk was always in his office on Friday nights, when the richest pickings of the week were up for grabs. People out for a good time were carefree – and careless. By eight o'clock, the city centre car parks were filling to near capacity. Locals and visitors jostled along Brighton's old, narrow streets, packing the pubs, bars and restaurants, and later on, the younger ones, high and drunk, would be starting to queue outside the clubs.

A large Tesco carrier bag swung from his arm as he progressed slowly through the teeming throng, squeezing his way at times past packed outdoor tables. The warm downtown air was laced with a thousand scents. Colognes, perfumes, cigarette smoke, exhaust fumes, olive oil and spices searing on cooking pans, and always the tang of salt in the air. His mind elsewhere, he tuned out the chatter, the laughter, the *clack-clack-clack* of high heels tripping along on paving stones, the boom of music from open doors and windows. Tonight he only vaguely clocked the Rolex watches on tanned wrists, the diamond brooches, necklaces and rings, the tell-tale bulges in men's jackets where a plump wallet sat for the taking.

Tonight he had bigger fish to fry.

Heading down East Street, he felt like he was pushing through an incoming tide. Forking right, past the Latin in the Lane restaurant, behind the Thistle Hotel, he then turned right along the seafront, stepping around a teenage girl having a screaming, tearful row with a spiky-haired boy, and made his way past the Old Ship, the Brighton Centre, the smart Grand and Metropole hotels – neither of which he had ever been inside. Finally, sticky with sweat, he reached Regency Square.

Avoiding the exit/entrance, where an NCP attendant sat, he walked up to the top of the square, then down concrete steps which stank of urine, into the centre of the second level of the car park. With the cash he was going to get from this job, he would buy himself another bag of brown, and then anything else that might come his way later on tonight at one of the clubs. All he had to do was find a car that matched the one on the shopping list folded in his trouser pocket.

Inside his carrier bag was a set of number plates, copied from the model he had seen earlier. When he found the right car, a new-shape Audi A4 convertible, automatic, low mileage, metallic blue, silver or black, he would simply put those plates on it. That way, if the owner reported it stolen, the police would be looking for a car with different plates.

There was almost bound to be something suitable here. If not, he'd try another car park. And if the worst came to the worst, he'd find one on the street. It was a rich bitch's car, and there was no shortage of rich, peroxided, nip-and-tucked bitches in this city. He wouldn't mind an Audi convertible himself. He could see himself, in some parallel universe, driving Bethany along the seafront, on a warm Friday night, the music up loud, the heater on his feet and the smell of new leather all around him.

One day.

One day, things would be different.

He found a car within minutes, at the back of the third level. A dark shade of opalescent blue or green – it was hard to tell in the shitty light down here – with a black roof and cream leather seats. Its licence plate indicated it was less than six months old, but when he reached the car and noticed the smell of freshly burnt oil rising from it, he realized, to his joy, it was brand new. Not a mark on it!

And the owner had very conveniently parked it nose in, close to a pillar.

Checking carefully there was no one around, he walked up the side of the car and put his hand on the bonnet. It felt hot. Good. That meant it must have just recently been driven in here; so, with luck, it would be some hours before its owner returned. But just as a precaution he still removed the two sets of licence plates from his carrier bag and stuck them, with double-sided tape, over the originals.

Then from his bag he removed what would look, to any police officer who stopped him, like a Sky TV remote control. He aimed it, through the driver's window, at the dash panel, punched in the code he had been given and then the green button.

Nothing happened.

He tried again. The red light showed on the remote but nothing else happened.

Shit. He looked around again, more nervously now, then went up to the front of the car and knelt by the right headlamp. Shielded by the car and the pillar, he relaxed a little. It was easy. He'd done this before; at least a dozen Audis. A five-minute job, max.

Removing a screwdriver from the plastic bag, he began unscrewing the front right headlight-restraining rim. When he had finished, he eased out the sealed headlamp unit and let it dangle on its flex. Then, taking a pair of pliers, he reached his arm through the empty headlight socket, felt around until he found the wire to the horn and cut it. Next he groped about, cursing suddenly as he accidentally touched the hot engine casing, burning his knuckles, until he located the auto locking mechanism. Then he cut through the wires, disabling it.

He replaced the headlamp, then opened the driver's door, setting off the headlamp flashers – all that the crippled alarm system now had left in its armoury. Moments later he plucked the fuse for the flashers out of the box and dropped it into his bag. Then he popped the bonnet and bridged the solenoid and the starter motor. Instantly the engine roared sweetly into life.

He slipped into the driver's seat and gave the steering wheel a hard wrench, snapping the lock. Then he saw to his joy that he was going to make himself a little bonus tonight. The owner had graciously left the car-park ticket on the passenger seat. And Barry Spiker, the tight bastard he did these jobs for, who had given him twenty-seven quid to cover the all-day parking charge penalty to get the car out of the NCP, would be none the wiser!

Two minutes later, having forked out just two pounds to the attendant, he drove the car gleefully up the ramp, already twenty-five pounds in profit. He was in such a good mood that he stopped at the top of the ramp, turned the music up loud, and lowered the roof.

It was not a smart move.

37

'How are you?' Sophie asked imploringly. 'What's happened? How—?'

'Try it on,' he said sharply, putting the package on the tray, ignoring her questions.

Out in the falling dusk, a siren wailed, momentarily drowning out the faint, low, four-beat *boom-boom-boom-boom* of dance music that was getting increasingly tiresome.

Sophie, astonished – and uneasy at his behaviour – meekly untied the bow, then peered into the gift box. All she could see for the moment was tissue paper.

Out of the corner of her eye, on the television screen, she saw Chris Tarrant mouth the words, 'Final answer?'

The geeky-looking guy in big glasses nodded.

A yellow flashing light encircled the name *Morocco*.

Moments later, on the screen, a flashing green light encircled *Tunisia*.

Chris Tarrant's eyebrows shot several inches up his forehead.

The lady in the wheelchair, who had looked earlier as if she was about to be hit by a cricket bat, now looked as if she had been hit by a sledgehammer. Meanwhile, her husband seemed to shrink in his seat.

Sophie lipread Tarrant saying, 'John, you had sixty-four thousand pounds . . .'

'You want to watch television or open the gift I've bought you?' he said.

Swinging her tray of food on to her bedside table, she said, 'The gift, of course! But I want to know how you are. I want to know about—'

'I don't want to talk about it. Open it!' he said in a tone suddenly so aggressive it startled her.

'OK,' she said.

'What are you watching that crap for?'

Her eyes still flicked back to the screen. 'I like it,' she said, trying to calm him. 'Poor guy. His wife's in a wheel-chair. He's just blown the hundred and twenty-five thousand pound question.'

'The whole show's a con,' he said.

'No, it isn't!'

'Life's a con. Haven't you figured that one out yet?'

'A con?'

Now it was his turn to point at the screen. 'I don't know who he is, nor did the rest of the world. A few minutes ago he sat in that chair and had nothing. Now he's going to walk away with thirty-two thousand pounds and feel dis-satisfied, when he should be rip-roaring with joy. You're going to tell me that's not a con?'

'It's a matter of perspective. I mean – from his point—'

'Turn the fucking thing off!'

Sophie was still shocked by the aggression in his voice, but at the same time a defiant streak made her reply, 'No. I'm enjoying it.'

'Want me to go, so you can watch your fucking sad little programme?'

She was already regretting what she had said. Despite her earlier resolve to end it with Brian, seeing him in the flesh made her realize she would a million times rather that he was here, with her, tonight than watch this show – or any show. And God, what the poor man must be going through . . . She punched the remote, turning it off. 'I'm sorry,' she said.

He was staring at her in a way she'd never seen before. As if blinds had come down behind his eyes.

'I'm really sorry, OK? I'm just surprised you're here.'

'So you're not pleased to see me?'

She sat up and threw her arms around his neck and kissed him on the lips. His breath was rancid and he smelled sweaty, but she didn't care. They were manly smells, his smells. She breathed them in as though they were the most intoxicating scents on the planet. 'I'm more than pleased,' she said. 'I'm just . . .' She looked into those hazel eyes she adored so much. 'I'm just so surprised, you know – after what you said earlier when we spoke. Tell me. Please tell me what's happened. Please tell me everything.'

'Open it!' he said, his voice rising.

She pulled away some of the tissue, but, like a Chinese box, there was another layer beneath, and then another again. Trying to bring him back down from whatever was angering him, she said, 'OK, I'm trying to guess what this is. And I'm guessing that it's a—'

Suddenly his face was inches in front of hers, so close their noses were almost touching.

'Open it!' he screeched. 'Open it, you fucking bitch.'

38

Skunk, driving along in falling, purple-tinted darkness, clocked the bright headlights again in his mirror. They had appeared from nowhere moments after he left the Regency Square car park. Now they were accelerating past the line of traffic and cutting in behind a blacked-out BMW that was right on his tail.

It wasn't necessarily anything to worry about, he thought. But as he reached the two solid lines of vehicles backed up at the roundabout in front of Brighton Pier, in his mirror he caught a fleeting glimpse of the face of the man in the passenger seat, flashlit under the neon glare of the street lighting, and began to panic.

He couldn't be completely sure, but it looked too fucking much like that young plain-clothes cop called Paul Packer, whose finger he'd bitten off after a run-in over a stolen car, for which he had been banged up in a young offenders' institute.

At full volume on the car's radio, Lindsay Lohan was singing 'Confessions of a Broken Heart', but he barely heard the words; he was looking at the traffic flow in and out of the roundabout, trying to decide which exit to take. The car behind hooted. Skunk gave him the bird. There was a choice of four exits. One would take him towards the town centre and clogged-up traffic. Too risky, he could easily get trapped there. The second was Marine Parade, a wide street with plenty of side roads, plus fast open road beyond it. The third would take him along the seafront, but the danger there was, with just one exit at either end, he could get blocked in easily. The fourth would take him back in the direction he had just come from. But there were roadworks and heavy traffic.

He made his decision, pressing the pedal all the way down to the metal. The Audi shot forward, across the bows of a white van. Fiercely concentrating, Skunk continued accelerating along Marine Parade, past shops, then the flash Van Alen building. He checked in the mirror. No sign of the Vectra. Good. Must be stuck at the roundabout.

Traffic lights ahead were red. He braked, then cursed. In his mirrors he saw the Vectra again, overtaking on the wrong side, making up ground, driving like a maniac. The car pulled up behind him. Right behind him. Like, one inch from his rear bumper. All shiny clean. Radio aerial on the roof. Two men in the front seats. And now, lit up in the glare of his own brake lights, there really was no mistaking one of them.

Shit.

In the mirror he saw Packer's eyes, remembered them from before, big, calm eyes, that sort of locked on you like lasers. He remembered even when he'd bitten the fucker's finger off, his eyes kept fixed on him, no surprise, no look of pain. Sort of weird, smiley eyes – almost like the man had been mocking him. And it was as if he was doing that again now, sitting there, neither cop making any move to get out of their car.

Why the fuck aren't you arresting me?

His nerves were jumping about inside him, like there was some crazed animal on a trampoline inside his stomach. He nodded his head to the music. But he was jangling. Needed something. Needed another hit. The mean amount he'd taken was wearing off fast. Tried to think of the best route.

Tried to think why the cops weren't getting out of their car.

The lights changed to green. He stamped on the pedal, accelerated halfway across the junction, then jerked the wheel hard left and slewed into Lower Rock Gardens, narrowly missing an oncoming taxi. In his mirror he saw, to his relief, the Vectra shoot over the junction.

He accelerated flat out up the Victorian terraced street, which was lined on both sides with cheap bed and breakfasts and bedsits. As he halted at another red light at the top, he saw the Vectra approaching quickly. And any last shred of doubt he might have had that he was being followed was now gone.

Checking both directions, he saw two buses were coming from his left, nose to tail. Waiting until the last possible moment, he accelerated, shooting across the front of the first bus, driving like the wind. He raced up Egremont Place, through a sharp S-bend, overtaking a dawdling Nissan on the wrong side, on a blind corner, but fortune was with him and nothing was coming from the other direction.

Then he waited anxiously at the junction with busy Elm Grove for a gap in the traffic. Two headlights suddenly pricked the darkness a long way back. Forgetting about a break in the traffic, he turned right, across it, ignoring squeals of brakes, blaring horns and flashing lights, laying a trail of rubber, up past Brighton racecourse, then down through the suburb of Woodingdean.

He debated about stopping to change the licence plates and revert back to the car's original ones, as it almost certainly had not yet been reported stolen, but he didn't want to take the risk of the Vectra catching him up again. So he pressed on, ignoring the flash of a speed camera with a wry smile.

Ten minutes later on a country road two miles inland from the Channel port of Newhaven, with his mirrors black and empty, and his windscreen spattered with dead insects, he slowed down and made a right turn at a sign which read *Meades Farm.*

He drove through a gap in a tall, ragged hedgerow on to a metalled, single-track farm road, following it through fields of corn overdue for harvesting, for half a mile, several kamikaze rabbits darting in and out of his path. He passed the massive derelict sheds that once housed battery hens, and an open-sided barn on his right containing a few shadowy pieces of long-disused and rusting farm machinery. Then, directly ahead, his headlights picked up the wall of a vast, steel-sided, enclosed barn.

He stopped the car. No light came from the building and there were no vehicles parked outside. Nothing at all to reveal that an active business was being carried on in here at this moment.

Pulling his mobile phone from his pocket, he called a number he knew by heart. 'Outside,' he said when it was answered.

Electronic doors slid open just wide enough to allow him to drive in, revealing a brightly lit, cavernous space, then began closing behind him instantly. Inside he saw about twenty cars, most of them the latest model, top-end luxury machines. He clocked two Ferraris, an Aston Martin DB9, a Bentley Continental, two Range Rovers, a Cayenne, as well as some less exotic cars, including a Golf GTI, a Mazda MX5, a classic yellow Triumph Stag and a new-looking MG TF. Some of the cars appeared to be intact, while others were in various stages of dismemberment. Despite the lateness of the hour, four boiler-suited mechanics were working on vehicles – two beneath open bonnets, one on his back under a jacked-up Lexus sports car, the fourth fitting a body panel to a Range Rover Sport.

Skunk switched off the engine and with that his music fell silent. Instead some cheesy old Gene Pitney song crackled out from a cheap radio somewhere in the building. A drill whined.

Barry Spiker stepped out of his glass-windowed office over on the far side, talking into a mobile, and walked towards him. A short, wiry, former regional champion flyweight boxer with close-cropped hair, he had a face hard enough to carve ice with. He was dressed in a blue boiler suit over a string vest, and flip-flops, and he reeked of a sickly sweet aftershave. A medallion hung from a gold chain around his neck. Without acknowledging Skunk, he walked all the way around the car, still talking on his phone, arguing, looking in a foul mood.

As Skunk got out of the car, Spiker ended his call, then, brandishing his phone like a dagger, walked up to him. 'What the fuck's this piece of shit? I wanted a three-point-two V6. This is a two-litre piss-pot. No use to me. Hope you're not expecting me to buy it!'

Skunk's heart sank. 'You – you didn't . . .' He dug the crumpled piece of paper from his pocket, on which he had taken down the instructions this morning, and showed it to Spiker. On it was written, in his shaky handwriting, *New-shape Audi A4 convertible, automatic, low mileage, metallic blue, silver or black.*

'You never specified the motor size,' Skunk said.

'So which fucking tree did you fall out of? People who buy nice cars happen to like nice engines to go with them.'

'This goes like hot shit,' Skunk said defensively.

Spiker shrugged, looked at the car again pensively. 'Nah, not for me.' His phone started ringing. 'Don't like the colour much either.' He checked the display, brought the phone to his ear and said abruptly, 'I'm busy. Call you back,' then he hung up. 'Sixty quid.'

'What?' Skunk had been expecting two hundred.

'Take it or leave it.'

Skunk glared at him. The bastard always found some way to screw him. Either there was a mark on the paint-work, or the tyres were knackered, or it needed a new exhaust. Something. But at least he was making a secret profit on the car park, getting back at the man in his own small – but satisfying – way.

'Where did you get it from?'

'Regency Square.'

Spiker nodded. He was checking the interior carefully, and Skunk knew why. He was looking for any mark or scratch he could use to beat the price down lower. Then Spiker's eyes alighted greedily on something in the passenger footwell. He opened the door, ducked down, then stood up, holding a small piece of paper, like a trophy, which he inspected carefully. 'Brilliant!' he said. 'Nice one!'

'What?'

'Parking receipt from Regency Square. Twenty minutes ago. Just two quid! Top man, Skunk! So you owe me twenty-five quid back from that float I gave you.'

Skunk cursed his own stupidity.

39

His words shook her. Scared her. His eyes were glazed and bloodshot. Had he been drinking? Taken some drug?

'Open it!' he said again. 'Open it, bitch!'

She was tempted to tell him to go to hell, and how dare he speak to her like that? But, knowing how much stress he must be under, she tried to humour him, to calm him down and bring him back from whatever place or space he was in. She removed another layer of tissue. This was one weird game. *First we shout and swear at you, then we give you a present, right?*

She removed another layer, balled it and dropped it on the bed beside her, but there was no thaw in his demeanour. Instead, he was worsening, quivering with anger.

'Come on, bitch! Why are you taking so long?'

A shiver of anxiety wormed through her. Suddenly she did not want to be here, trapped in her room with him. She had no idea what she was going to find in the gift box. He'd never bought her a gift before, except some flowers a couple of times recently when he'd come over to her flat. But whatever it was, nothing felt right; it was as if the world was suddenly skewed on its axis.

And with every layer she removed she was starting to have a really bad feeling about what was in the box.

But then she got down to the last layer of tissue paper. She felt something that was part hard, part soft and yielding, as if it was made of leather, and she realized what it might be. And she relaxed. Smiled at him. The sod was teasing her, it was all a wind-up! 'A handbag!' she said with a squeal. 'It's a handbag, isn't it? You darling! How did you know I desperately need a new bag? Did I tell you?'

But he wasn't smiling back. 'Just open it,' he said again, coldly.

And that brief moment of good feeling evaporated as her world skewed again. There was not one shred of warmth coming back from his expression or his words. Her fear deepened. And just how strange was it that he was giving her a present on the day his wife was found dead? Then, finally, she removed the last layer of tissue.

And stared down in shock at the object that was revealed.

It wasn't a handbag at all, but something strange and sinister-looking, a helmet of some kind, grey, with bug-eyed glass lenses and a strap, and a ribbed tube hanging down with some kind of filter on the end. A gas mask, she realized with dismay, the kind she'd seen on soldiers' faces out in Iraq, or maybe it was older. It had a musty, rubbery smell.

She looked up at him in surprise. 'Are we about to be invaded or something?'

'Put it on.'

'You want me to *wear* this?'

'Put it on.'

She held it to her face and instantly lowered it, wrinkling her nose. 'You really want me to wear this? You want to make love with me wearing it?' She grinned, a little stupefied, her fear subsiding. 'Is that going to turn you on or something?'

For an answer, he ripped it out of her hands, jammed it against her face, then pulled the strap over the back of her head, trapping some of her hair painfully. The strap was so tight it hurt.

For a moment, she was completely disoriented. The lenses were grimy, smeared and heavily tinted. She could only see him, and the room, partially, in a green haze. When she turned her head, he disappeared for a moment and she had to swivel her head back to see him again. She heard the sound of her own breathing, hollow exhalations like the roar of the sea in her ears.

'I can't breathe,' she said, panicking, claustrophobia gripping her, her voice muffled.

'Of course you can fucking breathe.' His voice was muzzy, distorted.

In panic she tried to pull the mask off. But his hands gripped hers, forcing them away from the strap, gripping them so hard they were hurting. 'Stop being a stupid bitch,' he said.

She was whimpering. 'Brian, I don't like this game.'

Almost instantly she felt herself pushed down on her back, on the bed. As the walls, then the ceiling scudded past her eyes, her panic worsened. 'Nooo!' She lashed out with her feet, felt her right foot strike something hard. Heard him roar in pain. Then she broke free from his hands, rolled away, and suddenly she was falling. She crashed painfully on to the carpeted floor.

'Fucking bitch!'

Struggling to get to her knees, she put her hands up to the mask, tugged at the strap, then felt an agonizing, crunching blow in her stomach which belted all the wind out of her. She doubled up in pain, shocked at the realization of what had happened.

He had hit her.

And suddenly she sensed that the stakes had changed. He had gone insane.

He hurled her on to the bed and the backs of her legs struck the edge. She screamed out at him, but her voice remained trapped inside the mask.

Have to get away from him, she realized. *Have to get out of here.*

She felt her T-shirt being torn off. For a moment, she stopped resisting, thinking, trying to make a plan. The booming of her breathing was deafening. *Have to get the damn mask off.* Her heart was thudding painfully. *Have to get to the door, downstairs, to the guys downstairs. They will help me.*

She snapped her head right, then left, checking what was on her bedside tables that she could use as a weapon. 'Brian, please, Brian—'

She felt his hand, hard as a hammer, strike the side of the mask, jarring her neck.

There was a book, a thick hardback Bill Bryson tome on science she had been given for Christmas and dipped into from time to time. She rolled over, fast, grabbed it and swung it at his head, striking him side on, flat. She heard him grunt in pain and surprise, and go down, over the side of the bed.

Instantly she was on her feet, running out of the bedroom, along the short hall, leaving the mask on, not wanting to waste precious time. She got to the front door, grabbed the Yale knob, turned and pulled.

The door opened a few inches and then halted, abruptly, with a sharp, metallic clank.

Brian had put the safety chain on.

A burst water main of icy fear exploded inside her. She grabbed at the chain, pushing the door shut again, tugging at it, trying to pull it free, but it was stuck, the damn thing was stuck! How could it be stuck? She was shaking, screaming, muffled echoing screams. 'Help! Help me! Help me! Oh, please, HELP ME!'

Then, right behind her, she heard a grinding, metallic whine.

She whipped her head round. And saw what he was holding in his hands.

Her mouth opened, silently this time, fear freezing her gullet. She stood, whimpering in terror. Her whole body felt as if it was collapsing in on itself. Unable to prevent herself, she began urinating.

40

I have read that devastating news has a strange impact on the human brain. It freezes time and place together, indelibly. Perhaps it is part of the way we humans are wired, to give us a warning signal marking a dangerous place in our lives or in the world.

I wasn't born then, so I cannot vouch for this, but people say they can remember exactly where they were and what they were doing when they heard the news, on 22 November 1963, that President John F. Kennedy had been assassinated by a gunman in Dallas.

I can remember where I was and what I was doing when I heard the news, on 8 December 1980, that John Lennon had been shot dead. I can also remember, very clearly, that I was sitting at my desk in my den, searching on the internet for the wiring loom for a 1962 Mark II Jaguar 3.8 saloon, on the morning of Sunday 31 August 1997, when I heard the news that Diana, Princess of Wales, had been killed in a car crash in a tunnel in Paris.

Above all I can remember where I was and exactly what I was doing on that July morning, eleven months later, when I received the letter that ruined my life.

41

Roy Grace sat at his desk in his small, airless office in Sussex House, waiting for any news of Brian Bishop and filling in time before the eleven o'clock briefing. He was staring gloomily at the equally gloomy face of the seven-pound, six-ounce brown trout, stuffed and mounted in a glass case fixed to a wall in his office. It was positioned just beneath a round wooden clock that had been a prop in the fictitious police station in *The Bill*, which Sandy bought for him in happier times in an auction.

He had bought the fish on a whim some years back, from a stall in the Portobello Road. He referred to it occasionally when briefing young, fresh-faced detectives, making an increasingly tired joke about patience and big fish.

On his desk in front of him was a pile of documents he needed to go through carefully, part of the preparations for the trial, some months ahead, of a man called Carl Venner, one of the most odious creeps he had ever encountered in his career. Hopefully, if he didn't screw up on the preparations, Venner would be looking at the wrong end of several concurrent life sentences. But you could never be sure with some of the barmy judges that were around.

His evening meal, which he had chosen a few minutes ago from the ASDA superstore, also lay on his desk. A tuna sandwich still in its clear plastic box, stickered in yellow with the word *Reduced!*, an apple, a Twix chocolate bar and a can of Diet Coke.

He spent several minutes scanning the waterfall of emails, answering a few and deleting a load. It didn't seem to matter how quickly he dealt with them, more poured in, and the number of unanswered ones in his inbox was rising towards the two hundred mark. Fortunately, Eleanor would deal with most of them herself. And she had already cleared his diary – an automatic process whenever he began a major crime investigation.

All she had left in was Sunday lunch with his sister, Jodie, whom he had not seen in over a month, and a reminder to buy a card and birthday present for his god-daughter, Jaye Somers, who would be nine next week. He wondered what to buy her – and decided that Jodie, who had three children either side of that age, would know. He also made a mental note that he would have to cancel the lunch if he went to Munich.

Over fifteen emails related to the police rugby team, which he had been made president of for this coming autumn. They were a sharp reminder that although it was gloriously warm today, in less than four weeks it would be September. Summer was coming to an end. Already the days were getting noticeably shorter.

He clicked on his keyboard to bring up the Vantage software for the force's internal computer system and checked the latest incident reports log to see what had happened during the past couple of hours. Scanning down the orange lettering, there was nothing that particularly caught his eye. It was still too early – later there would be fights, assaults and muggings galore. An RTA on the London Road coming into Brighton. A bag-snatch. A shoplifter in the Boundary Road Tesco branch. A stolen car found abandoned at a petrol station. A runaway horse reported on the A27.

Then his phone rang. It was Detective Sergeant Guy

Batchelor, a new recruit to his inquiry team, whom he had dispatched to talk to Brian Bishop's golfing partners from this morning.

Grace liked Batchelor. He always thought that if you asked a casting agency to provide a middle-aged police officer for a scene in a film, the man they sent would look like Batchelor. He was tall and burly, with a rugger-ball-shaped head, thinning hair and a genial but businesslike demeanour. Although not huge, he had an air of the gentle giant about him – more in his nature than his physical mass.

'Roy, I've seen all three people Bishop played golf with today. Just something I thought might be of interest – they all said he seemed in an exceptionally good mood, and that he was playing a blinder – better than any of them had ever seen him play.'

'Did he give them any explanation?'

'No, he's quite a loner apparently, unlike his wife, who was very gregarious, they say. He doesn't have any really close friends, normally doesn't say much. But he was cracking jokes today. One of the men, a Mr Mishon, who seems to know him quite well, said it was as if he had taken a happy pill.'

Grace was thinking hard. *Dead wife, big weight off his mind?*

'Not the sort of reaction of a man who's just killed his wife, is it, Roy?'

'Depends how good an actor he is.'

After Batchelor had finished his report, adding little further, Grace thanked him and said he would see him at the eleven p.m. briefing. Then, thinking hard about what Batchelor had just said, he tore away the film covering of the sandwich, levered it out and took a bite. Instantly he wrinkled his nose at the taste; it was some new exotic kind of bread he'd never tried before – and regretted trying now. It had a strong caraway flavour he did not like. He'd have been much happier with an egg and bacon all-day-breakfast sandwich, but Cleo had been trying to wean him on to a healthier diet by getting him to eat more fish – despite his regaling her with a detailed account of an article he'd read earlier in the year, in the *Daily Mail*, about the dangerous mercury levels in fish.

He exited Vantage, launched the website of expedia.com and entered a search for flights to Munich on Sunday, wondering whether it was possible to get out there and back on the same day. He *had* to go, no matter how slender the information from Dick Pope. *Had* to go and see for himself.

It was all he could do to stop himself from getting the next possible plane. Instead, he glanced at his watch. It was nine fifty. Ten fifty in Germany. But hell, Dick Pope would be up and about, he was on holiday. Sitting in some café or bar in Bavaria with a beer in his hand. He dialled Pope's mobile, but it went straight to voicemail.

'Dick,' he said. 'Roy again. Sorry to be a pest, but I just want to ask you a few more details about the beer garden where you think you saw Sandy. Call me when you can.'

He hung up and stared for a moment at his prize collection of three dozen vintage cigarette lighters, hunched together on the ledge between the front of his desk and the window, with its view down on the parking area and the cell block. They reflected how much Sandy loved trawling antiques markets, bric-à-brac shops and car-boot sales. Something he still did, when he had the time, but it had never been the same. Part of the fun had always been seeing Sandy's reaction to something he picked up. Whether she would like it too, in which case they would haggle the price, or whether she would reject it with a single, disapproving scrunch of her face.

Most of the space in his office was occupied by a television and video player, a circular table, four chairs and piles of loose paperwork, his leather go-bag containing his crime-scene kit, and ever-growing small towers of files. Sometimes he wondered if they bred at night, on their own, while he was away.

Each file on the floor stood for an unsolved murder. Murder files never closed until there was a conviction. There would come a point in every murder inquiry when every lead, every avenue, had been exhausted. But that did not mean the police gave up. Years after the incident room was shut down and the inquiry team disbanded, the case would remain open, the evidence stored in boxes, so long as there was a chance that the parties connected to it might still be alive.

He took a swig from his Coke. He'd read on a website that low-carb drinks were full of all kinds of chemicals hostile to your body, but he didn't care at this moment. It seemed that everything you ate or drank was more likely to kill you than provide you with nutrients. Maybe, he pondered, the next food fad would be pre-digested food. You would just buy it and then throw it straight down the lavatory, without needing to eat it.

He clicked his keyboard. There was a British Airways flight out of Heathrow at seven a.m. on Sunday morning. It would get him into Munich at nine fifty. He decided to call the police officer he knew there, Kriminalhauptkommissar Marcel Kullen, to see if he would be free.

Marcel had been seconded here in Sussex a few years back, on a six-month exchange, and they'd become friends during this period. The officer had extended an open invitation for Grace to come and stay with him and his family at any time. He looked at his watch. Nine fifty-five. Munich was one hour ahead, so it really was late to be calling, but there was a good chance of catching him in.

As he reached out to pick up the phone, it rang.

'Roy Grace,' he answered.

It was Brian Bishop.

42

Grace noted that Bishop had changed out of the golfing clothes he had been wearing earlier. He now had on an expensive-looking black blouson jacket over a white shirt, blue trousers and tan loafers, without socks. He looked more like a playboy on a night out than a man in mourning, he thought.

As if reading Grace's mind as he sat down uneasily on the red armchair in the cramped Witness Interview Suite, Bishop said, 'My outfit was selected from my wardrobe by your family liaison officer, Linda Buckley. Not quite my choice for the circumstances. Can you tell me when I will be allowed back in my house?'

'As soon as possible, Mr Bishop. In a couple of days, I hope,' Grace replied.

Bishop sat bolt upright, furious. 'What? This is ridiculous!'

Grace looked at a rather livid graze on the man's right hand. Branson came in with three beakers of water, set them down on the table and closed the door, remaining standing.

Gently, Grace said, 'It's a crime scene, Mr Bishop. Police practice these days is to preserve a scene like this as much as possible. Please understand it's in all our interests, to help catch the perpetrator.'

'Do you have a suspect?' Bishop asked.

'Before I come on to that, would you mind if we record

this interview? It will be quicker than if we have to write down notes.'

Bishop gave a thin, wintry smile. 'Does that mean I'm a suspect?'

'Not at all,' Grace assured him.

Bishop signalled his assent with his hand.

Glenn Branson switched on the audio and video recorders, announcing clearly, as he sat down, 'It is ten twenty p.m., Friday 4 August. Detective Superintendent Grace and Detective Sergeant Branson interviewing Mr Brian Bishop.'

'Do – do you have a suspect?' Bishop asked again.

'Not yet,' Grace replied. 'Is there anyone you can think of who might have done this?'

Bishop gave a half-laugh, as if the question was just too ridiculous. His eyes shot to the left. 'No. No, I don't.'

Grace watched his eyes, remembering from earlier. To the left was truth mode. Bishop had answered just a little too quickly, and almost a little too good-humouredly for a bereaved man. He'd seen this kind of behaviour before, the cool, slick, rehearsed answer to the questions; the lack of emotion. Bishop was displaying the classic signs of a man who had committed a murder. But that did not mean he had. That laughter could equally well have been from nerves.

Then his eyes dropped to the man's right hand. To the abrasion on the back of it, just in from his thumb; it looked recent. 'You've hurt your hand,' he said.

Bishop glanced at his hand, then gave a dismissive shrug. 'I – er – bashed it getting into a taxi.'

'Would that be the taxi you took from the Hotel du Vin to the Lansdowne Place Hotel?'

'Yes, I – I was putting a bag in the boot.'

'Nasty,' Grace said, making a mental note to get the taxi driver to verify that. He also noted that Bishop's eyes darted to the right. To construct mode. Which indicated he was lying.

'It looks quite a bad graze. What did the driver say?' Grace glanced at Branson, who nodded.

'Did he give you any first aid or anything?' Branson asked.

Bishop looked at each of them in turn. 'What is it with you guys? It's like the bloody Inquisition. I want to help you. What the hell's a graze on my hand got to do with anything?'

'Mr Bishop, in our work we ask an awful lot of questions. I'm afraid it's what we do. It's in our nature. I've had a long day, and so has DS Branson, and I'm sure you must be exhausted. Please bear with us and answer our questions, and we'll all be able to leave here quicker. The more you can help us, the sooner we'll be able to catch your wife's killer.' Grace took a gulp of water, then said gently, 'We're a little curious as to why you checked out of the Hotel du Vin and went to the Lansdowne Place. Could you explain your reasons?'

Bishop's eyes moved as if he was tracking the path of an insect across the carpet. Grace followed his line of sight but could see nothing.

'Why?' Bishop suddenly looked up, staring at him intently. 'What do you mean? I was told to move there.'

Now it was Grace's turn to frown. 'By whom?'

'Well – by the police. By you, I presume.'

'I'm not with you.'

Bishop opened his arms expansively. He gave a good impression of sounding genuinely surprised. 'I was called in my room. The officer said that the Hotel du Vin was being staked out by the press and you were moving me.'

'What was the name of the officer?'

'I – I don't remember. Umm – it may have been Canning? DS Canning?'

Grace looked at Branson. 'Know anything about this?'

'Nothing,' Branson replied.

'Was it a male or female officer?' Grace asked.

'Male.'

'DS Canning was his name? Are you sure?'

'Yes. Canning. DS Canning. I think it was DS. Definitely Canning.'

'What exactly did this man say to you?' Grace watched his eyes intently. They darted left again.

'That you'd booked me a room at the Lansdowne Place. A cab would be outside the rear entrance, by the staff door at the rear of the kitchens. That I should take the fire escape stairs down there.'

Grace wrote down the name *DS Canning* on his pad. 'Did this officer call you on your mobile or on the hotel phone?'

'On the room phone,' Bishop said after some moments' thought.

Grace cursed silently. That would make it harder to verify or trace. The hotel's switchboard could log the time of incoming calls, but not their numbers. 'What time was this?'

'About five thirty.'

'You checked into the Lansdowne Place and then went out. Where did you go?'

'I went for a walk along the seafront.' Bishop pulled out a handkerchief and dabbed his eyes. 'Katie and I used to love it down there. She loved going on the beach. She was a keen swimmer.' He paused and took a sip of water.

'I needed to call my kids – they're both abroad, on holiday. I . . .' He lapsed into silence.

So did Roy Grace. There was no police officer called Canning on his team.

Excusing himself, the Detective Superintendent slipped out of the room and walked down the corridor to MIR One. It took him just a few clicks on a workstation keyboard to establish that there was no officer of that name in the entire Sussex police force.

43

Shortly before midnight, Cleo opened her front door wearing an unlaced black silk camisole. It covered the top two inches of her pale, slender thighs and little else. In her outstretched hand was a tumbler of Glenfiddich on the rocks, filled to the brim. The only other things she had on were a tantalizing, deep, musky perfume and the dirtiest grin Roy Grace had ever seen on a woman's face.

'Wow! Now that's what I call a—' he started to say, when she kicked the door shut behind him, the camisole falling even further open over her large, firm breasts. And that was as far as he got as, still holding the glass, she put both arms around his neck and pressed her moist lips against his. Moments later a whisky-flavoured ice cube was sliding into his mouth.

Her eyes, blurry, smiling, danced in front of his own.

Tilting her head just far enough back that he still could only see her in blurred focus, she said, 'You've got far too many clothes on!' Then, placing the glass in his hand, she began, ravenously, to unbutton his shirt, kissing his nipples, then his chest, then pressing another ice cube, with her mouth, deep against his belly button. She looked up at him with eyes that seemed to burn into him with happiness, eyes the colour of sunlight on ice. 'You are so gorgeous, Roy. God, you are so, so gorgeous.'

Gasping, and crunching the remains of the ice cube, he said, 'You're sort of OK yourself.'

'Just sort of OK?' she echoed, distractedly tugging at his

belt buckle as if the world's survival depended on it, then jerking his trousers and boxer shorts sharply down over his shoes.

'In the sense of being the most beautiful, incredible, gorgeous woman on this planet.'

'So there are more beautiful women than me on other planets?' In one deft movement, Cleo dug her fingers into the glass, popped another ice cube in her mouth, then scooped more ice from the glass and pressed it against his balls.

For a reply, raw air shot out of Grace's throat. Pleasure burned in his stomach, so intense it hurt. He pulled the silky garment off her shoulders and buried his mouth into her soft neck, as she took him in her lips, deeply, all the way down the shaft, burying her face in his tangled pubic hairs.

Grace stood, intoxicated with the heat of the night, the smell of her perfume, the touch of her skin, wishing, somewhere in a recess of his brain, that he could freeze this moment, this incredible moment of sheer, utter joy, bliss, freeze it forever, stay here, with her gripping him in her icy lips, that smile in her eyes, that sheer joy dancing in his soul.

Somewhere, just inches away, a shadow hovered. *Munich.* He pushed it away. A ghost, that was all. Just a ghost.

He wanted this woman, Cleo, so much. Not just now, this moment, but wanted her in his life. He adored her to bits. He felt more in love at this moment than he could imagine any man on the planet had ever been before. More in love than he had ever dared to think could happen to him again, after these nine long wilderness years.

Forcing his hands through her long, silky hair, his words gasped breathlessly. 'God, Cleo, you are so –

– incredible –

– so amazing –

– so—'

Then, with his suit jacket still on, his trousers and striped boxer shorts around his ankles, half in and half out of his shirt, he was lying on top of her, on a thick, white pile rug on her polished oak floor, deep, so incredibly deep inside her, holding her in his arms, kissing this wild, writhing beast of so many contrasts.

He gripped her head tightly, pulling her mouth hard against his. Feeling her silky skin entwined around his. Feeling her insanely beautiful, lithe body. Sometimes she felt like a stunning, pedigree racehorse. Sometimes – now – as she suddenly broke her mouth away and stared at him in tense concentration, he saw a vulnerable little girl.

'You won't ever hurt me, will you, Roy?' she asked plaintively.

'Never.'

'You're incredible, you know that?'

'You're more incredible.' He kissed her again.

She gripped the back of his head, pressing her fingers in so hard they hurt. 'I want you to come staring into my eyes,' she whispered intently.

*

Some time later he woke up, his right arm hurting like hell, and blinked, disoriented, unable to figure out for a moment where he was. Music was playing. A Dido song he recognized. He was staring up at a square glass tank. A solitary goldfish was swimming through what looked like the remains of a submerged miniature Greek temple.

Marlon?

But it wasn't his fish tank. He tried to move his arm, but

it was dead, like a big lump of jelly. He shook it. It wobbled. Then a tangled fuzz of blonde pubic hairs filled his eye-line. The view was replaced by a glass of whisky.

'Sustenance?' Cleo said, standing naked over him.

He took the glass in his good hand and sipped. God, it tasted good. He put it down and kissed her bare ankle. Then she lay down and snuggled up beside him. 'OK, sleepy-head?'

Some life was returning to his arm. Enough to put it around her. They kissed. 'Wassertime?' he asked.

'Two fifteen.'

'I'm sorry. I – I didn't – didn't mean to fall asleep on you.'

She kissed each of his eyes in turn, very slowly. 'You didn't.'

He saw her beautiful face, and her blonde hair, in soft focus. Breathed in sweet scents of sweat and sex. Saw the goldfish again, swimming around, oblivious of them, having whatever kind of a good time a goldfish had. He saw candles burning. Plants. Funky abstract paintings on the walls. A floor-to-ceiling row of crammed bookshelves.

'Want to go up to bed?'

'Good plan,' he said.

He tried to stand up, and it was then that he realized he was still half-dressed.

Shedding everything, holding Cleo's hand in one hand and his tumbler in the other, he climbed, leadenly, up two flights of steep, narrow wooden stairs, then flopped on to a massive bed, with the softest sheets he had ever felt in his life, and Dido music still pumping out.

Cleo wrapped herself around him. Her hand slid down his stomach and wrapped around his genitals. 'Is Big Boy sleepy?'

'A little.'

She held the whisky to his lips. He sipped like a baby.

'So, how was your day? Or would you like to sleep?'

He was trying to put his thoughts together. It was a good question. How the hell was his day?

What day?

It was coming back. Bit by bit. The eleven o'clock emergency briefing. No one had anything significant to report, except for himself. Brian Bishop's move from the Hotel du Vin to the Lansdowne Place – and the strange explanation he had given.

'Complicated,' he said, nuzzling up against her right breast, taking her nipple in his mouth and then kissing it. 'You are the most beautiful woman in the world. Did anyone ever tell you?'

'You.' She grinned. 'Only you.'

'Goes to show. No other man on this planet has any taste.'

She kissed his forehead. 'Actually, this may come as a surprise from a slapper like me, but I haven't tried them all.'

He grinned back. 'Now you don't need to.'

She looked at him quizzically, shifted herself around and propped her chin up on one hand. 'No?'

'I missed you all week.'

'I missed you too,' she said.

'How much?'

'Not going to tell you – I don't want it going to your head!'

'Bitch!'

She raised her free left hand in the air and curled the index finger, provocatively mimicking a limp dick.

'Not for long,' he said.

'Good.'

'You are totally wicked.'

'You make me feel wicked.' She kissed him, then moved back a few inches, studying his face carefully. 'I like your hair.'

'You do?'

'Uh huh. Suits you. I do, I really like it!'

He blushed slightly at the compliment. 'I'm glad. Thank you.'

Glenn Branson had been going on about his hair for as long as he could remember, telling him it needed a make-over, and had finally booked him an appointment with a very hip guy called Ian Habbin, at a salon in Brighton's most fashionable quarter. For years Grace had just had his hair clipped to a short fuzz by a mournful, elderly Italian in an old-fashioned barber's shop. It had been a new experience to have his hair shampooed by a chatty young girl in a room hung with art and pounding with rock music.

Then Cleo asked, 'So, Sunday lunch with your sister – *Jodie*, right?'

'Yes.'

'Can you tell me about her? Is she protective of you? Am I going to get the third-degree interrogation? Like, *Is this old slapper good enough for my brother?*' She grinned at him quizzically.

Grace took a large gulp of whisky, trying to buy time to compose his thoughts and his response. Then he took another gulp. Finally he said, 'I've got a problem.'

'Go on.'

'I have to go to Munich on Sunday.'

'Munich? I've always wanted to go there. My friend Anna-Lisa, who's an air hostess, says it's the best place in the world to buy clothes. Hey, I could come with you! Check out some cheap tickets on easyJet or something?'

He cradled the glass. Took another sip, wondering

whether to tell her a white lie or the truth. He didn't want to lie to her, but at this moment it seemed to be less hurtful than telling her the truth. 'It's an official police visit – I'm going with a colleague.'

'Oh – who?' she was staring at him hard.

'It's a DI from another division. We're meeting to discuss a six-month exchange of officers. It's an EU initiative thing,' he said.

Cleo shook her head. 'I thought we'd made a pact never to lie to each other, Roy.'

He stared back at her for a moment, then dropped his eyes, feeling his face flushing.

'I can read you, Roy. I know how to read you. I can read your eyes. You taught me – remember? About that right and left stuff. Memory and construct.'

Grace felt something drop deep inside his heart. After some moments' hesitation, he told her about Dick Pope's possible sighting of Sandy.

Cleo's response was to pull away sharply from him. And suddenly he felt a chasm between them as large as the one separating Earth from the moon.

'Fine,' she said. She sounded like she had just bitten into a lemon.

'Cleo, I have to go there.'

'Of course you do.'

'I don't mean it like that.'

'No?'

'Cleo, please. I—'

'What happens if you find her?'

He raised his hands hopelessly. 'I doubt that I will.'

'And if you do?' she insisted.

'I don't know. At least I'll have found out what happened to her.'

'And if she wants you back? Is that why you lied to me?'

'After nine years?'

She rolled away from him and lay facing the far wall.

'Even if it is her, which I doubt.'

Cleo was silent.

He stroked her back and she shrank further from him.

'Cleo, please!'

'What am I – something to tide you over until you find your missing wife?'

'No way.'

'Are you sure?'

'Totally and utterly.'

'I don't believe you.'

44

There was software on the Time Billionaire's computer screen which he had written himself. It brought up analogue clock faces for cities in every time zone in the world. He was staring at it now. 'Taking stock,' he suddenly said aloud, then grinned at his joke.

Through the window he could see the dawn sky slowly lightening over the city of Brighton and Hove. It was coming up to five here in England. Six in Paris. Eight a.m. in St Petersburg. Eleven in Bangladesh. One in the afternoon in Kuala Lumpur. Three in the afternoon in Sydney.

People would be getting up here soon. And going to bed in Peru. Everyone in the world was subservient to the sun, except for himself. He had been liberated. It made no difference any more to him whether it was day or night, whether the stock exchanges of the world were open or shut, or the banks, or anything else.

There was one man he had to thank for that.

But he was no longer bitter. That was all packed away in another box that was his past. You needed to be positive in life, have goals. He'd found a site on the internet which was all about living longer. People who had goals lived longer, simple as that. And those people who achieved their goals – well, their life expectancy hit the jackpot! And now he had achieved two goals! He owned even more time, to lavish on whatever he liked.

Steam curled from the cup of tea beside him. English breakfast tea with a little milk. He picked the spoon up and stirred the tea seven times. It was very important to him always to stir tea exactly seven times.

Turning his attention back to the computer, he tapped the command for another piece of software he had created for himself. He had never been happy with any of the internet search engines – none of them were precise enough for him. All of them delivered information in the sequence they wanted. This one of his own, which linked and trawled all the major search engines, obtained quickly for him everything that *he* wanted.

And at this moment he wanted an original workshop manual for a 1966 Volkswagen Karmann Ghia.

Then he sucked the back of his right hand. The pain was getting worse, the stinging sensation deepening, which was what had woken him and prevented him from going back to sleep. Not that he was much of a sleeper anyway. He could see a slight swelling around it, which seemed to be affecting the movement of his thumb, although he might be imagining that. And his chest was still stinging.

'Bitch,' he said aloud.

He walked into the bathroom, switched on the light, unbuttoned his shirt and opened up the front, then peeled back the strip of Elastoplast. The fresh scratch, over an inch long, crusted with congealed blood, had been gouged from his chest some hours back by a long toenail.

45

Shortly after five a.m. Roy Grace left Cleo's house, in a trendy, gated development in the centre of Brighton, closing the front door as quietly as he could behind him, feeling terrible. The breaking dawn sky, a dark, marbled grey streaked with smudgy, crimson veins, was the colour of a frozen human cadaver. A few birds were beginning a tentative dawn chorus, firing off solitary tweets, briefly piercing the morning stillness. Signals to other birds, like radio signals beamed into space.

He shivered, as he pressed the red exit button on the wrought-iron gates, and let himself out of the courtyard into the street. The air was already warming up and it promised to be another blistering summer day. But it was raining in his soul.

He hadn't slept a wink.

During the past two months of their relationship, he and Cleo had never exchanged a solitary cross word. They hadn't really tonight either. Yet tossing and turning during these past few hours, he sensed that something had changed between them.

The street lighting was still on, useless orange glows emitting from each lamp in the rapidly encroaching daylight. A tabby cat slunk across the road ahead of him. He walked up past a line of cars, noticed a Coke can lying in the gutter, a pool of vomit, a Chinese takeaway carton. He passed Cleo's blue MG, covered in dew, then reached his Alfa, covered in less dew. It was parked in what had become his regular spot, on a single yellow line outside an antiques dealer that specialized in retro twentieth-century furniture.

He climbed in, started the car, blipped the accelerator, the engine snuffling, running lumpily and unevenly for a few moments until the damp burned off the electrics; the wipers clopped the dew from the screen. A hiss of static belted out from the radio; he punched a button to switch stations. Someone was talking, but he didn't listen. Instead he turned and stared at the closed gates, wondering whether to go back and say something.

Like what?

Cleo saw Sandy as a threat she could not deal with. He knew that he needed to get his head around that, to put himself in Cleo's position. What if she'd had a husband who'd vanished and it was she who was off to Munich to try to find him tomorrow? How would *he* be feeling?

He had no idea, that was the honest truth. In part because he was too dog-tired to think straight, and in part because he didn't know what he was feeling about the prospect – however slim – of seeing Sandy.

Ten minutes later he passed the red pillar box on New Church Road, which had been his landmark for twelve years, and made the next left turn. Apart from a milk float halted several feet out from the pavement, Grace's street was deserted. It was a quiet, pleasant residential avenue, lined on both sides with semi-detached mock-Tudor houses, most of them three-bedroomed, with integral garages. A few had rather ugly loft conversions and some – not his own – had hideous secondary double-glazing.

He and Sandy had bought the house just over two years before she disappeared, and sometimes he wondered if the move had had something to do with it, whether she hadn't been happy there. They'd been so content in the small flat in Hangleton that had been their nest in those first years of marriage, but they'd both fallen in love with this house, Sandy even more so than himself because it had a good-sized rear garden and she had always longed for a garden of her own.

Buying the place and then doing it up had stretched them both financially. Grace had been a detective sergeant then, still qualifying for overtime, and had worked all the hours he could. Sandy had been a secretary at a firm of accountants and had put in extra hours there, too.

She had seemed happy enough, taking charge of gutting and modernizing the interior. The previous owners had lived there for over forty years, and it had been drab and dark when they had bought it. Sandy had transformed it into light, modern spaces, with touches of Zen here and there – and she seemed so proud of all she had done. And the garden had become her pride and joy – although it was now in an embarrassing state of neglect, Grace thought guiltily. Every weekend he promised himself he would spend some time on it, sorting things out. But in the end he never seemed to have enough time – or the inclination. He kept the grass under reasonable control, and had convinced himself that most of the weeds were flowers anyway.

On his car radio, which he had tuned out of his brain for several minutes, he now heard a man earnestly explaining EU agricultural policy. Turning into his driveway, he pulled up in front of the single garage and switched off the engine, the radio dying with it.

Then, letting himself into the house, his solemn mood was suddenly replaced by a flash of anger. All the downstairs lights were on, burning brightly. So was his original juke box.

He saw that one of his rare vinyl records, 'Apache' by the

Shadows, was spinning round on the juke-box turntable, the needle stuck in the groove, making a steady *click-scrape-click-scrape-click-scrape* sound. His stereo was on also and part of his CD collection was scattered on the floor, along with several of his precious Pink Floyd LPs, out of their sleeves, an opened can of Grolsch lager, a couple of Harley-Davidson brochures, a set of dumb-bells and assorted other pieces of iron-pumping kit.

He stormed up the stairs, ready to yell blue murder at Glenn Branson, then stopped at the top, checking himself. The poor bastard was distraught. He must have gone home last night after the briefing meeting and been given his marching orders – hence the weights equipment. Let him sleep.

He looked at his watch. Five twenty. Although he felt tired, he was too wired to sleep. He decided he would go for a run, try to clear his head and energize himself for the heavy day ahead, which was starting with an eight-thirty team briefing, followed by a press conference at eleven a.m. And then he planned to have another session with Brian Bishop. The man smelled all wrong to him.

He went through to his bathroom, and immediately noticed the top was off the toothpaste. There was a large indent in the middle of the tube and some of the white paste had spewed out of the neck and on to the bathroom shelf. For some reason he could not immediately under-stand, this irked him even more than the mess downstairs.

Since entering this house just a few minutes ago, he was beginning to feel as if he'd slipped through a reality warp into the old TV sitcom *Men Behaving Badly*, with Martin Clunes and Neil Morrissey playing bachelor slobs sharing a pad. And then he realized about the toothpaste: it had been one of the very few things that had irritated him about

Sandy, the way she did that too. She always squeezed the damn tube in the middle rather than from the end, then left the top off so that part of the contents dribbled out.

That and the condition she always kept the interior of her car in – she treated the passenger side as a kind of permanent dustbin that never needed emptying. The elderly black VW Golf was so littered with shopping receipts, discarded sweet wrappers, empty shopping bags, Lottery tickets and a whole raft of other debris that Grace used to think it looked more like something you'd want to keep chickens in than drive.

It was still in the garage now. He'd cleaned out the rubbish long ago, been through every scrap of it in search of a clue, and found none.

'You're up early.'

He turned and saw Branson standing behind him, wearing a pair of white underpants, a thin gold chain around his neck and his massive diver's wristwatch. Although his body was stooped, his physique was in terrific shape, his muscles bulging through his gleaming skin. But his face was a picture of abject misery.

'I need to be, to clear up after you,' Grace retorted.

Either not registering this or deliberately ignoring it, Branson went on. 'She wants a horse.'

Grace shook his head, unsure whether he had heard correctly. 'What?'

'Ari.' Branson shrugged. 'She wants a horse. Can you believe, on what I earn?'

'More eco-friendly than a car,' Grace replied. 'Probably cheaper to run too.'

'Very witty.'

'What exactly do you mean, a *horse*?'

'She used to ride – worked in stables when she was a kid.

She wants to take it up again. She said if I agree to get her a horse, I can come back.'

'Where can I buy one?' Grace retorted.

'I'm being serious.'

'So am I.'

46

Roy Grace had been right. With Parliament long closed for its summer recess and the most significant world event during the past twenty-four hours being a train crash in Pakistan, the only stories vying for the front pages, particularly the tabloids, were the shock revelations of a Premiership footballer caught in a gay threesome, a panther apparently terrorizing the Dorset countryside and Prince Harry cavorting on a beach with an enviably pretty girl. All the nation's news editors were hungry for a big story, and what better than the murder of a wealthy, beautiful woman?

The conference room for the morning press briefing he had called had been so tightly packed that some reporters had been left out in the corridor. He kept it short and tight, because he didn't have a lot to tell them at this stage. No new information had come in overnight, and the earlier team briefing had been more about assigning tasks for the day than assessing any developments.

The one message he did put across clearly, to the sea of forty or so faces of press and media reporters and photographers in the room, was that the police were anxious to trace Mrs Bishop's recent movements, and they would like to hear from any members of the public who might have seen her during the previous few days. The press were to be issued with a set of photographs Grace had chosen from the Bishops' house, most of them from a montage of action pictures. One showed the dead woman in a bikini on a powerboat, another at the wheel of her convertible BMW, and in another she wore a long dress and a hat at a smart race meeting – Ascot or Epsom, Grace guessed.

He had chosen these photographs very carefully, knowing that they would appeal to news editors. They were the kind of pictures readers liked to feast their eyes on – the beautiful woman, the fast, glamorous lifestyle. With acres of column inches to fill, Grace knew they would be used. And wide coverage just might jog the memory of one key witness out there somewhere.

He slipped away quickly at the end, anxious to call Cleo before going into a further interview with Brian Bishop, which was scheduled for midday, leaving Dennis Ponds, the senior police public relations officer, to distribute the photographs. But only yards before reaching the security door leading through to the sanctuary of his office, he heard his name called out. He turned, and was irritated to see that the young *Argus* crime reporter, Kevin Spinella, had followed him.

'What are you doing here?' Grace said.

Spinella leaned against a wall, close to a display board on which was pinned a flow chart headed MURDER INVESTIGATION MODEL, an insolent expression on his sharp face, chewing gum, holding his black notebook open and a pen in his hand. Today he had on a cheap, dark suit that he seemed to have not quite yet grown into, a white shirt that was also too big for him and a purple tie with a large, clumsy knot. His short hair had that fashionable, mussed, just-got-up look.

'I wanted to ask you something in private, Detective Superintendent.'

Grace held his security card up to the lock. The latch clicked and he pulled open the door. 'I've just said everything I have to say to the press at the conference. I've no further comment at this stage.'

'I think you have,' Spinella said, his smug expression irritating Grace even more now. 'Something you omitted.'

'Then speak to Dennis Ponds.'

'I would have raised it at the conference,' Spinella said, 'but you wouldn't have thanked me for it. The thing about the gas mask?'

Grace spun round, shocked, taking a step towards the reporter, letting the door click shut again behind him. 'What did you say?'

'I heard there was a gas mask discovered at the murder scene – that it might have been used by the killer – some kinky ritual or something?'

Grace's brain raced. He was seething with anger, but venting it now wasn't going to help. This had happened before. A couple of months back, on another case, a vital piece of information about something found at a crime scene and withheld from the press – in that case a beetle – had been leaked to the *Argus*. Now it seemed it had happened again. Who was responsible? The problem was it could have been anyone. Although the information had been withheld from the press conference, half of Sussex Police would already know about it.

Instead of shouting at Spinella, Grace stared at the man, sizing him up. He was a smart lad and crime was clearly his thing. Quite likely in a year or two he would move on from this local paper to a bigger one, maybe to a national; there was nothing to be gained from making an enemy of him.

'OK, I appreciate your not raising it at the conference.'

'Is it true?'

'Are we on the record or off?'

Spinella shrewdly closed his notepad. 'Off.'

Grace hesitated, still wary of how much the man could be trusted. 'There was a Second World War gas mask found at the scene, but we don't know that it's connected.'

'And you're keeping that quiet because only the real killer will know it was there?'

'Yes. And it would be very helpful if you didn't print anything about it – yet.'

'So what would be in that for me?' Spinella retorted instantly.

Grace found himself grinning at the young man's cheek. 'You trying to cut a deal?'

'If I scratch your back now, it means you'll owe me one. Some time in the future. I'll bank it. Deal?'

Grace shook his head, grinning again. 'You cheeky monkey!'

'I'm glad we understand each other.'

Grace turned back to the door.

'Just one quick thing,' Spinella said. 'Is it true that you and Assistant Chief Constable Alison Vosper don't see eye to eye?'

'Are we still off the record?' Grace asked.

Spinella nodded, holding up the closed notebook.

'No comment!' Grace delivered his most acidic smile, and this time went through the door, closing it firmly behind him.

*

Ten minutes later, together with Branson, Grace sat down in one of the red, bucket-shaped chairs in the Witness Interview Suite, opposite a wretched-looking Brian Bishop. He had been driven over from his hotel by WPC Maggie Campbell, who was waiting outside.

Grace, his jacket off and wearing a short-sleeved shirt,

placed his notebook down on the small coffee table, then dabbed perspiration off his forehead with his handkerchief. Branson, wearing a fresh white T-shirt tight as skin, thin blue jeans and trainers, seemed in a less desolate mood today.

'OK if we record again, to save time, sir?' Grace asked Bishop.

'Whatever.'

Branson switched on the apparatus. 'The time is three minutes past twelve p.m. Saturday 5 August. Detective Superintendent Grace and Detective Sergeant Branson interviewing Mr Brian Bishop.'

Grace took a sip of water, observing that Bishop was dressed in the same clothes as yesterday, apart from a different top – today a lime-green polo shirt. He was looking much more grief-stricken than yesterday, as if the reality of his loss had hit him. Perhaps yesterday he had been running on adrenaline from the shock, which sometimes happened. Grief affected everyone in different ways, but there were long-trodden stages most bereaved people went through. Shock. Denial. Anger. Sadness. Guilt. Loneliness. Despair. Gradual acceptance. And, Grace was aware, some of the coolest killers he had encountered had delivered Oscar-nominee performances of these.

He watched Bishop leaning forward in his chair, very intently stirring the coffee that Branson had brought him with a plastic paddle, and frowned as he clocked the sudden intense concentration on Bishop's face. Was the man counting the number of times he stirred?

'How's your hand today?' Grace asked.

Bishop raised his right hand until it was in plain view. Grace could see scabbing on the grazes. 'It's OK,' he said. 'It's better. Thank you.'

'Are you normally an accident-prone person?' Grace went on.

'I don't think so.'

Grace nodded, then fell silent. Branson shot him a quizzical glance which Grace ignored.

If Bishop had killed his wife, he could have incurred the wound in the process. Or he could have just injured his hand through clumsiness. Bishop did not look like a man who was normally clumsy. It was perfectly conceivable that, distraught with grief, he was making misjudgements, but there were other possible explanations for his injury. Most criminals became a bag of wired nerves in the hours following their crime.

Are you in a red mist, Mr Bishop?

'What progress have you made?' Brian Bishop suddenly asked in a croaky voice, looking at each of them in turn. 'Have you any clue who might have done this?'

Yes, I have, and I've a feeling I'm looking at him, Grace thought, but ensured he did not let it show. 'I'm afraid we're not any further along than we were last night, sir. Have you had any more thoughts? Did you and Mrs Bishop have anyone you'd upset? Any enemies that you were aware of?'

'No – not – not at all. Some people were jealous of us, I think.'

'You *think*.'

'Well, Katie and I – we – we are – were – you know – one of the city's *golden* couples. I don't mean that in a vulgar or boasting sense. Just a fact. Our lifestyle.'

'Thrust upon you, was it?' Grace couldn't help himself saying, and caught Branson's smirk.

Bishop gave him a humourless smile. 'No, actually, it was our choice. Well – more Katie – she liked the limelight. Always had big social ambitions.'

A fly scudded erratically around the room. Grace followed its path for a few seconds before saying, 'That rather distinctive Bentley you drive – was that your choice or did your wife choose it?'

Bishop shrugged. 'My choice of car – but I think Katie had something to do with the colour – she really liked it.'

Grace smiled, trying to disarm him. 'Very diplomatic of you, I'm sure. Women can get a bit negative about boys' toys, if they're not involved.' He shot a pointed look. 'And vice versa sometimes.'

The DS grimaced back at him.

Bishop scratched the back of his head. 'Look – I – I need – I need some help from you – about – I need to make funeral arrangements – what do I do about that?'

Grace nodded sympathetically. 'I'm afraid it will be up to the coroner when the body is released. But in the meantime it would be a good idea to engage an undertaker. Linda Buckley will be able to help you with that.'

Bishop stared down at his coffee, looking like a small, lost boy suddenly, as if talk of undertakers made it all too real for him to bear.

'I just want to go back over a time sequence with you,' Grace said, 'to make sure I've got it right.'

'Yes?' Bishop gave him an almost pleading look.

Grace leaned towards the table and flicked back a few pages in his notebook. 'You spent Thursday night in London, then you drove down to Brighton to play golf early on Friday morning.' Grace turned back another page and read carefully for a moment. 'At half past six yesterday morning, your concierge, Oliver Dowler, helped you load your golf clubs and your luggage into your car, you told us. That's correct, is it?'

'Yes.'

'And you'd spent the night in London, after having dinner with your financial adviser, Mr Phil Taylor?'

'Yes. He could vouch for that.'

'He already has, Mr Bishop.'

'Good.'

'And your concierge has vouched that he helped you load your car at about six thirty in the morning.'

'So he should.'

'Indeed,' Grace said. He studied his note pages again. 'You are certain you didn't go out anywhere in between having dinner with Mr Taylor and leaving in the morning?'

Brian Bishop hesitated, thinking about the bizarre phone conversation yesterday with Sophie, when she had been insisting that he slept with her after his dinner with Phil Taylor. That made no sense. There was no way on earth he could have driven an hour and a half down to her flat in Brighton, then back up to London again and not remembered.

Was there?

Looking at each police officer in turn, he said, 'I didn't. No. Absolutely not.'

Grace observed the man's hesitation. Now wasn't the moment to reveal the piece of information he had, that Bishop's Bentley had been clocked by a camera heading towards Brighton at eleven forty-seven on Thursday night.

Grace had a number of detectives available to him in Sussex Police who were specifically trained in interviewing techniques and would put Bishop under pressure. He decided to hold back this nugget of information, so they could spring it on the man at the appropriate moment.

That interview process would begin when Grace decided to treat Bishop formally as a suspect. And he was fast approaching that decision.

47

On the two o'clock news on Southern Counties Radio, the murder of Katie Bishop remained the top story, as it had been on all of the bulletins he had caught throughout the past twenty-four hours. Each time he heard it, the story seemed a little more pepped up with carefully chosen words to make it increasingly glamorous. It was starting to sound like something from a soap opera, he thought.

Brighton *socialite*, Katie Bishop.

Wealthy businessman husband, Brian.

Millionaires' row, Dyke Road Avenue.

The news presenter, whose name was Dick Dixon, sounded young, although he looked older in his photograph on the BBC website, craggier and very different from his voice. His picture was up on the screen now, quite mean-looking, like the actor Steve Buscemi in *Reservoir Dogs*. Not a person you'd want to mess with, though you'd never have guessed that from his friendly voice.

With the help of the editorial team behind him, Dick Dixon was trying his best to turn this bulletin, in which there were no fresh developments to report on the murder investigation, into one which gave the impression that a breakthrough was imminent. A sense of urgency was created by cutting to the taped voice of Detective Superintendent Roy Grace, from a press conference earlier today.

'This is a particularly nasty crime,' the Detective Superintendent said. 'One in which the sanctity of a private home, protected by an elaborate alarm, was breached and a human life tragically and brutally destroyed. Mrs Bishop was a tireless worker for local charities and one of this city's most popular citizens. We offer our deepest sympathy to her husband and all her family, and we will work around the clock to bring the evil creature who did this to justice.'

Evil creature.

As he listened to the officer, he sucked his hand. The pain was getting worse.

Evil creature.

There was noticeable swelling, he could see it clearly if he put his two hands together. And there was something else he did not like the look of: thin red lines seemed to be tracking out, away from the wound and up his wrist. He continued sucking hard, trying to draw out any poison that might be in there. A freshly brewed mug of tea sat on his desk. He stirred it, counting carefully.

One, two, three, four, five, six, seven.

Dick Dixon was speaking again now, talking about a growing protest movement over a proposed third terminal at Gatwick airport. A local MP's voice came on, launching a savage attack.

Evil creature.

He stood up, fuming, and stepped away from his workstation, threading his way across the basement floor through stacks of computer equipment, piles of motoring magazines and motor car workshop manuals, towards the grimy bay window that was protected by net curtains. No one could see in, but he could see out. Looking up from his *lair*, as he liked to call it, he saw a pair of shapely legs cross his eye-line, striding by on the pavement, along the railings. Long, bare, brown legs, firm and muscular, with a mini-skirt that barely covered her bits.

He felt a prick of lust, then immediately felt bad about that.

Terrible.

Evil creature.

He knelt down on the spot, on the thin, faded carpet that smelled of dust, cupped his face in his hands and recited the Lord's Prayer. When he had reached the end, he continued with a further prayer: 'Dear God, please forgive my lustful thoughts. Please do not let them stand in my way. Please don't let me squander all the time you have graciously given me on these thoughts.'

He continued to pray for some minutes, then, finally, stood up, feeling refreshed, energized, happy that God was with him in the room now. He walked back over to his workstation and drank some tea. Someone on the radio was explaining how to fly a kite. He had never flown a kite in his life, and it had never, before, occurred to him to try. But maybe he should. Perhaps it would take his mind off things. Might be a good way to spend some of that time that was piling up in his account.

Yes, a kite.

Good.

Where did you buy one? In a sports shop? A toyshop? Or the internet, of course!

Not too big a kite, because he was tight on space in the flat. He liked it here, and the place was ideal for him, because it had three entrances – or, more importantly, three *exits*.

Perfect for an *evil creature*.

The flat was on the busy thoroughfare of Sackville Road, close to the junction with Portland Road, and there were always vehicles passing by, day and night. It was a down-market area, this end. A quarter of a mile to the south, closer to the sea, it became rapidly smarter. But here, close to an industrial estate, with a railway bridge running overhead and a few grime-fronted shops, it was a ragbag of unloved, modest-sized Victorian and Edwardian terraced houses, all of them split up into rooming houses, bedsits, cheap flats or offices.

There were always people around. Mostly students, as well as some transients and dossers, and the occasional dealer or two. Just sometimes, a few of Hove's elderly, gentrified, blue-rinse ladies could be seen out and about in daylight, waiting at the bus stop or waddling to a shop. It was a place where you could come and go, twenty-four/ seven, without attracting attention.

Which made it perfect for his purposes. Apart from the damp, the inadequate storage heaters and the leaking cistern which he kept fixing, over and over. He did all the maintenance down here himself. He didn't want workmen coming in. Not a good idea.

Not a good idea at all.

One exit was up the front steps. Another was out the back, through a garden belonging to the ground-floor flat, above him. The owner, a wasted-looking guy with straggly hair, grew rust and weeds in it very successfully. The third exit was for Doomsday, when it finally came. It was concealed behind a false, plywood wall, carefully and seamlessly covered in the same drab floral paper as the rest of the room. Over it, like over most of the wall space down here, he had stuck cuttings from newspapers, photographs and parts of family trees.

One photograph was brand new – he had added it just a quarter of an hour ago. It was a grainy head and shoulders of Detective Superintendent Roy Grace, from today's *Argus*, which he had scanned into his computer, blown up, and then printed.

He was staring at the policeman now. Staring at his sharp eyes, at the quiet determination in his expression. *You're going to be a problem for me, Detective Superintendent Grace. You are in my face. We're going to have to do something about you. Teach you a lesson. Nobody calls me an* evil creature.

Then suddenly he shouted out aloud, 'No one calls me an EVIL CREATURE, Detective Superintendent Roy Grace of Sussex CID. Do you understand me? I will make you sorry you called me an *evil creature.* I know who you love.'

He stood, hyperventilating, closing and opening his left hand. Then he paced around the room a couple of times, treading a careful path through the magazines, manuals and entrails of the computers that he was building on the floor, then returned to the photograph again, aware that circumstances had changed. There had been a call on his bank; he could no longer luxuriate in being a time billionaire. The stuff was running out.

48

Just before four o'clock, Holly Richardson stood at the till of Brighton's coolest new boutique, paying for the insanely expensive, seriously skimpy black dress, edged with diamantés, that she had decided she totally could not go to the party tonight without. She was buying it courtesy of a Virgin credit card that had conveniently landed on her doormat, followed by the pin code, just a few days ago. Her Barclaycard was already maxed out, and by her calculations, on her current rate of outgoings, her earnings from the Esporta fitness centre at Falmer, where she worked as a receptionist, would enable her to pay it off fully around the time of her ninety-fifth birthday.

Marrying someone rich was not an option, it was a necessity.

And maybe tonight *Mr Seriously Gorgeous Very Rich Who Likes Curly Dark Haired Girls With Very Slightly Big Noses* might just be at that party she and Sophie were going to. The guy throwing it was a successful music producer. The house was a stunning Moorish pad right on the beach, just a couple of doors along from the one Paul McCartney had bought his ex-beloved Heather.

And, *oh shit!* She just remembered that she had promised to call Sophie back yesterday, when she was out of the hairdresser's, and it had completely slipped her mind.

Carrying her extremely expensive purchase by the rope handles of the store's swanky carrier bag, she went out into busy East Street, dug her tiny, latest-model Nokia out of her handbag and dialled Sophie's. It went straight to voicemail. She left an apologetic message, suggested they meet for a drink about seven thirty, then share a taxi to the party. When she finished, she then dialled the landline in Sophie's flat. But that went to voicemail too.

She left a second message there.

49

Roy Grace didn't leave a message. He had already left one earlier on Cleo's home phone, as well as on her mobile, and he'd also left one on the mortuary's answering machine. Now he was listening to her breezy voicemail intro on her mobile for the third time today. He hung up. She was clearly avoiding him, still in her strop over Sandy.

Shit, shit, shit.

He was angry with himself for handling it so bloody clumsily. For lying to Cleo and breaking her trust in him. OK, it was a white lie, yadda yadda yadda. But that question she asked, that one simple question, was one he just could not answer, not to her, not to himself. Always the killer question.

What happens if you find her?

And the truth was he really did not know. There were so many imponderables. So many different reasons why people disappeared, and he knew most of them. He had been over this ground so many times with the team at the Missing Persons Helpline, and the shrink he had been seeing on and off for years. In his heart he clung to the slim hope that, if Sandy was alive, she was suffering from amnesia. That had been a realistic possibility in those first days and weeks after she had disappeared, but now, with so many years gone by, it was a straw almost too thin to clutch.

A pink-faced Swatch wristwatch with white letters and a white strap dangled in front of his face. 'I got my nine-year-old one of these. She was over the moon, like, totally wow, know what I mean?' the shop assistant said helpfully. He was a pale Afro-Caribbean, in his early thirties, smartly dressed and friendly, with hair that looked like a bunch of broken watch springs.

Grace focused back on his task. His sister had suggested he buy his goddaughter a watch for her birthday tomorrow, and he had phoned her mother to check they were not giving her one. There were ten laid out on the glass counter. His problem was that he had no idea what a nine-year-old would consider cool or horrid. Memories of the disappointment of opening dreary presents thrust on him by his own well-meaning godparents haunted him. Socks, a dressing gown, a jumper, a wooden replica of a 1920s Harrods delivery van where the wheels wouldn't even turn.

All the watches were different. The pink with the white face was the prettiest, the most delicate. 'I don't know what's in and out with watches – would a nine-year-old girl consider this one cool?'

'This one rocks, man. Totally. This is what they're all wearing. You ever see that show on Saturday morning, Channel Four?'

Grace shook his head.

'There was a kid on it last week wearing one of these. My daughter went mental!'

'How much is it?'

'Thirty quid. Comes in a nice box.'

Grace nodded, pulling out his wallet. At least that was one problem solved. Albeit the smallest of the current crop.

*

There were some much bigger problems presented to him at the six-thirty briefing in the conference room at Sussex House that evening, the stifling heat in the room being the least of them. All twenty-two of the team present had their jackets off, and most of the men, like Grace, wore short-sleeved shirts. They kept the door open, creating the illusion that cooler air was wafting in from the corridor, and two electric fans whirred away noisily and uselessly. Everyone in the room was perspiring. Just as the last of them sat down, there was a rumble of thunder in the darkening sky.

'There we go,' Norman Potting said, with large blotches of damp on his cream shirt. 'The traditional English summer for you. Two fine days followed by a thunderstorm.'

Several of the team smiled, but Grace barely heard him, he was wrapped up in so many thoughts. Cleo had still not called him back. He was booked on a seven a.m. flight to Munich, tomorrow, returning at nine fifteen p.m. But at least he had some help over there. Although he hadn't spoken to Marcel Kullen in over four years, the man had returned his call within an hour and – so far as Grace could understand from Kullen's erratic, broken English – the German detective was insisting on collecting him in person from the airport. And he had remembered to cancel Sunday lunch at his sister's tomorrow – much to her disappointment and Cleo's silent anger.

'The time is six thirty, Saturday 5 August,' he read out formally to the assembled company, from his notes prepared by Eleanor Hodgson. 'This is our fourth briefing of Operation Chameleon, the investigation into the death of Mrs Katherine Margaret Bishop – known as Katie – conducted on day two following the discovery of her body at eight thirty yesterday morning. I will now summarize events following the incident.'

He kept the summary short, skipping some of the details, then finished by stating angrily that someone had leaked the crucial piece of information about the gas mask to the *Argus* reporter, Kevin Spinella. Glaring around the room, he asked, 'Anyone know how this information got to him?'

Blank expressions greeted him.

Irritable because of the heat, and Cleo, and every damn thing at the moment, he thumped his fist down on the table. 'This is the second time this has happened in recent months.' He shot a glance at his deputy, Inspector Kim Murphy, who nodded as if in confirmation. 'I'm not saying it was anyone in this room,' he added. 'But by hell or high water I'm going to find out who was responsible, and I want you to all keep your ears to the ground. OK?'

There were general nods of consensus. Then a brief moment of heavy silence, broken by a flit of lightning and the sudden flicker of all the lights in the room. Moments later there was another rumble of thunder.

'On an organizational point, I won't be here for tomorrow's briefings – these will be taken by DI Murphy.'

Kim Murphy nodded again.

'I will be out of the country for a few hours,' Grace continued. 'But I'll have my mobile phone and my BlackBerry, so I will be reachable at all times by phone and email. OK, so let's have your individual reports.' He looked down at his notes, checking the tasks that had been assigned, although he could remember most if not all of them in his head. 'Norman?'

Potting's voice was a deep, sometimes mumbled growl, coarsened by a rural burr. 'I have something which may be significant, Roy,' the Detective Sergeant said.

Grace signalled for him to continue.

Potting, a stickler for detail, related the information in the rather formal and ponderous terminology he might have used when making a statement from a witness box. 'You asked me to check on all CCTV cameras in the area. I was looking through the Vantage log for all incidents that were reported during Thursday night, and observed that a plumber's van, which had been reported stolen in Lewes on Thursday afternoon, had been found abandoned on the slip road of a BP petrol station, on the westbound carriage-way of the A27, two miles west of Lewes, early yesterday morning.'

He paused to flick back a couple of pages of his lined notebook. 'I made the decision to investigate because it struck me as strange—'

'Why?' DS Bella Moy rounded on him. Grace knew that she couldn't stand Potting and would grab any opportunity to put him down.

'Well, Bella, it struck me that a van full of plumbing tools would hardly be the vehicle of choice for most joyriders,' he replied, provoking a ripple of mirth. Even Grace allowed himself a thin smile.

Stony-faced, Bella retorted, 'But it might be for a crooked plumber.'

'Not with what plumbers charge – they all drive Rollers.'

This time the laughter was even louder. Grace raised a silencing hand. 'Can we just keep to business, please? We're dealing with something very serious.'

Potting ploughed on. 'It just didn't feel right to me. A plumber's van being abandoned. Around the same time Mrs Bishop was killed. I can't explain why I made any con-nection – just call it a copper's nose.'

He looked at Grace, who responded with a nod. He knew what Potting meant. The best policemen had instincts. Intuition. The ability to tell – smell – when something was right or wrong, for reasons they could never logically explain.

Bella glared childishly at Norman Potting, as if trying to stare him out. Grace made a mental note to speak to her about her attitude afterwards.

'I went to the BP petrol station this morning and requested permission to view and interrogate the forecourt's CCTV camera footage for the previous night. The staff were obliging, partly because they'd had two people drive off without paying them.' Potting suddenly looked straight back at Bella smugly. 'The camera takes one frame every thirty seconds. When I studied the images, they revealed a BMW convertible, which had pulled in just before midnight, which I later ascertained was the vehicle belonging to Mrs Bishop. I was also able to identify a woman walking to the petrol station's shop as Mrs Bishop.'

'This could be significant,' Grace said.

'It gets better.' Now the veteran detective was looking even more pleased with himself. 'I checked the interior of the car afterwards, at the Bishops' residence in Dyke Road Avenue, and found a pay-and-display parking ticket, issued at five eleven p.m. on Thursday afternoon from a machine in Southover Road in Lewes. The stolen van was taken from a car park just behind Cliffe High Street – about five minutes' walk away.'

Potting said nothing further. After some moments Grace prompted him, 'And?'

'I can't add anything further at this stage, Roy. But I have a feeling that there's a connection.'

Grace looked at him, hard. Potting, with a disastrous personal life, and enough political incorrectness to inflame half of the United Nations, had, despite all that baggage, produced impressive results before. 'Keep on it,' he said, and turned to DC Zafferone.

Alfonso Zafferone had been assigned to the important but tedious job of working out the time-lines. Insolently chewing gum, he reported on his work with the HOLMES team, plotting the sequence of events surrounding the discovery of Katie Bishop's body.

The young DC reported that Katie Bishop had started the day of the night she died with a one-hour session at home with her personal trainer. Grace made a note that he was to be interviewed.

Next she had attended a beauty parlour in Brighton, where she had had her nails done. Grace jotted down that the staff there needed to be interviewed. That had been followed by lunch at Havana Restaurant in Brighton with a lady called Caroline Ash, the appeals organizer of a local charity for children, the Rocking Horse Appeal, to discuss plans for a fund-raising event that she and her husband were scheduled to host at their Dyke Road Avenue home in September. Grace wrote down that Mrs Ash was to be interviewed.

Mrs Bishop's gruelling day, Zafferone said, with considerable sarcasm, continued with a visit to her hairdresser at three o'clock. After that the trail on her went cold. The information that Norman Potting had provided clearly filled in the gap.

The next report was from the latest recruit to Grace's team, a tough, sharp-eyed female detective constable in her late thirties called Pamela Buckley – constantly confused by many with the family liaison officer Linda Buckley and so similar-looking, they could have been sisters. Both had blonde hair, Linda Buckley's cropped boyishly short, Pamela's longer, clipped up rather severely.

'I found the taxi driver who drove Brian Bishop from the Hotel du Vin to the Lansdowne Place Hotel,' Pamela Buckley said, and looked down at her notepad. 'His name's Mark Tuckwell and he drives for Hove Streamline. He has no recollection of Bishop hurting his hand.'

'Could Bishop have injured himself without this driver knowing?'

'It's possible, sir, but unlikely. I asked him that. He said Bishop was completely silent throughout the journey. He felt that if he had injured himself, he'd have said something.'

Grace nodded, making notes, not convinced this got them anywhere.

Bella Moy then gave a detailed character report on Katie and Brian Bishop. Katie Bishop did not come out of it particularly well. She had been married twice before, the first time to a failed rock singer, when she was eighteen. She had divorced him when she was twenty-two and then married a wealthy Brighton property developer, whom she had divorced six years later, when she was twenty-eight. Bella had been in touch with both men, who had described her, unflatteringly, as being obsessed with money. Two years later she had married Brian Bishop.

'Why didn't she have any children?' Grace asked.

'She had two abortions with her rock singer. Her property developer already had four children and didn't want any more.'

'Was that the reason for her divorcing him?'

'That's what he told me,' she said.

'Did she get a big settlement?'

'About two million, he said,' she replied.

Grace made another note. Then he said, 'She and Brian Bishop were married for five years. And we don't know the reason why they didn't have children. We need to ask him. Could have been an issue between them.'

Next on Grace's list was DS Guy Batchelor. One of the actions he had delegated to the detective sergeant was to conduct a thorough search of the Bishops' Brighton home, once the forensic work had been finished, and to act as a coordinator in the meantime.

'I have something which may be significant,' Batchelor said. He held up a red file folder, with an index tab clipped to the top. He opened it and removed a bunch of A4-sized papers, clipped together, bearing the logo of the HSBC bank. 'A SOCO found it in a filing cabinet in Bishop's study,' he said. 'It's a life insurance policy taken out six months ago in the name of Mrs Bishop. For three million pounds.'

50

Most of us have one BIG IDEA at some point in our lives. That Eureka! moment. It comes to us all in different ways, often by chance or serendipity. Alexander Fleming had it when he left some bacteria out overnight in his lab and discovered penicillin as a result. Steve Jobs had it when he looked at a Swatch watch one day and realized that offering computers in a range of colours was the way forward for Apple. Bill Gates must have had one of those moments too, at some point.

These ideas sometimes come to us when we least expect it: when we are lying in the bathtub fretting about this or that, or wide awake in bed in the middle of the night, or perhaps just sitting at our desk at work. The idea that no one has ever had before us. The idea that will make us rich, get us away from all the drudgery and daily crap we have to put up with. The idea that will change our lives and set us free!

I had mine on Saturday, 25 May 1996, at eleven twenty-five p.m. I was hating my job as a software engineer at a company located in Coventry that developed gearboxes for racing cars. I was trying to figure how to get my life together – and realizing, now I was soon turning thirty-two, that it was as together as it was ever going to get. I was on a charter plane coming back from a lousy week's holiday in Spain, and there was a sudden walk-out of staff at Malaga airport and all the planes got grounded.

The ground staff tried to put us into hotels for the night, but it was hopeless. There was one girl on the charter company desk, trying to find rooms for 280 people. And there were employees at all the other airline desks trying to do the same for their stranded passengers. There were probably three to four thousand people stranded and there was no way they were able to cope and book everyone in.

I lay down on a bench in the departure lounge. And then I had my moment! One computer software program installed in all the local hotels and in all the airlines could have solved their problems. Instant boost of profit for the hotels; instant solution to their nightmare for the airlines. Then I began to think of other applications beyond cancelled flights. Any organization that had to fit large numbers of people into places and any organization that had rooms to sell. Tour operators, prisons, hospitals, disaster relief agencies, the armed forces, were just some of the potential customers.

I had found my gold mine.

51

The tide was coming in on the Brighton and Hove waterfront, but there was still a wide expanse of exposed mudflats between the pebble beach and the frothing surf from the breakers. Although it was almost half past eight in the evening and the sun was fast closing on the horizon, there were still plenty of people on the beach.

Sweet barbecue smoke mingled with the smells of salt, weed and tar. Strains of steel-band music from a stoned group playing on the promenade drifted through the warm, still air. Two small naked children dug plastic spades into the mud, helped by a plump, badly sunburnt man in loud shorts and a baseball cap who was adding a further layer to an already fine-looking sandcastle.

Two young lovers, in shorts and T-shirts, walked barefoot across cool, wet mud. They stepped on whorls of lugworm casts, upturned shells, strands of weed, carefully avoiding the occasional rusted can, discarded bottle or empty plastic carton. Their hands were tightly linked and they stopped every few steps to kiss, dangling their flip-flops with their free hands.

Carefree, smiling, they passed a solemn, elderly man in a crumpled white hat pulled tight down over his ears, swinging a metal detector in an arc in front of him, inches above the surface of the mud. Then they passed a youth, in gumboots and khaki trousers, with an open shirt spilled over them, a fishing bag on the ground beside him, digging out worms for bait with a garden spade and shaking them off the blade into a rubber bucket.

A short distance ahead were the blackened girders of the ruin of the West Pier, rising out of the shallows, in the fading light, like an eerie sculpture. The water seemed to be travelling faster, more urgently, every minute, the breakers getting larger, louder.

The girl squealed and tried to pull her boyfriend away, towards the shore, as water suddenly ran in further than before, covering her bare feet. 'I'm getting wet, Ben!'

'Tamara, you're such a wuss!' he replied, standing firm as another breaker, even closer, sent water shooting over their ankles, and then a third, almost up to their knees. He pointed out towards the horizon, at the crimson orb of the sun. 'Watch the sunset. You get a green flash of light when it hits the horizon. You ever seen it?'

But she wasn't looking at the sun. She was looking at a log that was rolling over and over in the surf. A log with long tendrils of seaweed attached to one end, trailing from it. An even bigger breaker roared, and the log was sucked back. And for one brief, fleeting instant, as the log rolled, she saw a face. Arms and legs. And realized that it wasn't seaweed on the end of it. It was human hair.

She screamed.

Ben broke free of her hand and ran into the water, towards it. A breaker hit his knees, showering spray over his body and face, spattering the lenses of his sunglasses, blurring his vision. The body rolled again, a naked woman with her face partially eaten away, her skin the colour of tallow wax. She was being pulled back, away from Ben, reclaimed by the ocean as if she had merely been presented for a brief inspection.

The young man lunged forward, water up to his thighs

now, drenched completely as another breaker exploded around him, and grabbed an arm by the wrist, then pulled hard. The skin felt cold and slimy, reptilian. He shuddered but hung on resolutely. She seemed only slightly built, but with the pull of the ocean against him she felt as heavy as lead. He pulled back, locked in a grim tug-of-war. 'Tam!' he shouted. 'Call someone for help! Dial 999 on yer mob!'

Then suddenly, still gripping the wrist hard, he was falling. He landed flat on his back in the mud, as deafening surf from another breaker roared and sucked and gurgled over his face and around him. And there was another sound in his ears now, a dull, ragged whine, getting louder, more intense, more piercing.

It was Tamara. Standing rigid, her eyes bulging in shock, mouth open, the scream coming from deep within her.

Ben hadn't yet fully realized that the arm he was holding had torn clean away from the rest of the body.

52

Cleo's phone was ringing. Her home line. She eased herself forward on her sofa so she could read the caller display. It was Grace's mobile number.

She let it ring. Waited. Four rings. Five. Six. Then her voicemail kicked in and the ringing stopped. Must have been the fourth – maybe even the fifth – call from him today on this line. Plus all the ones on her mobile.

She was being childish not answering it, she knew, and sooner or later she was going to have to respond; but she was still not sure what she wanted to say to him.

Heavy-hearted, she picked up her wine glass and saw, to her slight surprise, that it was empty. Again. She picked up the bottle of Chilean Sauvignon Blanc and saw, to her even bigger surprise, there were no more than a couple of inches left. 'Shit,' she said, pouring it. It barely covered the bottom of her large glass.

She was on duty this weekend, which meant she shouldn't drink much, if anything at all, since she could be called out at any time of day or night. But today she felt badly in need of alcohol. It had been a shit day. A *really* shit day. After her row with Roy, and a totally sleepless remains of the night following it, she'd been called out to the mortuary at ten in the morning to receive the body of a six-year-old girl who had been hit by a car.

She'd become hardened to most things in the eight years she had been in this profession, but not to the bodies of children. They got her every time. There seemed to be a different kind of grief that people had for a child, deeper somehow than for the most loved adult, as if it was incomprehensible that a child could be torn from anyone's life. She hated seeing the undertaker bringing in a tiny coffin and she hated doing those post-mortems. This little girl's would be on Monday – making it a great Monday morning to look forward to.

Then, this afternoon, she'd had to go to a grim flat in a run-down terraced house near Hove station and recover the body of an elderly lady which had been there for a good month, at least, in the opinion of her colleague Walter Hordern, judging from the condition of the body and the level of infestation of flies and larvae.

Walter had gone with her, driving the coroner's van. A dapper, courteous man in his mid-forties, he was always smartly attired in the business clothes of someone who worked in a City office. His official role was chief of Brighton and Hove cemeteries, but his duties also included spending a part of his time helping in the process of collecting bodies from their scene of death and dealing with the considerable paperwork that was required for each one.

Walter and Darren had recently taken to challenging each other on how close they could get in estimating the time of death. It was an inexact science, subject to weather conditions and a raft of other factors, and one that got harder the longer it took to retrieve the body. Counting the stages of the life cycle of certain insects was one, unpleasant, very rough guide. And Walter Hordern had been boning up on that on a forensic medical site he had found on the internet.

Then, just a couple of hours ago she'd had a distraught phone call from her sister, Charlie, of whom she was hugely fond, saying she had just been dumped by her boyfriend of over six months. At twenty-seven, Charlie was two and a half years younger than she was. Pretty and tempestuous, she always went for the wrong men.

Like herself, she realized, more sadly than bitterly. Thirty in October. Her best friend, Millie – *Mad Millie*, she used to be called when they were teenage rebels at Roedean School – had now settled into landed life with a former naval officer who'd made a fortune in the conference business, and was expecting her second child. Cleo was a godmother to the first, Jessica, as well as to two other children of old schoolfriends. It was starting to feel as if this was her destiny in life. The godmother with the strange job who wasn't capable of doing anything *normal*, not even holding down a *normal* relationship.

Like Richard, the barrister she'd fallen madly in love with after he had come to the mortuary to view a body in a murder case he was defending. It wasn't until after they'd got engaged, two years later, that he'd sprung the *big surprise* on her. He had found God. And that became a problem.

At first she'd thought it was something she could deal with. But after attending a number of charismatic church services in which people had fallen to the ground, struck with the Holy Spirit, she had begun to realize she was never going to be able to connect with this. She had seen too much unfair death. Too many children. Too many bodies of young, lovely people, smashed up or, worse, incinerated in car accidents. Or dead from drug overdoses, deliberate or accidental. Or decent, middle-aged men and women who had died in their kitchens, falling off chairs or plugging in appliances. Or gentle elderly folk crushed by buses when crossing the road or struck down by heart attacks or strokes.

She watched the news avidly. Saw items about young

women in African countries who had been gang-raped, then had knives inserted up their vaginas, or revolvers, which had then been fired. And, she was sorry, she had told Richard, she just could not buy into a loving God who let all this shit happen.

His response had been to take her hand and enjoin her to pray to God to help her understand *His will*.

When that hadn't worked, Richard had stalked her fervently, relentlessly, bombarding her alternately with love and then hate.

Then Roy Grace, a man she had long considered a truly decent human being, as well as extremely attractive, had suddenly, this summer, become a part of her life. She even had, perhaps naïvely, started to believe that they were true soul mates. Until this morning, when she had realized that she was nothing more than a temporary substitute for a ghost. That was all she could ever be in this relationship.

All the sections of today's *Times* and *Guardian* lay spread out on the sofa beside her, mostly unread. She kept trying to settle down to work on her Open University course, but was unable to concentrate. Nor could she get into her new book, a Margaret Atwood novel, *The Handmaid's Tale*, which she had wanted to read for years and had finally bought this afternoon from her favourite bookshop in Hove, City Books. She had read and re-read the first page four times, but could not engage with the words.

Reluctantly, because she hated squandering time – and considered most television just that – she picked up the remote and began to surf through the Sky channels. She checked out the Discovery channel, hoping there was maybe a wildlife documentary, but some fossilized-looking professor was pontificating on the Earth's strata. Interesting, but not tonight, Josephine.

Now her phone was ringing again. She looked at the caller display. The number was withheld. Almost certainly business. She answered it.

It was an operator at the police call centre in Brighton. A body had been washed up on the beach, near the West Pier. She was required to accompany it to the mortuary.

Hanging up, she did a quick calculation. When had she opened that bottle of wine? About six o'clock. Four and a half hours ago. Two units of alcohol would put the average woman at the limit for driving. A bottle of wine contained six average units. You burned off one per hour. She should be OK to drive, just about.

Five minutes later she left her house, walked up the street and unlocked the door of her MG sports car.

As she climbed in and fumbled with her seat belt, a figure emerged from the shadows of a shop doorway, just a short distance down the street, and took the few short steps to his own car. She started the MG, revved the engine and pulled into the street. The small black Toyota Prius, running on just its electric motor, glided silently through the darkness behind her.

53

So far no one had said a word about her dress. Not Suzanne-Marie, not Mandy, not Cat, not a single one of the girlfriends she had bumped into at the party tonight had even seemed to notice it. Which was *very* unusual. Four hundred and fifty quid and not one comment. Maybe they were just jealous.

Or maybe it looked a disaster on her.

Sod them. Bitches! Wandering through into another room, which was pulsing with coloured lights, crammed with people, music pounding, the sharp, rubbery smell of hashish heavy in the air, Holly downed the last dregs of her third peach martini and realized she was starting to feel decidedly tipsy.

At least men were noticing her.

The black, diamanté-edged dress seemed even skimpier when she had put it on tonight than it had in the shop. It was so open at the front that there was no possibility of wearing a bra – and hell, she had great boobs, so why not flaunt them, the same the way the dress – or rather the lack of it – enabled her to flaunt her legs, almost every inch of them, most of the way up to her navel? And she did feel good in this, wickedly good!

'Cool dresshh. Where you from?'

The man, slurring his words through sharp, pointy little teeth that reminded her of a piranha's, swayed in her path, smoke from his cigarette curling in her eye. He was dressed in black leather trousers, a skin-tight black T-shirt, a rhinestone belt, and sported a large gold earring. He had one of the stupidest haircuts she had ever seen.

'Mars,' she said, sidestepping past him, looking around, increasingly anxiously, for Sophie.

'North or south?' he slurred, but she barely heard him. Sophie had not returned the two messages she had left about meeting for a drink before this party and sharing a taxi. It was now half past ten. Surely she should be here by now?

Pushing her way through the crowd, looking everywhere for her friend, she reached open French windows and stepped outside on to a relatively quiet terrace. One couple sat on a bench, locked in serious tonsil hockey. A very spaced-out man with long, fair hair was staring at the beach and sniffing, repeatedly. Holly dug her mobile phone out of her bag and checked for a text she might have missed, but there was nothing. Then she dialled Sophie's mobile phone.

Again it went straight to voicemail.

She tried Sophie's home number. That went to voicemail too.

'Ah – here you are! Losht shight of you!' His sharp incisors glinted demonically in the flash of a strobe. 'You come out for air?'

'And now I'm going in again,' she said, walking back into the mêlée. She was worried, because Sophie was reliable. This simply wasn't like her.

But not so worried it was going to stop her from enjoying herself tonight.

54

Because of a problem with a baggage door, the plane took off half an hour late. Roy Grace spent the entire journey bolt upright in his seat, which he didn't even think about reclining, staring out through the window at the rivets on the bulbous grey metal of the starboard engine casing.

For two interminable hours in the air he had been unable to concentrate on anything for very long, to pass the time, other than memorizing part of the street map of Munich city centre. The cardboard box containing the plastic wrap and empty box of the unpleasant cheese roll he had eaten out of sheer hunger, and the dregs of the second bitter coffee he had drunk, wobbled on his tray as the plane bumped through clouds, finally starting its descent.

He was frustrated about the loss of those precious thirty minutes, eating into the very short time he had ahead of him today. He barely noticed the hands of the stewardess reaching down in front of him and removing the detritus of his breakfast as he stared at the landscape now opening up below him.

At the vastness of it.

Butterflies swarmed in his stomach as he absorbed his first-ever sights of German soil. The patchwork of brown, yellow and green rectangles of flat farmland spread out over a seemingly endless, horizonless plain. He saw small clusters of white houses with red and brown roofs, copses, the trees an emerald green so vivid they looked like they had been spray-painted. Then a small town. More clusters of houses and buildings.

A great, yammering panic was building up inside him. Would he even recognize Sandy if he saw her? There were days when he could no longer recall her face without looking at her photograph, as if time, whether he liked it or not, was slowly erasing her from his memory.

And if she was down there, somewhere in that vast landscape, where was she? In the city that he couldn't yet see? In one of these remote villages beneath them that they were slowly passing? Was Sandy living her life somewhere in this vast open landscape below him? An anonymous German hausfrau whose background no one had ever questioned?

The stewardess's hand appeared again in front of him, pushing up the grey table and rotating the peg to secure it. The ground was getting closer, the buildings bigger. He could see cars travelling along roads. He heard the captain's voice on the intercom, ordering the cabin crew to take their seats for landing.

The captain then thanked them for flying British Airways and wished them a pleasant day in Munich. To Grace, until these last two days, Munich had just been a name on a map. A name in newspaper headlines in the deepest recesses of his mind. A name in television documentaries. A name in history lessons when he had been at school. A name where distant relatives of Sandy, whom she had never met, in a past she had been disconnected from, still lived.

The Munich where Adolf Hitler had made his home and been arrested as a young man for attempting a coup. The Munich where, in 1958, half the Manchester United football team had died in a plane crash on a snow-covered runway. The Munich where, in 1972, the Olympic Games were grimly immortalized by Arab terrorists who massacred eleven Israeli athletes.

The plane banged down hard and, moments later, he felt the seat belt digging into his stomach as it braked, the engines roaring in reverse thrust. Then it settled down to a gentle taxiing speed. They passed a windsock, the hull of an old, rusting plane with a collapsed undercarriage. There was an announcement on the intercom about passengers with connecting flights. And it felt to Roy Grace that every single one of the butterflies in his stomach was now trying to make its way up his gullet.

The man in the seat next to him, whom he had barely noticed, switched on his mobile phone. Grace dug his own out of his cream linen jacket and switched it on too, staring at the display, hoping for a message from Cleo. Around him he heard the *beep-beeps* of message signals. Suddenly his own phone beeped. His heart leapt. Then fell. It was just a service message from a German telecom company.

During the restless night, he had woken several times, and lain fretting about what to wear. Ridiculous, he knew, because in his heart he did not feel he would see Sandy today, even if she really was there, somewhere. But he still wanted to look his best, just in case . . . He wanted to look – and smell – the way she might remember him. There was a Bulgari cologne she used to buy him, and he still had the bottle. He'd sprayed it on this morning, all over himself. Then he'd dressed in a white T-shirt beneath his cream jacket. Lightweight jeans, because he had looked up the temperature in Munich, which was twenty-eight degrees. And comfortable sneakers, because he'd figured he might be doing a lot of walking.

Even so, he was surprised by the cloying, sticky, kerosene-laced heat that enveloped him as he walked down the plane's gangway and across the tarmac to the waiting bus. Minutes later, without any baggage, shortly after ten fifteen local time, he strode through the comfort of the quiet, air-conditioned customs hall into the arrivals hall, and instantly saw the tall, smiling figure of Marcel Kullen.

Cropped wavy black hair, some flopping loose over his forehead, a wide grin on his genial face, the German detective was dressed in Sunday casuals, a lightweight brown bomber jacket over a yellow polo shirt, baggy jeans and brown leather loafers. He clamped Grace's outstretched hand firmly with both hands, and said, in his guttural accent, 'Roy, nearly was not recognizing you. You are looking so young!'

'You too!'

Grace was so touched by the warmth of the greeting, from a man he had never really known that well. In fact he was so overwhelmed by the emotion of the occasion that he found himself, suddenly and very uncharacteristically, close to tears.

They exchanged pleasantries as they walked through the almost empty building, across the black and white chequerboard tiled floor. Kullen's English was good, but it was taking Grace time to get used to his accent. They followed a solitary figure pulling an overnight bag on wheels, past the striped awning of a gift shop and back outside into the cloying heat, past a long line of cream taxis, mostly Mercedes. On the short walk to the car park Grace compared the almost suburban calm of this airport to the hurly-burly of Heathrow and Gatwick. It felt like a ghost town.

The German had just had his third child, a boy, and if there was time today, he very much hoped to bring Grace to his home to meet his family, Kullen informed him with a broad grin. Grace, sitting in the cracked leather passenger seat of the man's ancient but shiny BMW 5-series, told him he would like that a lot. But secretly he had no desire to do that at all. He had not come here to socialize, he wanted to spend every precious minute finding a trail for Sandy.

A welcome current of cool air blew on his face from the asthmatic-sounding air conditioning, as they headed away from the airport, driving through the rural landscape he had scanned from the plane. Grace stared out of the windows, feeling overwhelmed by the sheer vastness of it all. And he realized he had not properly thought this through. What on earth could he hope to achieve in just one day?

Road signs flashed past, blue with white lettering. One bore the name of Franz Josef Strauss airport, which they had just left, then on another he read the word *München*. Kullen continued chatting, mentioning names of the officers he had worked with in Sussex. Almost mechanically, Grace gave him the download on each of them, as best he could, his mind torn between thinking about the murder of Katie Bishop, worrying about his relationship with Cleo and trying to concentrate on the task in front of him today. For some moments his eyes followed a silver and red S-bahn train running parallel with them.

Suddenly Kullen's voice became more animated. Grace heard the word *football*. He saw on his right the massive new white stadium, in the shape of a tyre, the words *Allianz Arena* in large blue letters affixed to it. Then beyond it, high on what looked like a man-made mound, was a solitary white wind-farm pylon with a propeller attached.

'I show you a little around, give you some feeling for Munich, then we are going to the office and then the Englischer Garten?' Kullen said.

'Good plan.'

'You have made a list?'

'I have, yes.'

The Lieutenant had suggested that before he came Grace write down a list of all Sandy's interests, then they could go to places she might have visited in pursuit of them. Grace stared down at his notepad. It was a long list. Books. Jazz. Simply Red. Rod Stewart. Dancing. Food. Antiques. Gardening. Movies, especially anything with Brad Pitt, Bruce Willis, Jack Nicholson, Woody Allen and Pierce—

Suddenly his phone was ringing. He pulled it from his pocket and stared down at the display, hoping to see one of Cleo's numbers.

But the number was withheld.

55

At ten fifteen on Sunday morning, David Curtis, a young probationary Police Constable on his second day at Brighton, was part-way through his shift. A tall nineteen-year-old with a serious demeanour and dark brown hair that was short and tidy, but with a nod towards fashion, he was in the passenger seat of the Vauxhall police patrol car, which smelled of last night's French fries, being driven by the John Street police station club's biggest bar bore.

Police Sergeant Bill Norris, a crinkly haired, pug-faced man in his early fifties, had been everywhere, seen it all and done it all, but never quite well enough to get raised above the level of sergeant. Now, just a few months short of his retirement, he was enjoying teaching this youngster the ropes. Or more accurately, was enjoying having a captive audience for all the old stories no one else wanted to hear yet again.

They were cruising down litter-strewn West Street, the clubs all shut now, the pavements littered with broken glass, discarded burger and kebab wrappers, all the usual detritus from Saturday night. Two road-sweeping vehicles were hard at work, grinding along the kerbs.

'Course it was different then,' Bill Norris was saying. 'In them days we could run our own informants, see? One time when I was in the drugs squad, we staked out this deli in Waterloo Street for two months from information I'd had. I knew my man was right.' He tapped his nose. 'Copper's nose, I got. You either got it or you haven't. You'll find out soon enough, son.'

The sun was in their eyes, coming obliquely at them across the Channel at the end of the street. David Curtis raised his hand to shield his eyes, scanning the pavements, the passing cars. *Copper's nose.* Yep, he was confident he had that all right.

'And a strong stomach. Got to have that,' Norris continued.

'Cast iron, I've got.'

'So we sat in this derelict house opposite – used to go in and out via a passage round the back. Bloody freezing it was. Two months! Froze our bollocks off! I found this old British Rail guard's overcoat some tramp had abandoned there, and wore it. Two months we sat there, day in and night out, watching with binoculars by day and night scopes in the dark. Nothing to do, just swinging the lantern – that's what we used to call it, you know? Telling stories – *swinging the lantern.* Well, anyhow, one evening this saloon car pulled up, big Jag—'

The probationary PC was reprieved, temporarily, from this story, which he had already heard twice before, by a call from Brighton Central Control.

'Sierra Oscar to Charlie Charlie 109.'

Using his personal radio set, sitting in its plastic cradle on the clip of his stab vest, David Curtis replied, '109, go ahead.'

'We've got a grade-two cause for concern on the queue. Are you free?'

'Yes, yes. Go ahead with details, over.'

'Address is Flat 4, 17 Newman Villas. The occupant is a Sophie Harrington. She didn't turn up to meet a friend yesterday, and she's not answered her phone or doorbell since yesterday afternoon, which is out of character. Can you do an address check so we can take it off the queue?'

'Confirm Flat 4, 17 Newman Villas, Sophie Harrington?' Curtis said.

'Yes, yes.'

'Received. En route.'

Relieved to have something to actually do this morning, Norris swung the car around in a U-turn so hard and fast that the tyres squealed. Then he made a left turn at the top into Western Road, accelerating faster than was strictly necessary.

56

Apologizing to Marcel Kullen, he put the phone to his ear and pressed the green button. 'Roy Grace,' he answered.

Then, when he heard the acerbic voice at the other end, he immediately wished he had left the damn phone ringing.

'Where are you, Roy? It sounds like you're abroad.' It was his boss, Assistant Chief Constable Alison Vosper, and she seemed a little astonished. 'That wasn't a UK ring tone,' she said.

This was one call he simply had not expected today and he had no answer prepared. When he had phoned Marcel in Germany he had noticed the ring tone was quite different, a steady, flat whine instead of the normal two-tone ring in the UK. There was no point in lying, he knew.

Taking a deep breath, he said, 'Munich.'

From the other end of the phone came a sound like a small nuclear device detonating inside a corrugated-iron shed filled with ball bearings. It was followed by some moments of silence. Then Vosper's voice again, very abrupt: 'I've just spilled some coffee. I'll have to call you back.'

As he finished the call he cursed for not having thought this through better. Of course, in a normal world he was perfectly entitled to a day off, and to leave his deputy SIO in charge. But the world in which Alison Vosper prowled was not normal. She had taken a dislike to him, for reasons he could not figure out – but no doubt in part because of his recent unfortunate press coverage – and was looking all the time for a reason to demote him, or freeze his career path, or transfer him to the other end of the country. Taking the day off on the third day of a major murder inquiry was not going to improve her opinion of him.

'Everything is OK?' Kullen asked.

'Never better.'

His phone was ringing again now. 'What exactly are you doing in Germany?' Alison Vosper asked.

Roy hated lying – as he knew from recent experience, lies weakened people – but he was also aware that the truth was not likely to be met with much civility, so he fudged. 'I'm following up a lead.'

'In Germany?'

'Yes.'

'And when exactly will we be able to expect your leadership back in England?'

'Tonight,' he said. 'DI Murphy is in charge in my absence.'

'Excellent,' she replied. 'So you will be able to meet me straight after your briefing meeting tomorrow morning?'

'Yes. I can be with you about nine thirty.'

'Anything to report on the case?'

'We're making good progress. I'm close to an arrest. I'm just waiting for DNA tests to come back from Huntington, which I expect tomorrow.'

'Good,' she said. Then, after a moment, she added, without any softening of her tone, 'I'm told they have excellent beer in Germany.'

'I wouldn't know.'

'I spent my honeymoon in Hamburg. Take it from me, they do. You should try some. Nine thirty tomorrow morning.'

She hung up.

Shit, he thought, angry with himself for being so badly prepared. *Shit, shit, shit!* And tomorrow morning she would ask him for sure to tell her about the lead he was following up here. He needed to think of something pretty damn good.

They were passing a high-rise block of flats, with the BMW roundel prominently displayed near the top. Then a Marriott hotel.

He quickly checked his BlackBerry for messages. There were a dozen emails waiting to be read that had come in since getting off the plane, most of them relating to Operation Chameleon.

'The old Olympic stadium!' Kullen said.

Grace looked over to his left and saw a building designed in the shape of a half-collapsed marquee. They forked right, down an underpass, then turned left over tramlines. He opened his map on his knees, trying to orient himself.

Kullen looked at his watch and said, 'You know, I am thinking, it was my plan we go to end up at my office first, and put up all the details of Sandy on the system, but I think it will be better we go to the Seehausgarten first. It will be busy now, many people. Perhaps you will have a chance of seeing her. Is better we go to the office after, is OK?'

'You're the tour guide, your decision!' Grace said. He saw a blue tram with a large advertisement for Adelholzener on its roof.

As if misinterpreting him, Kullen began pointing out the names of galleries as they drove down a wide avenue. 'Museum of Modern Art,' he said. Then, 'This over here is the Haus der Kunst – an art gallery built during the Hitler regime.'

Then, minutes later, they were driving down a long,

straight road with the tree-lined banks of the River Isar to their right and tall, old, elegant apartment building after apartment building to their left. The city was beautiful but large. So damn large. Shit. How the hell could he search for Sandy here, so far from home? And if she did not want to be found, then she sure as hell had picked a good place.

Marcel continued diligently pointing out the names of sights they were passing and the districts of the city they were in. He listened, continually staring down at the street map open on his knees, trying to fix the geography of the place in his mind, and thinking to himself, *If Sandy is here, what part of this city will she be living in? The centre? A suburb? A village outside?*

Each time he looked up he clocked everyone on the pavement and in every car, on the off-chance, however small, of spotting Sandy. For some moments he watched a thin, studious-looking man ambling along in shorts and a baggy T-shirt, a newspaper tucked under his arm, munching on a pretzel he was holding in a blue paper napkin. *Do you have a new man in your life? Does he look like this?* he wondered.

'We are go to the Osterwald Garten. It is also beer garden close to the Englischer Garten – easier we parking there and a nice foot walk to the Seehaus,' Kullen announced.

A few minutes later they turned into a residential area and drove along a narrow street with small, attractive houses on either side. Then they passed an ivy-clad pink and white columned building. 'For weddings – marriage registry. You can get married in this place,' Kullen said.

Something cold suddenly churned inside Grace. *Marriage.* Was it possible Sandy had married again in some new identity she had adopted?

They drove on down a leafy street, with a hedge on their right and trees on their left, then came into a small square, with a cobbled pavement and other ivy-clad houses, and if it weren't for the left-hand-drive cars and the German writing on the parking signs, it could have been somewhere in England, Grace thought.

The Kriminalhauptkommisar swung into a parking space and switched off the engine. 'OK, us start here?'

Grace nodded, feeling a little helpless. He was not sure exactly where he was on his map, and when the German helpfully pointed a finger, he realized he had been looking in the wrong place entirely. He then pulled out of his pocket the one-page map that Dick Pope had printed from the internet and faxed him, with a circle showing where he and his wife had seen the person they believed was Sandy on their day in this city. He handed it to Marcel Kullen, who studied it for some moments. '*Ja*, OK, super!' he said, and opened his door.

As they walked down the dusty street in the searing morning heat, it was clouding over. Grace, removing his jacket and slinging it over his shoulder, looked around for a bar or a café. Despite the adrenaline pumping, he felt tired and thirsty, and could have done with some water and a caffeine hit. But he realized he didn't want to waste precious time, he was anxious to get to that place, to that black circle on the fuzzy map.

To the only positive sighting, in nine years, of the woman he had loved so much.

His pace getting more urgent with every step, he strode with Kullen towards a large lake. Kullen navigated them across a bridge and left along the path, with the lake and a wooded island on their right and dense woodland to their left. Grace breathed in the sweet scents of grass and leaves, savouring the sudden delicious coolness of the shade and the slight breeze from the water.

Two cyclists swerved past them, then a young man and a girl, chatting animatedly, on roller blades. Moments later a large French poodle bounded along, with an irate man with a centre parting and tortoiseshell glasses running after it, shouting out, 'Adini! Adini! Adini!' He was followed by a very determined-looking Nordic walker in her sixties, wearing bright red Lycra, teeth clenched, walking poles clacking on the tarmac path. Then, rounding a bend, the landscape opened up in front of them.

Grace saw a huge park, teeming with people, and beyond the island now the lake was far larger than he had at first realized, a good half-mile long and several hundred yards wide. There were dozens of boats out on the water, some of them elegant, wooden, clinker-built rowing boats, and the rest white and blue fibreglass pedalos, and flotillas of ducks.

People crowded the benches that lined the water's edge, and there were sunbathing bodies lying everywhere, on every inch of grass, some with iPods plugged into their ears, others with radios, listening to music or perhaps, Grace thought, trying to shut out the incessant shrieks of children.

And blondes everywhere. Dozens. Hundreds. His eyes moved from face to face, scanning and discarding each one in turn. Two small girls ran across their path, one holding an ice-cream cornet, the other screaming. A mastiff sat on the ground, panting heavily and drooling. Kullen stopped beside a bench on which a man with his shirt completely unbuttoned was reading a book, holding it at an uncomfortable-looking arm's length as if he had forgotten his glasses, and pointed across the lake.

Grace saw a sizeable, attractive – if rather twee-looking

– pavilion, in a style that might have been interpreted from an English thatched cottage. Crowds of people were seated at the beer-garden tables outside it, and to the left there was a small boathouse and a wooden deck, with just a couple of boats tied up, and one pedalo pulled out of the water and lying on its side.

Grace suddenly felt his adrenaline surging at the realization of what he was looking at. This was the place! This was where Dick Pope and his wife, Leslie, reckoned they had seen Sandy. They had been out in one of those wooden rowing boats. And had spotted her in the beer garden.

Forcing the German to quicken his pace, Grace took the lead, striding along the tarmac path that girded the lake, past bench after bench, staring out across the water, scanning every sunbather, every face on every bench, every cyclist, jogger, walker, roller-blader that passed them. A couple of times he saw long, fair hair swinging around a face that reminded him of Sandy, and locked on to it like a Pavlovian dog, only to dismiss it when he looked again.

She might have had it all cut off. Dyed another colour, perhaps.

They passed an elegant stone monument on a mound. He absorbed the names engraved on the side: VON WERNECK . . . LUDWIG I . . . Then, as they reached the pavilion, Kullen stopped in front of a selection of menus pinned to an elegant, shield-shaped board, under the heading SEEHAUS IM ENGLISCHER GARTEN.

'You like we eat something? Perhaps we can go inside in the restaurant, where it is cooler, or we can be outside.'

Grace cast his eyes over at the rows and rows of densely packed trestle tables, some under the shade of a canopy of trees, some beneath a large green awning, but most out in the open. 'I'd prefer outside – for looking around.'

'Yes. Of course. We get a drink first – you like something?'

'I'd better have a German beer,' he said with a grin. 'And a coffee.'

'*Weissbier* or *Helles*? Or would you like a *Radler* – a shandy – or maybe a *Russn*?'

'I'd like a large, cold beer.'

'A *Mass*?'

'*Mass?*'

Kullen pointed at two men at a table drinking from glasses the size of chimney stacks.

'Something a little smaller?'

'A half-*Mass*?'

'Perfect. What are you going to have? I'll get them.'

'No, when you coming Germany, I buy!' Kullen said adamantly.

The whole thing was attractively done, Grace thought. Elegant lamp posts lined the waterfront; the outbuildings housing the bar and the food area were in dark green and white, and recently painted; there was a funky bronze of a naked, bald man, with his arms folded and a tiny penis, on a marble plinth; orderly stacks of plastic crates and green rubbish bins for empties and rubbish, and beer glasses, and polite signs in German and in English.

A cashier sat under a wooden awning, dealing with a long queue. Waiters and waitresses in red trousers and yellow shirts cleared away debris from tables as people left. Leaving the German police officer to queue at the bar, Grace stepped away a short distance, carefully studying the map, trying to pinpoint from it at which of the hundred or so eight-seater trestle tables Sandy might have sat.

There must be several hundred people seated at the tables, he estimated, a good five hundred, maybe more, and almost without exception they each had a tall beer glass in front of them. He could smell the beer in the air, along with wafts of cigarette and cigar smoke, and the enticing aromas of French fries and grilling meat.

Sandy drank the occasional cold beer in summer, and often, when she did, she would joke that it was because of her German heritage. Now he was starting to understand that. He was also starting to feel very strange. Was it tiredness, or thirst, or just the enormity of being here? he wondered. He had the ridiculous feeling that he was trespassing on Sandy's patch, that he wasn't really wanted here.

And suddenly he found himself staring into a stern, headmasterly face that seemed to be agreeing with him, admonishing him. It was a grey, stone head-and-shoulders sculpture of a bearded man that reminded him of those statues of ancient philosophers you often saw in junk shops and car-boot sales. He was still in the early stages of his studies, but this man definitely looked like one of them.

Then he noticed the name, PAULANER, embossed importantly on the cornerstone, just as Kullen came up to him, carrying two beers and two coffees on a tray. 'OK, you have decided where you want to sit?'

'This guy, Paulaner, was he a German philosopher?'

Kullen grinned at him. 'Philosopher? I don't think. Paulaner is the name of the biggest brewing house in Munich.'

'Ah,' Grace said, feeling decidedly dim-witted. 'Right.'

Kullen was pointing to a table at the water's edge, where some spaces were being freed up by a group of youngsters who were standing and hauling on backpacks. 'Would you like to sit there?'

'Perfect.'

As they walked over to it, Grace scanned the faces at table after table after table. Packed with men and women of all ages, from teens to the elderly, all in casual dress, mostly T-shirts, baggy shirts or bare-chested, shorts or jeans, and just about everyone in sunglasses, baseball caps, floppy hats and straw hats. They were drinking from *Mass* or half-*Mass* glasses of beer, eating plates of sausages and fries, or spare ribs, or tennis-ball-sized lumps of cheese, or something that looked like meatloaf with sauerkraut.

*

Was this where Sandy had been earlier in the week? Was this where she came regularly, walking past the naked bronze on the plinth and the bearded head in the fountain who was advertising Paulaner, to sit and drink beer and stare at the lake?

And with whom?

A new man? New friends?

And, if she was alive, what went on in her mind? What did she think about the past, about him, their life together, all their dreams and promises and times shared?

He took out Dick Pope's map and looked again at the fuzzy circle, orienting himself.

'Bottoms up!'

Kullen, wearing aviator sunglasses now, had raised his glass. Grace raised his own. '*Skol!*'

Shaking his head amiably, the German said, 'No, we say *Prost!*'

'*Prost!*' Grace returned, and they clinked glasses.

'To success,' Kullen said. 'Or perhaps that's not what you want, I think?'

Grace gave a short, bitter laugh, wondering if the German had any idea just how true that was. And almost as if on cue, his phone beeped twice.

It was a message from Cleo.

57

Probationary PC David Curtis and Sergeant Bill Norris climbed out of the patrol car a short distance up from the address they had been given. Newman Villas was an archetypal Hove residential street of tired Victorian terraced houses. Once they had been single-occupancy homes, with servants' quarters upstairs, but now they were carved up into smaller units. A battery of estate-agents' boards ran the length of the street, most of them advertising flats and bedsits to let.

The front door of number 17 looked like it hadn't seen a lick of paint in a couple of decades, and most of the names on the entry-phone panel were handwritten and faded. *S. Harrington* looked reasonably fresh.

Bill Norris pressed the button. 'You know,' he said, 'used to be just four of us on a stakeout. Today it can be twenty officers. I got into trouble once. There was a streetwalker who was a customer of this deli we was staking out. I wrote in the log, "Nice bum and tits." Didn't go down well. I got a right bollocking over that, I did, from the station inspector!' He rang the bell again.

They waited in silence for some moments. When there was still no answer, Norris pressed all the other buttons, one after another. 'Time to ruin someone's Sunday lie-in.' He tapped his watch. 'Maybe she's in church?' He chuckled.

'Yeah?' a wasted voice suddenly crackled.

'Flat 4. I lost me key. Could you let me in please?' Norris pleaded.

Moments later there was a sharp rasp, then a click from the lock.

The sergeant pushed the door open, turning to his young colleague and lowering his voice. 'Don't tell 'em it's the law – they won't let you in then.' He touched his nose conspiratorially. 'You'll learn.'

Curtis looked at him, wondering for how many more patrols he was going to have to endure this pain. And hoping to hell someone would pull out his plug if he ever started becoming like this sad git.

They walked along a short, musty-smelling corridor, past two bicycles and a shelf piled with post, mostly fliers from local pizza and Chinese takeaways. On the first-floor landing they heard the sound of gunshots, followed by James Garner's stentorian tones: 'Freeze!' It was coming from behind a door bearing the number '2'.

They climbed on, past the second-floor door numbered '3'. The staircase narrowed and at the top they reached a door numbered '4'.

Norris knocked loudly. No answer. He knocked again, more loudly. And again. Then he looked at the probationer. 'All right, son. One day this'll be you. What would you do?'

'Break the door open?' Curtis ventured.

'And if she's busy having nooky in there?'

Curtis shrugged. He didn't know the answer.

Norris knocked again. 'Hello! Ms Harrington? Anyone in? Police!'

Nothing.

Norris turned his burly frame sideways and barged hard against the door. It shook, but did not yield. He tried harder and this time the door burst open, splintering the frame, and he tumbled in to a narrow, empty corridor, grabbing the wall to steady himself.

'Hello! Police!' Norris called out, advancing forward, then he turned to his junior officer. 'Keep in my footsteps. Don't touch anything. We don't want to contaminate any evidence.'

Curtis tiptoed clumsily, holding his breath, in the sergeant's footsteps along the corridor. Ahead of him the sergeant pushed open a door, then froze.

'Bloody hell!' Norris said. 'Oh, bloody hell!'

When he caught up with the sergeant, the young PC stopped in his tracks, staring ahead in revulsion and shock. A cold sensation crawled in his guts. He wanted desperately to look away but could not. Morbid fascination that went way beyond professional duty held his gaze rooted to the bed.

58

Roy Grace stared at the message from Cleo on his phone's display:

> *Sort yourself out in Munich. Call me when*
> *you get back home.*

No signature. No kiss. Just a bald, pissed-off statement. But at least she had finally responded.

He composed a terse reply, in his mind, and instantly discarded it. Then he composed another, and discarded that. He had stood her up for a Sunday lunch date in order to go to Munich to try to find his wife. Just how good must that have sounded to her?

But surely she could be a little sympathetic? He'd never kept Sandy's disappearance a secret – Cleo knew all about it. What choice did he have? Surely anyone would be doing what he was doing now, wouldn't they?

All at once, fuelled by his tiredness, stress, the incessant heat of the sun beating down on his head, he felt a flash of anger at Cleo. *Hell, woman, can't you bloody understand?*

He caught Marcel Kullen's eye and shrugged. 'Women.'

'Everything is OK?'

Grace put down his phone and cradled his heavy glass in both hands. 'This beer is OK,' he said. 'More than OK.' He took a large swig. Then he sipped his scalding coffee. 'Nothing much else is. You know?'

The Kriminalhauptkommisar smiled, as if he was unsure how to respond.

A man at the next table was puffing on a briar pipe. Smoke drifted across them and the smell suddenly reminded Grace of his father, who also smoked a pipe. He remembered all the rituals. His father ramming long, slim white pipe cleaners, that rapidly turned brown, down the stem. Scraping out the rim with a small brass instrument. Mixing the tobacco with his large fingers, filling the bowl, lighting it with a Swan Vesta match, then tamping it down and relighting it. The living room instantly filling with the tantalizing aroma of the blue-grey smoke. Or, if they were out fishing in a small boat, or on the end of the Palace Pier, or on the mole of Shoreham Harbour, Roy use to watch the direction of the wind when his father took out his pipe, then ensure he stood downwind of him to catch those wisps.

He wondered what his father would have done in this situation. Jack Grace had loved Sandy. When he was sick in the hospice, dying far too young, at fifty-five, from bowel cancer, she used to spend hours at his bedside, talking to him, playing Scrabble with him, reading through the *Sporting Life* with him as he selected his bets for each day and placing them for him. And just chatting. They were like best friends from the day Grace had first brought Sandy home to meet his parents.

Jack Grace had always been a man contented with what he had, happy to remain a desk sergeant until his retirement, tinkering with cars and following the horses in his free time, never with any ambition to rise higher in the force. But he was a thorough man, a stickler for details, procedures, for tidying up loose ends. He would have approved of Roy coming here, of course he would. No doubt about it.

Bloody hell, Roy thought suddenly. *Munich is just full of ghosts.*

'Tell me, Roy,' Kullen asked, 'how well was Inspector Pope knowing Sandy?'

Bringing him back to reality, to his task here today, Grace replied, 'Good question. They were our best friends – we went on holiday with them, every year for years.'

'So he would not easily be mistook – ah – mistaken?'

'No. Nor his wife.'

A young man, tall and fit-looking, in a yellow shirt and red trousers, was clearing glasses away from the vacated places next to them. He had fashionable, gelled fair hair.

'Excuse me,' Grace asked him. 'Do you speak any English?'

'Too right!' he grinned.

'You're an Aussie?'

''Fraid so!'

'Brilliant! Maybe you can help me. Were you here last Thursday?'

'I'm here every day. Ten in the morning till midnight.'

From his jacket pocket Grace pulled a photograph of Sandy and showed it to him. 'Have you seen this person? She was here, on Thursday, lunchtime.'

He took the photograph and studied it intently for some moments. 'Last Thursday?'

'Yes.'

'No, mate, doesn't ring a bell. But that doesn't mean she wasn't here. There's like hundreds of people every day.' He hesitated. 'Shit, I see so many faces, they all become a blur. I can ask my colleagues if you like.'

'Please,' Grace asked. 'It's really important to me.'

He went off and returned, a few minutes later, with a whole group of young clearer-uppers, all in the same uniform.

'Sorry, mate,' he said. 'This is a bunch of the stupidest people on the planet. But the best I could do!'

'Yeah, you can fuck off, Ron!' one of the young men said, a short, stocky Aussie with a head of hair that looked like a pin cushion. He turned to Grace. 'Sorry about my mate, he's just retarded. Happened at birth – we try to humour him.'

Grace put on a forced smile and handed him the photograph. 'I'm looking for this person. I think she was here last Thursday at lunchtime. Just wondering if any of you guys recognize her?'

The stocky Australian took the photograph, studied it for some moments, then passed it around. Each of them in turn shook their head.

Marcel Kullen dug his hand in his pocket and pulled out a bunch of business cards. He stood up and handed one to each of the crew. Suddenly they all looked more serious.

'I will come back tomorrow,' the police officer said. 'I will have a copy of this photograph for each of you. If she comes back, please call me immediately on my mobile number on the card, or at the Landeskriminalamt number. It is very important.'

'No worries,' Ron said. 'If she comes back we'll call.'

'I would really appreciate that.'

'You got it.'

Grace thanked them.

As they returned to their duties, Kullen picked up his beer and held his glass out, staring Grace in the eye. 'If your wife is in Munich, I will find her for you, Roy. What is that you are saying in England? Whatever takes it?'

'Close enough.' Grace raised his glass and touched the German's. 'Thank you.'

'I have also been making a list for you.' He pulled a small

notepad from his inside pocket. 'If we imagine she is here, all her life she has lived in England. There are perhaps things that she would miss, yes?'

'Like?'

'Some foods? Are there any foods she might miss?'

Grace thought for a moment. It was a good question. 'Marmite!' he said. 'She loved the stuff. Used to have it on toast for breakfast every day.'

'OK. Marmite. There is a store in the Viktualienmarkt that sells English foods for your expatriates. I will go there for you. Did she have anything medical wrong with her? Allergies, perhaps?'

Grace thought hard. 'She didn't have any allergies, but she had a problem with rich foods. It was a genetic thing. She used to get terrible indigestion if she ate rich foods – she took medication for it.'

'You have the name of the medication?'

'Something like Chlomotil. I can check in the medicine cabinet at home.'

'I can make a search of the doctors' clinics in Munich – we find if anyone with her description is ordering this medication.'

'Good thinking.'

'There are many things we should be looking at also. What music did she like? Did she go to the theatre? Did she have favourite movies or movie stars?'

Grace reeled off a list.

'And sport? Did she do any sport?'

Suddenly Grace realized where the German was coming from. And what had seemed, just a couple of hours ago, to be an impossibly enormous task was getting narrowed down into something that could be done. And it showed him just how fogged his own thinking had become. That old expression of not being able to see the wood for the trees was so true. 'Swimming!' he said, wondering why the hell he hadn't thought of it himself. Sandy was obsessed with keeping fit. She didn't jog, or go to a gym, because she had a knee that played up. Swimming was her big passion. She used to go to the public swimming baths in Brighton daily. Either the King Alfred or the Regency, or, when it was warm enough, the sea.

'So we can monitor the baths in Munich.'

'Good plan.'

Staring at his notes again, Kullen said, 'Does she like to read?'

'Is the Pope a Catholic?'

The German looked at him, puzzled. 'The Pope?'

'Forget it. Just an English expression. Yes, she loved books. Crime, especially. English and American. Elmore Leonard was her favourite.'

'There is a bookstore, on the corner of Schelling Strasse, called the Munich Readery. It is run by an American. Many English-speaking persons go there – they can exchange books, you know? Swapping them? Is that the right word?'

'Will it be open today?'

Kullen shook his head. 'This is Germany. On Sunday, everything is closed. Not like England.'

'I should have picked a better day.'

'Tomorrow I go look for you. Now will you have something to eat?'

Grace nodded gratefully. Suddenly he had an appetite.

And then, as he looked yet again around the sea of faces, he caught a glimpse of a woman, blonde hair cropped short, who had been heading over in their direction with a group of people but suddenly turned and started walking very quickly away.

His heart exploding, Grace was on his feet, barging past a Japanese man taking a photograph, running, weaving through a group unloading their backpacks, locking on to her with his eyes, gaining on her.

59

Dressed in just a crumpled white T-shirt, Cleo sat in her favourite place, on a rug on the floor, leaning back against the sofa. The Sunday papers were spread all around her and she was cradling a half-drunk mug of coffee that was steadily getting more tepid. Up above her, Fish was busily exploring her rectangular tank, as ever. Swimming slowly for a few moments, as if stalking some invisible prey, then suddenly darting at something, maybe a speck of food, or an imaginary enemy, or lover.

Despite the room being in the shade, and having all the windows open, the heat was unpleasantly sticky. *Sky News* was on television, but the sound was down low and she wasn't really watching, it was just background. On the screen, a pall of black smoke was rising, people were sobbing, jerky images from a handheld camera showed a hysterical woman, dead bodies, stark buildings, the twisted, burning ball of metal that had been a car, a man covered in blood being carried off on a stretcher. Just another Sunday in Iraq.

Meanwhile, her own Sunday was ebbing away. It was half past twelve, a glorious day, and all she had done was get up and lie here, downstairs, in this shaded room, leafing through section after section of the papers until her eyes were too numb to read any more. And her brain was almost too numb to think. The place looked a tip, she needed to give it a good clean, but she had no enthusiasm, no energy. She stared down at her mobile phone, expecting to see a reply to the text she had sent Roy. *Bloody man*, she thought. But it was really herself she was cursing.

Then she picked up the phone and dialled her closest girlfriend, Millie.

A child answered. A long, drawn-out, faltering five-year-old voice saying, 'Hello, this is Jessica, who is speaking please?'

'Is your mummy there?' Cleo asked her goddaughter.

'Mummy's quite busy at the moment,' Jessica replied importantly.

'Could you tell her it's your Auntie Kilo?' Kilo was what Millie had called her for as far back as she could remember. It had started because Millie was dyslexic.

'Well, the thing is, you see, Auntie Kilo, she is in the kitchen because we have quite a lot of people coming to lunch today.'

Then a few moments later she heard Millie's voice. 'Hey, you! What's up?'

Cleo told her about what had happened with Grace.

The thing she had always liked about Millie was that, however painful the truth might be to hear, Millie never minced words. 'You're a bloody idiot, K. What do you expect him to do? What would you do in that situation?'

'He lied to me.'

'All men lie. That's how they operate. If you want a long-term relationship with a man, you've got to understand it's going to be with a liar. It's in their nature – it's genetic, it's a bloody Darwinian acquired characteristic for survival, OK? They tell you what they want you to hear.'

'Great.'

'Yep, well, it's true. Women lie too, in different ways. I've lied about most of the orgasms Robert ever thinks I've had.'

'Doesn't seem much of a basis to build a relationship on, lies.'

'I'm not saying it's all lies – I'm saying if you are looking for perfection, K, you're going to end up alone. The only guys who aren't ever going to lie to you are the ones lying in the fridges in your mortuary.'

'Shit!' Cleo said suddenly.

'What?'

'It's OK. You just reminded me of something I have to do.'

'Listen, I have an invasion coming any minute – Robert's got a bunch of clients coming to lunch! Can I call you back this evening?'

'No probs.'

When she hung up she looked at her watch and realized she had been so wrapped up in her thoughts about Roy that she had completely forgotten to go to the mortuary. She and Darren had left the woman's body they'd brought off the beach last night on a trolley, because all the fridges were full – one bank of them was out of commission, in the middle of being replaced. A local undertaker was due to collect two of the bodies at midday, and she was meant to let him in, and at the same time put the woman in one of the vacated fridges.

She hauled herself to her feet. There was a message on her answering machine from her sister, Charlie, who had phoned about ten o'clock. She knew exactly what it would be about. She would have to listen to Charlie's blow-by-blow account of being dumped by her boyfriend. Maybe she could persuade her to meet somewhere in the sun, in a park or down on the seafront, for a late lunch after the mortuary? She dialled the number and, to her relief,

Charlie agreed readily, suggesting a place she knew under the Arches.

Thirty minutes later, after crawling along in heavy traffic headed for the beaches, she drove in through the mortuary gates, relieved to see that the covered side entrance, where bodies were delivered and removed out of sight of the public, was empty – the undertaker had not yet arrived.

The car's roof was down and her spirits were up, a fraction, thinking about something Roy Grace had said to her a few weeks ago, as she had driven him out to a country pub in this car. *You know, on a warm evening, with the roof down like this and you beside me, it's pretty hard to think there is much wrong with the world!*

She parked the blue MG in its usual place, opposite the front door of the grey, pebbledash-rendered mortuary building, and then opened her bag to take out her phone and warn her sister she was going to be late. But her phone wasn't in it.

'Bugger!' she said out loud.

How the hell could she have forgotten it? She never, ever, *ever* left home without it. Her Nokia was attached to her via an invisible umbilical cord.

Roy Grace, what the hell are you doing to my head?

She closed the roof of the car, even though she was only intending to be a few minutes, and locked it. Then, standing beneath the exterior CCTV camera, she inserted her key into the lock of the mortuary's staff entrance and turned it.

*

One of the vehicles in that solid stream of traffic trickling along the Lewes Road gyratory system, on the far side of the mortuary's wrought-iron gates, was a black Toyota Prius.

Unlike most of the rest of the traffic, instead of continuing on down to the seafront, it made a left turn into the next street along from the mortuary, then cruised slowly up the steep hill, which was lined on both sides with small terraced houses, looking for a parking space. The Time Billionaire smiled. There was a space right ahead of him, just the right size. Waiting for him.

Then he sucked his hand again. The pain was getting worse; it was muzzing his head. It didn't look good either. It had swollen more during the night.

'Stupid little bitch!' he shouted, in a sudden fit of rage.

*

Even though Cleo had been working in mortuaries for eight years, she was still not immune to the smells. The stench that hit her today, as she opened the door, almost physically knocked her backward. Like all mortuary staff, she had long ago trained herself to breathe through her mouth, but the reek of decaying meat – sour, caustic, fetid – hung heavy and cloying, as if weighed down by extra atoms, cloaking her like an invisible fog, swirling around her, seeping in through every pore in her skin.

Just as quickly as she possibly could, holding her breath and forgetting about the call she was going to make, she hurried past her office and entered the small changing room. She pulled a fresh pair of green pyjamas off a hook, dug her feet into her white wellington boots, tore a fresh pair of latex gloves from a pack and wriggled her clammy hands into them. Then she put on a face mask; not that it was going to do much to reduce the smell, but it would help a little.

She turned right and walked down the short, grey-tiled corridor and into the receiving room, which adjoined the main post-mortem room, and switched the lights on. The dead woman had been booked in as *Unknown Female*, the name given to all unidentified women who fetched up here. Cleo always felt it was such a sad thing, to be dead and unidentified.

She was lying on a stainless-steel table, next to another three parked alongside each other, her severed arm placed between her legs, her hair hanging back, dead straight, with a tiny strand of green weed in it. Cleo strode up to her, flapping her hand sharply, sending a dozen bluebottles flying into the air and scudding around the room. Through the stench of decay, she could smell something else strongly as well. Salt. The tang of the sea. And suddenly, tenderly plucking the tendril of weed out of the woman's hair, she wasn't sure she wanted to meet her sister on the beach.

Then the back doorbell rang. The undertaker had arrived. She checked the image on the CCTV before opening the rear doors into the loading bay and helping the two casually dressed young men load the bodies, in their plastic body-bags, into the rear of the discreet brown van. They then drove off. She locked the bay doors carefully and returned to the receiving room.

From the cupboard in the corner she removed a white plastic body-bag and walked back to the body. She hated dealing with floaters. Their skin after a few weeks immersion had a ghostly, fatty-white colour and the texture seemed to change, so that it looked like slightly scaly pork. The terminology was *adipocere*. The first mortuary technician Cleo had worked under, who relished the macabre, told her with a gleam in his eye that it was also known as *grave wax*.

The woman's lips, eyes, fingers, part of her cheeks,

breasts, vagina and toes had been eaten away, by small fish or crabs. Her badly chewed breasts lay, wrinkled, splayed out to the right and left, with much of their inside tissue gone, along with every scrap of the poor creature's dignity.

Who are you? she wondered, as she opened up the bag, laying it out under her, lifting her slightly but being careful in case her flesh tore.

When they'd examined her last night, along with two uniformed police officers, a detective inspector and a police surgeon, and Ronnie Pearson, the coroner's officer, they had found no obvious signs to indicate she might have been murdered. There were no marks on her body, other than just the abrasions that might be expected for someone rolled along shingle by the surf, although she was in a considerable state of decomposition, and evidence might already have been lost. The coroner had been notified, and they had been authorized to recover the body to the mortuary for a post-mortem on Monday, for identification – most probably from dental records.

She was looking at her carefully again now, checking for a ligature mark around her neck that they might have missed, or an entry hole from a bullet, trying to see what she could learn about her. It was always hard to determine the age of someone who had been in the water a while. She could be anywhere from her mid-twenties to her forties, she guessed.

She could have been a drowned swimmer or someone who had gone overboard from a boat. A suicide victim, perhaps. Or even, as sometimes happened, a burial at sea that hadn't been properly weighted down and had broken free, although it tended to be men more than women who were buried at sea. Or she could have been one of the thousands of people who just disappear every year. A *misper*.

Carefully she lifted away the severed arm and placed it on the empty stainless-steel table next to her body. Then, very gently, she began the process of rolling her over on to her stomach, to check her back. As she did so, she heard a faint click from inside the building.

She raised her head and listened for a moment. It sounded like the front door opening, or closing.

60

'Sandy!' he yelled. 'SANDY!!!'

She was pulling away from him. Shit, she was running fast!

Wearing a plain white T-shirt, blue cycling shorts and trainers, clutching a small bag in her hand, the woman was racing along a path around the side of the lake. Grace followed her, dodging past a statue, and saw her weaving in between several children playing. She swerved around two Schnauzer dogs, each chasing the other. Back on to a path, past a smartly dressed woman on horseback and a whole crocodile of matronly women Nordic-walking in pairs.

Roy was now regretting his beer. Sweat was streaming down his face, stinging his eyes, semi-blinding him. Two roller-bladers were coming towards him. He swerved right. They swerved the same way. Left. They swerved the same way. He lunged right at the last minute, in desperation, his leg banging painfully into a small, free-standing bench, and fell flat on his face, the bench underneath him, digging into him.

'*T'schuldigen!*' One of the roller-bladers, a tall, teenage boy, was standing over him, looking concerned. The other knelt and held out a hand.

'It's OK,' he gasped.

'You are American?'

'English.'

'I am so sorry.'

'I'm OK, fine, thanks. My fault. I—' Shaken and feeling

foolish, he took the boy's hand and allowed himself to be hauled up. As soon as he was back on his feet, his eyes were hunting for Sandy.

'You have cut your leg,' the other said.

Grace barely gave it a glance. He saw there was a rip in his jeans on his left shin and blood was coming out, but he didn't care. 'Thank you – *Danke*,' he said, looking ahead, to the left, to the right, in panic.

She had vanished.

The path ran straight on, for several hundred yards, through dense woodland and way in the distance opened on to a clearing. But there was also a right fork over a narrow, metal-railed bridge.

Fuck, fuck, fuck, fuck, fuck.

He balled his hands in frustration. *Think!*

Which way had she gone? Which possible way?

He turned back to the two roller-bladers. 'Excuse me, which is the nearest way to a road over there?'

Pointing at the bridge, one said, '*Ja*, this is the shortest way to the road. It is the only road.'

He thanked them, stumbled on for some yards, thinking, then forked right, weaving through a group of cyclists coming towards him over the bridge, and began to run faster, ignoring the stinging pain in his leg. Sandy would head for an exit, he figured. Crowds. He broke into a limping sprint, keeping off the crowded path, running along the grass beside it, shooting the occasional glance down at the ground ahead for benches, darting dogs, sunbathers, but mostly keeping his eyes fixed on the distance, looking desperately for a flash of blonde hair.

It *was* her! OK, he'd only caught part of her profile, and had not had a good look at her face, but it had been enough.

It *was* Sandy. It *had* to be! And why the hell else would she have run off, if it wasn't her?

He raced on, desperation numbing the pain. He could not have come so far, so damn far, just to let her slip from his grasp like this.

Where are you?

A brilliant ray of sunlight shone straight in his eye, like a flashlight beam, for an instant. A reflection off a bus moving along the road, no more than a hundred yards away. Then he saw another glint. It wasn't sunlight this time.

He dodged around a jolly-looking group having their picture taken, just as the camera flashed, ran over a verge of ragged grass and reached an empty road with the woodland of the garden on either side and a bus pulled over. There was no sign of Sandy.

Then he saw her again, as the bus moved on, a hundred yards ahead of him, still running!

'SANNDDDDDYYYYYY!' he hollered.

She stopped in her tracks for a moment and stared in his direction, as if wondering whom he was shouting at.

Leaving her in no doubt, waving his arm frantically, he sprinted towards her, shouting, 'Sandy! Sandy! Sandy!'

But she was already running again and vanished around a bend. Two mounted policemen appeared, coming towards him, and for a moment he wondered whether to ask them for help. Instead he sprinted on past them, conscious of their wary stares.

Then in the distance he could see the yellow wall of a building. She was running past a red stop light and a skip, over a bridge, past the building and a cluster of buses.

Then she stopped by a parked silver BMW and appeared to be searching in her bag for something – the key, he presumed.

And suddenly he was alongside her, gasping for air. 'Sandy!' he said elatedly.

She turned her head, panting hard, and said something to him in German.

And then, staring at her properly for the first time, he realized it wasn't Sandy.

It wasn't her at all.

His heart plunged like an elevator with a snapped cable. She had the same profile, uncannily the same, but her face was wider, flatter, much plainer. He couldn't see her eyes, because they were behind dark shades, but he didn't need to. It wasn't Sandy's mouth; this was a small, thin mouth. It wasn't Sandy's fine, silky skin; this face was pockmarked from childhood acne.

'I'm – I'm sorry. I'm so sorry.'

'You are English?' she said with a pleasant smile. 'Can I help you?'

She had her key out now, hit the fob and the doors unlocked. She opened the driver's door and rummaged around for something inside. He heard the jangle of coins.

'I'm sorry,' he said. 'I – I made a mistake. I mistook you – I thought you were someone I knew.'

'I forgot the time!' She patted the side of her head, indicating stupidity. 'The police give you tickets very quickly here. Two hours only on the ticket!'

She pulled a handful of euros out of the door pocket.

'Can I ask you a question, please? Ah – were you here – in the Englischer Garten – on Thursday? At about this time?'

She shrugged. 'I think so. In this weather, I come often.' She thought for a moment. 'Last Thursday?' she said.

'Yes.'

She nodded. 'Definitely. For sure.'

Grace thanked her and turned away. His clothes were

clinging to his skin with perspiration. A ribbon of blood trailed across his left trainer. A short distance away he saw Marcel Kullen walking towards him. He felt totally crushed. He pulled out his mobile phone and raised it to his ear, as the woman walked across to the ticket-vending machine. But he wasn't making a phone call. He was taking a photograph.

61

Cleo continued listening. She had very definitely heard a *click*.

Halting midway in her process of rolling the slender, fragile, grey cadaver over, she gently lowered her back down on to the stainless-steel table. 'Hello?' she called out, her voice muffled by her mask.

Then she stood still, listening, staring uneasily through the door at the silent grey tiles of the corridor. 'Hello? Who's that?' she called out, louder, feeling a tightening in her throat. She lowered her mask, letting it hang by the tapes. 'Hello?'

Silence. Just the faint hum of the fridges.

A slick of fear shot through her. Had she left the outside door open? Surely not, she *never* left it open. She tried to think clearly. The smell when she had opened the door – could she have left it open to let some fresh air in?

No way, she would not have been so stupid. She always closed the door; it self-locked. Of course she had closed it!

So why wasn't the person out there replying?

And in her over-revving heart she already knew the answer to that. There were some weirdos around for whom mortuaries held a fascination. They'd had a number of break-ins in the past, but now the latest security systems had so far, for a good eighteen months, acted as an effective deterrent.

Suddenly she remembered the CCTV monitor on the wall and looked up at it. It was showing a static black and white image of the tarmac outside the door, and the flower bed and brick wall beyond. The tail lights and rear bumper of her car were just in frame.

Then she heard the distinct rustle of clothes out in the corridor.

Goosebumps broke out over her entire body. For an instant she froze, her brain spinning, trying to get traction. There was a phone on the shelf next to the cabinet, but she didn't have time to get to it. She looked around frantically for a weapon that was in reach. For an instant she considered, absurdly, the severed arm of the cadaver. Fear tightened her skin; her scalp felt as if she were wearing a skullcap.

The rustling came closer. She saw a shadow moving along the tiles.

Then, suddenly, her fear turned to anger. *Whoever the hell it was out there had no damn right to be here.* She decided she was not going to be scared or intimidated by some sicko who got kicks out of breaking into the mortuary. *Her* mortuary.

In a few fast, determined strides, she reached the cabinet, slid the door open, noisily, and pulled out the largest of the Sabatier carving knives. Then, gripping it tightly by the handle, she ran at the opened doorway. And collided, with a scream of terror, with a tall figure in an orange T-shirt and lime-green shorts, who gripped her arms, pinning them to her sides. The knife clattered to the tiled floor.

62

Marcel Kullen pulled over to the kerb and pointed across the street. Roy Grace saw a large, beige-coloured store on the corner. It had book-lined windows and the interior was dark. Lights inside, hanging from stalks, were switched on, providing decoration rather than any illumination. They reminded Grace of glow-worms.

Elegant grey letters on the store front read THE MUNICH READERY. Another announced SECOND-HAND BOOKS IN ENGLISH.

'I just wanted to show you the shop. I am asking in this tomorrow,' the German detective said.

Grace nodded. He had consumed two large beers, a bratwurst, sauerkraut and potatoes, and was feeling decidedly woozy. In fact, he was having a problem keeping his eyes open.

'Sandy was a big reader, you told me?'

Was. The word jarred in Grace's mind. He didn't like people referring to Sandy in the past tense, as if she were dead. But he let it slide. He used that tense himself often enough, subconsciously. Feeling more energized suddenly, he said, 'Yes, she's a big reader, always has been. Crime, thrillers – all kinds of mystery novels. Biographies as well – she liked reading about women explorers in particular.'

Kullen put the car in gear and drove on. 'What is it – you have this saying in England – keep your pecker up?'

Grace patted his friend on the arm. 'Good memory!'

'So now us will go to the police headquarters. There they

have the records for the missing persons. I have a friend, Sabine Thomas, the Polizeirat who is in charge of this department. She is coming in to meet us.'

'Thank you,' Grace said. 'That's kind of her, on a Sunday.'

His earlier optimism had deserted him and he was feeling flat, realizing again the enormity of what faced him here. He watched quiet streets, deserted shops, cars, pedestrians slide by. She could be anywhere. In a room behind any of these façades, in any of these cars, on any of these streets. And this was just one city. How many gazillion towns and cities in the world were there where she might be?

He found the button on his door and lowered his window. Sultry, humid air blew on his face. The foolishness he had felt earlier, as he had returned to the table after his fruitless chase, had gone, but now he felt lost.

Somehow, after Dick Pope's call, he had felt that all he had to do was go to the Englischer Garten and he would find Sandy there. Waiting for him. As if somehow letting Dick and Leslie Pope see her had been her subtle way of getting the message to him.

How dumb was that?

'If you like on the way to the office we can walk through Marienplatz. It is a small detour. We can go there to the Viktualienmarkt, the place I told you where I think an English person might go for food.'

'Yes, thank you.'

'Then you are come to my house and you meet my family.'

Grace smiled at him, wondering if the German had any idea just how much he envied him the apparent normality of his life. Then, suddenly, his mobile phone rang. Grace looked at the display.

Private number.

He let it ring a couple more times, hesitating. Probably work, and he wasn't in the right mood to speak to anyone from work right now. But he was aware of his responsibilities. With a heavy heart, he pressed the green button.

'Yo!'

It was Glenn Branson.

'Wassup?'

'Where are you?'

'Munich.'

'*Munich?* You're still there?'

'It's only been a few hours.'

'What the fuck are you doing there anyway?'

'Trying to buy you a horse.'

There was a long silence. 'A *what*?' And then, 'Oh, I get it. Very funny. Munich – shit, man. Ever see that movie *Night Train to Munich*?'

'No.'

'Directed by Carol Reed.'

'Never saw it. This is not a good time to discuss movies.'

'Yeah, well, you were watching *The Third Man* the other night. He directed that too.'

'Is that what you phoned to tell me about?'

'No.' He was about to add something, when Kullen leaned across Grace, pointing at a rather unimpressive-looking building.

'Hold on a moment.' Grace covered the mouthpiece.

'The *Bierkeller* where Hitler was thrown out from, because he did not pay his bill!' he said. 'A rumour, you know!'

'I'm just driving past Adolf Hitler's watering hole,' Grace informed Branson.

'Yeah? Well, keep on driving past it. We have a problem.'

'Tell me?'

'It's big. Massive. OK?'

'I'm all ears.'

'You sound pissed. Have you been drinking?'

'No,' Grace said, mentally sharpening himself up. 'Tell me?'

'We have another murder on our hands,' the DS said. 'Similarities with Katie Bishop.'

And suddenly Roy Grace was sitting bolt upright, fully alert. 'What similarities?'

'A young woman – name of Sophie Harrington. She's been found dead with a gas mask on her face.'

Cold fingers crawled up Grace's spine. 'Shit. What else do you have?'

'What else do you need? I'm telling you, man, you need to get your ass back here.'

'You have DI Murphy. She can handle it.'

'She's your understudy,' he said disparagingly.

'If you want to call her that. So far as I'm concerned, she's my deputy SIO.'

'You know what they said about Greta Garbo's understudy?'

Struggling to remember any movie he had ever seen the screen legend in, Grace replied testily, 'No, what did they say?'

'Greta Garbo's understudy can do everything that Greta Garbo does, except for *whatever it is* that Greta Garbo does.'

'Very flattering.'

'You geddit?'

'I geddit.'

'In that case get your ass on the next plane back here. Alison Vosper thinks she has your scalp. I don't give a toss about those politics, but I do give a toss about you. And we need you.'

'Did you remember to feed Marlon?' Grace asked.

'Marlon?'

'The goldfish.'

'Oh, shit.'

63

Cleo tried to scream, but the sound stayed trapped in her throat. She struggled manically, trying to free her arms, the man's face a blur to her unfocused eyes. She lashed out with her leg, kicking him in the shin.

Then she heard his voice.

'Cleo!'

Quiet, plaintive. 'Cleo! It's me! It's OK.'

Spiky black hair. A startled expression on his young, pleasant face. Dressed casually in an orange top and green shorts, headphones plugged into his ears.

'Oh, shit.' She stopped struggling, her mouth dropping open. 'Darren!'

He released her arms very slowly, warily, as if not yet quite sure he could trust her not to stab him. 'Are you all right, Cleo?'

Gulping down air, she felt as if her heart was trying to drill its way out of her chest. She stepped back, looking at her colleague, then at the knife on the floor, then back at his brown eyes. Numb. Too numb to say anything else for a moment.

'You gave me such a shock.' The words came out in a breathless, whispered rush.

Darren raised his hands and pulled out his earphones, letting them dangle by their white wires. Then he raised his hands again, in an attitude of surrender. He was trembling, she realized.

'I'm sorry.' She was still hyperventilating, her voice shaky. Then she smiled, trying to remedy the situation.

Still looking uncertain, he said, 'Am I that scary?'

'I – I heard the door,' she said, starting to feel foolish now. 'I called out and you didn't reply. I thought you were an intruder. I – I was . . .' she shook her head.

He dropped his hands, cupping his earpieces. 'I was listening to some heavy music,' he said. 'I didn't hear you.'

'I'm so sorry.'

He reached down and rubbed his shin.

'Did I hurt you?'

'Actually, yes! But I'll live.' There was a nasty mark on his shin. 'I suddenly remembered we'd left the body out. I thought, with this heat, it ought to go in a fridge. I called you, but there was no answer from your home or your mobile, so I decided to come in and do it.'

Feeling more normal now, Cleo apologized again.

He shrugged. 'Don't worry about it. But I never thought of working in a mortuary as being a contact sport.'

She laughed. 'I'm so, so sorry. I've just had a shit twenty-four hours. I—'

'Forget it. I'm OK.'

She looked at the red weal on his leg. 'It was good of you, that you came in. Thank you.'

'I'll think twice next time,' he said good-humouredly. 'Maybe I should have stayed in my last job – it was a lot less violent.'

She grinned. In his previous job, she remembered, Darren had been a butcher's apprentice. 'It's good of you to give up time on a Sunday,' she said.

'It got me out of a barbecue at my girlfriend's parents,' he said. 'That's the downside of this work. I can't cope with barbecues since I started working here.'

'That makes two of us.'

They were both thinking of burns victims. Usually their skin was blackened, crisp like pork crackling. Depending how long they had burned for, their flesh was sometimes grey and hard, sometimes raw and bloody liked seared, undercooked pork. Cleo had read once that cannibal tribes in central Africa called white man *long pig*. She understood exactly why. It was the reason many people who worked in mortuaries were uncomfortable at barbecues. Particularly when pork was involved.

Together they rolled the cadaver on to her stomach and examined her back for tattoos, birthmarks and bullet-entry wounds, but found nothing. With relief they finally eased her into a body-bag, zipped it up and slid it into fridge number 17. Tomorrow the process of identifying her would begin. The soft tissues from her fingers were gone, so there were no prints that could be taken. Her jaw was intact, so dental records could be checked. DNA was a longer shot – she would need to already be on a database to find a match. Her description and photographs and measurements would be sent to the Missing Persons Helpline, and Sussex police would contact friends and relatives of anyone who had been reported missing who fitted the description of this dead woman.

And in the morning the consultant pathologist, Dr Nigel Churchman, would conduct a post-mortem to establish the cause of death. If, during the course of this, he found any-thing suspicious, he would halt his work immediately, the coroner would be notified and a Home Office pathologist, either Nadiuska or Dr Theobald, would be called in to take over.

In the meantime, both Cleo and Darren had several

hours of a glorious August Sunday afternoon ahead of them.

Darren left first, in his small red Nissan, heading for the barbecue he really could have done without. Cleo stood in the doorway, watching him drive off, unable to stop herself from envying him. He was young, full of enthusiasm, happy in his relationship with his girlfriend and in his job.

She was rapidly heading for the wrong side of thirty. Enjoying her career but worrying about it at the same time. She wanted to have children before she was too old. Yet each time she thought she had found Mr Right, he would spring something on her from left field. Roy was such a lovely man. But just when she thought everything was perfect, his missing wife popped up like a bloody jack-in-the-box.

She set the alarm, stepped outside and locked the front door, with just one thought in her mind – to get home and see if there was a message from Roy. Then, walking across the tarmac drive to her blue MG, she stopped dead in her tracks.

Somebody had slashed the black canvas roof open. All the way from the windscreen to the rear window.

64

The woman behind the wooden counter and glass window handed him a buff-coloured rectangular form. 'Please put your name and address and other details on this,' she asked him in a weary voice. She looked as if she had been sitting there for too long, reminding him of an exhibit in a museum showcase that someone had neglected to dust. Her face had an indoors pallor and her shapeless brown hair hung around her face and shoulders like curtains that had become detached from some of their rings.

Above the reception desk of the Accident and Emergency Unit of the Royal Sussex County Hospital was a large LCD display of yellow letters on a black background, currently reading WAITING TIME 3 HOURS.

He considered the form carefully. A name, address, date of birth and next of kin were required. There was also a space for allergies.

'Everything all right?' the woman asked.

He raised his swollen right hand. 'Difficult to write,' he said.

'Would you like me to fill it in for you?'

'I can manage.'

Then, leaning on the counter, he stared at the form for some moments, his brain, muzzed by the pain, really not functioning that well at all. He was trying to think quickly, but the thoughts that he wanted didn't come in the right sequence. He felt a little dizzy suddenly.

'You can sit down and fill it in,' she said.

Snapping back at her, he shouted, 'I SAID I CAN MANAGE!'

People all around looked up from their hard grey plastic seats, startled. *Not smart*, he thought. *Not smart to draw attention.* Hastily he filled out the form and then, as if to make amends, beside *Allergies* he wrote, wittily, he thought, 'Pain.'

But she didn't appear to notice as she took the form back. 'Please take a seat and a nurse will come and see you shortly.'

'Three hours?' he said.

'I'll tell them it's urgent,' she said flatly, then watched warily as the strange man with long, straggly brown hair, a heavy moustache and beard, and large, tinted glasses, wearing a baggy white shirt over a string vest, grey slacks and sandals, walked over to an empty seat, between a man with a bleeding arm and an elderly woman with a bandaged head, and sat down. Then she picked up her phone.

The Time Billionaire unclipped the BlackBerry from its holster, which was attached to his belt, but before he had time to do anything, a shadow fell in front of him. A pleasant-looking, dark-haired woman in her late forties, in nursing uniform, was standing over him. The badge on her lapel read BARBARA LEACH – A&E NURSE.

'Hello!' she said breezily. 'Would you come with me?' She led him into a small booth and asked him to sit down. 'What seems to be the problem?'

He raised his hand. 'I hurt it working on a car.'

'How long ago?'

Thinking for a moment, he said, 'Thursday afternoon.'

She examined it carefully, turning it over, then comparing it to his left hand. 'It looks infected,' she said. 'Have you had a tetanus injection recently?'

'I don't remember.'

She studied it again for a while thoughtfully. 'Working on a car?' she said.

'An old car. I'm restoring it.'

'I'll get the doctor to see you as soon as possible.'

He went back to his chair in the waiting room and turned his attention back to his BlackBerry. He logged on to the web and then clicked on his bookmark for Google.

When that came up, he entered a search command for MG TF.

That was the car Cleo Morey drove.

Despite his pain, despite his muzzy thoughts, a plan was forming. Really quite a good plan.

'Fucking brilliant!' he said out loud, unable to control his excitement. Then immediately he shrank back into his shell.

He was shaking.

Always a sign that the Lord approved.

65

Reluctantly cutting short his precious hours in Munich, Grace managed to board an earlier flight. The weather in England had changed dramatically during the day, and shortly after six o'clock in the evening, as he went to get his car from the short-stay multi-storey car park at Heathrow, the sky was an ominous grey and a cold wind was blowing, flecking the windscreen with rain.

It was the kind of wind that you forgot even existed during the long, summer days they'd had recently, he reflected. It was like a stern reminder from Mother Nature that summer was not going to last much longer. The days were already getting shorter. In little over a month it would be autumn. Then winter. Another year.

Feeling flat and tired, he wondered what he had achieved today, apart from earning another black mark in Alison Vosper's book. Anything at all?

He pushed his ticket into the machine and the barrier rose. Even the rorty sound of the engine as he accelerated, which ordinarily he liked listening to, seemed off-key tonight. Definitely not firing on all cylinders. Like its owner.

Sort yourself out in Munich. Call me when you get back home.

As he headed towards the roundabout, taking the direction for the M25, he stuck his phone in the hands-free cradle and dialled Cleo's mobile. It started ringing. Then he heard her voice, a little slurred, and hard to decipher above a raucous din of jazz music in the background.

'Yo! Detective Shhuperintendent Roy Grace! Where are you?'

'Just left Heathrow. You?'

'I'm getting smashed with my little sister, we're on our third Sea Breezes – no – sorry – correct that! We're on our *fifth* Sea Breezes, down by the Arches. It's blowing a hooley, but there's a great band. Come and join us!'

'I have to go to a crime scene. Later?'

'Don't think we'll be conscious much longer!'

'So you're not on call today?'

'Day off!'

'Can I swing by later?'

'Can't guarantee I'll be awake. But you can try!'

*

When he was a kid, Church Road, Hove, was the dull back-water that Brighton's busy, buzzy, shopping street, Western Road, morphed into, somewhere west of the Waitrose supermarket. It had perked up considerably in recent years, with trendy restaurants, delis and shops displaying stuff that people under ninety might actually want to buy.

Like most of this city, many of the familiar names from his past along Church Road, such as the grocer's Cullens, the chemist's Paris and Greening, the department stores Hills of Hove and Plummer Roddis, had now gone. Just a few still remained. One was Forfars the baker's. He turned right shortly past them, drove up a one-way street, made a right at the top, then another right into Newman Villas.

As with most lower-rent residential areas of this transient city, the street was a riot of letting-agency boards. Number 17 was no exception. A RAND & Co. sign, prominently displayed, advertised a two-bedroom flat to let. Just inches below it, a burly uniformed police constable, holding a clipboard, stood in front of a barrier of blue and white crime-scene tape that was cordoning off some of the pavement. Parked along the street were a number of familiar vehicles. Grace saw the square hulk of a Major Incident Vehicle, several other police vehicles double-parked, making the narrow street even narrower, and a cluster of media reporters, with good old Kevin Spinella, he noted, among them.

Anonymous in his private Alfa, he drove past them all and found a space on double yellow lines around the corner, back in Church Road. Switching the engine off, he sat still for a moment.

Sandy.

Where did he go from here? Wait to see if Kullen came up with anything? Go back to Munich and spend more time there? He had over a fortnight's leave owing – Cleo and he had discussed going away somewhere together, with her perhaps accompanying him to a police symposium in New Orleans at the end of this month. But at this moment a big part of him was torn.

If Sandy was in Munich, given time he knew he could find her. Today had been stupid, really. He was never going to be able to achieve much in just a few hours. But at least he had started the ball rolling, done what he could. Marcel Kullen was reliable, would do his best for him. If he went back for a week, maybe that would be sufficient. He could have one week there and another in New Orleans with Cleo. That would work – if he could get her to buy it. A big *if.*

Switching his mind to the task immediately in front of him, he hefted his go-bag out of the boot and walked back to number 17. Several reporters shouted at him, an eager-looking girl shoved a foam-padded microphone in his face and flash bulbs popped.

'No comment at this stage,' he said firmly.

Suddenly Spinella was blocking his path. 'Is this another, Detective Superintendent?' he asked quietly.

'Another what?'

Spinella dropped his voice even more, giving him a knowing look. 'You know what I mean. Right?'

'I'll tell you when I've seen myself.'

'Don't worry, Detective Superintendent. If you don't, someone else will.' Spinella tapped the side of his nose. 'Sources!'

Harbouring the pleasant thought of punching the reporter's lights out, almost hearing the crunching sound of Spinella's nasal bones already, Grace pushed past him and signed his name on the clipboard. The constable told him to go up to the top floor.

He ducked under the tape, then removed a fresh white paper suit from his bag and began struggling clumsily into it. To his embarrassment, he almost fell over in front of the entire Sussex media as he jammed both feet into one leg. Red-faced, he sorted himself out, pulled on disposable overshoes and a pair of latex gloves and went inside.

Closing the front door behind him, he stopped in the hallway and sniffed. Just the usual musty smell of old carpet and boiled vegetables that was typical of a thousand tired buildings like this he'd been into in his career. No stench of a decaying cadaver, which meant the victim hadn't been dead long – it wouldn't take many days of a summer heat-wave for the stench of a putrefying corpse to start becoming noticeable. A small relief, he thought, noticing the strip of tape that had been laid all the way up the stairs, marking the entry and exit route – which he was pleased to see. At least the police team that had arrived here knew what they were doing, avoiding contamination at the scene.

Which was what he needed to do himself. It would not be smart for him to go upstairs, because of the risk of giving the defence team a cross-contamination situation they could crawl all over. Instead, he pulled out his mobile phone and called Kim Murphy, telling her he was downstairs.

Up on the first floor above him, he suddenly saw a white-suited and hooded SOCO officer called Eddie Gribble come into view. He was kneeling on the floor, taking a scraping. He nodded in acknowledgement. A second, identically clad SOCO, Tony Monnington, also came into view, dusting the wall for fingerprints.

'Evening, Roy!' he called down cheerily.

Grace raised a hand. 'Having a nice Sunday?'

'Gets me out of the house. And Belinda's able to watch what she wants on the telly.'

'There's always a silver lining!' Grace replied grimly.

Moments later two further suited and hooded figures appeared and came down the stairs towards him. One was Kim Murphy, holding a video camera, the other was Detective Chief Inspector Brendan Duigan, a tall, large-framed, genial officer with a gentle, ruddy face and prematurely white hair that was cropped into a buzz-cut. Duigan was the duty SIO called to this scene earlier, Grace had learned on his way here. Duigan had subsequently called Kim Murphy over, because of similarities with the Katie Bishop murder.

After exchanging brief pleasantries, Murphy played Grace the video that had been taken of the scene. He watched it on the small screen on the back of the camera.

After you had done this job for a number of years, you

started thinking that you were immune to horrors, that you had seen it all, that nothing could surprise or shock you any more. But the footage that confronted him now sent a black chill worming deep through him.

Staring at the slightly jerky footage of the white-suited and hooded figures of two more SOCO officers on their hands and knees and another standing, and Nadiuska De Sancha on her knees at the end of the bed, he saw the alabaster-coloured naked body of a young woman with long brown hair lying on the bed, with a gas mask over her face.

It was as near as possible a carbon copy of the way Katie Bishop had been found.

Except that Katie did not appear to have put up a fight. The camera now started to show that this young woman certainly had. There was a smashed plate on the floor, with a mark gouged out of the wall above it. A shattered dressing-table mirror, bottles of perfume and jars of make-up lying all over the place, along with a smear of blood on the wall, just above the white headboard. Then a lingering shot of a framed, abstract print of a row of deckchairs, lying on the floor, the glass shattered.

Brighton had had its share of murders over the years, but one thing, mercifully, it had never been clouded by before was the spectre of a serial killer. It wasn't even an area Grace had needed to know much about – before now.

Nearby, a car alarm *beep-beep-beeped* loudly. He blanked it out as he stared at the freeze-frame of the dead young woman. He had regularly attended lectures given by SIOs on serial-killer cases at the International Homicide Investigators Association annual symposium, which was mostly held in the USA. He was trying to recall the common features. So far, Spinella had kept his word and there had been no mention in the press about the gas mask, so a copy-cat killing was unlikely.

One thing he did remember clearly from a lecture was a discussion of the fear that could be created in a community when it was announced that a serial killer was out there. But equally, the community had a right to know, a *need* to know.

Grace then turned to DCI Duigan. 'What do we have so far?' he asked.

'Nadiuska's best guess is the young woman has been dead for about two days, give or take.'

'Any idea of how she died?'

'Yes.' Kim Murphy started the camera running and zoomed in, pointing to the young woman's throat. A dark red ligature mark was visible, then even more clearly for an instant as the burst of flash from a police photographer's camera strobed across it.

And Grace's own leaden innards sank before Kim confirmed it.

'Identical to Katie Bishop,' she said.

'We're looking at a serial killer – whatever that description actually means?' Grace queried.

'On what I've seen so far, Roy, it's too early to be able to say anything,' Duigan replied. 'And I'm not exactly an expert on serial killers. Luckily, I've never experienced one.'

'That makes two of us.'

Grace was thinking hard. Two attractive women killed, apparently, in the same manner, twenty-four hours apart. 'What do we know about her?'

'We believe her name is Sophie Harrington,' Murphy said. 'She's twenty-seven and employed by a film production company in London. I answered a phone call a little earlier, from a young woman called Holly Richardson, who claims to be her best friend. She had been trying to contact her all yesterday – they were meant to be going to a party together last night. Holly last spoke to her about five on Friday afternoon.'

'That helps us,' Grace said. 'At least we know she was alive then. Has anyone interviewed Holly Richardson?'

'Nick's gone to find her now.'

'And Ms Harrington clearly put up one hell of a fight,' Duigan added.

'The place looks smashed up,' Grace said.

'Nadiuska's found something under the nail of one of her big toes. A tiny bit of flesh.'

Grace felt a sudden surge of adrenaline. 'Human flesh?'

'That's what she thinks.'

'Could it have been gouged out of her assailant in the struggle?'

'Possibly.'

And suddenly, his memory pin-sharp now, Roy Grace remembered the injury on Brian Bishop's hand. And that he had gone AWOL for several hours on Friday evening. 'I want a DNA test on that,' he said. 'Fast-tracked.'

As he spoke, he was already using his mobile phone.

Linda Buckley, the family liaison officer, answered on the second ring.

'Where's Bishop?' he asked.

'Having supper with his in-laws. They are back from Alicante,' she replied.

He asked for the address, then he called Branson's mobile.

'Yo, old-timer – wassup?'

'What are you doing right now?'

'I'm eating some unpleasantly healthy vegetarian cannelloni from your freezer, listening to your rubbish music and watching your antique television. Man, how come you don't have widescreen, like the rest of the planet?'

'Put all your problems behind you. You're going out to work.' Grace gave him the address.

66

The silence was fleetingly broken by the tinkle of the tea-spoon, as Moira Denton stirred the tea in her delicate, bone china teacup. Brian Bishop had never found his in-laws easy to get along with. Part of the reason, he knew, was that the couple didn't really get along with each other. He remembered a quote he had once come across, which talked about people *leading lives of quiet desperation*. Nothing, it seemed to him, sadly, could be a truer description of the relationship between Frank and Moira Denton.

Frank was a serial entrepreneur – and a serial failure. Brian had made a small investment in his last venture, a factory in Poland converting wheat into bio-diesel fuel, more as a token of family solidarity than from any real expectation of returns, which was just as well, as it had gone bust, like everything else Frank had touched before it. A tall man just shy of seventy, who had only just recently started looking his age, Frank Denton was also a serial shagger. He wore his hair stylishly long, although it was now tinged a rather dirty-looking orange, from the use of some dyeing product, and his left eye had a lazy lid, making it look permanently half-closed. In the past he had reminded Brian of an amiable, raffish pirate, although at this moment, sitting silent, hunched forward in his armchair in the tiny, boiling-hot flat, unshaven, his hair unbrushed, dressed in a creased white shirt, he just looked like a sad, shabby, broken old man. His brandy snifter stood untouched with a stubby bottle of Torres 10 Gran Reserva beside it.

Moira sat opposite him on the other side of a carved-wood coffee table, on the top of which was yesterday's *Argus* with its grim headline. In contrast to her husband, she had made an effort with her appearance. In her mid-sixties, she was a handsome-looking woman, and would have looked even better if she had not allowed bitterness to so line her face. Her dyed black hair, coiled abundantly above her head, was neatly coiffed, she was wearing a plain, loose grey top, a pleated navy blue skirt and flat, black shoes, and she had put make-up on.

On the television, with the sound turned down low, a moose was running across open grassland. Because the Dentons now lived most of the time in their flat in Spain, they found England, even at the height of summer, unbearably cold. So they kept the central heating in their flat, close to Hove seafront, several degrees north of eighty. And the windows shut.

Seated in a green-velour armchair, Brian was perspiring. He sipped his third San Miguel beer, his stomach rumbling, even though Moira had just served them a meal. He'd barely touched his cold chicken and salad, nor the tinned peach slices afterwards. He just had no appetite at all. And was not up to much conversation either. The three of them had been sitting in silence for much of the time since he'd come round a couple of hours earlier. They had discussed whether Katie should be buried or cremated. It was not a conversation Brian had ever had with his wife, but Moira was adamant that Katie would have wanted to be cremated.

Then they had discussed the funeral arrangements – all on hold until the coroner released the body, which both

Frank and Moira had viewed yesterday at the mortuary. The talk had reduced both of them to tears.

Understandably, his in-laws were taking Katie's death hard. She had been more than just their only child – she had been the only thing of real value in their lives, and the glue that had kept them together. One particularly uncomfortable Christmas, when Moira had drunk too much sherry, champagne and then Baileys, she had confided sourly to Brian that she'd only taken Frank back after his affairs for Katie's sake.

'Like that beer, do you, Brian?' Frank asked. His voice was posh English, something he had cultivated to mask his working-class roots. Moira had an affected voice also, except when she drank too much and then lapsed back into her native Lancastrian.

'Yes, good flavour. Thank you.'

'That's Spain for you, you see? Quality!' Suddenly becoming animated for a moment, Frank Denton raised a hand. 'A very underrated country – their food, wines, beers. And the prices, of course. Some of it is developed out, but there are still great opportunities if you know what you're doing.'

Despite the man's grief, Brian could sense that Katie's father was about to launch into a sales pitch. He was right.

'Property prices are doubling every five years there, Brian. The smart thing is to pick the next hot spots. Building costs are cheap, and they're jolly efficient workers, those Spaniards. I've identified an absolutely fantastic opportunity just the other side of Alicante. I tell you, Brian, it's a real no-brainer.'

The last thing Brian wanted or needed at this moment was to hear the details of yet another of Frank's plausible-sounding but ultimately fatally flawed schemes. The miserable silence had been preferable – at least that had left him to his thoughts.

He took another sip of his beer and realized he had almost drained the glass. He needed to be careful, he knew, as he was driving, and he didn't know how the family liaison officer, waiting in her car downstairs like a sentinel, would react to the smell of alcohol on his breath.

'What have you done to your hand?' Moira asked suddenly, looking at the fresh plaster on it.

'I – just bashed it – getting out of a car,' he said dismissively.

The doorbell rang.

The Dentons exchanged glances, then Frank hauled himself up and shuffled out into the hallway.

'We're not expecting anyone,' Moira said to Brian.

Moments later Frank came back into the room. 'The police,' he said, giving his son-in-law a strange look. 'They're on their way up.' He continued staring at Brian, as if some dark thought had entered his head during those moments he had been out of the room.

Brian wondered if there was something else the police had said that the old man was not relaying.

67

In the Witness Interview Suite, Glenn Branson switched on the audio and video recorders announcing clearly as he sat down, 'It is twenty-one twelve, Sunday 6 August. Detective Superintendent Grace and Detective Sergeant Branson interviewing Mr Brian Bishop.'

The CID headquarters were becoming depressingly familiar to Bishop. The walk up the entrance stairs, past the displays of police truncheons on blue felt boards, then through the open-plan offices and the cream-walled corridors lined with diagrams, and into this tiny room with its three red chairs.

'This is starting to feel like *Groundhog Day*,' he said.

'Great movie,' Branson commented. 'Best thing Bill Murray did. I preferred it to *Lost in Translation*.'

Bishop had seen *Lost in Translation* and was starting to empathize with the character Murray played in that movie, wandering sleep-deprived through an unfamiliar world. But he wasn't in any mood to start discussing films. 'Are your people finished in my house yet? When can I move back in?'

'I'm afraid it will be a few days yet,' Grace said. 'Thank you for coming up here tonight. I apologize for disrupting your Sunday evening.'

'That's almost funny,' Bishop said acidly. He nearly added, but didn't, that it hadn't been any great hardship to escape from the grim misery of his in-laws and Frank's sales pitch for his new business venture. 'What news do you have for me?'

'I'm afraid we have nothing further to report at this stage, but we are expecting results from DNA analysis back during tomorrow and that may give us something. But we have some questions that our investigations have thrown up, if that's all right with you?'

'Go ahead.'

Grace noted Bishop's apparent tetchiness. It was a considerable change from his sad, lost-looking state at their last interview. But he was experienced enough not to read anything into it. Anger was one of the natural stages of grief, and a bereaved person was capable of lashing out at anyone.

'Could you start, Mr Bishop, by explaining the nature of your business?'

'My company provides logistical systems. We design the software, install it and run it. Our core business is rostering.'

'Rostering?' Grace saw that Branson was frowning also.

'I'll give you an example. An aeroplane that should be taking off from Gatwick, for instance, gets delayed for some reason – mechanical, bad weather, whatever – and cannot take off until the following day. Suddenly the airline is faced with finding overnight accommodation for three hundred and fifty passengers. It also has a knock-on series of problems – other planes in the wrong places, the crew schedules all mucked up, with some crew going over their permitted working hours, meals, compensations. Passengers having to be put on different flights to make connections. All that kind of stuff.'

'So you are a computer man?'

'I'm a businessman. But yes, I have a pretty good grasp

of computing. I have a degree in cognitive sciences – from Sussex University.'

'It's successful, I presume?'

'We made the *Sunday Times* list of the hundred fastest-growing companies in Britain last year,' Bishop said. There was a trace of pride beneath his gloom.

'I hope all this won't have a negative impact on you.'

'It doesn't really matter any more, does it?' he said bleakly. 'Everything I did was for Katie. I—' His voice faltered. He pulled out a handkerchief and buried his face in it. Then suddenly, in a burst of rage, he shouted out, 'Please catch the bastard. This creep! This absolutely fucking—' He broke down in tears.

Grace waited some moments, then asked, 'Would you like a drink of anything?'

Bishop shook his head, sobbing.

Grace continued to wait until he had calmed down.

'I'm sorry,' Bishop said, wiping his eyes.

'You don't need to apologize, sir.' Grace gave him a little more time, then asked, 'How would you describe your relationship with your wife?'

'We loved each other. It was good. I think we comple-ment—' He stopped, then said heavily, '*Complemented* each other.'

'Had you had any arguments recently?'

'No, I can honestly say we hadn't.'

'Was there anything bothering your wife? Troubling her?'

'Apart from maxing out her credit cards?'

Both Grace and Branson gave thin smiles, uncertain whether this was a lame stab at humour.

'Could you tell us what you did today, sir?' Grace said, changing tack.

He lowered the handkerchief. 'What I did today?'

'Yes.'

'I spent the morning trying to deal with my emails. Phoned my secretary, going through a list of meetings that I needed her to cancel. I was meant to be flying to the States on Wednesday, to see a possible new client in Houston, and I got her to cancel that. Then I had lunch with a friend of mine and his wife – I went round to their house.'

'They could vouch for that?'

'Jesus! Yes.'

'You've had a dressing put on your hand.'

'My friend's wife is a nurse – she thought it ought to be covered.' Bishop shook his head. 'What is this? Are we back to the Spanish Inquisition again?'

Branson raised both hands. 'We're just concerned for your welfare, sir. People in a state of bereavement can overlook things. That's all.'

Grace would have loved to have told Bishop at this point that the taxi driver, in whose taxi he claimed to have injured his hand, remembered Bishop clearly but had absolutely no recollection of his hurting himself. But he wanted to keep his powder dry on this one for later. 'Only a couple more questions, Mr Bishop, then we can call it a day.' He smiled, but received a blank stare back.

'Does the name Sophie Harrington mean anything to you?'

'Sophie Harrington?'

'A young lady who lives in Brighton and works in London for a film production company.'

'Sophie Harrington? No,' he said decisively. 'No, it doesn't.'

'You've never heard of this young lady?' Grace persisted.

Both Grace and Branson clocked his hesitation.

'I haven't, no.'

The man was lying, Grace knew. The swing of his eyes towards *construct* had been unmistakable. Twice.

'Should I know her?' he asked clumsily, fishing.

'No,' Grace responded. 'Just a question, on the off-chance. The last thing I'd like to talk to you about tonight is a life insurance policy you took out for Mrs Bishop.'

Bishop shook his head, looking genuinely astonished. Or making a good act of it.

'Six months ago, sir,' Grace said, 'you took out a life insurance policy with HSBC bank, in your wife's name, for the amount of three million pounds.'

Bishop grinned inanely, shaking his head vigorously. 'No way. I'm sorry, I don't believe in life insurance. I've never taken out a policy in my life!'

Grace studied him for some moments. 'Can I get this straight, sir? You are telling me that you didn't take out any life insurance policy on Mrs Bishop?'

'Absolutely not!'

'There's one in place. I suggest you take a look at your bank statements. You are paying for it in monthly instalments.'

Bishop shook his head, looking stunned.

And this time, from the movement of his eyes, Grace saw that he was not lying.

'I don't think I should say any more,' Bishop said. 'Not without my solicitor present.'

'That's probably a good idea, sir.'

68

A few minutes later Roy Grace stood with Glenn Branson outside the front of Sussex House, watching the tail lights of Bishop's dark red Bentley disappear around the right-hand bend, below them, past the massive warehouse of British Bookstores.

'So what do you think, old-timer?' Branson asked him.

'I think I need a drink.'

They drove down to the Black Lion pub at Patcham, went in and stood at the bar. Grace bought Glenn a pint of Guinness and ordered a large Glenfiddich on the rocks for himself, then they installed themselves in a booth.

'I can't figure this guy out,' Grace said. 'He's smart. There's something very cold about him. And I have a feeling that he does know Sophie Harrington.'

'His eyes?'

'You saw that?' Grace said, pleased at the way his protégé learned from him.

'He knows her.'

Grace drank a little whisky and suddenly craved a cigarette. Hell. One more year and smoking in pubs was going to be banned. Might as well take advantage. He went over to the machine and bought himself some Silk Cut. Ripping off the cellophane, he took out a cigarette and then went to get a light from the young female bartender. He inhaled deeply, loving every sweet second of the sensation as he drew the smoke in.

'You should quit. Those things don't do you any good.'

'Living doesn't do you any good,' he replied. 'It kills us all.'

Branson's face descended into gloom. 'Tell me about it. That bullet. Yeah? One inch to the right and it would have taken out my spine. I'd have been in a wheelchair for the rest of my life.' He shook his head, then drank a long gulp of his beer. 'I go through all that goddamn recovery, get home, and instead of finding a loving, nurturing wife, what do I get? Fucking shit!'

He leaned forward, cradling his face in his hands.

'I thought you just had to get her a horse,' Grace probed gently.

His friend did not respond.

'I don't know how much a horse costs to buy or keep, but you'll get compensation for your injury – quite a lot of money. More than enough, I would have thought, to buy a horse.'

The young barmaid who had given him the light was suddenly standing over them. 'Can I get you anything else? We're going to be closing up soon.'

Grace smiled at her. 'We're done, thanks.' He put an arm around Branson, feeling the soft suede of his bomber jacket.

'You know the irony?' the Detective Sergeant said. 'I told you, didn't I? I joined the force so my kids could be proud of me. Now I'm not even allowed to kiss them goodnight.'

Grace drank some more whisky and took another drag on his cigarette. It still tasted good, but not so good as before. 'Matey, you know the law. She can't stop you.'

He stared at the long wooden counter of the bar. At the upturned bottles and the optics beyond; at the empty bar stools and the empty tables around them. It had been a long day. Hard to believe he'd had lunch beside a lake in Munich.

'You,' Glenn Branson said suddenly. 'I didn't even ask you how it went. What happened?'

'Nothing,' he replied. 'Nothing.'

'Don't do what I did, Roy. Don't screw it all up. You've got a good thing going with Cleo. Cherish her. She's well lovely.'

*

Cleo was smashed when he got to the wrought-iron gates of her townhouse, shortly after half past eleven.

'Need your help,' she said through the intercom. 'God, I'm pisshed!'

The electronic lock opened with a sharp click, like a pistol being cocked. Grace went in, walking across stone slabs that were lit by a faint neon glow, towards Cleo's house. As he neared the front door, it opened. Cleo was standing there, beside what looked like the upturned shell of a giant, mutant blue crab.

She turned her cheek towards him as he attempted to kiss her on the lips, signalling through her inebriated state that she was still angry with him. 'The hard top for my MG. Some bastard slashed my roof open today. Can you help me put the hard top on?'

He could not remember ever lifting anything so heavy in his life. 'You OK?' he asked, grunting repeatedly as they staggered out into the street with it. He was disappointed by her frostiness.

'Much lighter than a body!' she replied breezily, then nearly fell over sideways.

They walked down the dark, silent street, past his Alfa Romeo, until they reached her MG, then they put it down. Grace looked at the clean slit in her roof.

'Bastards!' he said. 'Where was it done?'

'At the mortuary this afternoon. No point getting it repaired. It will just happen again.'

With an unsteady hand she fumbled with the key fob, then unlocked the car, climbed inside and lowered the soft roof. Struggling, sweating, cursing, they proceeded to manoeuvre the hard top into place.

All their concentration was taken up by the task in hand. Neither Roy Grace nor Cleo Morey noticed the figure standing in the shadow of an alley a short distance away, watching them with a smile of satisfaction.

69

Roy Grace began his Monday morning with a seven-thirty meeting in his office with DI Kim Murphy, DCI Brendan Duigan, Crime Scene Manager Joe Tindall and Glenn Branson. He was heaping as much responsibility on his friend as possible to take his mind off his domestic problems. Eleanor, his Management Support Assistant, was also there. Duigan agreed to schedule his morning and evening briefing meetings half an hour apart from Murphy's, so that Grace could preside over both, but for this morning they would combine them, to give both teams a complete overview of events to date.

Shortly before eight Grace went to get his second coffee of the morning. Returning to his office, he downloaded from his mobile phone the three photographs he had taken yesterday of the blonde German woman in the Englischer Garten, then typed an email to Dick Pope, who would be back at work today.

> *Dick, is this the woman you and Leslie saw*
> *in the Englischer Garten last week? Roy*

Then he checked the photographs. A full-on shot of her face and one of each profile. All in reasonable close-up. He sent them.

Next he fired off a quick email, with the same photographs, to Marcel Kullen. He had already shown them to him on the tiny screen of his mobile, but they would be clearer on his computer screen. Then he opened the incident serials and ran his eye down the overnight incidents log. Sunday nights tended to be quiet, apart from the roads in summer, with day trippers tired, and some boozed up, heading home. There were a number of minor RTAs, some street crimes, car crimes, a domestic in Patcham, a hit-and-run involving an elderly pedestrian, a break-in at an angling club and a fight in a restaurant among the dozens of incidents he scanned. Nothing immediately apparent that was relevant to Katie Bishop's death or Sophie Harrington's.

He sent another couple of emails, then collected the agenda for the eight-thirty briefing from Eleanor, and headed along the corridors to the conference room, where the combined team numbered over forty.

He began by welcoming everybody and explaining, particularly for the benefit of the new team, the structure of the investigation. He told them that he would be the officer in overall command of both investigations, with DI Kim Murphy the SIO for the investigation into the murder of Katie Bishop and DCI Duigan the SIO for the investigation into the murder of Sophie Harrington. Next he informed them that he would be showing the video taken at the Sophie Harrington murder scene, and then run through both investigations to bring everybody up to date.

When the video finished there was a brief silence, broken by Norman Potting, sitting with his elbows on the table, hunched up in his crumpled, food-stained cream linen suit.

'Seems like we're hunting a killer with smelly feet, if you ask me,' he growled, then looked around with a broad smirk on his face. The only person to smile back was Alfonso Zafferone. But there was no humour in the young detective's expression; it was more a smile of pity.

'Thank you, Norman,' Grace said coldly, annoyed with Potting for being so crass and insensitive. He did not want to digress from the typed agenda in front of him, which he had carefully prepared with Kim Murphy and his MSA earlier that morning, but he decided to seize the moment to put Norman back in his box. 'Perhaps you'd like to start this morning off for us with your evidence to back up this assertion.'

Potting straightened the clumsy knot of his Sussex County Cricket Club tie, which was as frayed as his hair, looking rather pleased with himself. 'Well, I think I've got a bit of a result in another direction.' He continued working on his knot.

'We're all ears,' Grace said.

'Katie Bishop was having an affair!' the veteran DS announced triumphantly.

And now forty pairs of eyes were on him in sharp focus.

'As some of you may recall,' Potting continued, glancing down at his notepad for reference, 'I had ascertained that a BMW convertible, registered to Mrs Bishop, was recorded by CCTV camera. It was at a BP petrol station on the A27, two miles west of Lewes, just before midnight last Thursday – the night she was killed,' he reminded them all needlessly. 'And I subsequently identified Mrs Bishop on the video footage at the petrol station. Then, in an examination of said vehicle at the Bishops' residence on Friday afternoon, I found a pay-and-display parking ticket, with a time of –' he checked his notes again – 'five eleven on Thursday afternoon, issued from a machine in Southover Road, Lewes.'

He paused and fiddled with his knot again. Grace glanced at the window. Outside the sky was blue and clear. Summer was back again. As if yesterday afternoon had been a small glitch in the weather, a wrong lever pulled by someone.

'I called in a favour owed to me by John Smith in the Telecoms Unit here at the CID HQ,' Potting continued. 'Got him to come in yesterday to examine the mobile phone belonging to Mrs Bishop. As a result of a Lewes number found stored in the mobile phone's speed-dial memory, I was able to identify a Mr Barty Chancellor – a portrait painter of some international standing, I understand – at an address in Southover Street, Lewes.'

Potting now looked even more pleased with himself. 'I went to question Mr Chancellor at four yesterday afternoon, at his premises, where he admitted that he and Mrs Bishop had been seeing each other for about a year. He was in a state of considerable distress, having read the news of Mrs Bishop's death, and seemed quite pleased – if that's the right way to say it – to have someone to pour his heart out to.'

'What did you learn from him?' Grace asked.

'Seems like the Bishops weren't quite the happy golden couple that the little local world thought they were. According to Chancellor, Bishop was obsessed with work and was never around. He didn't seem to understand that his wife was lonely.'

'Excuse me,' Bella Moy interrupted angrily. 'Norman, that's just so typical of a man trying to justify an affair. *Oh, her husband doesn't bloody understand her, that's why she fell into my arms, that's the truth, gov!*' The young DS looked around at the team, her face flushed. 'Honestly, how many times has everyone heard that? It's not *always* the husband who's at fault – there are plenty of women who are real slappers out there!'

'Tell me about it,' Potting said. 'I married three of them.'

'Did Bishop know?' Glenn Branson interrupted.

'Chancellor doesn't think so,' the DS replied.

Grace wrote the name down on his pad thoughtfully. 'So now we have another potential suspect.'

'He's quite a good painter. Mind you, he should be,' Potting said. 'Charges between five to twenty grand for a painting. Could buy a bloody car for that! Or a house, where my new missus comes from.'

'Is that significant, Norman?' Grace queried.

'These arty types, some of 'em can be a bit kinky, that's what I'm thinking. Read about Picasso still shagging women in his nineties.'

'Oh, he's a painter, so he must be a pervert. Is that what you are saying?' Bella Moy was in a seriously bad mood with Potting today. 'So he must have stuck a gas mask on Katie Bishop's head and strangled her, right? So why don't we stop wasting time – let's go along to the Crown Prosecution Service with our evidence, get an arrest warrant for Chancellor and have done with it?'

'Bella!' Grace said firmly. 'Thank you, that's enough!'

She glared at Potting, her face flushed. Grace wondered for a moment whether her hostility towards the Detective Sergeant had something deep-rooted behind it. Had they ever been an item? He doubted it, looking at them now, contrasting the plug-ugly old warhorse with the fresh-faced, attractive thirty-five-year-old brunette divorcee. No way.

'So did you discover anything in his premises to indicate he might be kinky?' Kim Murphy asked. 'Any gas masks hanging on the wall? Or in any of his paintings?'

'He had a few raunchy nudes on the walls, I'm telling you! Not the kind of paintings you'd want your elderly mum to see. And there's something very interesting I got out of him: he was with Mrs Bishop on Thursday night. Until nearly midnight.'

'We need to bring him in for questioning, ASAP,' Grace said.

'He's coming in at ten.'

'Good. Who will be with you?'

'DC Nicholl.'

Grace looked at Nick Nicholl. The young, fledgling father was stifling a yawn, barely keeping his eyes open. Clearly he'd had another bad night with his baby. He didn't want a sleep-deprived zombie interviewing such an important witness. He looked at Zafferone. Much though he disliked the cocky youngster, Zafferone would be perfect, he thought. His arrogance would rub anyone up the wrong way, and particularly a sensitive artist. And often the best way to get something out of a witness was to wind them up, so they lost their rag.

'No,' Grace said. 'DC Zafferone will interview him with you.' He looked down at his typed agenda, then up at shaven-headed middle-aged Joe Tindall, with his narrow strip of beard and blue-tinted glasses. 'OK,' he said formally. 'We will now have a report from the Crime Scene Manager.'

'First off,' Joe Tindall informed them, 'I'm expecting DNA results back this afternoon from Huntington from semen found in the vagina of Mrs Bishop.' He looked down at his notes. 'We are sending several exhibits from Ms Harrington's flat off to the lab this morning. These include a small piece of flesh removed from her right big toenail, and a gas mask found on the victim's face, which appears similar in type and manufacture to the one present at Mrs Bishop's house.'

He took a swig of bottled water. 'We are also sending

clothing fibres recovered from Ms Harrington's flat and blood samples. We believe the blood samples may be significant. We found blood smeared on the wall just above the bed where the victim was found, which is not consistent with the injuries found on the victim. So it may be the perp's blood.' He looked down at his notes. 'All fingerprints found at both scenes to date have been eliminated from our inquiries, which would indicate that the killer of both women was either wearing gloves – the most likely scenario – or wiped them. However, using chemical enhancement we have found footprints on the tiled bathroom floor that are clearly not the victim's. We will be analysing these for shoe type.'

Next, tough, sharp-eyed DC Pamela Buckley reported on a check she had run on all accident and emergency departments in hospitals in the area – the Sussex County, Eastbourne, Worthing and Haywards Heath – for people coming in with hand injuries.

'We're up against patient confidentiality,' she said with more than a hint of sarcasm in her voice. Then she read out the list of hand-injury types that had been seen at each hospital – with no names attached – and treated. None were consistent with those Grace had seen on Brian Bishop's hand, and none of the staff she had interviewed identified Bishop from his photograph.

Then DS Guy Batchelor gave his report. The tall, burly officer spoke in his usual businesslike way. 'Well,' he said, 'I think I have something rather interesting.' He gave Norman Potting an appreciative nod. 'Norman did a good job getting his mate John Smith in the Telecoms Unit to give up his Sunday. John stayed on to look at the mobile phone taken from Sophie Harrington's flat.'

He paused to take a sip of coffee from a large Starbucks

Styrofoam cup, then looked up with a smile. 'The last
number that Ms Harrington dialled, according to information retrieved from her phone, was –' he paused to read
from his notes – '07985 541298. So I checked that number
out.' He looked Roy Grace squarely and triumphantly in the
eye. 'It's Brian Bishop's mobile phone.'

70

*They say the recipe for success in life is 1 percent
inspiration and 99 percent perspiration. The bit they
don't tell you when you start a new business is the cash
you need to find. You need the lawyer and the
accountants to set up the company, the Patent Agent to
file for your copyright on your software, the design
company to create your logo and your corporate image,
and the packaging for your product, which you need to
have if you intend to be a global player, and of course
your website. You need an office, furniture, phones, fax
and a secretary. None of this stuff comes cheap. Twelve
months on from my Big Idea, I was over one hundred
thousand pounds out of pocket and not yet ready to
rock and roll. But close.*

*I had taken out a second mortgage on my flat, sold
everything I could sell, and, on top of that, a bank
manager who believed in me had given me a bigger
loan than he really should have. I had, as the
Americans say, bet the ranch.*

*I was reading all the financial pages of the
newspapers and subscribed to the trade magazines of
every business I intended to target. So imagine my
dismay one day when I opened a supplement of the
Financial Times to see an article written by a journalist
called Gautam Malkani on my business.*

*It was a complete carbon copy of everything I had
thought of doing. And it was already up and running.*

And my photograph was staring out at me from the pink page.

Except the name of the company was different from the name I had chosen.

And the name beneath my photograph was the name of someone else, a man I had never heard of.

71

Marija Djapic pressed the entry code and let herself in through the wrought-iron gates. It was just gone nine a.m. and she was a little later than usual, thanks to her daughter. She noticed the man immediately, standing outside the front door of number 5, looking as if he had been waiting for a while.

She strode across the cobbled courtyard, puffing from the exertion of her long walk here, made harder by the weight of the bag which she lugged everywhere, containing her work clothes, shoes, lunch and a drink. And she was perspiring heavily from the heat. She was also in a foul mood after yet another row with Danica. Who was this man? What did he want from her? Was he from another of the collection agencies she owed money to on a credit card?

The thirty-five-year-old Serbian woman walked everywhere, to save money on bus fares. She could reach all of her employers on foot in less than an hour from the council flat in Whitehawk she shared with her bolshy, fourteen-year-old prima donna. Almost every hard, sweated penny that she earned went on buying Danica the best she could afford in their new life here in England. She tried to buy decent food, made sure Danica had the clothes she wanted – well, some of them, at any rate. As well as all the stuff she needed to keep up with her friends: a computer, a mobile phone and, for her birthday two weeks ago, an iPod.

And her reward was for the girl to arrive home at ten

past four this morning! Make-up all smeared, pupils dilated.

And now this smarmy-looking man was standing by the doorstep, doubtless waiting to snatch the cash that would have been left for her on the kitchen table out of her hand. She looked at him warily as she rummaged in her bag for the keys to Cleo Morey's house. He was tall, with slicked-back brown hair, handsome in a way that reminded her of a movie actor whose name she couldn't place and dressed respectably enough in a white shirt and plain tie, blue trousers, black shoes and a dark blue cotton jacket that looked as if it was a uniform of some sort, with a badge sewn on the breast pocket.

Marija glanced warily around for signs of life elsewhere in the courtyard and, to her relief, saw a young woman in Lycra shorts and top pulling a mountain bike out of a front door a couple of houses down. Emboldened, she put the key in the lock and turned it.

The man stepped forward, holding out an identity card bearing his photograph. It was laminated and hung from his neck on two thin white cords. 'Excuse me,' he said very politely. 'Gas Board – would it be convenient to read the meter?' Then she noticed the small metal machine with a keypad on it which he was holding.

'You made appointment with Miss Morey?' she said sharply and a tad aggressively.

'No. I'm doing this area today. It won't take me more than a couple of minutes, if you could show me where the meters are.'

She hesitated. He looked normal enough to her and he had the identification. Several times in her work in different houses people had turned up to read meters. It was normal. So long as they had the identification. But she was on strict instructions to let no one into the house. Maybe she should phone Miss Morey and ask. But to bother her at her important work because a man had come to read the meter? 'I see identification again, please.'

He showed her the card again. Her English wasn't that good, but she could see his face and the word SEEBOARD. It looked important. Official. 'OK,' she said.

Even so, she was wary of him, stepping in ahead of him, leaving the front door open. Then she marched straight through the open downstairs living area, up a couple of steps into the kitchen, not letting him out of her sight for a moment.

Her money was sitting on the square pine table, weighted down by a ceramic bowl of fruit. Next to it was a handwritten note from Cleo, with her instructions on what housework to do this morning. Marija beadily picked up the two twenty-pound notes and pushed them into her purse. Then she pointed up at a wall panel to the left of the huge silver fridge. 'I think meter's there,' she said, noticing for the first time the bandage on his hand.

'Sharp edges!' the man said, seeing her eyes widen a fraction. 'You wouldn't believe the places some people have their meters! Makes my life quite hazardous.' He smiled. 'Do you have something I can stand on, to reach?'

She pulled a wooden kitchen chair over for him and he thanked her, kneeling down to remove his shoes, his eyes not on the meter at all, but on the cleaning lady's set of keys lying on the table. He was thinking hard about how to distract her and get her out of the room, when her mobile phone suddenly rang.

He watched as the woman pulled a little green Nokia out of her handbag, glanced at the display, then, visibly shaking, said, 'Yes, Danica?' followed by furious gabbling in a language he did not recognize. After some moments the row this woman was having with this person, Danica, seemed to intensify. She paced up and down the kitchen, talking increasingly loudly, then stomped out and stood at the top of the stairs to the living area, where the conversation turned into what sounded like a full-scale yelling match.

She had her eyes off him for less than sixty seconds, but that was more than enough for his hand to shoot out, grab the key, press it into the soft wax in the tin concealed in the palm of his hand and return it to the table.

72

Malling House, the headquarters of Sussex Police, was a fifteen-minute drive from Grace's office. It was a ragbag complex of buildings, situated on the outskirts of Lewes, the county town of East Sussex, from where the administration and key management for the five thousand officers and employees of the force were handled.

Two buildings dominated. One, a three-storey, futuristic glass and brick structure, contained the Control Centre, the Crime Recording and Investigation Bureau, the Call Handling Centre and the Force Command Centre, as well as most of the computing hardware for the force. The other was an imposing red-brick, Queen Anne mansion, once a stately home and now a Grade-1 listed building, kept in fine condition, which had given its name to the HQ. Although next to the ramshackle sprawl of car parks, single-storey pre-fabs, modern low-rise structures and one dark, windowless building, complete with a tall smokestack that always reminded Grace of a Yorkshire textile mill, it stood proudly aloof. Inside were housed the offices of the Chief Constable, the Deputy Chief Constable and the Assistant Chief Constables, of which Alison Vosper was one, together with their support staff, as well as a number of other senior officers working either temporarily or permanently out of here.

Vosper's office was on the ground floor at the front of the building. It had a view through a large sash window out on to a gravel driveway and a circular lawn beyond. As he strode towards her desk, Grace caught a glimpse of a thrush standing on the grass, washing itself under the throw of a sprinkler.

All the reception rooms contained handsome wood-work, fine stucco and imposing ceilings, which had been carefully restored after a fire nearly destroyed the building some years back. The house had originally been built both to provide gracious living and to impress upon visitors the wealth of its owner.

It must be nice to work in a room like this, he thought, in this calm oasis, away from the cramped, grotty spaces of Sussex House. Sometimes he thought he might enjoy the responsibility, and the power trip that came with it, but then he would wonder whether he could cope with the politics. Especially that damn insidious political correct-ness that the brass had to kow-tow to a lot more than the ranks. However, at this moment it wasn't so much promo-tion that was on his mind as avoiding demotion.

Some years ago, because of her mood swings, a wit had nicknamed Alison Vosper 'no. 27', after a sweet-and-sour dish on the local Chinese takeaway menu, and it had stuck. The ACC could be your new best friend one day and your worst enemy the next. It seemed a long time since she had been anything but the latter to Grace, as he stood in front of her desk, used to the fact that she rarely invited visitors to sit down, in order to keep meetings short and to the point.

So it surprised him, in a way that created a rather ominous sensation in the pit of his stomach, that, without looking up from a document bound with green string, she waved him to one of the two upright armchairs by the large expanse of her glossy rosewood desk.

In her early forties, with blonde hair cut in a short,

severe style that framed a hard but not unattractive face, she was power-dressed in a crisp white blouse buttoned up at the neck, despite the heat, and a tailored navy blue two-piece, with a small diamanté brooch pinned to one lapel.

As always, the morning's national newspapers were fanned out on her desk. Grace could smell her usual, slightly acidic perfume; it was tinged with the much sweeter smell of freshly mown grass wafting in on a welcome breeze through the opened window.

He couldn't help it. Every time he came into this office his confidence ebbed away, as it used to when, as a child, he was summoned to the headmaster's study. And the fact that she continued to ignore him, still reading, made him more nervous with each passing second. He listened to the *swish . . . swish . . . swish* of the sprinkler outside. Then two rings of a mobile phone, faint, in another room.

Munich was going to be the first point of Alison Vosper's attack, and he had his – admittedly somewhat lame – defence ready. But when she finally looked up at him, while not exactly beaming with joy, she gave him a pleasant smile.

'Apologies, Roy,' she said. 'Been reading this bloody EU directive on standardization of the treatment of asylum seekers who commit crimes. Didn't want to lose my thread. What bloody rubbish this is!' she went on. 'I can't believe how much taxpayers' money – yours and mine – is wasted on stuff like this.'

'Absolutely!' Grace said, agreeing perhaps a little too earnestly, waiting warily for her expression to change and whatever nuke she had ready to land on him.

She raised a fist in the air. 'You wouldn't believe how much of my time I have to waste reading things like this – when I should be getting on with my job of helping to police

Sussex. I'm starting to really hate the EU. Here's an interesting statistic: you know the Gettysburg Address?'

'Yes. What's more, I can probably quote it completely – I learned it at school for a project.'

She barely took that in. Instead, she splayed her hands out on her desk, as if to anchor herself. 'When Abraham Lincoln gave that speech, it led to the most sacrosanct principles in the world, *freedom* and *democracy*, becoming enshrined in the American Constitution.' She paused and drank some water. 'That speech was less than three hundred words long. Do you know how long the European directive on the size of cabbages is?'

'I don't.'

'Sixty-five thousand words long!'

Grace grinned, shaking his head.

She smiled back, more warmly than he could remember her ever smiling before. He wondered if she was on some kind of happy pill. Then, abruptly changing the subject, but still good-humoured, she asked, 'So how was Munich?'

Wary suddenly, his guard up again, Roy said, 'Well, actually it was a bit of a Norwegian lobster.'

She frowned. 'I beg your pardon? Did you say *Norwegian lobster*?'

'It's an expression I use for when something is less than you've been expecting.'

She cocked her head, still frowning. 'I'm lost.'

'A couple of years ago I was in a restaurant in a pub at Lancing. There was something on the menu described as *Norwegian lobster*. I ordered it, looking forward to a nice bit of lobster. But what I in fact got were three small prawns, about the size of my little finger.'

'You complained?'

'Yes, and I was then confronted by Sussex's own Basil Fawlty, who produced an ancient cookbook which said these particular prawns were sometimes called *Norwegian lobsters*.'

'Sounds like a good restaurant to avoid.'

'Unless you feel in particular need of going out for a disappointment.'

'Quite.' She smiled again, a little less warmly, as if realizing that she and this particular man would always be on different planets. 'So, I take it you didn't find your wife in Munich?'

Wondering how she knew that this had been his mission, he shook his head.

'How long has it been now?'

'Just over nine years.'

She seemed to be about to say something further, but instead she refilled her glass. 'Do you want any water? Tea? Coffee?'

'I'm OK, thanks. How was your weekend?' he said, anxious to move the subject on from Sandy, and still wondering why he had been summoned here.

'I was at an ACC's conference in Basingstoke on the subject of improving police performance – or rather, public perceptions of police performance. Another of Tony Blair's cosmetic tinkerings. A bunch of slick marketing gurus telling us how to leverage our results and how to strategize and drive that process.' She shrugged.

'What's the secret?' Grace asked.

'To go after the low-hanging fruit first.' Her mobile phone rang. She glanced at the display and abruptly terminated the call. 'Anyhow, for the moment murders are still a priority. What progress? And by the way, I'm going to come to this morning's press conference.'

'You are?' Grace was pleasantly surprised, and relieved that he wasn't going to be carrying it all on his shoulders. He had a feeling that with the news of the second murder the conference, which was scheduled for eleven, was going to be a tough one.

'Can you bring me up to speed on where we're at?' she asked. 'Any bones we can throw to them? Do we have any suspects? And what about the body found yesterday? Do you have enough staff on your team, Roy? Are there any extra resources you need?'

The relief he felt now that she appeared to be letting Munich drop was almost palpable. In brief summary, he brought the Assistant Chief Constable up to speed. After telling her that Brian Bishop's Bentley had been picked up by a camera heading to Brighton at eleven forty-seven on Thursday night, and then giving her details about the life insurance policy, she raised a hand, stopping him.

'You've got enough right there, Roy.'

'Two people have provided him with pretty strong alibis. His financial adviser, with whom he had dinner, was interviewed and can distinctly remember the timeframe – which is not helpful to us. If he is telling the truth, Bishop could not have reached that camera at eleven forty-seven. And the second person is the concierge at his London flat, a Mr Oliver Dowler, who has been interviewed and confirms that he was up early that morning and helped Bishop load his golfing equipment into his car at around half-past six.'

Vosper was silent for some moments, thinking, absorbing this. Then she said, 'That's the elephant in the room.'

Grace smiled, grimly.

Suddenly her phone rang. Raising an apologetic finger, she answered it.

Moments later his mobile phone rang. The words *private number* on the display indicated it was probably work. He stood up and stepped away from the desk to answer it. 'Roy Grace.'

It was DS Guy Batchelor. 'I think we have something significant, Roy. I've just had a call from a Sandra Taylor, an analyst at the Force Intelligence Unit, who's been allocated to this case. Did you know that Brian Bishop has a criminal record?'

73

Paul Packer sat at a table outside the Ha! Ha! bar in Pavilion Parade, in front of the entrance gates to Brighton's Royal Pavilion, sipping a latte and watching the world go by. He had a smile on his face. At ten thirty on a hot, sunny August Monday morning, there were a lot worse places to be in the world than here, he reckoned. And this sure as hell beat working! Which was a private joke to himself, because, of course, he was working.

Not that it looked that way to the waitress, or to the people passing by. All they saw was a figure in his twenties, short and burly, with a shaven head and goatee beard, scruffily dressed in a shapeless grey T-shirt, with an exercise book open in front of him, in which he appeared to be jotting down notes, just one of the scores of students hanging out in cafés all over the city.

He missed nothing. He clocked every face that passed by in either direction.

People in business clothes, some carrying bags or briefcases, rushing around to meetings, or in some instances just very late for work. He observed the tourists; one elderly couple were walking around in circles, both trying to read a map, the man pointing in one direction, the woman shaking her head and pointing in the other. He saw a middle-aged couple, Dutch he guessed, striding determinedly in ridiculous clothes and heavy backpacks, as if they were on some kind of safari and needed to carry their own supplies. Then he watched two kids in baggy clothes practising a parcour jump over a free-standing information sign.

Several homeless down-and-outs, all of whom he knew by sight, had passed by in the last half-hour. Probably going to spend the day on the Pavilion lawns before moving to their next doorstep or archway, lugging their worldly goods in shopping bags, or plastic sheeting, or in supermarket trolleys, leaving the sour reek of damp sacks in their wake. And steadily Brighton's lowlife – the dealers, the pushers, the runners and the users – were all starting to surface. The junkies, their last fixes all but worn off, were starting out on their relentless daily grind to find the money, by whatever means they could, for their next hits.

In the lulls between passers-by, Detective Constable Packer did make real notes in his exercise book. He had ambitions to be a writer, and at this moment he was working on a film script about a group of aliens whose navigation system had broken down and they landed on Earth, just outside Brighton, in search of help. After just a few days they were desperate to leave. Two of them had been mugged, their spacecraft had been vandalized and then impounded, because they had no money to pay for the charge of towing it off the main road, where they had parked it, and they didn't like the food. Furthermore, they couldn't get the help they wanted without filling in an online form, which required a postcode and a credit card number, and they had neither. Sometimes Packer wondered whether his job made him too cynical.

Then he was jolted back to reality. Out of the corner of his eye he saw a familiar, round-shouldered figure slouching along. And his already pleasant morning suddenly became even more pleasant when the figure walked straight past without clocking him.

Paul stared at the emaciated, gaunt-faced young man in a ragged hoodie, tracksuit bottoms and filthy trainers with an even measure of loathing, disgust and sympathy. The young man's ginger hair was shaven, like his own, in a number one, and he, as usual, had a thin, vertical strip of beard running from the centre of his lower lip to his chin. Paul watched him walk slowly through a photograph being taken by a young man of his girlfriend or wife, oblivious to just about everything around him. He weaved through a gaggle of tourists being shepherded by a tour guide, and now the Detective Constable knew exactly where he was heading.

To the wall across the square from them, where there were cashpoint machines, side by side. And sure enough, the young man sat down between them. It was a popular spot for begging. And already he had a target, a young woman who was entering her bank card.

Paul Packer seized the moment, strode across and stood squarely in front of the man just as he heard him croak feebly, 'Can you spare us any change, love?'

By way of a greeting, Packer held out the shortened stump of his right hand index finger. 'Hi, Skunk,' he said. 'Remember me?'

Skunk looked up at him warily. The woman was digging in her purse. Packer turned to her. 'I'm a police officer. Begging is illegal. Anyhow, this fellow knows better ways to get a pound of flesh, don't you?' he said, turning back to Skunk, waggling his bitten-off index stump, and making a series of rapid bites, clacking his teeth noisily, mocking his former assailant.

'Don't know what you mean,' Skunk said.

'Memory need a jog, does it? Would a day in a custody cell help? Be difficult to get your drugs there, wouldn't it?'

'Fuck off. Leave me alone.'

Packer looked at the young woman, who did not seem to know where to put herself. She grabbed her cash and her card and fled.

'I'm clean,' Skunk suddenly added sullenly.

'I know that, mate. I don't want to bust you. Just wondered if you'd like to give me some information.'

'What's in it for me?'

'What do you know about Barry Spiker?'

'Never heard of him.'

A fire engine screamed down North Street, siren louder than a ship's foghorn, and Packer waited for it to pass by. 'Yes, you have. You do jobs for him.'

'Never heard of him.'

'So that Audi convertible you were swanning around the seafront in on Friday night – that was your car, was it?'

'Dunno what you mean.'

'I think you do. There was a car following you, an unmarked police car. I was in it. You drive pretty well,' he said, with grudging admiration.

'Na. Dunno what you mean.'

Packer put his stump of an index finger right up close to Skunk's face. 'I've got a long memory, Skunk. Understand.'

'I did time for that.'

'And then you came out, but my finger didn't come back, and I'm still pretty pissed off, so I'm going to make a deal with you. Either I'm going to be in your face for the rest of your shitty little life, or you help me.'

After some moments' silence, Skunk said, 'What kind of help?'

'Information. Just a phone call, that's all. Just a phone call from you next time Spiker gives you a job.'

'And then?'

Packer explained what he wanted Skunk to do. When he had finished he said, 'Then we'll call it quits.'

'And I get arrested, right?'

'No, we don't touch you. And I'm out of your face. Do we have a deal?'

'Is there any cash in it for me?'

Packer looked down at him. He was such a pathetic figure, the DC suddenly felt sorry for him. 'We'll bung you something afterwards, as a reward. Deal?'

Skunk gave a limp, indifferent shrug.

'I'll take that as a yes.'

74

Saturday's press conference had been bad enough, but this one now was even worse. Around fifty people were crammed into the briefing room and a lot more than on Saturday were packed along the corridor. A capacity house, Grace thought grimly. The only good thing was that he had heavyweight support here this morning.

Flanking him on either side, so they formed a line of three in front of the concave board carrying the Sussex Police website address and the Crimestoppers legend, were Assistant Chief Constable Alison Vosper, who had changed clothes since he left her office and was now wearing her spotless, freshly pressed uniform, and the Brighton Police Divisional Commander, Chief Superintendent Ken Brickhill, a blunt, plain-speaking policeman of the old school, in his equally immaculate uniform. A tough individual, Brickhill had no time for the politically correct lobby, and would happily hang most of the villains in Brighton and Hove, given half a chance. Unsurprisingly, he was respected by just about everyone who had ever served under him.

Some of the windows in here actually opened, but even so, with sunlight beating through the blinds, it was stiflingly hot. Someone made a quip about the Black Hole of Calcutta, while the press officer, flamboyantly but slightly shabbily dressed Dennis Ponds, squeezed his way around the table to join the trio, muttering an excuse for being late.

Ponds started by leaning too closely to the microphone,

so that his first words were almost lost in squawk-back. 'Good morning,' he said, starting again, his rather unctuous, ingratiating voice clearer this time. 'This press conference will start with Detective Superintendent Grace running through the investigations into the deaths of Mrs Katherine Bishop and Miss Sophie Harrington. Then Assistant Chief Constable Vosper and Chief Superintendent Brickhill, Divisional Commander of Brighton Police, will talk about the community and the public at large.' He handed over to Grace with a theatrical sweep of his arm and stepped away.

Flashbulbs strobed for some moments, as Roy Grace outlined the details of the investigation so far. He of course didn't tell them everything, but kept to the facts on times and events, confirming a lot of information that they already knew. He appealed in respect of both investigations for witnesses to come forward, particularly anyone who knew either woman and had seen her in the last few days. He stated, also, that he was keen to talk to anyone who had seen anything suspicious near either murder scene.

Having concluded all he wanted to say about the murders at this stage, Grace then asked those present if they had any questions.

A female voice, someone at the back whom Grace could not see, shouted out, 'We understand there is a serial killer at large. Can you reassure us that the people of Brighton and Hove are safe, Detective Superintendent?'

Grace had the usual problem of what to do with his hands, well aware that his body language was as important as what he said. Resisting the temptation to clasp his hands in front him, he dropped them firmly to his sides, and leaned into the microphone. 'At present there is nothing to indicate that this is a serial killer. But people should take care and be a little more vigilant than usual.'

'How can you say this isn't a serial killer, when two women have been murdered within twenty-four hours of each other?' demanded a squeaky-voiced old stringer for a bunch of provincial papers. 'Detective Superintendent Grace, can you give an assurance to young women living in Brighton that they are safe?'

A bead of perspiration dropped, stinging, into Grace's right eye. 'I think it best now that my colleagues, who are here to talk about community issues, respond to that,' he said, looking first at Alison Vosper and then at Ken Brickhill.

They nodded and the Chief Superintendent then said, in his no-nonsense voice, 'No one can ever give a 100 per-cent guarantee like that in a modern city. But police and local community leaders are doing everything they can, with additional resources, to catch the killer – or killers.'

'So it might be one person responsible for both killings?' the reporter persisted.

Evasively, Brickhill replied, 'If anyone has concerns they should contact the police. Police patrols are going to be increased. Anyone who sees anything suspicious should contact us. We don't want the public to panic. A lot of resources have been allocated to the investigation and we are doing everything to ensure the citizens of Brighton and Hove are safe.'

Then Kevin Spinella, who was standing a short distance away, at the front of the pack, said, 'Are you not going to admit, Detective Superintendent, that there is a crazed serial killer at large in Brighton somewhere?'

Grace responded calmly by reiterating the overview from both murder scenes. Then he continued by adding, 'We are still in the early stages of our investigation, but there would appear to be some similarities between the two cases, yes.'

'Detective Superintendent, do you have a prime suspect?' asked a young reporter from the *Mid-Sussex Times*.

'We are following a number of lines of inquiry and every day we are getting more information in. We would like to thank the public for all the information they have supplied so far. At this moment our teams are sifting through a large volume of phone calls and we are waiting for forensic results back from the labs. We have detectives working around the clock to identify who is responsible and bring them to justice.'

'So what you are saying,' Kevin Spinella said, in a loud, important voice, 'is that people in Brighton and Hove should lock themselves in their houses and not go out until the killer has been caught.'

'No,' Grace retorted, 'that's not what we are saying. The police have no idea who or where the killer of either woman is, and all women must be at risk. But that does not mean anyone needs to panic.' He turned to his chief. 'I'll let Assistant Chief Constable Vosper respond to that in more detail.'

If looks could kill, Vosper's smile would have sliced Grace open and then disembowelled him.

A solidly built earth mother standing near the back called out loudly, 'Assistant Chief Constable, will you be allowing Detective Superintendent Grace to consult a medium?'

There was a titter of laughter. The woman had touched a raw nerve. Maintaining a poker face, Grace smiled inwardly, watching Alison Vosper's sudden discomfort and really quite enjoying it. He had been pilloried over a previous case, a few months back, when it had come out in court that he had taken a shoe, a key piece of evidence in a murder trial, to a medium. The press had had a field day. And so had Vosper – with him.

'It is not normal practice for the police to follow such a line of inquiry,' she replied sharply. 'That said, we listen to anyone who can provide us with information, and then assess how it may progress the investigation.'

'So you don't rule it out?' the reporter persisted.

'I think I've already given you my answer.' Then she looked around the room. 'Any more questions?'

*

At the end of the conference, as Grace was leaving, Alison Vosper collared him and they stepped into a vacant office.

'We've got the whole eyes of the city on us, Roy. If you are planning to go and see any of your psychics, please discuss it with me first.'

'I don't have any plans, not at this stage.'

'Good!' she said, with the gusto of someone praising a puppy for urinating in the right place. For a moment he thought she was going to pat him on the head and give him a biscuit.

75

Half an hour later, Grace stood in the cramped changing room at the mortuary, fumbling with the tapes on the green gown, then stepping into a pair of white gumboots. As he did so a very hung-over, gowned-up Cleo popped her head around the door and gave him a look he could not read.

'Sorry about last night!' she said. 'Didn't mean to pass out on you, honest!'

He smiled back. 'Do you always get that wrecked when you go out with your sister?'

'She's just been dumped by her dickhead boyfriend and wanted to get smashed. It seemed rude not to join her.'

'Quite. How are you feeling?'

'Only marginally better than Sophie Harrington looks. I had the roundabouts earlier!'

'Coca-Cola, full strength – the best thing,' he said.

'I've already drunk two cans.' She again gave him a look he could not read. 'I don't think I asked you how Germany went. Did you find your wife? Have a cosy reunion?'

'You did ask, about five times.'

She looked astonished. 'And you told me?'

'How about we have a meal tonight and I'll give you the full low down?'

She looked hard at him again and, for a sudden, panicky moment, he thought she was going to tell him to get lost. Then she gave him a thin smile – but with no warmth. 'Come over to me. I'll cook something very simple and non-alcoholic. Comfort food. I think we need to talk.'

'I'll come over as soon as I can after the evening briefing.' He took a step towards her and gave her a quick kiss.

At first she pulled away sharply. 'I'm very hurt and I'm very angry with you, Roy.'

'I like it when you are angry,' he said.

Suddenly she melted a little. 'Bastard,' she said and grinned.

He gave her another quick kiss, which turned into a longer kiss. Their gowns rustled as they held each other tighter, Grace keeping one eye on the door in case anyone came in.

Then Cleo broke away and looked down at herself, grinning again. 'We're not meant to be doing this. I'm still angry with you. Turns you on, this gear, does it?'

'Even more than black silk underwear!'

'Better get back in and do some work, Detective Superintendent. A centre-spread in the *Argus* that you got caught shagging in the mortuary changing room wouldn't be the best thing for your image.'

He followed her down the tiled corridor, his mind a maelstrom of thoughts, about Cleo, about Sandy and about work. The press had given them a rough ride this morning and he could understand where they were coming from. One murder of an attractive young woman could be an isolated incident, something personal. Two could put a city, or an entire county, into a state of panic. If the press got hold of the information on the gas mask there would be a feeding frenzy.

He hadn't released the information that Sophie Harrington had made a call to Brian Bishop, the prime suspect in Katie Bishop's murder. And that Brian Bishop, behind his veneer of respectability as a successful businessman, respected citizen of Brighton and Hove, golf club committee member and charity benefactor, whose equally outwardly respectable Rotarian wife had been having an affair, had a deeply unpleasant criminal record.

At the age of fifteen, according to the information on the PNC – the Police National Computer database – Bishop had been sentenced to two years in a young offenders' institute for raping a fourteen-year-old girl at his school. Then, at the age of twenty-one, he was given two years' probation for violently assaulting a woman, causing her grievous bodily harm.

It seemed that the deeper his team dug into Bishop's life, the stronger the evidence against the man was becoming. Earlier today Alison Vosper had talked about his alibi in London being the elephant in the room. But there was another elephant in the same room at this moment. And that was Bishop's vehement denial of any knowledge of the insurance policy taken out on his wife's life. Because he appeared to be telling the truth about that, and that was bothering Grace.

Still, it was equally clear that Brian Bishop was a sharp operator. Not many people achieved his level of financial success by being a nice guy, in Grace's view – something now borne out by the man's ugly, violent past. And he knew he shouldn't read too much into Bishop's ignorance – or feigned ignorance – of the life insurance policy.

The complexities were starting to hurt his brain. He wanted to go somewhere and sit in a quiet, dark corner and run through every element of the Bishop and Harrington cases. The SOCO team would be in the Bishops' house for a good few days yet, and Grace was glad about that. He wanted the man to be uncomfortable, out of his natural habitat. In a hotel room, like a caged animal, he would be insecure and therefore would respond better to questioning.

They were definitely stacking up material against Bishop, but it was too early to arrest the man. If they did that, they could only keep him inside for twenty-four hours – with an extension of a further twelve hours – without charging him. There wasn't enough hard evidence yet, and although the man's alibi wasn't watertight, there was enough room for doubt. Two independent witnesses to say he had been in London either side of the time of the murder, against one Automatic Number Plate Recognition camera, which said he hadn't. There had been far too many cases of villains using copied number plates – particularly these days, to avoid speeding fines from cameras; a clever brief could easily sow doubt in a jury's mind about whether this number plate was real or a fake.

He was also very interested in the artist that Katie Bishop had been seeing. At this point the man was a potential suspect, for sure.

Deep in thought, he entered the stark, bright glare of the post-mortem room. Sophie Harrington's body was obscured from his view, crowded by green-gowned figures peering intently, like students in a classroom, as Nadiuska De Sancha pointed out something.

In the room, in addition to the pathologist, Cleo and Darren, were DCI Duigan and the lean figure of the Coroner's Officer, Ronnie Pearson, a retired police officer in his early fifties.

Grace walked over to the pathologist's side, and experienced the same uncomfortable surprise he got every time he saw a cadaver in here or anywhere else. They always looked almost ethereal, the skin of Caucasians – except for burnt or badly decomposed victims – a ghostly alabaster colour. It was as if the process of death made them appear in black and white, while everything around them remained in colour.

Sophie Harrington had been turned over on to her stomach. Nadiuska was pointing her latex-gloved finger at dozens of tiny dark crimson holes on the dead woman's back. It was like a tattoo all the way down her torso, covering much of the skin.

'Can you all read what it spells out?' she asked.

As he looked closer, all Grace could see at first was an indecipherable pattern.

'I would say, from the neatness and consistency of the holes, that it has been done with something like a power drill,' the pathologist continued.

'While the victim was alive?' DCI Duigan asked. 'Or after she was dead?'

'I would say post-mortem,' Nadiuska responded, leaning over and peering closely at a section of the dead woman's back. 'These are deep holes and there's very little bleeding. Her heart wasn't pumping when they were made.'

Some small mercy for the poor woman, Grace thought. Then, like suddenly being able to read the hidden writing inside a visual puzzle, he could see the words clearly now.

BECAUSE YOU LOVE HER.

76

The grumpy cleaning woman left Cleo Morey's house just after twelve thirty. The Time Billionaire made a note of this, from behind the wheel of his Toyota Prius. It was good timing, just minutes before his parking voucher expired. As she stomped off up the hill, talking angrily into her mobile phone, he wondered if she had spent the whole of the last three and a half hours on the phone. He was sure Cleo Morey would be interested to know what she was getting for the money she paid this woman. Although of course that wasn't really his business.

He put the car in gear and, running silently on the electric motor, glided up past her, then threaded his way through the complex network of streets up to Queens Road, then down past the clock tower, and turned right along the seafront.

He drove across the Hove border, along past the King Alfred development, stopped at the lights at the bottom of Hove Street, then made a right turn a couple of streets further along, into Westbourne Villas, a wide terrace of large semi-detached Victorian houses. Then he made another right turn into a mews where there was a row of lock-ups. The ones he rented were at the end, numbers 11 and 12.

He parked outside number 11 and got out of his car. He then unlocked the garage door and hauled it up, went inside, switched on the light, then pulled the door back down hard. It closed with a loud, echoing clang. Then silence. Just the faintest whir from the two humidifiers.

Peace!

He breathed in the warm smells he loved in here: engine oil, old leather, old bodywork. This was his home. His *temple*! In this garage – and sometimes in the one next door, where he kept the covered trailer – he used up so many of those hours he had stashed away in the bank. Dozens of them at a time! Hundreds of them every month! Thousands of them every year!

He stared lovingly at the fitted dust cover, at the flowing contours of the car it was protecting, the gleaming moonstone-white 1962 3.8 Jaguar Mk II saloon, which took up so much of the floor space that he had to edge past it sideways.

The walls were hung with his tools, arranged in patterns, each item so spotless it might have been fresh out of its box, all in their correct places. His hammers formed one display. His ring spanners, his wrenches, his feeler gauges, his screwdrivers – each formed a separate artwork. On the shelves were laid out his tins and bottles of polish, wheel cleaner, chrome cleaner, window cleaner, leather polish, his sponges, chamois leathers, bottle brushes, pipe cleaners – all looking brand new.

'Hello, baby!' he whispered, caressing the top of the dust cover, running his hand over the curved hard roof he could feel beneath. 'You are beautiful. So, so beautiful.'

He edged along the side of the car, running his hand along the cover, feeling the windows, then the bonnet. He knew every wire, every panel, every nut and bolt, every inch of her steel, chromium, leather, glass, walnut and Bakelite. She was his baby. Seven years of painstaking reassembly from a wreck inhabited by rats and mice in a derelict farmyard barn. She was in better condition now than the day, well over forty years ago, she had left the factory. Ten

Concours d'Elégance rosettes for First Place pinned to the garage wall attested to that. They had come from all over the country. He had won dozens of second-, third- and even fourth-place rosettes as well. But they always went straight into the bin.

Later today, he reminded himself, he needed to work on the insides of the bumpers, which were invisible to the normal observer. Judges looked behind them sometimes and caught you out, and there was an important Jaguar Drivers' Club concourse coming up at the end of this month.

But at this moment he had something more important on his mind. It was a key-cutting machine, complete with a wide set of blanks – for any lock, the advertisement on the internet had said – that had been sitting in the brown packaging marked FRAGILE on the floor beside his work-bench since its arrival a couple of months ago.

That was the big advantage of being a Time Billionaire. You were able to plan ahead. To think ahead. He had read a quotation in a newspaper from someone called Victor Hugo, who had said, 'There is one thing stronger than all the armies in the world, and that is an idea whose time has come.'

He patted the tin full of wax, with the indentation of Cleo Morey's front door key, that sat heavily in his jacket pocket. Then he began to open the package with a smile on his face. Ordering this had definitely been a very good idea.

Its time had come.

77

Grace pulled his Alfa Romeo into the front car park of the Royal Sussex County Hospital, where he had come to visit an injured officer, and cruised slowly along, looking for a space. Then he patiently waited for an elderly lady to unlock the door of her little Nissan Micra, climb in, do up her seat belt, get her ignition key in the slot, fiddle with the interior mirror, start the engine, figure out what the round wheel in front of her did, remember where the gear stick was and finally find reverse. Then she backed out with the speed of a torpedo propelled from a tube, missing the front of his car by an inch. He drove into the space she had vacated and switched off the engine.

It was shortly before half past two and his stomach rumbled, reminding him he needed some food, although he had no appetite. Visits to the mortuary seldom left him feeling like eating, and the image of the grim tattoo on Sophie Harrington's back was still vividly with him, puzzling and disturbing.

BECAUSE YOU LOVE HER.

What the hell did that mean? Presumably *her* referred to the victim, Sophie Harrington. But who was *you*? Her boyfriend?

His phone rang. It was Kim Murphy to update him on the day's progress so far. The most important news was that the Huntington laboratory had confirmed they would have the DNA test results by late afternoon. As he was finishing the call, the phone beeped with a caller-waiting signal. It was DCI Duigan, also calling in with a progress report on Sophie Harrington, and he was sounding pleased.

'An elderly neighbour living opposite went over and spoke to the scene guard officer about an hour ago. She said she had noticed a man acting strangely in the street outside Sophie Harrington's building at about eight on Friday night. He was holding a red carrier bag and wearing a hoodie. Even so, it sounds like she had a good look at him.'

'Was she able to give a description of his face?'

'We've someone on their way to interview her now. But what she has said so far fits Bishop, in terms of height and build. And am I right in understanding from the time-line report he has no alibi for his whereabouts around that time?'

'Correct. Could she pick him out in an identity parade?'

'That's right at the top of the list.'

Grace asked Duigan if they'd managed to find out if Sophie had had a boyfriend. The SIO responded that there was no information on that yet, but they would shortly be interviewing the friend who had reported her missing.

When his colleague had finished, Grace checked his emails on his BlackBerry, but there was nothing relevant to either of the two investigations. He slotted the gadget back in its holster on his belt and thought for some moments. Duigan's news was potentially very good indeed. If this woman could positively identify Bishop, then that was another significant piece of evidence stacked up against the man.

His stomach rumbled again. Fierce sunlight burned through his opened sunroof and he pulled it shut, grateful for the momentary shade. Then he picked up the bacon and egg sandwich he had bought in a petrol station on the way here, tore off the cellophane wrapper and levered the sandwich out. The first bite tasted vaguely of bacon-flavoured cardboard. Chewing slowly and unenthusiastically, he picked up the copy of the latest edition of the *Argus* newspaper he had bought at the same time, and stared at the front-page splash, amazed how fast, as so often, they managed to get a story out. At some point he was going to have to get to the bottom of Spinella's insider sources. But right now this was the bottom of his list of priorities.

BRIGHTON SERIAL KILLER CLAIMS SECOND VICTIM.

There was a particularly attractive head and shoulders photograph of Sophie Harrington, wearing a T-shirt and simple beaded necklace, her long brown hair billowing in sunlight. She was smiling brightly at the camera, or the person behind it.

Then he read the article, bylined *Kevin Spinella*, which spilled over into the second and third pages. It was well dressed up with a series of lifestyle photographs of Katie Bishop, as well as all the usual grief-stricken sound-bites from Sophie Harrington's parents and her best friend that he would have expected to see. And the small photograph of himself that the paper always wheeled out.

It was typical Spinella, sensational reporting intended to create maximum possible panic in the city, and boost the circulation of the paper over the coming days, as well as to enhance Spinella's CV and the oily creep's undoubted ambitions for a position with a national paper. Grace supposed he could not blame the man, or his editor – he would probably have done the same in their positions. But all the same, deliberate misquotes such as '*Brighton Police Divisional Commander, Chief Superintendent Ken Brickhill, advised all women in the city of Brighton and Hove to lock their doors,*' were not helpful.

Part of the purpose of carefully managed press conferences, such as the one earlier today, was to inform the
public of the crimes that had been committed, with the
hope of getting leads. But all scaremongering like this did
was to jam the police switchboards with hundreds of calls
from frightened women.

He ate as much of the sandwich as he could manage,
washed it down with a tepid Diet Coke, then climbed out
and dumped the remnants of his meal and its packaging
into a bin. He dutifully bought a pay-and-display ticket and
stuck it on the windscreen. Then he walked over to the pre-
fab Hospitality Flowers booth and chose a small bouquet
from the stall. He walked along in front of the sprawling
front façade of the hospital, some of it painted white, some
cream and some grey, and entered under the large Perspex
awning, past an ambulance with the wording on its bonnet
in large green letters in mirror-image.

Roy hated this place. It angered and embarrassed him
that a city of Brighton and Hove's stature had such a
disgusting, run-down dump of a hospital. It might have
a grand name, and an impressive, sprawling complex of
buildings, and sure, some departments, such as the cardiac
unit, were world class, but in general the average makeshift
shack of a medical centre in a Third World nation put this
place to shame.

He had read once that the Second World War was the
first time in history that more soldiers died from their
actual wounds than from infections they picked up in
hospitals while being treated for their wounds. Half of the
citizens of Brighton and Hove were terrified to come into
this place because rumour was rife you were more likely
to die from something you picked up inside than from
whatever brought you in here in the first place.

It wasn't the fault of the medical staff, who were mostly quality people who worked their tired butts off – he had seen that with his own eyes enough times. He blamed the management, and he blamed the government, whose policies had allowed healthcare standards to fall so low.

He went past the gift shop and the chintzy Nuovo Caffè snack bar, which looked like it belonged in a motorway service station, and sidestepped an elderly, vacant-faced patient in her hospital gown who was wandering down the sloping floor straight towards him.

And then his anger at the place rose further as he walked over to the curved wooden counter of the unmanned reception desk and saw the sign, lying beside a spray of plastic flowers.

APOLOGIES THE RECEPTION DESK IS CLOSED.

Fortunately, Eleanor had managed to locate his young officer for him – she had been moved out of the orthopaedic ward a few days ago into one called Chichester. A list on the wall informed him that it was on the third floor of this wing.

He climbed up a spiral staircase, on the walls of which a cheery mural had been painted, walked along a blue linoleum-covered corridor, up two further flights of wooden-banistered stairs and stopped in a shabby, grimy corridor. A young female Asian nurse in a blue top and black trousers walked towards him. There was a faint mashed potatoes and cabbage smell of school dinners. 'I'm looking for Chichester ward,' he said.

She pointed. 'Go straight ahead.'

He walked past a row of gas cylinders through a door with a glass window covered in warning notices, and entered a ward of about sixteen beds. The smell of school dinners was even stronger in here, tinged by a faint, sour smell of urine and disinfectant. There was an old linoleum floor and the walls were filthy. The windows were wide open, giving a view out on to another wing of the hospital, with a vent from which steam was rising. Horrible curtains were partially drawn around some beds.

It was a mixed ward of what looked mostly like geriatrics and mental patients. Grace stared for a moment at a little old lady with tufts of hair the colour of cotton wool, matching the complexion of her sunken cheeks, fast asleep, her toothless mouth open wide. Several televisions were on. A young man in bed was babbling loudly to himself. Another old woman, in a bed at the far end, kept shouting out something loud and unintelligible to no one in particular. In the bed immediately to his right was a shrivelled little old man, fast asleep, unshaven, his bedclothes pushed aside, two empty bottles of Coke on the table that straddled him. He was wearing striped pyjamas, the bottoms untied, his limp penis clearly visible, nestling against his testicles.

And in the next-door bed, to his horror, surrounded by dusty-looking apparatus, he saw the person he had come to visit. And now, as he slipped his hand into his pocket and removed his mobile phone, storming past the busy nursing station, his blood was really boiling.

One of his favourite young officers, DC Emma-Jane Boutwood, had been badly injured trying to stop a van in the same operation in which Glenn Branson had been shot. She had been crushed between the van and a parked car, and suffered massive internal damage, including losing her spleen, as well as multiple bone fractures. The twenty-five-year-old had been in a coma on life support for over a week, and when she came round, doctors had been worried she might never walk again. But in recent weeks she had made a dramatic improvement, was able to stand unaided and had already been talking eagerly about when she could get back to work.

Grace really liked her. She was a terrific detective and he reckoned she had a great future ahead of her in the force. But at this moment, seeing her lying there, smiling palely at him, she looked like a lost, bewildered child. Always thin, she now looked emaciated inside her loose hospital gown, and the orange tag was almost hanging off her wrist. Her blonde hair, which had lost its lustre and looked like dried straw, was clipped up untidily, with a few stray wisps falling down. On the table next to her bed lay a crowded riot of cards, flowers and fruit.

Her eyes said it all before they even spoke, and something snapped inside him.

'How are you?' he asked, holding on to the flowers for the moment.

'Never better!' she said, making an effort to perk up for him. 'I told my dad yesterday that I was going to beat him at tennis before the end of the summer. Mind you, that should be easy. He's a crap player!'

Grace grinned, then asked gently, 'What the hell are you doing in this ward?'

She shrugged. 'They moved me about three days ago. Said they needed the bed in the other ward.'

'Did they, hell. You want to stay here?'

'Not really.'

Grace stepped back and scanned the ward, looking for a free nurse, then walked over to a young Asian girl in nursing uniform who was removing a bedpan. 'Excuse me,' he said. 'I'm looking for whoever is in charge here.'

The nurse turned around, then pointed to a harassed-looking nurse of about forty, with pinned-up hair and a bookish face behind large glasses, who was entering the ward, holding a clipboard.

In a few quick, determined paces, Grace cut her off, blocking her path. The badge hanging from her blue top read ANGELA MORRIS, WARD MANAGER.

'Excuse me,' he said, 'can I have a word with you?'

'I'm sorry,' she replied, in a brittle, distinctly hostile and haughty voice. 'I'm dealing with a problem.'

'Well, you have another one right now,' he said, almost shaking with anger, pulling out his warrant card and holding it up to her face.

She looked alarmed. 'What – what is this about?' Her voice had suddenly dropped several decibels.

Grace pointed at Emma-Jane. 'You have exactly five minutes to get that young woman out of this stinking hell-hole and into either a private ward or a women-only one. Do you understand?'

Haughty again, the Ward Manager said, 'Perhaps you should try to understand some of the problems we have in this hospital, Detective Superintendent.'

Raising his voice almost to a shout, Grace said, 'This young woman is a heroine. She was injured performing an act of supreme bravery in the line of duty. She helped to save this city from a monster, who is now behind bars awaiting trial, and to save the lives of two innocent people. She nearly damn well sacrificed her life! And her reward is to get put in a mixed, geriatric ward, in a bed next to a man with his dick hanging out. She's not spending one more hour in this ward. Do you understand me?'

Looking around edgily, the nurse said, 'I will see what I can do, later.'

Raising his voice even more, Grace said, 'I don't think you heard me properly. There's no *later* about this. You're going to do this now. Because I'm going to stay here, in your face, until she's moved into a bed in a ward that I'm happy about.' Then he held up the phone and showed it to the woman. 'Unless you'd like me to email the photos I've just taken of Brighton heroine DC Boutwood being stripped of all dignity by you cruel incompetents to the *Argus* and every damn newspaper in the land, you're going to do this right now.'

'You are not allowed to use mobile phones in here. And you've no right to take photographs.'

'You've no right to treat my officer like this. Get me the hospital manager. NOW!'

78

Thirty minutes later, Emma-Jane Boutwood was wheeled along a network of corridors, into a much more modern section of the hospital.

Grace waited until the young DC was installed in her sunny, private room, with a view out across the rooftops to the English Channel, then gave her the flowers and left, after receiving a promise from the hospital's Mr Big, down a phone line from his ivory tower, that she would remain in this room until she was discharged.

Following the directions he had been given back to the front entrance, he stopped at an elevator and hit the button. After a lengthy wait, he was about to give up and walk down when suddenly the doors slid open. He stepped in and nodded at a tired-looking young Indian man, who was taking a bite on an energy snack bar.

Dressed in green medical pyjamas, with a stethoscope hanging from his neck, the man was wearing a name tag which read DR RAJ SINGH, A&E. As the doors closed, Grace suddenly felt stifling heat; it was like being in an oven. He noticed the doctor was staring at him curiously.

'Hot day,' Grace said politely.

'Yes, a little too hot,' the man replied in a cultured English accent, then he frowned. 'Excuse me asking, but you look familiar. Have we met?'

Grace had always had a good memory for faces – almost photographic at times. But this man's did not ring any bells. 'I don't think so,' he replied.

The lift stopped and Grace stepped out. The doctor followed him. 'In the *Argus* today, is it your photograph?'

Grace nodded.

'That explains it! I was just reading it, a few minutes ago. Actually, I had been thinking of contacting your inquiry team.'

Grace, distractedly anxious to get on and back to the office, was only giving Dr Singh half an ear now. 'Really?'

'Look, it's probably nothing, but the paper says you've asked people to be vigilant and report anything suspicious?'

'Yes.'

'Well – I have to be careful about patient confidentiality, but I saw a man in here yesterday and he really made me feel uncomfortable.'

'In what way?'

The doctor glanced around the empty corridor, looked sternly at a fire hydrant, then turned back to check the lift doors were closed. 'Well, his behaviour was very erratic. He shouted at the receptionist, for instance.'

Nothing erratic about that, Grace thought privately. He was sure plenty of people got shouted at in here regularly, with good reason.

'When I saw him,' the doctor continued, 'he seemed extremely agitated. Don't get me wrong, I see plenty of people with psychiatric problems, but this man just seemed to be in a state of high anxiety about something.'

'What was his injury?'

'Here's the thing. It was an infected wound in his hand.'

Suddenly Grace was paying a lot more attention. 'From what?'

'Well, he said he had shut it in a door, but it didn't look like that to me.'

'Shut it in a door?' Grace queried, thinking hard about

380

Bishop's explanation for his injury – that he had bashed it getting into a taxi.

'Yes.'

'So what did it look like to you?'

'A bite. I would say a human bite quite possibly. You see, there were marks on both sides of the hand – on the wrist, then on the underside just below the thumb.'

'If he'd shut a car door or a boot lid on it, there would have been marks both sides.'

'Yes, but not curved ones,' the doctor replied. 'They were semi-lunar upper and lower, consistent with a mouth. And there were puncture marks of varying depths, consistent with teeth.'

'What makes you think they were human? Could they have been from an animal? A large dog?'

The doctor blushed. 'I'm a bit of a crime fiction addict – I love reading forensic crime novels, when I get the time – and watch programmes like *CSI* on television.' His beeper went. He paused a moment, then carried on, 'But you see, there's another thing I deduced.' He paused again, looking stressed, to read the message on the machine's display. 'The thing I deduced is that if it was a dog bite, then why would he have denied it? If it was a human bite that he received during an attack, I can of course see why he denied it. Then, when I saw the horrible news about this murdered young woman, I sort of put two and two together.'

Grace smiled. 'I think you'd make a good detective! But it's a big two and two,' he replied. 'Can you describe this man to me?'

'Yes. He was about six foot, very lean, with quite long brown hair, dark glasses and a heavy beard. It was quite hard to see his face clearly. He was wearing a blue linen jacket, a cream shirt, jeans and trainers. He looked a bit of a scruff.'

Grace's heart sank; this did not sound like Bishop at all, unless he had gone to the trouble of disguising himself, which was always a possibility. 'Would you recognize him if you saw him again?'

'Absolutely!'

'Would this man have been picked up on some of the hospital's CCTV cameras?'

'We have one in A&E, he'd be on that for sure.'

Grace thanked him, wrote down his name and phone numbers, then went off in search of the hospital's CCTV monitoring suite, unclipping his BlackBerry and checking his emails as he walked.

There was one from Dick Pope, in response to the email he had sent him earlier this morning with the photographs he had taken in Munich. It stopped him in his tracks.

Roy, this is not the woman Leslie and I saw last week. We really are convinced we saw Sandy. Best, Dick

79

It was nearly three thirty by the time that Nadiuska De Sancha had completed her post-mortem and left the mortuary, along with DCI Duigan and the Coroner's Officer.

From the ligature marks on Sophie Harrington's neck and the petechial haemorrhaging in her eyes, the Home Office pathologist was drawn towards the conclusion that the poor young woman had been strangled. But she would need to wait for blood toxicology reports and test results on the contents of her stomach, and the samples of fluids she had taken from the woman's bladder, to eliminate other possible causes of death. The presence of semen in her vagina indicated the likelihood that she had been raped either before or after her death.

Cleo and Darren still had several hours of work ahead of them. There was the post-mortem to be carried out on the 'unknown female' washed up from the sea. In addition they had the grim task of the post-mortem on the six-year-old girl who had been killed on Saturday by a car. And they had four other cadavers to deal with, including that of a forty-seven-year-old HIV-positive man whom they had earlier placed in the sealed isolation room for his post-mortem.

The parents of the little girl had wanted to come up to visit late yesterday afternoon, and Darren had let them in. They had come for a further visit a couple of hours ago and Cleo had seen them. She was still feeling upset now.

Dr Nigel Churchman, the local consultant pathologist,

who would carry out these much less intensive post-mortems, was due here in half an hour. Christopher Ghent, the forensic odontologist, who had come to assist in the identification of the unknown female, was currently in the office, having a cup of tea, tetchy at being kept waiting.

Cleo and Darren removed the woman from her fridge and unwrapped her. The smell of her rotten body instantly permeated the place again. Then they left Ghent to get on with his work.

Ghent, a tall, intense, bespectacled man in his mid-forties, with thinning hair, had an international reputation on two counts. He had written a well-respected book on forensic dentistry, in an attempt to rival Montreal odontologist Robert Dorion's definitive *Bitemark Evidence,* which had long been the profession's standard reference work. He was also an accomplished bird-watcher – or twitcher – and a world authority on seagulls.

Fully gowned up in his hospital greens, Ghent worked swiftly but thoroughly, against the background sounds of Darren crunching the ribs and grinding away at the skulls of the other cadavers with the band-saw. The mood was particularly sombre in here, with none of the banter between the team that usually went on. The presence of a small child's body subdued them all far more than that of a murder victim.

Ghent took a series of photographs, both normal and with a portable X-ray camera, then noted details of each tooth on a chart, finishing by taking a soft clay impression of the upper and lower sets. Acting on instructions from the coroner, he would later send his detailed records to every dentist within a fifteen-mile radius of the city of Brighton and Hove. If that failed to produce results, he would gradually broaden the circulation list until, if necessary, every registered dentist in the UK was covered.

There was as yet no international system of coordinated dental records. If no dentist in the UK could make an identification, and fingerprints and DNA failed to produce results, the woman would eventually end up in a grave paid for by the city of Brighton and Hove, recorded for posterity as one tiny fraction of a tragic statistic.

*

Nigel Churchman had calculated recently that he had performed over seven thousand post-mortems in this mortuary during the past fifteen years. Yet he approached each cadaver with the same, almost boyish enthusiasm, as if it were his first. He was a man who genuinely loved his work, and believed that each person who came under his scrutiny deserved the very best from him.

A handsome, fit man, with a passion for racing cars, he had a youthful face – much of it concealed at the moment behind his green mask as he peered down at the unknown female – making him seem much younger than his forty-nine years.

He flapped away some bluebottles from around her brain, which was lying on the metal examining tray above her opened chest cavity, and began work. He sliced the brain carefully with a long-bladed carving knife, checking for foreign bodies, such as a bullet, or damage from a knife, or evidence of haemorrhaging which could indicate death by a heavy blow. But the brain seemed healthy, undamaged.

Her eyes, which had been eaten almost entirely away, yielded no information. Her heart seemed robust, typical of a fit person, with no scaling in the arteries. He was not able to gauge her age very accurately at this stage. Judging from the condition and colour of her teeth, her general physique, the condition of her breasts, which were partly gone also, he was guessing mid-twenties to early forties.

Darren carried the heart to the weigh scales and marked it up on the wall chart. Churchman nodded; it was within the correct range. He moved on to the lungs, cutting them free, then lifting them with both gloved hands on to the examining tray, dark fluid dripping from them as he set them down.

Within a couple of minutes of starting to examine them, he stopped and turned to Cleo. 'Interesting,' he said. 'She hasn't drowned. There's no water in the lungs.'

'Meaning?' Cleo asked. It was a stupid question, blurted out without thinking, the result of her distress after being with the dead girl's parents, her hangover, her stress at the workload, and her worries about the spectre of Sandy clouding her relationship with Roy Grace. Of course she knew the answer, she knew exactly what it meant.

'She was already dead when she went into the water. I'm going to have to stop this p-m, I'm afraid. You'll need to inform the coroner.'

A Home Office pathologist – probably Nadiuska De Sancha again – would have to take over the post-mortem. Unknown female was now elevated to the status of a suspicious death.

80

Roy Grace made a mental note to never again find himself closeted with Norman Potting in a small room on a hot day. They were seated next to each other in front of a video monitor in the cubicle-sized viewing room that adjoined the Witness Interview Suite. The late-afternoon sun was beating mercilessly against the closed venetian blinds of the one window and the air conditioning was useless. Grace was dripping with perspiration. Potting, in a white short-sleeve shirt, with wide, damp patches in the armpits, smelled like the inside of an old hat.

Further, the Detective Sergeant had eaten something heavily laced with garlic and his breath reeked of the stuff. Grace fished a pack of peppermint gum out of his jacket, on the back of his chair, and offered a piece to Potting in the hope he would chew it and spare him his death-breath.

'Never touch it, Roy, thanks,' he said. 'Pulls my fillings out.' He was fiddling with the controls, fast-rewinding a recording. Grace watched the screen, as Potting, Zafferone and a third man all walked backward out of the room, in speeded-up motion, disappearing through the door one at a time. Potting stopped the tape, then started it and each of the three men reappeared, walking in through the door this time. 'Got yourself a MySpace profile yet, Roy?' he asked, suddenly.

'MySpace? I thought I was a bit old for a MySpace profile.'

Potting shook his head. 'All ages. Anyhow, Li's only

twenty-four. She and I got a joint profile. *Norma-Li.* Geddit?
She already has three Thai friends in England – one in
Brighton. Good, don't you think?'

'Genius,' Grace replied, his mind more on avoiding
Potting's breath than the conversation.

'Mind you,' Potting chuckled, 'there's some fancy-
looking tottie on there. Phwwoaaah!'

'Thought you were a happily married man now – with
your new bride.'

For a moment, Potting looked genuinely happy, his
pug-like face creased into a look of contentment. 'She's
something, I tell you, Roy! Taught me some new tricks.
Blimey! You ever had an Oriental woman?'

Grace shook his head. 'I'll take your word for it.' He was
trying to concentrate on the screen. Trying to put Sandy
to the back of his mind and focus on his work. He had
a massive responsibility on his shoulders, and how he
handled events over the coming days could have a major
impact on his career. He was aware, with the high profile of
this case, that it wasn't only Alison Vosper's critical eyes that
were focused on him.

On the screen a lean, angular man was lowering himself
into one of the three red chairs in the Witness Interview
Suite. He had a striking face, interesting rather than handsome, with untidy, tangled hair and a Dutch settler's beard.
He wore a baggy Hawaiian shirt hanging loose, blue jeans
and leather sandals. His complexion was pale, as if he had
spent too much of the summer indoors.

'That's Katie Bishop's lover?' Grace asked.

'Yes,' Potting replied. 'Barty Chancellor.'

'Poncy name,' Grace said.

'Poncy git,' Potting replied, turning up the sound.

Grace watched the interview progress, with both

detectives making frequent jottings in their notebooks. Despite his odd appearance, Chancellor spoke in an assured, faintly superior, public school accent, his body language relaxed and confident, the only hint of any nerves showing when he occasionally twisted a fabric bracelet on his wrist.

'Did Mrs Bishop ever talk to you about her husband, Mr Chancellor?' Norman Potting asked him.

'Yes, of course she did.'

'Did that give you a kick?' Zafferone asked.

Grace smiled. The young, arrogant DC was doing exactly what he had hoped – winding Chancellor up.

'What exactly do you mean by that?' Chancellor asked.

Zafferone held his gaze. 'Did you enjoy the knowledge that you were sleeping with a woman who was cheating on her husband?'

'I'm here to help you with your inquiries in finding the killer of my darling Katie. I don't think that question is relevant.'

'We'll be the judge of what's relevant, sir,' Zafferone replied coolly.

'I came here voluntarily,' Chancellor said, visibly riled now, his voice rising. 'I don't like your tone.'

'I appreciate you must be very distressed, Mr Chancellor,' Norman Potting cut in, speaking courteously, playing classic *good cop* to Zafferone's *bad*. 'I can understand something of what you must be going through. It would be very helpful if you could tell us a little bit about the nature of the relationship between Mr and Mrs Bishop.'

Chancellor toyed with his bracelet for some moments. 'The man was a brute,' he said suddenly.

'In what way?' Potting asked.

'Did he beat Mrs Bishop up?' Zafferone asked. 'Was he violent?'

'Not physically but mentally. He was very critical of her – the way she looked, the way she kept the house – he's a bit of an obsessive. And he was extremely jealous – which was why she was extra careful. And . . .' He fell silent for a moment, as if hesitating whether to add something. 'Well – I don't know if this is significant, but he's quite kinky, she told me.'

'In what way?' Potting asked.

'Sexually. He's into bondage. Fetish stuff.'

'What kind of stuff?' Potting asked again.

'Leather, rubber, that sort of thing.'

'She told you all this?' Zafferone asked.

'Yes.'

'Did that turn you on?'

'What the hell kind of a question is that?' Chancellor flared at him.

'Did it excite you, when Katie told you about these things?'

'I'm not some kind of a sick pervert, if that's what you think,' he retorted.

'Mr Chancellor,' Norman Potting said, playing *good cop* again, 'I don't suppose Mrs Bishop ever mentioned a gas mask to you?'

'A *what*?'

'Did Mr Bishop's fetishes ever include a gas mask, to the best of your knowledge?'

The artist thought for a moment. 'I don't – I – no – I don't recall her mentioning a gas mask.'

'Are you sure?' Zafferone said.

'It's not the kind of thing you forget easily.'

'You seemed to forget she was a married woman easily enough.' Zafferone pushed his barb in.

'I think it's time I had my solicitor present,' Chancellor said. 'You are out of order.'

'Did you kill Mrs Bishop?' Zafferone asked coolly.

Chancellor looked fit to explode. 'WHAT?'

'I asked you if you killed Mrs Bishop.'

'I loved her – we were going to spend the rest of our lives together – why on earth would I have killed her?'

'You just said you wanted your solicitor present,' Zafferone continued, like a Rottweiler. 'In my experience, when people want their lawyer in the room it's because they are guilty.'

'I loved her very much. I—' His voice began to crack. Suddenly he hunched forward, cradling his face in his hands, and began to sob.

Potting and Zafferone glanced at each other, waiting. Finally Barty Chancellor sat up, composing himself. 'I'm sorry.'

Then Zafferone lobbed the question Grace had been desperate for one of them to ask. 'Did Mr Bishop know about your relationship?'

'Absolutely not.'

Norman Potting cut in again. 'Mr Bishop is by all accounts a very bright man. You and Mrs Bishop had an affair that had been going on for over twelve months. Do you really think he had no inkling?'

'We were very careful – and, besides, he was away in London most weekdays.'

'Perhaps he knew and never said anything,' Zafferone suggested.

'Possibly,' Chancellor conceded grudgingly. 'But I don't think so – I mean, Katie was sure he didn't know.'

Zafferone flicked back some pages in his notebook. 'You said earlier that you have no alibi for the time when Mrs Bishop left your house and the estimated time, perhaps less than an hour later, when she was killed.'

'Correct.'

'You fell asleep.'

'It was nearly midnight. We'd been making love. Perhaps you've never tried making love? You'll find out if you do that it can make you sleepy.' He glared at Zafferone.

Grace was making some mental notes himself. The affair had been going on for twelve months. Six months ago Brian Bishop had taken out a three-million-pound insurance policy on his wife's life. He had a history of violence. What if he had found out about the affair?

Chancellor had said that he and Katie were planning to spend the rest of their lives together. This was more than just a fling. Perhaps Bishop couldn't bear the thought of losing his wife.

All the right boxes were getting ticked. The man had a motive.

Maybe he had planned this carefully for many months. The perfect alibi in London, except for one small slip-up that he wasn't even aware of. The photograph of his car from the hidden camera near Gatwick airport.

Grace watched the interview continue, Zafferone winding Chancellor up more and more. Sure, this artist was a possible suspect. He had clearly been desperately in love with the woman. Enough to kill her if she dumped him? Perhaps. Smart enough to murder her and set it up so it looked like her husband had done it? It could not be discounted. But at this moment the weight of the evidence seemed to be stacking up solidly against Brian Bishop.

He looked at his watch. It was five fifteen. He had

brought the video of the man in the Accident and Emergency waiting room from the Royal Sussex County Hospital CCTV straight to the film unit here at Sussex House for enhancement. He just had time now to go down and see how they were getting on, before his team meeting with Kim Murphy and Brendan Duigan to prepare for the six-thirty joint briefing.

On the hospital's low-grade recording, it was hard to make out the man's features, because his face was so extensively obscured by his long hair, dark glasses, moustache and beard. With the technology they had here, they would be able to sharpen the image considerably. As he stepped out into the corridor, his phone rang. It was DS Bella Moy, talking excitedly through what sounded like a mouthful of Maltesers. The DNA test results on Katie Bishop were back.

When she told him what they showed, he punched the air for joy.

81

There was no air conditioning in Robert Vernon's office, on the second floor of a fine Queen Anne house in Brighton's Lanes, with a view straight down a narrow street of flint-walled houses to the seafront. The din from a road-drilling machine outside came straight in through the open windows, worsening the headache that Brian Bishop had woken with this morning, after yet another virtually sleepless night.

It was a pleasant, airy office, with much of the wall space taken up by shelves crammed full of legal tomes and by filing cabinets. Two fine old Brighton prints hung on the pastel-blue walls, one showing the chain pier, the other a view of the Old Steine. Piles of correspondence were stacked on the desk and some on the floor.

'Forgive the mess please, Brian,' Vernon said, ever courteous. 'Just back from holiday this morning – not quite sure where to begin!'

'I often wonder if it's even worth going on holiday,' Bishop said, 'because of all the bloody paperwork you have to clear before you go, and the stuff that's waiting when you come back.'

He stirred his delicate china cup of tea seven times, staring at a framed colour photograph of Vernon's wife, Trish, on the window ledge behind the desk. An attractive, fair-haired woman, she was in golfing attire, posing by a tee. Next to it was another silver frame, with three oval holes, each containing the smiling face of one of the

Vernons' young children. Taken many years ago, Bishop realized, because they were all in their teens now. It was all right for Vernon, he suddenly thought bitterly. All his family were fine. His whole world was fine. It didn't matter what problems any client dragged in here. He would study the facts, dispense his advice, watch them drag it all back out of the door again behind them, then jump into his Lexus and head off to the golf course with a sunny smile on his face.

The man, who was approaching his mid-sixties, had an elegant, courtly charm. His silver hair was always neat, his clothes conservative and immaculate, and his whole manner exuded an air of wisdom and confidence. He had been Bishop's family solicitor forever, it seemed. He had handled all the formalities following the death of Bishop's father, then his mother. It was Vernon whom Brian Bishop had turned to when, on going through the papers in his mother's bureau in her bedroom soon after her death, nearly five years ago, he had discovered something that had been kept from him throughout his life. That he was adopted.

It was Vernon who had dissuaded him from embarking on the journey to discover his birth parents. Bishop had had a charmed childhood, Vernon had told him. Doting adoptive parents, who had married too late to have children of their own, had totally indulged him and his sister, who had followed two years later – but died tragically of meningitis when she was thirteen.

They had been comfortably off, and they'd brought him up in a pleasant, detached house overlooking Hove recreation ground, stretching their finances to educate him at a private school, taking him abroad on holidays, and buying him a small car the moment he passed his driving test. Bishop had loved them both very much, as well as most of their relatives. He had been deeply upset when his father died, but it was worse after his mother died. Despite the fact that he had been married to Katie for only a few months, he suddenly felt desperately lonely. Very lost.

Then he had found that document in his mother's bureau.

But Vernon had calmed him down. He pointed out that Bishop's parents had kept it from him because they thought it was in his best interests. They had wanted only to give him love and security, for him to enjoy the present and be strong for the future. They'd been worried that by telling him, they might pitch him into a life of turmoil, searching for a past that might no longer exist – or, worse, be very different from how he would have wanted it.

Vernon had agreed with him that this was an old-fashioned view, but that it had validity nonetheless. Brian was doing well in life, he was confident – outwardly at least – successful and reasonably content. Sure there could be big emotional rewards in finding one or both of his birth parents, but equally it could be a profoundly unsettling experience. What if he was really dismayed by the kind of people they were? Or if they just rejected him?

Yet the nagging desire to find out about his background got stronger all the time. And it was fuelled by the knowledge that, with each passing year, the chance of one or both of his birth parents still being alive diminished.

*

'I'm just so sorry about the news, Brian – and that I couldn't see you earlier today. I had to be in court.'

'Of course, Robert. No problem. I've had a load of business stuff to deal with. It kept my mind occupied.'

'It's unbelievable, isn't it?'

'Yes.' Bishop did not know whether to say anything about Sophie Harrington. He desperately wanted to open up to someone, but at the same it didn't feel right, not now, not at this moment.

'And how are you? Are you coping?'

'Just about.' Bishop smiled thinly. 'I'm sort of grounded here in Brighton. I can't get into the house for several more days. The police don't want me going up to London, so I'm having to stay down here – and carry on with the business as best I can.'

'If you need a bed, you're welcome to stay with Trish and me.'

'Thanks, but I'm OK.'

'And do they have any idea what happened? Who did this terrible thing?'

'The way they're treating me, I think they're convinced I did it.' The two men locked eyes briefly.

'I'm not a criminal lawyer, Brian, but I do know that the immediate family are always suspects in most murder inquiries, until eliminated.'

'I'm sure.'

'So don't be too worried by that. The faster they can eliminate you, the faster they can get on with finding who did do it. Out of interest, where are the kids at the moment?' Then the solicitor raised a pacifying hand. 'I'm sorry. Not that I meant to infer—'

'No, of course not, understood. Max is with a friend in the south of France. Carly's staying with cousins in Canada. I've spoken to them both, told them to stay on – there's nothing they can do by coming back. I understand from the police it will be about a month before I can –

before the coroner – will—' He stumbled over his words, emotion taking over.

'I'm afraid there are a lot of formalities. Bureaucracy. Red tape. Not helpful when I'm sure all you want to do is be alone with your thoughts.'

Bishop nodded, pulling out a handkerchief and dabbing his eyes.

'Talking of which, we have a few things we need to deal with. OK to make a start?'

'Yes.'

'First, what about Katie's assets – do you know if she made a will?'

'There's something very odd. The police asked me about a life insurance policy – for three million pounds – which they said I had taken out on Katie.'

The solicitor ignored an incoming call and looked at him. 'And you hadn't?'

Mercifully, the drilling suddenly stopped outside.

'No. Absolutely not – that I can remember, and I bloody well would remember that.'

Vernon was pensive for some moments. 'Didn't you remortgage your Dyke Road Avenue house quite recently? To raise cash for your rights issue?'

Bishop nodded. 'Yes, I did.'

His company was doing well at the moment, but almost too well ironically, and it had suffered from the cash-flow problems that many fast-expanding businesses experienced. When he had started up, it had been funded by himself and a small group of wealthy friends, on a relatively small amount of cash. Recently, to take it to the next level, they had needed to invest substantially in new technology, larger premises and more skilled computer staff. Bishop and his friends had decided to find the money themselves, rather than try to float, or raise it by other means, and he had provided his own portion from remortgaging his house.

'The mortgage companies normally require some life-insurance cover on a large loan – perhaps that's what you did.'

The solicitor might be right, he thought. Life-insurance cover was ringing a faint bell. But the amount seemed wrong. And he couldn't check his files because they were in the bloody house.

'Perhaps,' he said dubiously. 'And yes, she did make a will – it was a very short one. I'm one of the executors, along with David Crouch, my accountant. It's in the house.'

'Of course, I'd forgotten. She had some assets, didn't she? She got a reasonable settlement in her previous marriage. Can you remember what the will contained?'

'I can remember. She bequeathed a few quid to her parents, but she's an only child and the bulk of it she left to me.'

An alarm bell rang suddenly inside Robert Vernon's head. He frowned, just very slightly. Too slightly for Bishop to notice.

82

'The time is six thirty p.m., Monday 7 August,' Roy Grace read out briskly from his notes, feeling in a distinctly upbeat mood, for a change. 'This is our second joint briefing of Operation Chameleon and Operation Mistral.'

Mistral was the name the police computer had chosen, at random, for the Sophie Harrington inquiry. The conference room at Sussex House was filled to capacity, with police officers and support staff packed around the table in tight rows of chairs. There was an almost electric sense of expectation in the room. And for once the air conditioning was working properly.

Grace sped through the summaries, then concluded by saying, 'There have been a number of significant developments during the course of today, I am pleased to report.' He looked at the beanpole of a young father, DC Nick Nicholl. 'Would you like to start?'

Nicholl, with his jacket off, his top button undone and his tie slack, read formally from the notes on his pad. 'I interviewed Ms Holly Richardson at her place of work, the Regent Public Relations Agency, 71 Trafalgar Road, Brighton, at eleven o'clock this morning. She stated that she and Miss Harrington had been at secretarial college together and had remained best friends since then. Ms Richardson informed me that Sophie had confided in her that she had been carrying on a secret relationship with Brian Bishop for approximately six months. Sophie had related to her that on occasions recently Bishop behaved in

400

a violent manner towards her, which frightened her. And he made a number of increasingly sadistic and perverted sexual demands on her.'

He mopped his brow and continued, turning the page of his notepad. 'A technician in the Telecoms Unit here, John Smith, who has been examining both Miss Harrington's mobile phone records and Brian Bishop's, has informed me that each party made a large number of phone calls daily to the other during this six-month period. The most recent was a call from Miss Harrington to Mr Bishop at four fifty-one on Friday afternoon, a few hours before her estimated time of death.'

Grace thanked him, then turned to the burly figure of Guy Batchelor.

The Detective Sergeant told the assembled teams about the cash call Brian Bishop had made on the investors in his company, International Rostering Solutions PLC. He concluded by saying, 'Although his business seems to be expanding and is well regarded, Bishop is hocked up to his eyeballs in debt.'

The significance was not lost on anyone in the room. Then he delivered his nuke. He told the two teams about Bishop's criminal record.

Grace watched all their faces. There was a sense of progress in this room that was palpable.

Next, he had arranged for an abbreviated cut of Norman Potting and Alfonso Zafferone's interview with Barty Chancellor to be played on the video screen. When it finished, Potting informed the team that he had made inquiries about the particular make and model of gas mask that had been found on both victims. The manufacturer had been identified, and they were awaiting information on the number that had been produced and a full list of UK stockists.

Next was DCI Duigan, who related what the neighbour who lived opposite the house where Sophie Harrington had her flat claimed to have seen. She had positively identified Bishop from the photograph that had been in the *Argus* and would be very happy to attend a formal identity procedure.

Theatrically saving the best to last, Roy Grace turned to Bella Moy.

The DS produced a photograph of the number plate of Brian Bishop's Bentley, relating that it had been taken by an ANPR camera, on the southbound carriageway of the M23, near to Gatwick airport at eleven forty-seven on Thursday night. She pointed out that despite Bishop's alibi that he was in London, his car was seen heading in the direction of Brighton, no more than thirty minutes away, well within the frame of the estimated time of his wife's murder.

But Grace privately had concerns about this, as the photograph had been taken at night. The number plate was clearly visible, but it was impossible to determine the make of the car. It was helpful secondary evidence, but no slam-dunk. A half-competent barrister would kick it into touch in seconds. But it was worth keeping in the mix. One more fact for jurors to debate.

Bella added that Bishop's home computer contents were currently being analysed by Ray Packham, in the High Tech Crime Division, and she was awaiting his report. And then she delivered the killer blow.

'We received the lab reports back on the DNA analysis of semen found present in Mrs Bishop's vagina,' she said, reading from her notes in a matter-of-fact voice. 'There were two different spermatozoa ejaculates present in the samples taken by the Home Office pathologist at the post-

mortem,' she announced. 'In the opinion of the pathologist, based on the mobility of the spermatozoa present in
Mrs Bishop's vagina, both ejaculates occurred on the night
of Thursday 3 August, within a few hours of each other. One
is as yet unidentified – but we believe DNA tests will show
it to be that of Mrs Bishop's lover, who has admitted they
had sexual intercourse on Thursday evening. The other
contains a 100 percent match with DNA taken from Brian
Bishop.'

She paused for a moment. 'This means, of course, that
contrary to his alibi that he was in London, Bishop was in
Brighton and had sexual intercourse with his wife – at some
point close to the time of her death.'

Grace waited patiently, letting the information sink in.
He could feel the tension in the room. 'You've all done a
great job. We will arrest Brian Bishop tonight, on suspicion
of the murder of his wife. But I'm not yet confident that
he killed Sophie Harrington. So I don't want to read in
tomorrow's *Argus* that we've solved these murders. Is that
clear?'

The silence that greeted him told him it was abundantly
clear.

83

Brian Bishop stepped out of the hotel bathroom shower, dried himself, then rummaged in the overnight bag that Maggie Campbell had brought up to his room an hour ago, containing fresh clothes she had collected from his house.

He pulled on a dark blue polo shirt and navy slacks. The smell of a barbecue wafted in on the light breeze through the open window. It was tantalizing, even though, with his churned-up stomach, he had little appetite. He was regretting accepting an invitation to dinner with Glenn and Barbara Mishon, who were his and Katie's closest friends. Normally he loved their company and when Barbara had rung, earlier today, she had persuaded him to come over.

At the time it had seemed a more attractive proposition than spending another evening alone in this room with his thoughts and a room service trolley. But his meeting this afternoon with Robert Vernon had brought home to him the full reality of what had happened, and left him feeling deeply depressed. It was as if, up until then, it had all been just a bad dream. But now the enormity weighed down on him. There was so much to think about, too much. He really just wanted to sit alone and gather his thoughts.

His brown suede loafers were on the floor. It was too warm really to put on socks, but it would look too relaxed, too disrespectful to Katie, if he was overly casual. So he sat down on the bed and tugged on a pale blue pair, then pushed his feet into his shoes. Outside, in one of the back

gardens his window overlooked, he heard people chatter-
ing, a child shouting, music playing, a tinkle of laughter.

Then there was a knock on his door.

Probably room service wanting to turn down the beds,
he thought, opening it. Instead he saw the two police
officers who had first broken the news of Katie's death
to him.

The black one held up his warrant card. 'Detective
Sergeant Branson and Detective Constable Nicholl. May
we come in, sir?'

Bishop did not like the expression on their faces. 'Yes, of
course,' he said, stepping back into the room and holding
the door open for them. 'Do you have some news for me?'

'Brian Desmond Bishop,' Branson said, 'evidence has
come to light, as a result of which I'm arresting you on
suspicion of the murder of Mrs Katherine Bishop. You do
not have to say anything, but it may harm your defence
if you do not mention when questioned something which
you later rely on in court. Anything you do say may be given
in evidence. Is that clear?'

Bishop did not respond for a moment. Then he said,
'You can't be serious.'

'My colleague, DC Nicholl, is going to give you a quick
body search.'

Almost mechanically, Bishop raised his arms, to allow
Nicholl to frisk him. 'I'm – I'm sorry,' Bishop then said. 'I
need to call my solicitor.'

'I'm afraid not at the moment, sir. You will be given that
opportunity when we are at the Custody Centre.'

'My rights are—'

Branson raised his broad hands. 'Sir, we know what your
rights are.' Then he dropped his hands and unclipped a pair

of handcuffs from his belt. 'Please put your hands behind your back.'

What little colour there was in Bishop's face now drained away completely. 'You're not going to handcuff me, please! I'm not going to do a runner. There's a misunderstanding here. This is all wrong. I can sort this out with you.'

'Behind your back please, sir.'

In a total panic, Bishop stared wildly around the room. 'I need some things. My jacket – wallet – I – please let me put a jacket on.'

'Which is it, sir?' Nicholl asked.

Bishop pointed to the wardrobe. 'The camel-coloured one.' Then he pointed to his mobile phone and his Black-Berry, on the bedside table. Nicholl patted down his jacket, then Branson allowed him to put it on, and cram his wallet, mobile phone, BlackBerry and a pair of reading glasses into the pockets. Then he asked him to put his hands behind his back again.

'Look, do we really have to do this?' Bishop pleaded. 'It's going to be so embarrassing for me. We're going to walk through the hotel.'

'We've arranged with the manager to go via a fire exit at the side. Is your hand all right, sir?' Branson asked, clicking shut the first cuff.

'It wouldn't have a bloody plaster on it if it was all right,' Bishop snapped back. Still looking around the room, he said, panicking suddenly, 'My laptop?'

'I'm afraid that's going to be impounded, sir.'

Nick Nicholl picked up Bishop's car keys. 'Do you have a vehicle in the car park, Mr Bishop?'

'Yes. Yes, I do. I could drive it – you could come with me.'

'I'm afraid that's going to be impounded too, for forensic testing,' Branson said.

'This is unbelievable,' Bishop said. 'This is unfucking believable!'

But he got no sympathy from either man. Their demeanour from when they had first broken the bad news to him last Friday morning had changed completely.

'I need to make a quick call to the friends I'm having dinner with, to tell them I'm not coming.'

'Someone will call them for you, from the Custody Centre.'

'Yes, but they're cooking dinner for me.' He pointed at the hotel phone. 'Please – let me call them. It'll take thirty seconds.'

'I'm sorry, sir,' Branson said, repeating himself like an automaton. 'Someone will call them for you, from the Custody Centre.'

Suddenly Brian Bishop was scared.

84

Bishop sat next to DC Nicholl on the back seat of the grey, unmarked police Vectra. It was just past eight p.m., and the daylight beyond the car's windows was still bright.

The city that was sliding by, playing like a silent movie projected on to the car's windows, seemed different from the one he knew – and had known all his life. It was as if he was seeing the passing streets, houses, shops, trees, parks, for the first time. Neither officer spoke. The silence was broken only by the occasional crackle of static and a garbled burst from a controller's voice on the two-way radio. He felt as if he was a stranger here, looking out at some parallel universe in which he did not belong.

They were slowing suddenly and turning in towards a green, reinforced-steel gate that had started to slide open. There was a high, spiked fence to the right and a tall, drab brick structure beyond.

They stopped beside a blue sign with white lettering displaying the words BRIGHTON CUSTODY CENTRE until a wide enough gap had opened. Then they drove on up a steep ramp, along past what looked like factory loading bays in the rear of the brick building, and made a left turn into one of them. Instantly, the interior of the car darkened. Bishop saw a closed green door directly in front of them, with a small viewing window.

DS Branson switched off the engine and climbed out, the weak roof light barely changing the gloom inside the vehicle. Then he opened the rear door and motioned Bishop to step out.

Bishop, his hands cuffed behind his back, worked his way awkwardly sideways, then swung his feet out of the car and down on to the concrete screed. Branson put a steadying hand on his arm to help him up. Moments later the green door slid open and Bishop was ushered through into a narrow, completely bare holding room, fifteen feet long by eight wide, with another green door with a viewing window at the far end.

There was no furniture in here at all, just a hard bench seat running its full length,

'Take a seat,' Glenn Branson said.

'I'm happy to stand,' Bishop said defiantly.

'We may be a while.'

Bishop's mobile phone began ringing. He struggled for a moment, as if forgetting his hands were cuffed. 'Could one of you answer that for me?'

'It's not permitted, I'm afraid, sir,' DC Nicholl said, fishing it out of his pocket and terminating the call. The young detective studied the phone for some moments, then switched it off and returned it to Bishop's pocket.

Brian Bishop stared at a laminated plastic notice that was fixed to the wall by four strips of Sellotape. It was headed, in blue letters, CRIMINAL JUSTICE DEPARTMENT. Beneath was written:

ALL DETAINED PERSONS WILL BE
THOROUGHLY SEARCHED BY THE CUSTODY OFFICER.
IF YOU HAVE ANY PROHIBITED ITEMS
ON YOUR PERSON OR IN YOUR PROPERTY
TELL THE CUSTODY AND ARRESTING OFFICERS NOW.

Then he read another sign, above the second green door:

NO MOBILE PHONES TO BE USED IN THE CUSTODY AREA.

A third notice said:

YOU HAVE BEEN ARRESTED. YOU WILL HAVE YOUR
FINGERPRINTS, PHOTOGRAPH, DNA TAKEN RIGHT AWAY.

The two detectives sat down. Bishop remained standing. Anger was raging inside him. But, he reasoned, he was dealing with two robots. There was nothing to be gained by losing his rag. He just had to ride this out, for the moment. 'Can you tell me what all this is about?' he was addressing both of them.

But the door was sliding open as he spoke. Branson walked through. DC Nicholl gestured with his hand for Bishop to follow. 'This way please, sir.'

Bishop entered a large, circular room, dominated by an elevated central pod like a command centre that could have been a set for *Star Trek*, he thought, surprised by how futuristic it looked. It was constructed from a shiny, speckled grey composite that reminded him of the granite work surfaces Katie had chosen for their insanely expensive kitchen. Several men and women, some police officers and some Reliance Security staff, dressed in uniform white shirts with black epaulettes, manned individual workstations around the pod. Around the outside of the intensely brightly lit room were heavy-duty green doors, with some internal windows looking on to waiting rooms.

There was an air of quiet, orderly calm. Bishop noticed the pod had been designed with extended arms in front of each workstation, to create an area affording some privacy. A tattooed, shaven-headed youth in baggy clothes stood dejectedly, between two uniformed police officers, in one of them now. It all felt totally surreal.

Then he was escorted across to the central console, into a marbled portioned space, with a counter that was neck-high. Behind it sat a plump, crew-cut man in shirt sleeves. His black tie was clipped with a gold English Rugby Team pin that Bishop, who was a debenture holder at Twickenham, recognized.

On a blue video monitor screen, set into the face of the counter, just below his eye level, Bishop read:

BRIGHTON DETAINEE HANDLING CENTRE
DON'T LET PAST OFFENCES COME BACK TO HAUNT YOU.
A POLICE OFFICER WILL SPEAK TO YOU ABOUT ADMITTING
OTHER CRIMES YOU HAVE COMMITTED.

Branson outlined to the custody officer the circumstances of Bishop's arrest. Then the shirt-sleeved man was speaking directly, from his elevated seating position, down at him, in a flat voice devoid of emotion. 'Mr Bishop, I am the custody officer. You have heard what has been said. I'm satisfied that your arrest is lawful and necessary. I am authorizing your detention for the purpose of securing and preserving evidence and so you can be interviewed regarding the allegation.'

Bishop nodded, lost for the moment for a reply.

The custody officer handed him a folded yellow A4 sheet, headed, SUSSEX POLICE, NOTICE OF RIGHTS AND ENTITLEMENTS.

'You may find this helpful, sir. You have the right to have someone informed of your arrest, and to see a solicitor. Would you like us to provide you with a duty solicitor or do you have your own?'

'Can you please phone Mr Glenn Mishon and tell him that I won't be able to come to dinner tonight?'

'May I have his number?'

Bishop gave it to him. Then he said, 'I would like to speak to my own solicitor, Robert Vernon, at Ellis, Cherril and Ansell.'

'I will make those calls,' the custody officer said. 'In the meantime, I am authorizing your arresting officer, Detective Sergeant Branson, to search you.' The custody officer then produced two green plastic trays.

To his horror, Bishop saw DS Branson pulling on a pair of latex surgical gloves. Branson began patting him down, starting with his head. From Bishop's breast pocket, the DS removed his reading glasses and placed them in one tray.

'Hey! I need those – I can't read without them!' Bishop said.

'I'm sorry, sir,' Branson replied. 'I have to remove these for your own safety.'

'Don't be ridiculous!'

'It may be at a later stage that the custody officer will allow you to keep them with you, but for now they need to go into your property bag,' Branson replied.

'Don't be fucking stupid! I'm not about to kill myself! And how the hell am I supposed to read this document without them?' he said, flapping the A4 sheet at him.

'If you have reading difficulties, I'll arrange for someone to read it aloud to you, sir.'

'Look, come on, let's be reasonable about this!'

Ignoring Bishop's repeated pleas to have his glasses returned, Branson removed the man's hotel key, wallet, mobile phone and BlackBerry, placing each object in turn in a tray. The custody officer noted each item, counting the amount of cash in the wallet and writing that down separately.

Branson removed Bishop's wedding band, his Marc Jacobs wristwatch and a copper bracelet from his right wrist, and placed those in a tray also.

Then the custody officer handed Bishop a form, listing his possessions, and a biro to sign with.

'Look,' Bishop said, signing with clear reluctance, 'I'm happy to come in here and help you with your inquiries. But this is ridiculous. You've got to leave me with the tools of my trade. I must have email and my phone and my glasses, for God's sake!'

Ignoring him, Glenn Branson said to the custody officer, 'In view of the gravity of the offence and the suspect's potential involvement, we are asking to seize this person's clothing.'

'Yes, I authorize that,' the custody officer said.

'What the fuck?' Bishop shouted. 'What do you—'

With each of them holding one of his arms, Branson and Nicholl escorted him away from the console and out through yet another dark green door. They walked up a sloping floor, with dark cream walls on either side, and a red panic strip running the whole length on the left, past a yellow bollard printed with a warning triangle showing a figure falling over, and in large letters the words CLEANING IN PROGRESS. Then they rounded a corner into the corridor containing the custody cells.

And now as he saw the row of cell doors, Bishop began to panic. 'I – I'm claustrophobic. I—'

'There'll be someone to keep an eye on you round the clock, sir,' Nick Nicholl said gently.

They stepped to one side to allow a woman pushing a

trolley laden with dog-eared paperbacks to pass, then stopped outside a cell door that was partially open.

Glenn Branson pushed it wider open and went through. Nicholl, holding Bishop's arm firmly, followed.

The first thing that struck Bishop as he entered was the overpowering, sickly smell of disinfectant. He stared around the small, oblong room, bewildered. Stared at the cream walls, the brown floor, the same hard bench as in the holding room, topped in the same fake granite surface as in the pod outside, and a thin blue mattress on top of that. He stared at the barred, borrowed-light window with no view at all, at the observation mirror, out of reach on the ceiling, that was angled towards the door, and at the CCTV camera, also out of reach, pointing down at him as if he was a participant in *Big Brother*.

There was a modern-looking lavatory, with more fake granite for the seat and a flush button on the wall, and a surprisingly modern-looking washbasin, finished in the same speckled material. He noticed an intercom speaker grille with two control knobs, an air vent covered in mesh, the glass panel in the door.

Christ. He felt a lump in his throat.

DC Nicholl was holding a bundle in his arm, which he began to unfold. Bishop saw it was a blue paper jump-suit. A young man in his twenties, dressed in a white shirt bearing the Reliance Security emblem and black trousers, came to the doorway holding a clutch of brown evidence bags, which he handed to DS Branson. Then Branson closed the cell door.

'Mr Bishop,' he said, 'please remove all your clothes, including your socks and underwear.'

'I want my solicitor.'

'He is being contacted.' He pointed at the intercom

grille. 'As soon as the custody officer reaches him, he'll be patched through to you here.'

Bishop began stripping. DC Nicholl placed each item inside a separate evidence bag; even each sock had its own bag. When he was stark naked, Branson handed him the paper jump-suit and a pair of black, slip-on plimsolls.

Just as he got the jump-suit on and buttoned up, the intercom crackled sharply into life and he heard the calm, assured but concerned voice of Robert Vernon.

With a mixture of relief and embarrassment, Bishop padded over in his bare feet. 'Robert!' he said. 'Thanks for calling me. Thank you so much.'

'Are you all right?' his solicitor asked.

'No, I'm not.'

'Look, Brian, I imagine this is very distressing for you. I've had a little bit of a briefing from the custody officer, but obviously I don't have all the facts.'

'Can you get me out of here?'

'I'll do everything I can for you as your friend, but I'm not an expert in this area of law and you must have an expert. We don't really have anyone in my firm. The best chap down here is someone I know. His name's Leighton Lloyd. Very good reputation.'

'How quickly can you get hold of him, Robert?' Bishop was suddenly aware that he was alone in the cell and the door had been closed.

'I'm going to try right away and hope he's not on holiday. The police want to start interviewing you tonight. So far, they've just brought you in for questioning, so they can only hold you for twenty-four hours, I think it is, with another possible twelve-hour extension. Don't speak to anyone or do or say anything until Leighton gets to you.'

'What happens if he's away?' he asked, panicky.

'There are some other good people. Don't worry.'

'I want the best, Robert. The very best. Money's no object. It's ridiculous. I shouldn't be here. It's absolutely insane. I don't know what the hell's going on.'

'I'd better jump off the line, Brian,' the solicitor said, a little tersely. 'I need to get cracking for you.'

'Of course.' Bishop thanked him, then the intercom fell silent. He realized he was alone now and the door had been shut.

The cell was completely silent, as if he were in a sound-proof box.

He sat down on the blue mattress and pushed his feet into the plimsolls. They were too tight and pinched his toes. Something was bothering him about Robert Vernon. Why wasn't the man sounding more sympathetic? From his tone just now, it was almost as if he had been expecting this to happen.

Why?

The door opened and he was led into a room where he was photographed, his fingerprints were taken on an electronic pad and a DNA swab was taken from the inside of his mouth. Then he was returned to his cell.

And his bewildered thoughts.

85

For some officers, a career in the police force meant a constant, not always predictable series of changes. You could be moved from a uniform beat patrol one day to the Local Support Unit the next, executing arrest warrants and dealing with riots, then into plain clothes as a covert drug squad officer, then out at Gatwick airport, seconded to baggage crimes. Others found their niche, the way a snake finds its hole, or a squid finds its crevice in a sea wall, and stayed put in it all the way through their thirty years to retirement and, the bait on the hook, a very decent pension, thank you.

Detective Sergeant Jane Paxton was one of those who had found their niche and stayed in it. She was a large, plain-faced woman of forty, with lank brown hair and a brusque, no-nonsense attitude, who worked as an interview coordinator.

She had endeared herself to the entire female staff of Sussex House some years ago, legend had it, when she slapped Norman Potting on the face. Depending on who you talked to, there were half a dozen versions of what had happened. The one that Grace had heard was that Potting had put his hand on her thigh under the table during a meeting with the previous Chief Constable.

DS Paxton was now sitting opposite Grace at the round table in his office, wearing a loose-fitting blouse so voluminous it gave the appearance that her head was sticking out of the top of a tent. On either side of her sat Nick

Nicholl and Glenn Branson. DS Paxton was drinking water. The three men were drinking coffee. It was past eight thirty on Monday evening and all four of them knew they would be lucky to get out of the CID headquarters before midnight.

While Brian Bishop was alone, contemplating his navel in his custody block cell, awaiting the arrival of his solicitor, the team were creating their interview policy for Bishop's interrogation. Branson and Nicholl, who had both received specialist training in interviewing techniques, would carry out the series of interviews. Roy Grace and Jane Paxton would watch from an observation room.

The textbook procedure was to put suspects through three consecutive, strategized interviews within the twenty-four-hour period they could hold the person in custody. The first, which would take place tonight after the suspect's solicitor had arrived, would be mostly Bishop talking, setting down his facts. He would be encouraged to establish his story, his family background, and give an account of his movements during the twenty-four hours immediately before his wife's death.

In the second interview, which would take place in the morning, there would be specific questions on all that Bishop had said in the first interview. The tone would be kept courteous and constructive, while all the time the officers would be making notes of any inconsistencies. It was not until the third interview, which would follow later in the day, after Bishop and the team had had a break – and the team had had a chance to assess everything – that the gloves would come off. In that third interview, any inconsistencies or suspected lies would be challenged.

The hope was that by the end of that third interview, information extracted from the suspect, combined with whatever evidence they already had – such as the DNA in this instance – would give them enough for one of the Crown Prosecution solicitors, who operated from an office in the CPS headquarters in Dyke Road, to agree there was sufficient evidence to potentially secure a conviction, and to sanction the suspect being formally charged.

Key to any successful interrogation were the questions that needed to be asked and, very importantly, what information should be held back. They were all agreed that the sighting of Bishop's Bentley heading towards Brighton shortly before Mrs Bishop's murder should be held back to the third interview.

Then they debated for some time when to raise the question of the life insurance policy. Grace pointed out that since Bishop had already been questioned about this, and had denied all knowledge of the policy, it should be revisited as part of the first interview, to see if he had changed his story at all.

It was agreed to spring the gas mask on him during the second interview. Jane Paxton suggested it be raised as part of a series of specific questions about Bishop's sex life with his wife. The others agreed.

Grace asked Branson and Nicholl for a detailed account of how Bishop had behaved under arrest and his attitude generally.

'He's a bit of a cold fish,' Branson said. 'I couldn't believe it when me and Nick went to break the news about his wife being found dead.' He looked for confirmation to Nicholl, who nodded. Branson continued, 'Yeah, OK, he did the grief bit to start with, but do you know what he said next?' He looked at Grace, then Paxton. 'He said, "This is really not a good time – I'm halfway through a golf tournament." Can you believe it?'

'If anything, I think that comment works the other way,' Grace replied.

All of them looked at the Detective Superintendent with interest.

'What other way?' Branson asked.

'From what I've seen of him, Bishop's too smart to have made such a callous, potentially incriminating remark,' Grace replied. 'It's more the kind of remark of someone who is totally bewildered. Which would indicate the shock was genuine.'

'You're saying you think he's innocent?' Jane Paxton asked.

'No, what I'm saying is we have some strong evidence against this man. Let's stick to the hard facts for the moment. A comment like that could be useful during the trial – the prosecuting counsel could use it to help sway the jury against Bishop. We should keep it back, not bring it up in any of the interviews, because he'll probably say you've misunderstood him, and then you've blown its surprise value.'

'Good point,' Nick Nicholl said, and yawned, apologizing immediately.

Grace knew it was harsh, keeping Nicholl here until late, with his young baby at home, but that wasn't his problem. Nicholl was exactly the right soft-man foil to Branson's hard man for this series of interviews.

'The next item on my list,' Jane Paxton said, 'is Bishop's relationship with Sophie Harrington.'

'Definitely the third interview,' Grace said.

'No, I think we should bring it up in the second,' Branson replied. 'We could ask him again whether he knew her and if so what their relationship was. It would give us a good steer on how truthful he is, whether or not he still denies knowing her. Right?'

'It's a good point,' Grace said. 'But he'll know that we're analysing all his phone calls, so he'd have to be pretty stupid to deny knowing her.'

'Yeah, but I think it's worth asking him in the second interview,' Branson persisted. 'My reasoning is this: we got that witness opposite Sophie Harrington's house, who has positively identified him at around the time of her murder. Depending on how he answers the phone question in the second interview, we can spring that on him in the third.'

Grace looked at Jane Paxton. She was nodding in agreement.

'OK,' he said. 'Good plan.'

His internal phone rang. He stepped away from the table and over to his desk to answer it. 'Roy Grace?' He listened for some moments, then said, 'Fine. OK. Thanks. We'll be ready.'

He replaced the phone and joined them back at the round table. 'Bishop's solicitor will be here at half past nine.' He glanced at his watch. 'Forty-five minutes.'

'Who is it?' Jane Paxton asked.

'Leighton Lloyd.'

'Yeah, well.' Branson shrugged. 'Who else?'

They turned their focus on exactly what Lloyd would be told and what at this stage would be held back from him. Then the four of them left the building and walked briskly to the ASDA supermarket, taking a short cut through the bushes at the back, to grab a quick sandwich for their evening meal.

Ten minutes later they crossed back over the road. Branson and Nicholl walked through the side gate and up towards the custody block. Inside, they were taken to an interview room, where they would outline to Bishop's solicitor the background, and why Bishop had been arrested, without Bishop present. Then he would be brought into the room, too, for an interview.

Jane Paxton and Grace went back to their respective offices, Grace intending to use the next half-hour to catch up on some emails. He sat at his desk and rang Cleo, and discovered she was still at work at the mortuary.

'Hi, *you*!' she said, sounding pleased to hear from him.

'How are you?' he said.

'I'm shattered. But it's nice that you rang.'

'I like your voice when you're tired. It goes sort of croaky – it's sweet!'

'You wouldn't think that if you saw me. I feel about a hundred. And you? What's happening?'

He filled her in briefly, telling her he wouldn't be finished until around midnight, and asked if she'd like him to come over then.

'I would love to see you, my darling, but as soon as I'm out of here I'm going to fall into a bath and then crash. Why don't you come over tomorrow?'

'Sounds like a plan!'

'Are you eating properly?' she asked, motherly suddenly. 'Have you had some dinner?'

'Sort of,' he said evasively.

'An ASDA pot noodle?'

'A sandwich,' he confessed.

'That's not healthy! What kind of a sandwich?'

'Beef.'

'God, Roy. Fatty meat and carbohydrate!'

'It had a lettuce leaf in it.'

'Oh, well, that's all right then,' she said sarcastically.

Then her voice changed. 'Can you hang on a sec? There's someone outside the building.' She sounded worried.

'Who's there with you?'

'No one, I'm on my own. Poor Darren and Walter came in at four this morning. I sent them home a little while ago. I'm just going to check this out, OK? Call you back in a sec.'

The phone went dead.

86

I received a letter this morning from someone called
Lawrence Abramson at a firm of solicitors in London
called Harbottle and Lewis. It is a really unpleasant
letter.

I recently wrote to the man who looks just like me,
who started this company, suggesting that, as it was my
idea – and I have all the paperwork from my patent
agent, Mr Christopher Pett at Frank B. Dehn & Son,
to prove it – he should be paying me a royalty on his
revenues.

Mr Abramson is threatening to obtain an
injunction against me if I ever approach his client
again.

I'm really very angry.

87

Leighton Lloyd looked as if he'd had a hard day. Exuding a faint smell of tobacco smoke, he was sitting in this windowless, airless, enclosed interview room, dressed in an expensive-looking but crumpled grey suit, cream shirt and a sharp silk tie. A well-travelled leather attaché case was on the floor beside him, from which he extracted a black, lined A4 notebook.

Lloyd was a lean, wiry man, with close-cropped hair and an alert, predatory face that reminded Branson a little of the actor Robert Carlyle when he was playing a Bond villain in *The World Is not Enough*. Branson got a kick out of matching a movie villain's face to all lawyers – and he found it helped him to avoid feeling intimidated by them, particularly when being cross-examined by defence barristers in court.

Plenty of officers got on fine with solicitors. They took it in their stride, saying that it was all a game that sometimes they won, sometimes they lost. But for Branson it was more personal than that. He knew that criminal solicitors and barristers were only doing their job, and formed an important part of the freedoms of the British nation. But for nearly a decade before joining the police, he'd worked several nights a week as a nightclub bouncer in this city. He'd seen and tangled with just about every bit of scum imaginable, from drunk braggarts, to ugly gangsters, to some very smart criminals. He felt an intense obligation to try to make this city a better place for his own children to grow up in than it had been for him as a kid. That was his beef with the man sitting opposite him right now, in his hand-made suit and his black, tasselled loafers, with his big swinging dick of a BMW parked out front, and no doubt a flash, secluded house somewhere in one of Hove's swankier streets, all paid for out of the rich pickings from keeping scumbags out of jail – and on the streets.

Branson's mood had not been improved by a blazing row with his wife, Ari, on his mobile phone as he had walked over to the custody block. He'd called to say goodnight to the children and she had pointed out acidly that they had been asleep in bed for some time. To which his response, that it was not much fun still being at work at nine o'clock, received a torrent of sarcasm. It had then degenerated into a shouting match, ending with Ari hanging up on him.

Nick Nicholl closed the door, pulled up a chair opposite Branson and sat down. Lloyd had positioned himself at the head of the table, as if arranging the stage to assert himself from the getgo.

The solicitor made a note in his black book with a rollerball pen. 'So, gentlemen, what information do you have for me?' He spoke in a brisk, clipped voice, his tone polite but firm. Above them, an air-conditioning unit was starting, noisily, to pump out cool air.

Lloyd made Branson nervous. The detective could deal with brute force, no problem, but cunning intellects always unnerved him. And Lloyd was observing them both with an inscrutable, unreadable expression. He spoke slowly, articulating each word as if he were addressing a child, thinking very carefully about what he was going to say next.

'We have spoken to Mr Bishop over the last four days, as you will appreciate is normal in these circumstances, in order to get background information regarding himself and his wife. There is some information that we have been given which we will be covering during the interview, concerning his movements and location around the time of the murder.'

'OK,' Leighton Lloyd said, a tad impatiently, as if flagging that he wasn't here to listen to waffle. 'Can you bring me up to speed on why my client has been arrested?'

Branson then handed him the Pre-Interview Disclosure document that had been prepared. 'If you would like to read this, we can go through any questions you may have.'

Lloyd reached across the desk and took the short document, a single A4 sheet, and read it in silence. Then he read parts of it out aloud. 'Possible strangulation by ligature, subject to further pathology tests . . . We have certain DNA evidence which will form part of the interview.'

He looked up at the two officers for a moment, then continued reading out aloud, his voice now sounding quizzical: 'We have reason to believe that Mr Bishop has not been telling the complete truth. Accordingly, we wish to put certain questions to him under caution.'

The solicitor dropped the sheet back down on the table. 'Can you put any flesh on this document?' he asked Branson.

'How much information do you have?' Branson asked.

'Very little. Obviously I've been following the report on the murder of Mrs Bishop in the papers and on the news. But I haven't spoken to my client yet.'

For the next twenty minutes, Lloyd quizzed the police officers. He started by asking about the cleaning lady and the details of the crime scene. Glenn Branson gave him the very minimum information he felt he needed to. He outlined the circumstances surrounding the discovery of Katie Bishop's body, and the pathologist's estimate of the approximate time of death, but held back the information about the gas mask. And he firmly refused to reveal any information on their DNA evidence.

The solicitor finished by trying to trip up Branson into revealing why they believed that Brian Bishop had not been telling the truth. But Branson would not be drawn.

'Has my client given you an alibi?' he asked.

'Yes, he has,' Branson replied.

'And presumably you are not satisfied with it.'

The Detective Sergeant hesitated, then said, 'That is something we will be dealing with during the interview process.'

Lloyd made another note with the roller-ball pen in his book. Then he smiled at Branson. 'Is there anything else you can tell me at this stage?'

Branson glanced at Nicholl and shook his head.

'Right. I'd like to see my client now.'

88

It was now almost completely dark outside. Distractedly, Roy Grace ran his eye down the pages and pages on his screen of today's incident reports log, looking for anything that might be relevant to the two cases. He found nothing. He scanned through his email inbox, deleted several where he had just been copied in and fired off a few quick responses. Then he looked at his watch. It was fifteen minutes since Cleo had said she would call him right back.

He felt a sudden knot of anxiety in his stomach, thinking how much he cared for her; how he could not bear the thought of anything happening to her. As Sandy had been for so many years, Cleo was starting to feel like the rock to which his life was moored. A good, solid, beautiful, funny, loving, caring and wise rock. But sometimes in shadow, not sunlight.

Roy, this is not the woman Leslie and I saw last week. We really are convinced we saw Sandy. Best, Dick

God, he thought, it would have been so much simpler if Dick had replied to him that yes, this was the woman they had seen. It still wouldn't have given him the closure he sought, but at least it would have put Munich back in its box. Now it was drawing him towards another journey there. But at this moment, he wasn't able to think about that. He was remembering only too vividly that some creep had slashed the roof of Cleo's MG yesterday, in broad daylight, outside the mortuary.

The place attracted every imaginable kind of weirdo and sicko, of which Brighton had more than its fair share. He still found it hard to understand how she could enjoy working there as much as she claimed she did. Sure, you could get used to just about anything. But that didn't mean you could *like* anything.

Car roofs mostly got slashed in urban streets, either by people breaking in to steal something or by swaggering yobs late at night, high or drunk, who were passing by. People didn't *pass by* the mortuary car park, especially not on a hot Sunday afternoon. Nothing had been stolen from the car. It was just a nasty, malicious piece of vandalism. Probably some lowlife jealous of the car.

But was that person outside the mortuary now?

Call me. Please call me.

He opened an attachment and tried to read through the agenda for this year's International Homicide Investigators Association annual symposium, in New Orleans, now just a few weeks away. It was impossible to concentrate.

Then his phone rang. Grabbing it, he blurted in relief, 'Hi!'

But it was Jane Paxton, telling him that Bishop was about to see his solicitor and she was heading over to the observation room at the custody block. She suggested that he come over in about ten minutes.

89

Brian Bishop sat alone in his silent cell, hunched forward on the edge of the bench that was also the bed. He could not remember ever feeling so low in his entire life. It seemed that half his world had been ripped away from him and the other half was turning against him. Even gentle, non-judgemental Robert Vernon had sounded less friendly than usual on the phone earlier. Why? Had word got round that he was damaged goods, to be left alone? Poisonous to touch?

Would it be Glenn and Barbara next? And the other couple he and Katie saw a lot of, Ian and Terrina? And the rest of the people he had once considered his friends?

His blue paper suit felt tight under the armpits and his toes could barely move inside the plimsolls, but he didn't care. This was all a bad dream and some time soon he was going to wake up, and Katie would be all big smiles, sitting up in bed next to him, reading the *Daily Mail* gossip column, the page she always turned to first, a cup of tea beside her.

In his hands he held the yellow sheet he had been given, squinting at the blurred words, struggling to read them without his glasses.

SUSSEX POLICE
Notice of Rights and Entitlement
REMEMEMBER YOUR RIGHTS

His cell door was opened suddenly by a pasty-faced

man of about thirty, with no neck and the physique of a jelly baby, who looked as if he used to pump iron but had recently let his muscles run to fat. He was wearing the Reliance Security uniform of monogrammed white shirt with black epaulettes, black tie and black trousers, and was perspiring heavily.

He spoke in a courteous, slightly squeaky voice, avoiding eye contact, as if this was standard practice for addressing the scum behind the barred doors of this place. 'Mr Bishop, your solicitor is here. I'll take you through to him. Walk in front of me, please.'

Bishop walked as directed from behind, navigating a network of blank, cream corridors, the only relief on the walls being the continuous red panic strip set in a metal rim. Then he entered the interview room, which Branson and Nicholl had temporarily vacated, to allow him privacy with his lawyer.

Leighton Lloyd shook his hand and ushered him to a seat. He then checked that all the recording and monitoring equipment was switched off, before sitting back down himself.

'Thank you for coming over,' Bishop said.

The solicitor gave him a sympathetic smile, and Bishop found himself instantly warming to the man – although he knew that, at this moment, he would have probably warmed to Attila the Hun if he'd said he was here to help.

'That's my job,' Lloyd said. 'So, have you been treated all right?'

'I don't have much to compare with,' Bishop said, attempting a stab of humour that bypassed the lawyer. 'Actually, there's one thing I'm really angry about – they took my reading glasses.'

'Normal, I'm afraid.'

'Oh, great. So if I had contact lenses, I could keep those, but because I choose to have reading glasses, I'm now not able to read anything.'

'I'll do my best to get them back for you quickly.' He noted this down in his book. 'So, Mr Bishop, I'm conscious that it's late and you are tired. The police want to conduct one interview tonight – we'll keep it as brief as we can – then they'll continue again tomorrow morning.'

'How long am I going to be here? Can you get me out on bail?'

'I can only apply for bail if you are charged. The police are entitled to keep you for twenty-four hours without charging you, and they can get a further twelve hours' extension. After that they have to release you, charge you or go to court to apply for further time.'

'So I could be in here until Wednesday morning?'

'Yes, I'm afraid so.'

Bishop fell silent.

Lloyd held up a sheet of paper. 'This is what's called the Pre-Interview Disclosure document – it is a summary of the information the police are prepared to let us have at this stage. If you're having problems reading, would you like me to read it aloud to you?'

Bishop nodded. He felt sick and so drained that he did not even have the will to speak.

The lawyer read out the contents, then expanded, filling him in on the little extra that he had been able to glean from DS Branson. 'Is that all clear?' he asked Bishop, when he had finished.

Bishop nodded again. Hearing the words was making everything worse. They sank like dark stones, deep into his soul. And his gloom deepened even more. He felt as if he was sitting at the bottom of the deepest mineshaft in the world.

For the next few minutes, Bishop was briefed on the questions he would probably be asked at his first interview, and how he should reply. The solicitor told him to speak economically and be helpful but to give short answers. If there were any questions that either of them felt were inappropriate, the solicitor would step in. He also asked Bishop about his health, whether he was up to the ordeal ahead, or whether he needed to see a doctor or to have any medication. Bishop told him he was fine.

'There's one final question I have to ask,' Leighton Lloyd said. 'Did you murder your wife?'

'No. Absolutely not. That's ridiculous. I loved her. Why would I kill her? No, I didn't, I really didn't. You have to believe me. I just don't know what's going on.'

The solicitor smiled. 'OK. That's good enough for me.'

90

As Grace walked across the tarmac separating the back entrance of Sussex House from the custody centre, passing a row of wheelie bins, shadows jumped inside his mind. His mobile phone was clamped to his ear and the knot of anxiety inside his gullet was tightening more and more. His mouth was dry with worry. It was now over twenty minutes. Why hadn't Cleo called back? He listened as her mobile phone went yet again straight to voicemail without ringing, then dialled the mortuary phone. As before, it was picked up on the fourth ring by the answering machine. He toyed with just jumping in a car and driving over there. But that would be irresponsible. He had to be here, scrutinizing the interview all the way through.

So he phoned the resourcing centre and explained to the controller who he was and what his concerns were. To his relief, the man replied that there was a unit in that part of the city at the moment, so he would send it straight up to the mortuary. Grace asked if he could call him back, or have one of the officers in the patrol car call him when they were on site, to let him know the situation.

He had a bad feeling about this. Really bad. Even though he knew Cleo always kept the mortuary doors locked, and there were security cameras, he did not like the idea of her being there alone at night. Particularly not after what had happened yesterday.

Then, holding his security card up to the grey Interflex eye beside the door, he entered the custody centre, walked across past the central pod, where, as usual, some sad bit of lowlife – this one a skinny Rasta youth in a grubby vest, camouflage trousers and sandals – was being booked in, and headed through an internal security door up the stairs to the first floor.

Jane Paxton was already seated in the small observation room, in front of the colour monitor, which was switched on but blank. Both the video and audio would be off to give Brian Bishop privacy with his lawyer, until the interview formally started. She had thoughtfully brought over two bottles of water for them. Grace put his notepad on the work surface in front of his empty chair, then went down to the small kitchenette at the end of the corridor and made himself a mug of strong coffee. It was a cheap brand in a big tin that looked like it had been there a while and smelled stale. Some prat had left the milk out and it had gone off, so he left his coffee black.

As he carried it back into the room he said, 'You didn't want any tea or coffee, did you?'

'Never *use* them,' she said primly, with a faint reprimand in her voice, as if he had just offered some Class A drugs.

As he set his mug down, the speaker crackled and the monitor flickered into life. Now he could see the four men in the interview room, Branson, Nicholl, Bishop and Lloyd. Three of them had removed their jackets. The two detectives had their ties on but their shirt sleeves rolled up.

In the observation room they had a choice of two cameras and Grace switched to the one that gave him the best view of Bishop's face.

Addressing Bishop, with the occasional deferential glance at the man's solicitor, Glenn Branson started with the standard opening of all interview sessions with suspects: 'This interview is being recorded on tape and video, and this can be monitored remotely.'

Grace caught his fleeting, cheeky, upward glance.

Branson again cautioned Bishop, who nodded.

'It is ten fifteen p.m., Monday 7 August,' he continued. 'I am Detective Sergeant Branson. Can each of you identify yourselves for the benefit of the tape?'

Brian Bishop, Leighton Lloyd and DC Nicholl then introduced themselves. When they had finished, Branson continued, 'Mr Bishop, can you run us through, in as much detail as possible, your movements during the twenty-four hours leading up to the time when DS Nicholl and myself came to see you at the North Brighton Golf Club on Friday morning?'

Grace watched intently as Brian Bishop gave his account. He prefaced it by stating that it was normal for him to take the train to London early on Monday mornings, spend the week alone at his flat in Notting Hill, working late, often with evening meetings, and return to Brighton on Friday evenings for the weekend. Last week, he said, because he had a golf tournament that began early on Friday morning, as part of his club's centenary celebrations, he had driven to London late on Sunday evening, in order to have his car up there, so that he could drive straight down to the golf club on Friday morning.

Grace noted this exception to Bishop's normal routine down on his pad.

Bishop related his day at work, at the Hanover Square offices of his company, International Rostering Solutions PLC, until the evening, when he had walked down to Piccadilly to meet his financial adviser, Phil Taylor, for dinner at a restaurant called the Wolseley.

Phil Taylor, he explained, organized his personal annual

tax planning. After dinner, he had left the restaurant and gone home to his flat, a little later than he had planned and having drunk rather more than he had intended. He had slept badly, he explained, partly as a result of two large espressos and a brandy, and partly because he was worried about oversleeping and arriving late at the golf club the next morning.

Keeping rigidly to his script, Branson went back over the account, asking for specific details here and there, in particular regarding the people he had spoken to during the day. He asked him if he could recall speaking to his wife, and Bishop replied that he had, at around two p.m., when Katie had rung him to discuss the purchase of some plants for the garden, as Bishop was planning a Sunday lunch garden party early in September for his executives.

Bishop added that he had phoned British Telecom for a wake-up call at five thirty a.m. when he had arrived home after his dinner with Phil Taylor.

As Grace was in the middle of writing that down, his mobile phone rang. It was a young-sounding officer, who introduced himself as PC David Curtis, telling him they were outside the Brighton and Hove Mortuary, that the lights of the premises were off, and everything looked quiet and in order.

Grace stepped outside the room and asked him if he could see a blue MG sports car outside. PC Curtis told him that the parking area was empty.

Grace thanked him and hung up. Immediately he dialled Cleo's home number. She answered on the second ring.

'Hi!' she said breezily. 'How's it going?'

'Are you OK?' he asked, relieved beyond belief at hearing her voice.

'Me? Fine! I've got a glass of wine in my hand and I'm about to dive into my bath!' she said sleepily. 'How are you?'

'I've been worried out of my wits.'

'Why?'

'Why? Jesus! You said there was someone outside the mortuary! You were going to call me straight back! I was – I thought—'

'Just a couple of drunks,' she said. 'They were looking for Woodvale Cemetery – mumbling about going to pay their respects to their mother.'

'Don't do this to me!' he said.

'Do what?' she asked, all innocence.

He shook his head, smiling in relief. 'I have to get back.'

'Of course you do. You're an important detective, on a big case.'

'Now you're taking the piss.'

'Already had one of those, when I got home. Now I'm going to have my bath. Night-night!'

He walked back into the observation room, smiling, exasperated and relieved. 'Have I missed anything?' he asked Jane Paxton.

She shook her head. 'DS Branson's good,' she said.

'Tell him that later. He needs a boost. His ego's on the floor.'

'What is it with you men and ego?' she asked him.

Grace looked at her head, poking out of her tent of a blouse, her double chin and her flat-ironed hair, and then at the wedding band and solitaire ring on her podgy finger. 'Doesn't your husband have an ego?'

'He wouldn't bloody dare.'

91

The Time Billionaire knew all about *happy pills*. But he had never taken one. No need. Hey, who needed *happy pills* when you could come home on a Monday night to find the postman had delivered to your doormat the workshop manual for a 2005 MG TF sports car that you had ordered on Saturday?

It was the last year that this model was manufactured before MG ceased production and were bought up by a Chinese company. It was the model that Cleo Morey drove. Navy blue. Now fitted with its matching blue hardtop, despite the blistering hot weather, because some jerk had vandalized the soft-top roof with a knife. What a son of a bitch! What a creep! What a goddamn piece of lowlife shit!

And it was Tuesday morning! One of the days that the stupid, grumpy cleaning woman with the ungrateful daughter didn't come! She had told him that herself, yesterday.

Best of all, Brian Bishop had been arrested. It was the front-page splash of the morning edition of the *Argus*. It was on the local radio! It would be on the local television news, for sure. Maybe even the national news! Joy! What goes around comes around! Like the wheels of a car! Cleo Morey's car!

Cleo Morey had the top of the range, the TF 160, with its variable valve controlled engine. He listened to it now, 1.8 litres revving up sweetly in the cool, early-morning air. Eight o'clock. She worked long hours, had to credit her that.

Now she was pulling out of her parking space, driving up the street, holding first gear too long, but maybe she was enjoying the echoing blatter of the exhaust.

Getting in through the front gates of the courtyard development where Cleo Morey lived was a no-brainer. Just four numbers on a touch pad. He'd picked those up easily enough by watching as other residents returned home through his binoculars, from the comfort of his car.

The courtyard was empty. If any nosy neighbour was peeking from behind their blinds, they would have seen the same neatly dressed man with his clipboard, the Seeboard crest on his jacket pocket, as yesterday and assumed he had come to recheck the gas meter. Or something.

His freshly cut key turned sweetly in the lock. Thanks to God's help! He stepped inside, into the large, open-plan downstairs area, and shut the door behind him. The silence smelled of furniture polish and freshly ground coffee beans. He heard the faint hum of a fridge.

He looked around, taking everything in, which he had not had the time to do yesterday, not with the grumpy woman on his back. He saw cream walls hung with abstract paintings that he did not understand. Modern rugs scattered on a shiny oak floor. Two red sofas, black lacquered furniture, a big television, an expensive stereo system. A copy of *Sussex Life* magazine on a side table. And unlit candles. Dozens of them. Dozens and bloody dozens, on silver sticks, in opaque glass pots, in vases – was she a religious freak? Did she hold black masses? Another good reason why she had to go. God would be happy to be rid of her!

Then he saw the square glass fish tank on a coffee table, with a goldfish swimming around what looked like the remains of a miniature Greek temple.

'You need releasing,' the Time Billionaire said. 'It's wrong to keep animals imprisoned.'

He wandered across to a floor-to-ceiling row of crammed bookshelves. He saw Graham Greene's *Brighton Rock*. Then a James Herbert novel, *Nobody True*. A Natasha Cooper crime novel. Several Ian Rankin books and an Edward Marston historical thriller.

'Wow!' he said aloud. 'We have the same taste in literature! Too bad we'll never get a chance to discuss books! You know, in different circumstances you and I might have been pretty good friends.'

Then he opened the drawer in a table. It contained elastic bands, a book of parking vouchers, a broken garage-opener remote control, a solitary battery, envelopes. He rummaged through but did not find what he was looking for. He closed it. Then he looked around, opened two more drawers, closed them again, without luck. The drawers in the kitchen yielded nothing either.

His hand was still hurting. Stinging all the time, getting worse, despite the pills. And he had a headache. His head throbbed constantly and he was feeling a little feverish, but it was nothing he couldn't cope with.

He wandered upstairs slowly, taking his time. Cleo Morey had only just gone to work. He had all the time in the world. Hours of the stuff if he wanted!

On the next floor he found a small bathroom. Opposite was her den. He went in. It was a chaotically untidy room, lined again with crammed bookshelves; almost all of the books seemed to be on philosophy. A desk piled with papers, with a laptop in the middle of them, sat in front of a window overlooking the rooftops of Brighton, towards the sea. He opened each drawer of the desk, tidily inspecting the contents before closing them carefully. Then he opened and shut each of the four drawers of the metal filing cabinet.

Her bedroom was on the next floor, on the other side of a spiral staircase that appeared to lead up to the roof. He went in and sniffed her bed. Then he pulled back the purple counterpane and pressed his nose into her pillows, inhaling deeply. The scents tightened his groin. Carefully he peeled back the duvet, sniffing every inch of the sheet. More of her! More of her still! No scents of Detective Superintendent Grace! No semen stains from him on the sheet! Just her scents and smells! Hers alone! Left there for him to savour.

He replaced the duvet, then the counterpane carefully. So carefully. No one would ever know he had been here.

There was a modern, black lacquered dressing table in the room. He opened its one drawer and there, nestling in between her jewellery boxes, he saw it! The black leather fob with the letters *MG* embossed in gold. The two shiny, unused keys, and the ring that was hooped through them.

He closed his eyes and said a brief prayer of thanks to God, who had guided him to them. Then he held up the keys to his lips and kissed them. 'Beautiful!'

He closed the drawer, pocketed the keys and went back downstairs, then made his way straight over to the fish tank. He pushed up the cuff of his jacket, then the sleeve of his shirt, and sank his hand into the tepid water. It was like trying to grab hold of soap in the bathtub! But finally he managed to grip the wriggling, slippery goldfish, closing his fingers around the stupid creature.

Then he tossed it on to the floor.

He heard it flipping around as he let himself back out of the front door.

92

The joint morning briefing for Operations Chameleon and Mistral ended shortly after nine o'clock. There was a mood of optimism now that a suspect was in custody. And this was heightened by the fact that there was a witness, the elderly lady who lived opposite Sophie Harrington and had identified Brian Bishop outside her house around the time of the murder. With luck, Grace hoped, that DNA analysis on semen present in Sophie Harrington's vagina would match Bishop's. Huntington was fast-tracking the analysis and he should get the results later today.

There was now little doubt in anyone's mind that the two murders were linked, but they were still keeping the exact details back from the press.

Names of people and times given by Bishop in his first interview were being checked out, and Grace was particularly interested to see whether the British Telecom phone records would confirm that Bishop had requested an early-morning alarm call after he had returned to his flat on Thursday night. Although, of course, that call could have been made by an accomplice. With three million pounds to be gained from the life insurance policy on his wife, the possibility that Bishop had an accomplice – or indeed more than one – had to be carefully explored.

He left the conference room, anxious to dictate a couple of letters to Eleanor, his MSA, one regarding preparations for the trial of the odious character Carl Venner, who had been arrested on the last murder case Grace had run. He walked hurriedly along the corridors and through into the large, green-carpeted, partially open-plan area that housed all the senior officers of the CID and their support staff.

To his surprise as he went through the security door that separated this area from the Major Incident Suite, he saw a large crowd of people gathered around a desk, including Gary Weston, who was the Chief Superintendent of Sussex CID and technically his immediate boss – although in reality it was Alison Vosper to whom he answered mostly.

He wondered for a moment if it was a raffle draw. Or someone's birthday. Then, as he got closer, he saw that no one seemed to be in a celebratory mood. Everyone looked as if they were in shock, including Eleanor, who tended to look that way most of the time.

'What's up?' he asked her.

'You haven't heard?'

'Heard what?'

'About Janet McWhirter?'

'Our Janet, from the PNC?'

Eleanor nodded at him encouragingly, through her large glasses, as if she was helping him to a solution in a game of charades.

Janet McWhirter had, until four months ago, held a responsible position here in Sussex House as head of the Police National Computer department, a sizeable office of forty people. One of their main functions was information and intelligence gathering for the detectives here.

A plain, single girl in her mid-thirties, quiet and studious and slightly old-fashioned-looking, she had been popular because of her willingness to help, working whatever hours were needed while always remaining polite. She had reminded Grace, both in appearance and in her quietly earnest demeanour, of a dormouse.

Janet had surprised everyone back in April, when she resigned, saying that she'd decided to spend a year travelling. Then, very secretively and coyly, she had told her two closest friends in the department that she had met and fallen in love with a man. They were already engaged, and she was emigrating with him to Australia and would get married there.

It was Brian Cook, the Scientific Support Branch Manager and one of Grace's friends here, who turned to him. 'She's been found dead, Roy,' he said in his blunt voice. 'Washed up on the beach on Saturday night – been in the sea some considerable time. She's just been identified from her dental records. And it looks like she was dead before she went in the water.'

Grace was silent for a moment. Stunned. He'd had a lot of dealings with Janet over the years and really liked her. 'Shit,' he said. For a moment it was as if a dark cloud had covered the windows and he felt a sudden cold swirl, deep inside him. Deaths happened, but something instinctively felt very wrong about this.

'Doesn't look like she made it to Australia,' Cook added sardonically.

'Or the altar?'

Cook shrugged.

'Has the fiancé been contacted?'

'We only heard the news a few minutes ago. He could be dead too.' Then he added, 'You might want to pop along and say something to the team in her department – I imagine they're all going to be extremely upset.'

'I'll do that when I get a gap. Who's going to head the inquiry?'

'Don't know yet.'

Grace nodded, then led his shocked MSA away from the

group and back to her office. He had barely ten minutes to give her his dictation, then get over to the custody centre for the second interview with Brian Bishop.

But he couldn't clear the image of Janet McWhirter's plain little face from his mind. She was the most pleasant and helpful person. Why would someone kill her? A mugger? A rapist? Something to do with her work?

Mulling on it, he thought to himself, *She spends fifteen years working for Sussex Police, much of it in the PNC unit, falls in love with a man, then goes for a career change, a lifestyle change. Leaves. Then dies.*

He was a firm believer in always looking at the most obvious things first. He knew where he would start, if he was the SIO on her investigation. But at this moment, Janet McWhirter's death, although deeply shocking and sad, was not his problem.

Or so he thought.

93

'Jeezizzz, mon! Will you turn that fekkin', bleedin', soddin' thing off! It's been goin' all bloody mornin'! Can't you fekkin' answer it or summat?'

Skunk opened one eye, which felt as if it had been hit recently with a hammer. So did his head. It also felt as if someone was sawing through his brain with a cheese-wire. And the whole camper seemed to be pitchpoling like a small boat in a storm.

Preeep-preeep-bnnnzzzzz-preeep-preeeep-bnnnzzzzz. His phone, he realized, was slithering around on the floor, vibrating, flashing, ringing.

'Answer it yousself, you fuckwit!' he mumbled back at his latest, unwelcome, lodger-du-jour – some scumbag he'd encountered in a Brighton bat-cave in the early hours of this morning, who'd bummed a bed off him for the night. 'This isn't the fucking Hilton! We don't have fucking twenty-four-hour room service.'

'If I answer it, laddie, it's going straight up yer rectum, so fekkin' far ye'll have ter stick yer fingers down yer tonsils ter find it.'

Skunk opened his other eye as well, then shut it again as blinding morning sunlight lasered into it, through his brain, through the back of his skull and deep into the Earth's core, pinning his head to his sodden, lumpy pillow like a pin through a fly. He closed his eye and made an effort to sit up, which was rewarded by a hard crack on his head from the Luton roof above him.

'Fuck! Shit!'

This was the gratitude he got for letting fucking useless tossers crash in his home! Wide awake now, on the verge of throwing up, he reached out an arm that felt totally disembodied from the rest of him, as if someone had attached it to his shoulder by a few threads during the night. Numb fingers fumbled around on the floor until they found the phone.

He lifted it up, hand shaking, his whole body shaking, thumbed the green button and brought it to his ear. 'Urr?' he said.

'Where the hell have you been, you piece of shit?'

It was Barry Spiker.

And suddenly he was really wide awake, a whole bunch of confused thoughts colliding inside his brain.

'It's the middle of the fucking night,' he said sullenly.

'Maybe on your planet, shitface. On mine it's eleven in the morning. Missed holy communion again, have you?'

And then it came to Skunk. *Paul Packer. Detective Constable Paul Packer!*

Suddenly his morning was feeling a bit better. Recollections of a deal he had made with DC Packer were now surfacing through the foggy, drug-starved maelstrom of pain that was his mind. He was on a promise to Packer. To let him know the next time Barry Spiker gave him a job. It would be cutting his nose off to spite his face, to shop Spiker. But the pleasure the thought gave him overrode that. Spiker had stiffed him on their last deal. Packer had promised him a payment.

Cash payments from the police were crap. But if he was really smart, he could do a deal, get paid by Spiker and the police. That would be cool!

Ching. Ching. Ching.

Al, his hamster, was busy on his treadmill, going round and round, as usual, despite his paw in its splint. Al needed another visit to the vet. He owed money to Beth. Two birds with one stone! Spiker and DC Packer. Al and Beth! It was a done deal!

'Just got back from mass, actually,' he said.

'Good. I've a job for you.'

'I'm all ears.'

'That's your fucking problem. All ears, no brains.'

'So what you got for me?'

Spiker briefed him. 'I need it tonight,' he said. 'Any time. I'll be there all night. One-fifty if you get the spec right this time. Are you capable of it?'

'I'm fit.'

'Don't fuck up.'

The phone went dead.

Skunk sat up in excitement. And nearly split his skull open, again, on the roof.

'Fuck!' he said.

'Fek you, Jimmy!' came the voice from the far end of his van.

94

Glenn Branson terminated the second interview with Brian Bishop at twelve twenty p.m. Then, leaving Bishop alone with his solicitor in the interview room for a lunch break, the interviewing team regrouped in Grace's office.

Branson had kept to the script. They had held back, as planned, the really big questions for the third interview, this afternoon.

As they sat down at the small round table in Grace's office, the Detective Superintendent gave Branson a pat on the back. 'Well done, Glenn, good stuff. OK, now, as I see it –' and he used a phrase of Alison Vosper's which he rather liked – 'here's the elephant in the room.'

All three of them looked at him expectantly.

'Bishop's alibi. His evening meal at the Wolseley restaurant in London with this Phil Taylor character. That's the elephant in the room.'

'Surely the DNA result kicks his alibi into touch,' Nicholl said.

'I'm thinking about a jury,' Grace replied. 'Depends how credible this Taylor man is. You can be sure Bishop's going to have a top brief. He'll milk the alibi for all it's worth. An honest citizen versus the vagaries of science? Probably with evidence from British Telecom, showing the time Bishop booked his alarm call, to back his time-frame up?'

'I think we should be able to nail Bishop in this third interview, Roy,' Jane Paxton said. 'We've got a lot to hit him with.'

Grace nodded, thinking hard, not yet convinced they had everything they needed.

*

They started again shortly after two. Roy Grace was conscious, as he sat back down in the slightly unstable chair in the observation room, that they had just six hours left before they would have to release Brian Bishop, unless they applied for an extension or charged him. They could of course go to court for a Warrant of Further Detention, but Grace did not want to do that unless it was absolutely necessary.

Alison Vosper had already rung him to find out how close they were to charging Bishop. When he related the facts to date to her, she sounded pleased. Still in *sweet* mode.

The fact that a man had been arrested so quickly after Katie Bishop's murder was making the force look good in the eyes of the media, and it was reassuring for the citizens of Brighton and Hove. Now they needed to charge him. That, of course, would do Grace's career prospects no harm at all. And with the positive DNA results, they had sufficient evidence to secure consent from the Crown Prosecution Service to charge Bishop. But it wasn't just charging the man that Grace needed. He needed to ensure a conviction.

He knew he should be elated at the way it was all going, but something was worrying him, and he couldn't put his finger on what it was.

Suddenly, Glenn Branson's voice sounded loud and clear, followed an instant later by the image of the four men in the interview room appearing back on the monitor. Brian Bishop was sipping a glass of water, looking sick as a parrot.

'It is three minutes past two p.m., Tuesday 8 August,'

Branson was saying. 'Present at this interview, interview number 3, are Mr Brian Bishop, Mr Leighton Lloyd, DC Nicholl and myself, DS Branson.' He then looked directly at Bishop.

'Mr Bishop,' he said. 'You've told us that you and your wife were happily married and that you made a great team. Were you aware that Mrs Bishop was having an affair? A sexual relationship with another man?'

Grace watched Bishop's eyes intently. They moved to the left. From his memory of last watching Bishop, this was to truth mode.

Bishop shot a glance at his lawyer, as if wondering whether he should say anything, then looked back at Branson.

'You're not obliged to answer,' Lloyd said.

Bishop was pensive for some moments. Then he spoke, the words coming out heavily. 'I suspected she might have been. Was it this artist fellow in Lewes?'

Branson nodded, giving Bishop a sympathetic smile, aware the man was hurting.

Bishop sank his face into his hands and was silent.

'Do you want to take a break?' his solicitor asked.

Bishop shook his head, then removed his hands. He was crying. 'I'm OK. I'm OK. Let's just get on with all this bloody stuff. Jesus.' He shrugged, staring miserably down at the table, dabbing his tears with the back of his hand. 'Katie was the loveliest person but there was something inside driving her. Like a demon that always made her dissatisfied with everything. I thought I could give her what she wanted.' He started crying again.

'I think we should take a break, gentlemen,' Leighton Lloyd said.

They all stepped out, leaving Bishop alone, then

resumed the interview after ten minutes. Nick Nicholl, playing *good cop*, asked the first question.

'Mr Bishop, could you tell us how you felt when you first suspected your wife was being unfaithful?'

Bishop looked at the DC sardonically. 'Do you mean, did I want to kill her?'

'You said that, sir, not us,' Branson slammed in.

Grace was interested to see Bishop's display of emotion. Perhaps they were just crocodile tears for the benefit of the interviewing team.

In a faltering voice Bishop said, 'I loved her, I never wanted to kill her. People have affairs, it's the way of the world. When Katie and I first met, we were both married to other people. We had an affair. I think I knew in my heart then that if we did marry, she would probably end up doing the same to me.'

'Is that why you were unfaithful to her?' Nicholl asked.

Bishop took his time to respond. 'Are you referring to Sophie Harrington?'

'I am.'

His eyes moved left again. 'We'd been having a flirtation. Nice for my ego, but that's as far as it's gone. I never slept with her, although she seems – seemed,' he corrected, 'to enjoy fantasizing that it had happened.'

'You have never slept with Miss Harrington? Not once?'

Grace watched the man's eyes intently. They went left again.

'Absolutely. Never.' Bishop smiled nervously. 'I'm not saying I wouldn't have liked to. But I have a moral code. I was stupid, I was flattered by her interest in me, enjoyed her company – but you have to remember, I've been down that road before. You sleep with someone and if you're lucky, it's a crap experience. But if you are unlucky, it's a gosh-wow experience and you are smitten. And then you are in big trouble. That's what happened to Katie and me – we were smitten with each other.'

'So you never slept with Ms Harrington?' Glenn Branson pressed.

'Never. I wanted to try to make my marriage work.'

'So you thought kinky sex might be a way to achieve that?' Branson asked.

'Pardon? What do you mean?'

Branson looked at his notes. 'One of our team spoke yesterday to a Mrs Diane Rand. We understand from her that she was one of your wife's best friends, is that correct?'

'They spoke to each other about four times a day. God knows what they had to say to each other!'

'Plenty, I think,' Branson responded humourlessly. 'Mrs Rand told our officer, a WPC, that your wife had been expressing concerns recently over your increasingly kinky sexual demands on her. Would you like to elaborate on this?'

Leighton Lloyd interjected quickly and firmly. 'No, my client would not.'

'I have one significant question on this issue,' Branson said, addressing the lawyer. Lloyd gestured for him to ask it.

'Mr Bishop,' Branson said, 'do you possess a replica Second World War gas mask?'

'What is the relevance of that question?' Lloyd asked the DS.

'It's extremely relevant, sir,' Branson said.

Grace watched Bishop's eyes intently. They shot to the right. 'Yes,' he said.

'Is it something you and Mrs Bishop used in your sex life?'

'I'm not allowing my client to answer.'

Bishop raised a pacifying hand at his solicitor. 'It's OK. Yes, I bought it.' He shrugged, blushing. 'We were experimenting. I – I read a book about how to keep your love life going – you know? It sort of flags after a while between two people, when the initial excitement – novelty of the relationship – is over. I got stuff for us to try out.' His face was the colour of beetroot.

Branson turned his focus on to Bishop's dinner with his financial adviser, Phil Taylor. 'Mr Bishop, it's correct, isn't it, that one of the cars you own is a Bentley Continental, in a dark red colour?'

'Umbrian red, yes.'

'Registration number Lima Juliet Zero Four November Whiskey Sierra?'

Unused to the phonetic alphabet, Bishop had to think for a moment. Then he nodded.

'At eleven forty-seven last Thursday night, this vehicle was photographed by an Automatic Number Plate Recognition camera, on the south-bound carriageway of the M23 motorway, in the vicinity of Gatwick airport. Can you explain why it was there and who was driving it?'

Bishop looked at his solicitor.

'Do you have the photograph?' Leighton Lloyd asked.

'No, but I can let you have a copy,' Branson said.

Lloyd made a note in his book.

'There's a mistake,' Bishop said. 'There must be.'

'Did you lend your car to anyone that evening?' Branson asked.

'I never lend it. I had it in London that night because I needed to drive down to the golf club in the morning.'

'Could anyone have borrowed it without your permission – or your knowledge?'

'No. Well, I don't think so. It's extremely unlikely.'

'Who else has keys to the vehicle, apart from you, sir?'

'No one. We've had some problems in the underground car park – beneath my flat. Some cars broken into.'

'Could joyriders have taken it out for a spin?' Leighton Lloyd interjected.

'It's possible,' Bishop said.

'When joyriders take a car they don't usually bring it back,' Grace said. He watched Lloyd making a note in his book. The lawyer would have a field day with that.

Next, Glenn Branson said, 'Mr Bishop, we have already mentioned to you that during the course of a search of your house at 97 Dyke Road Avenue, a life insurance policy with the Southern Star Assurance Company was found. The policy is on your wife's life, with a value of three million pounds. You are named as the sole beneficiary.'

Grace swung his eyes from Bishop to the lawyer. Lloyd's expression barely changed, but his shoulders sank a little. Brian Bishop's eyes were all over the place and his composure seemed suddenly to have deserted him.

'Look, I told you – I – I already told you – I know nothing about this! Absolutely nothing!'

'Do you think your wife took this policy out herself, secretly, from the goodness of her heart?' Branson pressed him.

Grace smiled at this, proud of the way his colleague, to whom he had given so much guidance over the past few years, because he adored him and believed in him, was really growing in stature.

Bishop raised his hands, then let them flop down on to the table. His eyes were all over the place still. 'Please believe me, I don't know anything about this.'

'On three million pounds, I imagine there'd be a hefty premium,' Branson said. 'Presumably we'd be able to see from your bank account – or indeed Mrs Bishop's – how this was paid? Or perhaps you have a mystery benefactor?'

Leighton Lloyd was now scribbling fast in his book, his expression continuing to give nothing away. He turned to Bishop. 'You don't have to answer that unless you want to.'

'I don't know anything about it.' Bishop's tone had become imploring. Heartfelt. 'I really don't!'

'We seem to be stacking up quite a few things you claim not to know anything about, Mr Bishop,' Glenn Branson continued. 'You don't know anything about your car being driven towards Brighton shortly before your wife was murdered. You don't know anything about a three-million-pound life insurance policy, taken out on your wife just six months before she was murdered.' He paused, checked his own notes, then drank some water. 'In your account last night, you said that the last time you and your wife had sexual intercourse was on the morning of Sunday 30 July. Have I got that correct?'

Bishop nodded, looking a little embarrassed.

'Then can you explain the presence of a quantity of your semen that was found in Mrs Bishop's vagina during her post-mortem on the morning of Friday 4 August?'

'There's no way!' Bishop said. 'Absolutely not possible!'

'Are you saying, sir, that you did not have sexual intercourse with Mrs Bishop on the night of Thursday 3 August?'

Bishop's eyes swung resolutely left. 'Yes, that's exactly what I am saying. I was in London, for God's sake!' He turned to look at his solicitor. 'It isn't possible! It isn't bloody possible!'

Roy Grace had seen many solicitors' expressions over the years, as one client after another had clearly told yet another barefaced lie to them. Leighton Lloyd's face remained inscrutable. The man would make a good poker player, he thought.

At ten past five, after Glenn Branson had gone doggedly back over Bishop's statement from last night's interview, the questions that had been put to him in the second interview, this morning, and challenged virtually every single word that Bishop had said, he judged that they had got as much from the man as they were going to get at this stage.

Bishop was not budging on the three key elements: his London alibi, the life insurance policy and the last time he had had sex with his wife. But Branson was satisfied – and more than a little drained.

Bishop was led back to his cell, leaving the solicitor alone with the two police officers.

Lloyd pointedly looked at his watch, then addressed the two men. 'I presume you are aware that you will have to release my client in just under three hours' time, unless you are planning to charge him.'

'Where are you going to be?' Branson asked him.

'I'm going to my office.'

'We'll call you.'

Then the detectives went back over to Sussex House, up to Roy Grace's office, and sat at the round table.

'Well done, Glenn, you did well,' Grace said again.

'Extremely well,' Nick Nicholl added.

Jane Paxton looked pensive. She wasn't one for handing out praise. 'So we need to consider our next step.'

Then the door opened and Eleanor Hodgson came in, holding a thin wodge of papers, clipped together. Addressing Grace, she said, 'Excuse me interrupting, Roy, I thought you would want to see this – it just came back from the Huntingdon lab.'

It was two DNA analysis reports. One was on the semen

that had been found present in Sophie Harrington's vagina; the other was on the minute fleck of what had looked like human flesh that Nadiuska De Sancha had removed from under the dead woman's toenail.

Both were a complete match with Brian Bishop's DNA.

95

Cleo Morey left the mortuary, together with Darren, just before five thirty. Closing the front door and standing in the brilliant, warm sunlight, she said, 'What are you doing tonight?'

'Was going to take her to the cinema, but it's too hot,' he said, squinting back at his boss with the sun in his eyes. 'We're going to go down the Marina, have a few drinks. There's a cool new place I'm going to check out, Rehab.'

She looked at him dubiously. Twenty years old, spiky black hair, a cheery face sporting some designer stubble, he could have so easily, with just a brief turn in his life, have ended up like so many of the no-hoper youngsters draped along the pavements and doorways of this city every night, strung out, dossing, begging, mugging. But he'd clearly been born with a spirited streak in him. He worked hard, he was pleasant company, he was going to do OK in life. 'Rehab?'

'Yep, it's a bar and restaurant place. Classy. I'm splashing out – bit of a special bird. I would say join us, but, you know, two's company and all that!'

She grinned. 'Cheeky sod! And hey, who's to say I don't have a date myself tonight?'

'Oh yes?' He looked pleased for her. 'Now, let me guess who.'

'None of your business!'

'Don't suppose he works for the CID, does he?'

'I said it's none of your business!'

'Then you shouldn't snog him in the front office, should you?' He winked.

'What?' she exclaimed.

'Forget about the CCTV camera in there, did you?'

With a broad grin, he gave her a cheery wave and walked over to his car.

'Peeping Tom!' she called after him. 'Voyeur! Perve!'

He turned as he opened the door of his small red Nissan. 'Actually, if you want my opinion, you make quite a nice-looking couple!'

She flipped him the bird. Then added for good measure, 'And don't drink too much. Remember we're on call tonight.'

'You're a fine one to talk!'

She was still grinning some minutes later as she drove around the gyratory system and into the covered car park of Sainsbury's. Her mind was now on what she was going to give the CID officer she had *snogged in the front office* – as Darren had so crudely put it – to eat. As it was such a glorious evening, she decided to barbecue up on her roof terrace. Roy Grace liked seafood and fish.

Ahead of her she saw a parking space and manoeuvred in to it. She would go to the wet fish counter first and buy some uncooked prawns in their shells, if they had them, and tuna steaks. A couple of corn on the cobs. Some salad. And some sweet potatoes in their jackets, which were totally yummy on a barbecue. And a really nice bottle of rosé wine. Well, perhaps not just *one* bottle.

She was looking forward to this evening and hoped Grace would be able to escape from his investigation at a reasonable hour tonight. It seemed a long while since they had actually spent a proper evening together and it would be good to have a catch-up. She missed him, she realized, missed him all the time when he wasn't around. But there was still the spectre of Sandy and his visit to Munich – she wanted the full lowdown on that.

She had learned from her last relationship that just when you thought everything was perfect, life could turn round and bite you.

96

'His alibi,' Grace said, slapping the palm of his left hand against his balled right fist. 'We need to deal with it. I've said it before, it's the elephant in the room.'

Paxton, Branson and Nicholl, still seated around the table in his office with him, were looking pensive. Jane topped up her beaker of water from a bottle. 'Don't you think we've got enough evidence now, Roy?' she said. 'You're going to be cutting it fine for keeping Bishop in tomorrow, unless we apply to the court this evening for an extension.'

Grace considered this for some moments. The time that Bishop had been arrested yesterday, at eight p.m., was working against them. It meant they had to release him at eight tonight. They would be able to get a twelve-hour extension easily enough. But that would only take them to eight tomorrow morning. If they wanted to keep him beyond that, they would have to go before a magistrate in court with a Warrant of Further Detention application. And that would have to be arranged this evening if they wanted to avoid making phone calls at dawn and disturbing people who had every right to be left in peace to sleep.

He looked at his watch. It was five thirty-five. He picked up the phone and rang Kim Murphy.

'Kim, you had one of the team interview Bishop's financial adviser chap, Phil Taylor. I need Taylor's number urgently. Can you get it for me? Or better still, get him on the phone and patch him through to me?'

While he was waiting, they discussed the ramifications of the latest evidence. Grace maintained his stance.

'But what about the DNA evidence on Sophie Harrington, Roy?' Nick Nicholl asked. 'Surely that's pretty conclusive?'

Roy was feeling impatient, but managed to hold his temper. 'Nick, do you not get it? If Bishop's alibi stands up, that he was in London at the time of his wife's murder, it's going to nix that DNA evidence – the defence will argue that somehow it got planted there. If we are too hasty in linking the murders together, we could get that DNA evidence thrown out also, on the same grounds.'

Justice, Grace had come to learn from bitter experience, was elusive, unpredictable and only occasionally actually done. Far too many things could go wrong in a court. Juries, which often consisted of people who were totally out of their depth in a court of law, could be led, swayed, bamboozled, seduced and confused; often they were prejudiced, or just plain stupid. Some judges were way past their sell-by dates; others seemed, at times, to have come from another planet. It wasn't enough to have a watertight case, backed up with damning evidence. You still needed a lot of luck to get a conviction.

'We have the witness who saw Bishop outside her home,' Jane Paxton reassured him.

'Yes?' He was getting more irritable now by the minute. Was it the heat, he wondered? Or being so dog-tired? Or having to put up with his bloody lodger? Or Sandy pressing on a raw nerve?

'Well – I think that's strong,' she said, sounding defensive.

'We need to go through a formal identification process with that witness and double-check the time-lines there before we can really make it stand up. And there may be some other evidence that comes to light over the next few days. If we've got Bishop inside on a charge, then for the moment the time pressure's off on Ms Harrington. At least we'll have thrown the press a bone.'

The phone rang. It was Kim, telling Grace that she had Phil Taylor on the line and was putting him through. Grace stepped away from the table and took the call on the phone on his desk.

When he finished, Grace stood up again. 'He's agreed to meet me tonight in London. Sounds a straightforward enough man.' He looked at Branson. 'We'll apply for a twelve-hour extension for Bishop, then go up to London straight after the six-thirty briefing. I'd like you to come with me.'

Next he rang Norman Potting and asked him to contact the on-call PACE superintendent to make an application for a twelve-hour extension. Then he turned back to the trio in his office. 'OK, I'll see you all in the conference room at six thirty. Thanks very much, everyone.'

He sat back down at his desk. Now he had another task that was just as hard, in its own, very different way. How to explain to Cleo that he was going to have to go to London this evening and, with the best will in the world, was unlikely to be back down this side of midnight.

To his surprise, probably because she understood the twenty-four/seven nature of police work, she took it cheerfully.

'That's OK,' she said. 'I'm standing at the checkout in Sainsbury's with a load of fresh prawns and scallops. Be a shame to waste them, so I'll just have to eat them all myself.'

'Shit, I'm so sorry.'

'It's OK. These murders are a lot more important than a

few prawns. But you'd better hurry round when you get back down!'

'I'll probably have eaten – I'll grab something in the car.'

'I'm not talking about food!'

He blew her a kiss.

'Times ten!' she replied.

As he hung up, he smiled, relieved that Cleo seemed – for the moment at any rate – to have put his visit to Munich behind her.

But had he?

That would depend, he knew, on whether Marcel Kullen's inquiries provided any leads. And suddenly, for the first time, he found himself – almost – hoping that he wouldn't.

97

Unusually, there were no empty spaces in the street outside the front gates of her home, so Cleo had to circle around, looking for one. Keeping a safe distance back, the Time Billionaire watched the tail of the blue MG disappear around a corner, its right-hand indicator winking. Then he smiled.

And he sent a small, quick message of thanks to God.

This street was so much better! Tall, windowless walls on the right. A sheer cliff face of red brick. On the left, running the whole length of the street, was a blue construction site hoarding, with padlocked gates. Rising above it was a ten-foot-tall artist's impression of the finished development – a complex of fancy flats and shops – boasting the wording:

LAINE WEST

MORE THAN JUST A DEVELOPMENT
– AN URBAN ECO-FRIENDLY
LIFESTYLE!

She had found a space and was reversing into it. Joy!

He fixated on her brake lights. They seemed to be getting brighter as he watched them. Glowing red for danger, red for luck, red for sex! He liked brake lights; he could watch them the way some people could watch a log fire. And he knew everything about the brake lights on Cleo Morey's car. The size of bulb; the strength; how they could be replaced; how they were connected into the wiring loom of the vehicle; how they were activated. He knew *everything* about this car. He'd spent the whole night reading the workshop manual, as well as surfing the net. That was the good thing about the internet. Didn't matter what time of the day or the night, you could find some saddo enthusiast who could tell you more about the door-locking mechanism of a 2005 MG TF 160 than the manufacturer had ever known.

She was out of the car! Wearing jeans that stopped at her calves. Pink plimsolls. A white T-shirt. Hefting three Sainsbury carrier bags out of the boot and slinging the strap of her big, canvas handbag over her shoulder.

He drove past her and turned right at the end of the street. Then right again. Then right again, and now he was approaching the front of her building. He saw her standing outside the gates, doing an awkward balancing act of holding the grocery bags and tapping the number on the keypad. Then she went inside and the gate clanged shut behind her.

Hopefully she wasn't going out again tonight. He would have to take a gamble on that one. But of course he had God's assistance.

He made one more complete circuit, just to make sure she hadn't forgotten something in the car and gone running back for it. Women did that sort of thing, he knew.

After ten minutes he decided it was safe. He doubled-parked his Prius alongside a dusty Volvo covered in bird droppings that didn't look like it had gone anywhere in a while, temporarily blocking the street, although there was nothing coming. Then he unlocked the MG, drove it out of its spot, double-parked that also for a moment, while he jumped back into the Prius, and glided into the now empty space, between the Volvo and a small Renault.

Job done.

The first part.

It was a shame the MG had its hardtop on, he thought, as he headed towards his lock-up. It would have been a pleasant evening to drive with the roof down.

98

As soon as the six-thirty briefing was over, Grace grabbed the keys of the pool car that Tony Case had organized for him and, with Glenn Branson in tow, hurried down to the car park beneath the building.

'Let me drive, man!'

'You know your driving scares me,' Grace replied. 'Actually, let me rephrase that. Your driving terrifies the living daylights out of me.'

'Oh yeah?' Branson said. 'That's rich coming from you – your driving is rubbish. You drive like a girl. No, actually, you don't. You drive like an old git – which is what you are!'

'And you recently failed your Advanced Police Driving test!'

'The examiner was an idiot. My instructor said I had *natural aptitude* for high-speed pursuit driving. My driving rocks!'

'He should be sectioned under the Mental Health Act.'

'Wanker!'

Grace tossed him the keys as they approached the unmarked Mondeo. 'Just don't try to impress me.'

'Did you see *The Fast and the Furious*, with Vin Diesel?'

'He's got the most stupid name for an actor.'

'Yeah? Well, he doesn't think much of yours either.'

Grace wasn't sure what sudden mental aberration had prompted him to give his friend the keys. Maybe he was hoping that if Glenn was concentrating on driving, he'd be spared an endless discussion – or more likely monologue –

about all that was wrong with his marriage, yet again. He'd endured three hours of his friend's soul-searching last night, after they'd got back home following the interview with Bishop. The bottle of Glenfiddich, which they had demolished between them, had only partially mitigated the pain. Then he'd had to listen to Glenn again this morning while getting shaved and dressed, and then over his breakfast cereal, with the added negative of a mild hangover.

To his relief, Branson drove sensibly, apart from one downhill stretch, near Handcross, where he wound the car up to 130 mph especially so he could give Grace the benefit of his cornering skills through two, sharp, uphill bends. 'It's all about positioning on the road and balancing the throttle, old-timer,' he said.

From where Grace was sitting, stomach in his mouth, it was more about not flying off into the seriously sturdy-looking trees that lined both bends. Then they reached the M23 motorway and Grace's repetition of his warning about speed traps, and traffic cops who loved nothing better than to book other officers, had some effect.

So Branson slowed down, and instead tried to phone home on his hands-free mobile.

'Bitch!' he said. 'She's not picking up. I've got a right to speak to my kids, haven't I?'

'You've got a right to be in your house,' Grace reminded him.

'Maybe you could tell her that. Like – you know – give her the official police point of view.'

Grace shook his head. 'I'll help you all I can, but I can't fight your battle for you.'

'Yeah, you're right. It was wrong of me to ask. I'm sorry.'

'What happened about the horse?'

'Yeah, she was on about it again when we spoke. She's

decided she wants to try show-jumping. That's serious money.'

Grace decided, privately, that she needed to see a psychologist. 'I think you guys should go to Relate,' he said.

'You already said that.'

'I did?'

'About two o'clock this morning. And the day before. You're repeating yourself, old-timer. Alzheimer's kicking in.'

'You know your problem?' Grace said.

'Apart from being black? Bald? From an underprivileged background?'

'Yep, apart from all that.'

'No, tell me.'

'Lack of respect for your peers.'

Branson took one of his hands from the wheel and raised it. 'Respect!' he said deferentially.

'That's better.'

*

Shortly after nine, Branson parked the Mondeo on a single yellow line in Arlington Street, just past the Ritz Hotel and opposite the Caprice restaurant.

'Nice wheels,' he said, as they walked up the hill, passing a parked Ferrari. 'You ought to get yourself a set of those. Better than that crappy Alfa you pootle around in. Be good for your image.'

'There's a small matter of a hundred grand or so separating me from one,' Grace said. 'And lumbered with you on my team, my chances of a pay rise of that magnitude are somewhat reduced.'

At the top of the street they rounded the corner into Piccadilly. Immediately on their right they saw a handsome, imposing building, in black and gold paintwork. Its massive, arched windows were brightly illuminated, and the interior seemed humming with people. A smart sign on the wall said *The Wolseley.*

They were greeted effusively by a liveried doorman in a top hat. 'Good evening, gentlemen!' he said with a soft Irish accent.

'The Wolseley restaurant?' Grace asked, feeling a little out of place here.

'Absolutely! Very nice to see you both!' He held the door open and gestured them through.

Grace, followed by Branson, stepped inside. There was a small crowd of people clustered around a reception desk. A waiter hurried past with a tray laden with cocktails, into a vast, domed and galleried dining room, elegantly themed in black and white, and packed with people. There was a noisy buzz. He looked around for a moment. It had an old-world Belle Epoque grandeur about it, yet at the same time it felt intensely modern. The waiting staff were all dressed in hip black and most of the clientele looked cool. He decided Cleo would like this place. Maybe he would bring her up for a night in London and come here. Although he thought he had better check out the prices first.

A young woman receptionist smiled at them, then a tall man, with fashionably long and tangled ginger hair, greeted them. 'Gentlemen, good evening. Can I help you?'

'We're meeting Mr Taylor.'

'Mr Phil Taylor?'

'Yes.'

He pointed at a bar area, off to the side. 'He's in there, gentlemen, first table on the right! We'll take you to him!'

As Grace entered the bar, he saw a man in his early forties, wearing a yellow polo shirt and blue chinos, looking up at him expectantly.

'Mr Taylor?'

'Aye!' He half stood up. 'Detective Superintendent Grace?' He spoke in a distinct Yorkshire accent.

'Yes. And Detective Sergeant Branson.' Grace studied him fleetingly, weighing him up on first impression. He was relaxed and fit-looking, a tiny bit overweight, with a pleasant open face, a sunburnt nose, thinning fair hair and alert, very keen eyes. No flies on this man, he thought instantly. A set of car keys, with a Ferrari emblem on the fob, was lying on the table in front of the man next to a tall glass containing a watery-looking cocktail with a sprig of mint in it.

'Very pleased to make your acquaintance, gentlemen. Have a seat. Can I get you a drink? I can recommend the Mojitos, they're excellent.' He waved a hand to summon a waiter.

'I'm driving – I'll have a Diet Coke,' Branson said.

'The same,' Grace said, although, still faced with the nightmare of the drive back with Branson, he could have used a pint of single malt. 'We'll pay for these, sir. It's very good of you to see us at such short notice,' Grace began.

'It's not a problem. How can I help you?'

'Can I ask you how long you have known Brian Bishop?' Branson said, putting his pad down on the table.

Grace watched the movement of the man's eyes, as he thought.

'About six years – yes – almost exactly six years.'

Branson noted this down.

'Am I under caution?' Phil Taylor asked, only half in jest.

'No,' Branson replied. 'We're just here to try to confirm some times with you.'

'I gave them to one of your officers already. What exactly is the problem? Is Brian in trouble?'

'We'd rather not say too much at the moment,' Grace replied.

'How did you meet him?' Branson asked.

'At a P1 meeting.'

'P1?'

'It's a club for petrol heads that Damon Hill – the racing driver – former world champion – runs. You pay an annual subscription and get the use of various sports cars. We met at one of their cocktail parties.'

Eyeing the key fob, Glenn Branson asked, 'Is that your Ferrari, around the corner in Arlington Street?'

'The 430? Yes – but that's my own car.'

'Nice,' Branson said. 'Nice motor.'

'Be even nicer without all your damned speed cameras!'

'Can you give us a little bit of background about yourself, Mr Taylor?' Grace asked, not rising to the bait.

'Me? I qualified as a chartered accountant, then I spent fifteen years with the Inland Revenue, most of it on their Special Investigations team. Looking into tax abuse scams, mostly. Through it I saw how much money the IFA community – the Independent Financial Advisers – made. I decided that's what I should be doing. So I set up Taylor Financial Planning. Never looked back. Wasn't long after I started that I met Brian. He became one of my first clients.'

'How would you describe Mr Bishop?' Branson asked.

'How would I describe him? He's a top man. One of the best.' He thought for some moments. 'Absolute integrity, smart, reliable, efficient.'

'Did you ever arrange any life insurance for him?'

'We're getting into an area of client confidentiality, gentlemen.'

'I understand,' Grace said. 'There is one question I would like to ask, and if you don't want to answer it, that is fine. Did you ever arrange a life insurance policy on Brian Bishop's wife?'

'I can answer that with a categorical no.'

'Thank you.'

'Is it correct, Mr Taylor, that you and Mr Bishop had dinner here, in this restaurant, last week on Thursday 3 August?' Grace continued.

'Yes, we did.' His demeanour had become a little defensive now.

'This a regular haunt of yours?' Branson asked.

'It is. I like to meet clients here.'

'Can you remember what time, approximately, you left the restaurant?'

'I can do better than that,' Phil Taylor said, a little smugly. Fishing his wallet from his jacket, which was lying beside him on the bench seat, he rummaged inside and pulled out a credit card receipt from the restaurant.

Grace looked at it. Bishop hadn't been lying, he thought, when he saw the items of drink that the two men had consumed. Two Mojito cocktails. Two bottles of wine. Four brandies. 'Looks like you had a good evening!' he said. He also privately noted that the prices were no higher than decent Brighton restaurants. He could afford to bring Cleo here. She would love it.

'Aye, we did.'

Grace did a mental calculation. Assuming both men drank more or less equally, Bishop would have been way over the drink-drive limit when he left the restaurant. Could the drink have brought on a rage about his wife's infidelity? And given him the courage to drive recklessly?

Then, studying the receipt carefully, he found towards the top right what he was looking for. *TIME 22.54.*

'How did Brian Bishop seem to you last Thursday evening?' Grace asked Phil Taylor.

'He was in a great mood. Very cheerful. Good company. He had a golf match in Brighton next morning, so he didn't want to be late, or drink too much – but we still managed to!' He chuckled.

'Can you remember how soon after you got the bill you left this place?'

'Immediately. I could see Brian was anxious to get home – he needed to make an early start next morning.'

'So he got a taxi?'

'Aye. Doorman, John, got one. I let him take the first.'

'So that was about eleven.'

'Around then, yes. I couldn't say exactly. Maybe a few minutes before.'

Grace paid the bill for the drinks, then they thanked him and left. As they turned the corner into Arlington Street, Grace was silent, doing some mental arithmetic. Then, just as they reached the Mondeo, he slapped Branson warmly on the back. 'Every dog has his day!'

'What's that supposed to mean?'

'Suddenly, my friend, it is all your birthdays rolled into one!'

'Sorry, old-timer, you've lost me!'

'Your driving skills. I'm going to give you a chance to show them off. We're going to drive first, at a steady legal speed to Bishop's flat in Notting Hill. From there, you're going to drive like the clappers! We're going to see just how quickly Bishop could have made that journey.'

The Detective Sergeant beamed.

99

So what the fuck was this all about? Yesterday in Brighton you could throw a stick in any direction and you'd hit an MG TF. Now there wasn't one to be seen anywhere in the whole city. Skunk stared angrily out of the windscreen of Beth's mother's little Peugeot.

'Make me come!' Beth said.

'Fuck off,' he said. 'Find me a fucking MG.' Women. Shite!

It was half past ten. They'd done the round of all the regular car parks. Nothing. Nothing, at any rate, that matched Barry Spiker's specification, and after his last experience with the car handler, he wasn't going to repeat the mistake of getting the wrong model. An MG TF 160. Blue. Any spec. Couldn't be clearer than that.

He was wired as hell. Needed some brown badly. He had it all worked out two hours ago. DC Packer had agreed. He would grab the car, take it to Spiker. Packer would wait until he'd left with his cash from Spiker. All organized. Packer would pay him tomorrow. He'd buy his brown tonight with Spiker's money.

Now came the hitch. There were no blue MG TF 160s to be found anywhere. Not one. It was like they'd been hoovered up from the planet.

They were heading up Shirley Drive, one of the central and smartest arteries of Hove. It flowed with conspicuous cash instead of blood. Swanky houses, showy wheels on the driveways. Anything you could ever imagine you might want to buy if your lottery number came up. Beemers, Mercs, Porsches, Bentleys, Ferraris, Range Rovers, you name it. Gleaming, expensive metal as far as the eye could see and the credit cards could stretch.

'Turn right,' he commanded.

'At least finger me!'

'I'm busy, I'm working.'

'You shouldn't be in the office this late!' she scolded.

'Yeah? Tell you what. Find that car and I'll fuck you all night. I'll get some stuff we'll do together.'

Bethany leaned over and kissed him. The ring in her lip tingled his cheek. 'You know I adore you, don't you?'

Skunk looked at her. She was quite pretty from some angles, with her snub nose and cropped black hair. Something welled up deep inside him. Something he'd never felt during all the shitty years of his childhood, and didn't know how to handle now. He took a deep breath, fighting back tears. 'You know, Beth, you're the only nice thing that ever happened to me in my life.' He shrugged. 'I mean it. I want you to know that. Now fuck off and drive. We've got work to do.'

And then, as she made the right turn, he suddenly leaned forward in excitement. His seat belt jerked him sharply back. 'Accelerate! Quick!'

Bethany stoked the gears and the Peugeot surged forward, up past the smart, detached houses of Onslow Road, gaining on the tail lights in front of them. They caught up with the MG, waiting for a gap in the traffic, to turn right into Dyke Road.

Skunk stared ahead, the headlights giving him a clear view of the little MG. It was a TF 160, dark blue, with a blue hardtop. Why the driver had the hardtop on during glorious summer weather like this mystified him, but that wasn't his problem. And surely Spiker would be pleased. The hardtop would be an added bonus.

The MG pulled out.

'Follow him! Don't let him see us, but don't lose him!'

'What's going on, Bear?' *Bear* was her pet name for him, because she didn't like to call him *Skunk*.

'I'm working. Don't ask questions.'

Grinning, amused by his strange ways, Bethany pulled out, right in front of another car. Blinding lights. A squeal of brakes and the blast of a horn.

'Shite!' he said. 'You're a fucking lunatic driver.'

'You said follow him!'

'Don't let him see us.'

She slowed. The MG sped away down the road. Then stopped at traffic lights. Bethany pulled up behind it. Skunk saw the back of the driver's head at the wheel. Long, dark hair. It looked like a woman.

'When are you going to tell me what this is all about?' Bethany demanded.

'Just follow her. Keep your distance.'

*

The Time Billionaire was concerned about the headlights right behind him. Was the car following him? A police car? The lights turned green and he accelerated, keeping rigidly below the 30-mph speed limit. To his relief, the car behind stayed put, then moved forward very slowly.

It pulled up behind him again at the next lights, the junction with the Old Shoreham Road. It was halted right beneath a lamp post and he could see that it was just a crappy little old Peugeot 206. Definitely not a police vehicle. Just some slapper and a prat she was driving. No worries.

Five minutes later he pulled up in the street alongside Cleo Morey's home and double-parked beside the bird-shit-spattered Volvo. He moved his Prius out of the parking space, then drove the MG back into it. Perfect! The bitch would have no reason at all to suspect a thing.

*

Skunk, standing at the top of the street, concealed in the shadows, watched the curious manoeuvre with interest. He had no idea what was going on. Nor what the woman was doing spending so much time in the MG, fiddling about, with the Prius double-parked, blocking the street.

Then the woman climbed out of the car, and he saw that he was wrong, it was a bearded *bloke*. Skunk watched him get into the Prius and glide off.

Then he walked back to the Peugeot, parked a short distance away, and dialled PC Paul Packer's number.

'Hi, mate!' Packer said. 'What's up?'

'I've found me car.'

'OK. I've a slight problem for a couple of hours – I've been called to a job. Can you hang tight?'

'For how long?'

'Couple of hours, max.'

Skunk looked at the Peugeot's clock. It was ten fifty. 'No more,' he said. 'I can't wait no more than that.'

'Gimme the location. I'll get it sorted.'

Skunk told him where he was. Then he hung up and turned to Bethany. 'Get your panties off.'

'I'm not wearing any!' she said.

100

Grace checked his watch. Seven minutes past eleven. Then he glanced at the speedometer. They were doing a steady 135 mph. Lights streaked past; darkness rushed at them. He was concentrating on the cars ahead, trying to keep Glenn out of trouble. As they closed on each vehicle, he tried to check whether it was a police car. It was hard because there were so many unmarked patrol cars used on this stretch of road, but he knew some of the tell-tale signs to look for – two figures in the car, a clean, late-model four-seater and external aerials were the best clues – and he also knew there weren't many out late at night – there was a preference for marked cars then, a visible police presence.

He was already going to have to pull some strings – not an easy task when the police were under ever-increasing public scrutiny – to avoid Branson getting fined and points on his licence for the four Gatso cameras that had double-flashed them on their way out of London. Four cameras, three points each – maybe even more for the speed at which they had hit a couple of them. At least twelve points on his licence. An instant ban.

He grinned at the thought, imagining his friend's protests.

'What's funny?' Branson asked, having to raise his voice above the Bubba Sparxxx rap song that was playing at maxed-out volume on the radio. 'What you grinning at?'

Grace was tolerating the din because Glenn had told

him he needed the music to *put him in the zone* for a fast drive. 'My life,' he replied.

Eight minutes past. They were well beyond Junction 8 and Junction 9 should be coming up at any moment. He scanned the dark road ahead for the signs.

'Your life? I thought your life was just sad. Didn't realize it was a comedy.'

'Just drive! I'm having one of those – what do you call them? – *near-death experiences*. When your whole life flashes in front of your eyes. It's been like that since we left Notting Hill.'

The big blue and white sign for the Gatwick airport turn-off and the Junction 9 marking were now looming ahead. They hurtled past. A short way in the distance Grace could see the silhouette of the flyover across the motorway.

Thirty seconds later, as they passed under it, Grace's eyes swung from his watch to the car's milometer. 'OK, you can slow down now!'

'No way!'

Bubba Sparxxx ended, to Grace's relief. He leaned forward to turn down the volume, but Branson protested. 'It's Mobb Deep coming on next, man. He's like well out of your depth, but he's my kind of music.'

'If you don't slow down, I'm going to find some Cliff Richard!' Grace threatened.

Branson slowed down, a fraction, shaking his head.

For a moment, Grace tuned out Branson and his music and concentrated on some mental calculations. They had covered just over twenty-eight miles from outside Bishop's apartment building in Westbourne Grove, Notting Hill, some of which was through built-up, urban areas and some on dual carriageway and motorway.

There were several different routes that Bishop could

have taken, and analysis of all speed cameras and CCTV cameras covering them might in time reveal the one he had chosen. There had been some heavy traffic coming out of London, and Grace knew that on different days, at different times, you could be lucky or unlucky.

Tonight they had covered this distance in thirty-six minutes. At legal speeds, the journey would have taken closer to an hour. Branson really had been driving like the wind, and it was a miracle they hadn't been stopped anywhere. With lighter traffic, or taking a different route, he reckoned it might be possible to knock five to ten minutes off this time. Which meant Bishop could have driven it in twenty-six minutes.

There were a number of factors to be considered. Phil Taylor's restaurant receipt showed the bill had been paid at ten fifty-four on Thursday night. The clock on the credit card machine wouldn't necessarily be 100 percent accurate – it could easily be a few minutes fast or slow. He made an assumption for the moment, erring on the side of caution to give Bishop the benefit of the doubt, that it was five minutes slow. So, he assumed Bishop had left the restaurant more or less exactly at eleven on Thursday night. The cab journey, assuming no traffic hold-ups, could have been done in fifteen minutes. Add on a couple of minutes for Bishop to get his car out of the underground parking area beneath his flat.

Bishop could have been in his car, on Westbourne Grove, by eleven twenty. The ANPR camera on the bridge of Junction 9 at Gatwick had clocked him at eleven forty-seven.

Twenty-seven minutes to do a journey that had just taken them thirty-six. And Bishop had a much more powerful car. The fastest saloon car in the world.

The ANPR camera clock wouldn't necessarily be dead accurate either. There was a whole bunch of moving parts to this time-line. But what he was now certain of was that it was possible.

He turned the radio off.

'Hey!' Branson protested.

'And don't start playing that stuff in my house, or you'll be out in the chicken shed.'

'You don't have a chicken shed.'

'I'll buy one in the morning.'

'You're crap at DIY. You'd never put it together.'

'So you'll have to hope it's not raining.' Then, serious, he asked, 'Give me your assessment of Phil Taylor as a witness.'

'He's straight. Well flash, with that car and all. Cocksure.'

'Covering for his client? In league with Bishop for the insurance money?'

Branson shook his head. 'Didn't strike me as the type. Ex-Inland Revenue special investigator? Nothing to say anyone isn't a villain, but he just seemed straight to me. Regular guy, he was all right. But that car, though, bastard! I hate him for that!'

'I think he's straight too. And he'd come over as a credible witness in court.'

'So?'

'You did the journey in thirty-six minutes. On my calculations, Bishop would have needed to have done it in twenty-seven, but there's give or take on either side.'

'I could have gone faster.'

Grace winced at the thought. 'You did it exactly right.'

'So?'

'We're going to charge him.'

Grace pulled out his mobile phone and dialled the home number of the Crown Prosecution Service solicitor,

Chris Binns, with whom he had already been liaising over the past couple of days, whose sanction he would require in order to formally charge Bishop. He informed the lawyer of his latest findings tonight, and the time constraints they were under with Bishop's detention.

They arranged to meet at six thirty a.m. at Sussex House.

101

Cleo lay on a sofa in the downstairs living area, with an almost empty bottle of rosé wine on the floor and a completely empty glass lying next to it. A DVD of *Memoirs of a Geisha* was playing on the large television screen, but she was struggling to keep her eyes open.

She shouldn't really have drunk anything, she knew, being on call tonight – and she had an essay to write for her philosophy course – but finding Fish on the floor had really upset her. It was strange, she was thinking, that she saw dead human beings all day long and, with the exception of children, remained emotionally detached from them. Seeing little Fish lying sideways across the join between two oak planks, much of her vivid gold colour faded to a dull bronze, her opaque eye staring up at her, accusatory, as if saying, *Why didn't you come home and rescue me?* was different.

And how the hell had the little creature got there? If it had been yesterday, she could have blamed her cleaning lady, Marija, because the clumsy woman was always breaking things. But she didn't come on Tuesdays. Could a cat have got in here? A bird? Or had poor Fish been trying out some wild new exercise?

She reached out her arm, poured the last drops into her glass and drained it. On the screen, the Geisha was being taught the arts of pleasuring a man. She watched keenly, suddenly feeling more awake now, getting her second wind. She had put this film on in the hope of learning a few things she could try out on Roy.

Which was why all she had on beneath her silk dressing gown was some very slinky and revealing cream lace underwear that she had bought, at an outrageous cost, from a specialist shop in Brighton. All evening she had been planning what she would do when he arrived. She would open the door, kiss him, then stand back and let the front of the dressing gown fall open.

She was longing to see his reaction! She had once read that men got turned on by women who took the lead. And it was a real turn-on for her just lying here, in this outfit, thinking about it. The clock on the front of the video player read eight minutes past midnight. Where are you? she wondered.

As if in response, her home phone rang. She put the cordless handset to her ear and answered. It was Roy, on a crackly mobile.

'Hey,' he said. 'How are you doing?'

'I'm OK. Where are you, you poor thing?'

'Five minutes from the office. I've got a couple of things to quickly sort for the morning – I could be with you in half an hour. Is it going to be too late to come over?'

'No, it won't be too late at all! Just get here when you can. I'll have a drink waiting for you. How's it gone?'

'Good. It was very good. Tiring, but worth the journey. Are you really sure you'd like me to come over?'

'I'm totally sure, my darling! Making love is really a lot more fun with two people than one!'

She heard the *call-waiting* beep just as she hung up. The phone instantly rang again.

'Hello?' she answered.

And then, *Shit!* she thought, her heart sinking as she heard the voice at the other end. *Bugger, bugger, bugger! Why now?*

102

Skunk's phone pinged. An incoming text. He disentangled himself from a half-undressed Bethany, desperately trying to get his bearings. He'd been asleep, his body was all cramped up, he couldn't find the fucking phone. And he had the shakes badly now.

'Ouch!' Beth said as he dug his hand under her thigh.

'Trying to find me phone.'

'Think I broke my back earlier,' she said, then giggled.

'You're a dirty cow.'

He found it, on the floor in the front passenger footwell. It was a text from DC Paul Packer:

In place. u ready?

Skunk texted back:

yes

The time display showed fourteen minutes past midnight.

Awkwardly wiggling around, with Bethany complaining that he was squashing her, Skunk got his shell-suit bottoms back up. He still had his sneakers on. He gave Bethany a quick peck on the cheek. 'See ya!'

'What are you doing? Where are you going?'

'Got a meeting in me office!'

'Tell me about it!'

'I gotta go.'

He climbed out of the car with difficulty, his body still

stiff and very shaky, and stood in the dark shadow of the construction site hoarding, one hand on the car, the other on the hoarding wall. He was breathing heavily, palpitating, and thought for a moment he was going to throw up. Rivulets of sweat were guttering down his head and body. He saw Beth's face peering out anxiously at him, caught like a ghost by the glare of a street lamp opposite.

He took a step forward and realized he was giddy. He swayed and nearly fell over, just catching the side of the car in time to steady himself. *Gotta do this!* he told himself. *Gotta do this, hang it out a little longer, just take those steps forward, can't screw this up, gotta do it, gotta. Gotta!*

He pulled the hood of his thin cagoule up over his head, then launched himself forward. A breeze had started and the hoarding rattled a little. There were silent cars parked along both sides of the street, bathed in orange sodium glow from the street-lighting. The MG was about fifty yards ahead.

He was conscious that he was walking unsteadily. And aware that he was being watched. He didn't know where they were, but he knew they were somewhere in this street. Probably in one of the cars or vans. He passed a black Prius. A 2CV Citroën. A dusty Mitsubishi people-carrier blurred out of focus as he reached it, then came back into focus again. The nausea was even stronger now. He felt an insect crawling on his left arm and slapped it with his hand. Then there were more insects crawling over him; he could feel their tiny, sharp feet on his skin. He patted his chest, reached around and patted his neck. Then his stomach. 'Gerroff!' he blurted.

In a sudden panic, he thought he had forgotten his levers kit. Had they fallen out in the car? Or had he left them in the camper?

He checked his pockets, each one in turn. *No! Shite, no!*

Then he checked them again. And they were there, nestling in the right-hand pocket of the cagoule, closed up in their hard, plastic casing.

Get a grip!

As he reached the rear of the MG, he was suddenly lit up with bright, white light. He heard the roar of an engine and stepped aside. Bethany hurtled past, flat out in first gear, waved, then gave him a toot.

Stupid cow! He grinned. Watched her tail lights disappear. Then, moving swiftly, feeling a little better suddenly now he was actually here, he removed the lever set from his pocket, opened the one he wanted and eased the tip into the door lock. It popped open within a few seconds. Instantly the alarm went off, a loud beeping, combined with all the lights flashing.

He stayed calm. They were not easy to nick, these cars, they had shock sensors and immobilizers. But some of the key wiring was right behind the dash. You could short it out, neutralizing the shock sensor and the immobilizer, and start the engine with just one bridge.

The interior smelled nice, all new upholstery, leather and a faint tang of a woman's scent. He climbed in, leaving the door open, to keep the interior light on, ducked his head under the dash and immediately found what he was looking for. Two seconds later and the alarm stopped.

Then he heard a shout. A woman's voice. Bellowing in fury.

'HEY! THAT'S MY BLOODY CAR!'

*

Cleo sprinted down the street, her blood boiling. She was irritated enough that her carefully planned evening, already messed up by Roy's unexpected trip to London, had now been totally and utterly ruined by a call-out, to recover the body of a dead wino from a bus shelter in Peacehaven. Seeing some lowlife fuckwit in a hoodie trying to steal her car, she was ready to rip his limbs off.

The car's door slammed shut. She heard the engine turn over. The tail lights came on. Her heart was sinking. The bastard was getting away. Then just as she drew level with the Volvo parked behind it, the whole interior of the MG suddenly lit up in a bright flash, as if a massive light bulb had been switched on.

There was no bang. No sound of any explosion. It was just suddenly filled with silent, leaping flames, contained inside the cockpit. Like a light show.

She stopped, staring in numb shock, wondering for an instant if the fuckwit hoodie was just a vandal, deliberately setting it on fire. Except he was still inside the car.

Throwing herself forward, she reached the driver's door and saw his desperate, emaciated face at the window. He seemed to be struggling with the interior handle, throwing his weight against the door, as if it were stuck, then frantically hammering on the door window with his fist, looking at her with pleading eyes. She could see his hood was on fire. And his eyebrows. And she could feel the heat now. In panic, she reached out for the door handle and pulled it. Nothing happened.

Suddenly there were two men beside her, police officers in black boiler suits and stab jackets, a stocky one with a shaven head and a taller one with a brush cut.

'Get back, please, lady,' the stocky one said. He put both hands on the door handle and pulled, as the other ran around to the other side and tried that door.

Inside, the figure in the burning cagoule was turning his

head frantically, his mouth twisted open in an expression of utter terror and agony, his skin blistering in front of her eyes.

'Unlock the door! Skunk, for God's sake unlock the door!' the stocky one was yelling.

The figure inside mouthed something.

'It's my car!' Cleo jumped forward and put her key in the lock, but it would not turn.

The policeman tried for a moment, then, giving up, he pulled out his truncheon. 'Stand back, miss,' he said to Cleo. 'Stand right back!' Then he hit the window hard, cracking it. He hit it again and the blackening glass buckled. Then he hit it again, punched it through with his fists, showering the squealing occupant, ignoring the flames that were leaping out of the window, the dense black smoke, the stinking fumes of burning plastic. Putting his hands on the window frame, he pulled frantically on the door.

It would not give.

Then, taking a deep breath, the officer leaned right in through the window, into the inferno, put his arms around the figure and somehow, with his colleague's help now, slowly, far too slowly for the poor, squealing man, it seemed to Cleo, dragged him out through the window and laid him down on the street. All his clothes were on fire. She saw the laces of his trainers burning. He was writhing, thrashing, moaning, in the most terrible agony she had ever seen a human being experience.

'Roll him!' yelled Cleo, desperate to do something to help him. 'Roll him over to get the flames out!'

Both officers knelt, nodding, and rolled him, then over again, then one more time, away from the burning car, the stocky one ignoring or oblivious to his own singed brows and burnt face.

The burning hood had partially melted into the victim's face and head, and his shell-suit trousers had melted around his legs. Through the stench of molten plastic, Cleo suddenly caught a momentarily tantalizing smell of roasting pork, before revulsion kicked in, at the realization of what it actually was. 'Water!' she said, her first aid course from years ago coming back to her. 'He needs water and he needs covering, seal the air off.' Her eyes jumped from the terrible suffering of the man in the road to the fiercely burning interior of her car, frantically trying to think if she had anything she needed in the glove compartment or boot, not that there was much she could do about it. 'There's a blanket in the boot!' she said. 'A picnic blanket – could wrap him – need to stop the air—'

One of the officers sprinted up the road. Cleo stared down at the writhing, blackened figure. He was shaking, vibrating, as if he was plugged into an electrical socket. She was scared that he was dying. She knelt beside him. She wanted to hold his hand, to comfort him, but it looked so painfully blackened. 'You'll be OK,' she said gently. 'You'll be OK. Help's coming. There's an ambulance coming! You're going to be fine.'

He was rolling his head from side to side, his mouth open, the lips blistered, making pitiful croaking sounds.

He was just a kid. Maybe not even twenty. 'What's your name?' she asked him gently.

He was barely able to focus on her.

'You'll be OK. You will!'

The officer came running back, holding two coats. 'Help me wrap these around him.'

'He's covered in molten fabric – do you think we should try and get it off?' she asked.

'No, just get these around him, tight as we can.'

She heard a siren in the distance, faint at first, but rapidly getting louder. Then another. Followed by a third.

From the darkness of the interior of his Prius, the Time Billionaire watched Cleo Morey and the two police officers kneeling on the ground. He heard the sirens. A splinter of blue light skittered past his eyes. He watched the first police car arrive. Two fire engines, then a third. An ambulance.

He watched everything. He didn't have anything else to spend his time on tonight. He was still there, watching, as dawn was breaking, and the low-loader arrived and craned the MG, its interior all blackened but the exterior looking fine, considering, out of its space and carted it away.

Suddenly the street seemed quiet. But inside his car the Time Billionaire was raging.

103

The alarm was due to go off in a few minutes, at five thirty, but Roy Grace was already wide awake, listening to the dawn chorus, thinking. Cleo was awake too. He could hear the scratching of her eyelashes on the pillow each time she blinked.

They lay on their sides, two spoons. He held her naked body tightly in his arms. 'I love you,' he whispered.

'I love you so much,' she whispered back. Her voice was full of fear.

He had still been in the office at one a.m., preparing for his meeting with the CPS solicitor, when she'd rung him, sounding truly terrible. He'd gone straight over to her house and then, in between comforting her, had spent much of the next hour on the phone, tracking down the two officers who had first arrived on the scene. Eventually he had got through to an undercover PC on the Car Crime Unit called Trevor Sallis, who explained what they had been doing. It had been a sting to catch the ringleader of a gang.

According to Sallis, a local lowlife villain had been cooperating with the police and, in one of life's coincidences, it had been Cleo's car that was targeted. Something had gone badly wrong, it appeared, in the thief's attempt to hot-wire it. MG TF cars were, it appeared, notoriously hard to steal.

The explanation had calmed Cleo down. But something that he couldn't quite put a finger on bothered Grace deeply about the incident. The would-be thief was now in the intensive care unit at the Royal Sussex County Hospital – God help him in that place, he thought privately – and was due to be transferred, if he survived the next few hours, to the burns unit at East Grinstead. The other officer, Paul Packer, was also in the same hospital, with severe, but not life-threatening, burns.

What could make a car catch fire? A lowlife jerk, fiddling with wires he did not understand, rupturing a fuel pipe?

The thoughts were still churning through his tired brain when the alarm started beeping. He had exactly one hour to get home, shower, put on a fresh shirt – there was another press conference scheduled for later this morning – and get to the office.

'Take the day off,' he said.

'I wish.'

He kissed her goodbye.

*

Chris Binns, the CPS solicitor who had been allocated to the Katie Bishop case, was in Grace's opinion – which was one shared by a good many other officers – several miles up his own backside. The two of them had had plenty of encounters in the past, and there wasn't a huge amount of love lost.

Grace viewed his own job as, principally, to serve decent society by catching criminals and bringing them to justice. Binns viewed his priority as saving the Crown Prosecution Service unwarranted expense in pursuing cases where they might not secure a conviction.

Despite the early hour, Binns entered Grace's office looking – and smelling – as fresh as a rose. A tall, trim man in his mid-thirties, sporting a bouffant hairstyle, he had a large, aquiline nose, giving his face the hawkish look of a bird of prey. He was dressed in a well-cut dark grey suit that was too heavy for this weather, Grace thought, a white shirt, sharp tie and black Oxfords that he must have spent the whole night buffing.

'So nice to see you, Roy,' he said in his supercilious voice, giving Grace's hand a limp, moist shake. He sat down at the small, round conference table and placed his upright black calfskin attaché case down on the floor beside him, giving it a stern look for a moment, as if it was a pet dog he had commanded to sit. Then he opened the case and produced a large, hard-bound notebook from it, and a Montblanc fountain pen from his breast pocket.

'I appreciate your coming in so early,' Grace said, stifling a yawn, his eyes heavy from tiredness. 'Can I get you any tea, coffee, water?'

'Some tea. Milk, no sugar, thanks.'

Grace picked up the phone and asked Eleanor, who had also come in early, at his request, to get them one tea, and a coffee that was as strong as she could possibly make it.

Binns read through the notes in his book for a moment, then looked up. 'So you arrested Brian Desmond Bishop at eight p.m. on Monday?'

'Yes, correct.'

'Can you recap on your grounds for charging him? Any issues we should be concerned about?'

Grace summarized the key evidence as being the presence of Bishop's DNA in the semen found in Katie Bishop's vagina, the insurance policy taken out on her life just six months previously, and her infidelity. He also pointed out Bishop's two previous convictions for violent acts against women. He raised the issue of Bishop's alibi, but then showed the solicitor the time-line sheet he had typed up last night, after getting back from London, demonstrating that Bishop would have had enough leeway to get to Brighton and murder his wife – and then return to London.

'I imagine he would have been a bit tired on the golf course on Friday morning,' Chris Binns said drily.

'Apparently he was playing a blinder,' Grace said.

Binns raised an eyebrow and for a moment Grace's spirits sank, wondering if Binns was now going to nitpick and request witness statements from Bishop's golfing partners. But to his relief, all he added was, 'Could have been on an adrenaline rush. From the excitement of the kill.'

Grace smiled. For a welcome change, the man was on his side.

The CPS solicitor shot his cuff, revealing elegant gold links, and frowned at his watch. 'So, how are we doing now?'

Grace had been keeping a tight eye on the time. It was five to seven. 'Following our conversation last night, Bishop's solicitor was contacted. He's meeting with his client at seven. DS Branson, accompanied by DC Nicholl, will charge him.'

*

At seven thirty Glenn Branson and Nicholl, accompanied by a custody sergeant, entered the interview room, where Brian Bishop was already seated with his solicitor.

Bishop, in his paper suit, had dark rings under his eyes and his skin had taken on a prison pallor. He had shaved, but clearly in a poor light or in a hurry, and had missed a couple of spots, and his hair was not looking as neat as before. After just thirty-six hours he was already looking like an old lag. That's what prison did to people, Glenn knew. It institutionalized them more quickly than they realized.

Leighton Lloyd looked up at Branson and Nicholl. 'Good morning, gentlemen. I hope you are now going to release my client.'

'I'm afraid, sir, that following inquiries made last night, we have sufficient evidence to charge your client.'

Bishop's whole body sagged; his mouth fell open and he turned to his solicitor, bewildered.

Leighton Lloyd jumped to his feet. 'What about my client's alibi?'

'Everything has been looked into,' Branson said.

'This is preposterous!' the solicitor protested. 'My client has been completely open with you. He's answered everything you've asked him.'

'That will be noted at trial,' Branson responded. Then, cutting to the chase, he addressed Bishop directly. 'Brian Desmond Bishop, you are charged that on or about 4 August of this year, at Brighton in the county of East Sussex, you did unlawfully kill Katherine Margaret Bishop. You do not have to say anything, but it may harm your defence if you do not mention when questioned something which you later rely on in court. Anything you do say may be given in evidence. Is that clear?'

Bishop glanced at his solicitor again, then back at Branson. 'Yes.' The word came out as a whisper.

Branson turned to Leighton Lloyd. 'We will be making arrangements to put your client before Brighton Magistrates' Court at two o'clock this afternoon, when we will be requesting a remand in custody.'

'We will be making an application for bail,' Lloyd said resolutely, then shot a comforting smile at Bishop. 'My client is an upstanding member of the community and a pillar of society. I'm sure that he would be prepared to surrender his passport, and he is in a position to offer a substantial surety.'

'That will be for the magistrates to decide,' Branson replied. Then he and Nick Nicholl returned to Sussex House, leaving Bishop in the hands of his lawyer and his jailer.

104

After the CPS solicitor had departed, Grace made an internal call to his friend and colleague Brian Cook, the Scientific Support Branch Manager, and asked him what he knew about the burnt-out MG that had been taken to the police pound last night.

'Haven't allocated that to anyone from SOCO yet, Roy,' he said. 'Got so many people on holiday, everyone here is worked off their feet on the two murder cases. Why, do you think there's a link?'

'No, I'm just curious about what happened.' Despite indiscretions by Glenn Branson, his relationship with Cleo Morey was not yet public knowledge and Grace was happy to keep it that way, worried that some people, for whatever reason, might look on it as unprofessional.

'I understand it belonged to Cleo Morey at the mortuary,' Cook said.

Grace was unsure if there was deliberate innuendo in the man's voice or not. Then, dispelling any doubt, Cook added, with very definite innuendo now, 'She's your friend, isn't she?'

'We're *friendly*, yes.'

'So I hear. Good on you! Look, I'll keep you posted. We've got an officer in hospital, and I gather there's a man connected with it who's on life support, so I'm going to have to do a full report. Just double my budget and give me ten more SOCOs!'

Grace thanked him, then checked the briefing notes

that Eleanor had typed up. When he had finished, he opened the diary on his BlackBerry and glanced through his schedule for the day. At least they had some good news to give out at this morning's press conference. At two p.m. he needed to attend Bishop's remand hearing, in case there were any problems. Later he had the six-thirty briefing meeting. And perhaps an early night if there were no major new developments. He badly needed to catch up on some sleep, before he became so tired he started making mistakes. He felt precariously close to that state now.

*

Three magistrates – two women and a man – sat at the bench in Court 3 in the Edward Street courthouse. It was a small, plain room, with tiered rows of wooden seats and a small public and press area to the side. With the exception of the *Dieu et Mon Droit* crest displayed solemnly on the back wall, it had more the feel of a school classroom than the inquisitional air of some of the grander court-rooms in this part of Sussex.

Brian Bishop, changed back into his own clothes now, a camel-coloured jacket over a polo shirt and navy slacks, was standing in the dock, still looking utterly wretched.

Facing the bench were the CPS solicitor, Chris Binns, Bishop's own solicitor, Leighton Lloyd, Grace and Branson, as well as about thirty journalists, packing out the side gallery.

To Grace's dismay, the chairman of the bench today was peroxide-haired Hermione Quentin, lording it in an expensive-looking dress. She was the one magistrate in the city that he really disliked, having had a run-in with her earlier this year, in this same court, over a suspect he had wanted to hold in custody and she had, totally illogically –

and dangerously, in his view – refused. Was she going to do the same today?

The appearance was brief. Leighton Lloyd delivered a passionate and cogent argument why Bishop should be released on bail. Chris Binns did a swingeing demolition job on it. It took the magistrates only a few moments of conferring before Hermione Quentin spoke.

'Bail is denied,' she said haughtily, enunciating each word with the precision of an elocution teacher, alternately addressing Bishop and his solicitor. 'The reason is the seriousness of the offence. We believe Mr Bishop presents a flight risk. We are aware that the police are inquiring into a second serious offence, and custody would prevent Mr Bishop from interfering with any witnesses. We feel it is important to protect the public.' Then, as if doing Bishop a huge favour, she said, 'Because you are a local man, we think it would be helpful all round for you to be detained in Lewes prison until your trial. You are to be remanded in custody until next Monday, when you will appear before this court again.'

She then picked up a pen and proceeded to write something.

The court began to empty. Grace stepped out from behind his pew, satisfied. But as he walked past the dock, Bishop spoke to him.

'May I please have a quick word, Detective Superintendent?'

Lloyd sprang from his pew and positioned himself between them. 'I don't think that's advisable,' he said to his client.

'You haven't done such a good job yourself,' Bishop replied angrily. Then he turned to Roy Grace. 'Please, I didn't do it. Please believe me,' he implored. 'There is somebody out there who has killed two women. My darling wife and another good friend of mine. Don't give up looking for that person just because I'm locked away. Please!'

'Mr Bishop!' Leighton Lloyd admonished. 'Don't say any more.'

Grace left the courtroom with Bishop's words ringing in his ears. He'd heard this kind of last-minute, desperate plea before, from villains who were guilty as hell.

But all the same, he suddenly felt a deep sense of unease.

105

Brendan Duigan had alerted Roy Grace to a problem at the planning meeting, in advance of the six-thirty joint briefing for Operations Chameleon and Mistral.

So straight after his introduction, and his brief summary of the events of the day, Grace informed the key members of the two investigating teams, who were crammed into the conference room at Sussex House, that a time-line issue, connecting Brian Bishop to Sophie Harrington's murder, had arisen. He turned to DC Corbin, one of Duigan's team members, and asked her to give her report.

Adrienne Corbin, who was dressed in denim dungarees over an orange T-shirt, was short and sturdy, with the build of a tomboy. The twenty-eight-year-old detective had a butch haircut and a round, blunt face that reminded Grace of a pug. She looked more aggressive than she really was and turned out to be a surprisingly nervous speaker, he observed, as she addressed this large group.

'I have pieced together the movements of Brian Bishop during the afternoon and evening of Friday 4 August from information supplied to me by family liaison officer WPC Buckley, from a Hove Streamline taxi driver, Mr Mark Tuckwell, from CCTV footage obtained from Brighton Police Monitoring, as well as from civilian sources, Bishop's mobile phone call records and from a plot of mobile phone cell masts, provided by British Telecom, indicating the geographical movements of Bishop's phone.'

She stopped, blushing and perspiring heavily. Grace felt sorry for her. Being a good detective did not mean you were necessarily a confident public speaker. She turned back a page in her notes, as if checking something, then continued, 'Of interest to Operation Chameleon will be the report that there was no activity from Bishop's mobile phone from eleven twenty p.m. on Thursday 3 August until six thirty-six a.m. on Friday 4 August.'

'Can we extrapolate from the information whether it was because Bishop didn't move during that time period, or, if he did, he had left the phone behind, or that it was switched off?' Grace asked.

'I understand that if a phone is on stand-by or in use, it exchanges constant signals with the nearest base station – basically it *talks* to it, telling the base station where it is. There were a series of signals received from Bishop's phone from masts sited in London, indicating he was travelling from Piccadilly back to Notting Hill, from approximately eleven to eleven fifteen that night. The last signal was at eleven twenty, from a base station at a mast in Bayswater, west London, close to Notting Hill. The next signals were exchanged at six thirty-six a.m., from the same base station, sir.'

Although that fitted with the times given by Phil Taylor for when Bishop left the Wolseley restaurant, it wasn't helpful information, Grace realized. Bishop could have turned the phone off, so that his journey to Brighton and back in the middle of the night wouldn't be plotted on the phone masts; and he could easily argue that he'd switched it off in order to get a night's sleep without being disturbed. But it was what DC Corbin said next that made him sit up.

'The movements of Bishop's phone during Friday 4 August, up until six forty-five p.m., correspond with his story, and what we ourselves know. They show he came straight down from London to the North Brighton Golf Club, and from there he travelled directly to Sussex House. They also plot his journey from here to the Hotel du Vin. Then it appears he switched off his phone between twelve twenty-eight and two seventeen. This coincides with a period of time in which he was reported missing from the Hotel du Vin by WPC Buckley.'

She paused, looking around the silent room. Everyone was watching her, concentrating hard, with notes being taken. Grace gave her a smile of encouragement. She ploughed on.

'During this same time period, Bishop was sighted on three CCTV cameras. One at the junction of Dukes Lane and Ship Street, just up the road from the Hotel du Vin, one opposite St Peter's Church in the London Road, and one on Kings Parade, opposite Brighton Pier. The reason he gave for his absence was that he went out for some air.'

'Seems a bit odd to me,' Norman Potting said, 'that both times Bishop does a disappearing act, he switches his phone off.'

Grace nodded, thinking, then signalled for her to continue.

'From two seventeen until six forty-seven on Friday 4 August, the phone signals remained static, indicating that Bishop stayed in his hotel room. This is consistent with family liaison officer WPC Linda Buckley's report that Bishop returned to the hotel at around two twenty and was in his room each time she checked up on him, using the house phone, the last time being at six forty-five. Then the phone plot shows that Bishop moved one and a half miles west, which tallies with information obtained by DC Pamela Buckley from taxi driver Mark Tuckwell, who claims he drove Bishop to the Lansdowne Place Hotel at that time. I understand that Hove Streamline Taxis have confirmed this from their log.' She looked at the female detective constable.

'Yes, that is correct,' Pamela Buckley said.

Corbin turned to the next page. 'Bishop checked into the Lansdowne Place Hotel at five past seven – just over three hours after a member of the hotel reception staff received a phone call from an unidentified male making a reservation for a room for several nights, in Bishop's name,' she read.

Grace quickly turned back through his own notes. 'Bishop claimed that he received a call from a CID officer informing him that he was being moved to a different hotel and that a taxi had been arranged to collect him, from a back entrance. This was so he could leave the hotel without being seen by the press, who were staking the hotel out. He gave the name of this officer as DS Canning – but we have checked and there is no officer called Canning in the Sussex police force.'

'And is it correct, Adrienne, that there's no record of any phone call to the Lansdowne Place Hotel being made on Bishop's mobile phone?' DCI Duigan asked.

'That is correct, sir.' Then she added, 'The Hotel du Vin have also confirmed that there were no calls made by any of their internal phones to the Lansdowne Place during the time Bishop was there.'

'When he was out!' Norman Potting said suddenly, excitedly. 'When he went on his lunchtime walkabout, he could have bought one of them pay-as-you-go phones and disposed of it later. He could have bought it specifically to make those calls – and others we might not know about.'

'An interesting thought,' Grace conceded. 'A good point, Norman.'

'The Lansdowne Place Hotel is closer to Sophie Harrington's home than the Hotel du Vin,' Duigan said. 'That might be significant.'

'I'd like to add one more thought here,' Grace said. 'It's possible that Bishop had an accomplice helping him with his alibi for the night of Mrs Bishop's murder. The same accomplice could have been responsible for this switch of hotels.'

DCI Duigan said, 'Roy, we can see the attraction for an accomplice with the murder of Mrs Bishop and the substantial life insurance policy. Do we have any grounds yet for believing there would have been an accomplice for Bishop in the murder of Sophie Harrington?'

'No. But it's early days.'

Duigan nodded and noted something down.

Adrienne Corbin continued with her time-line report. 'Bishop was observed by staff leaving the hotel at approximately seven thirty. His phone mast plot shows that he then headed west. This was confirmed by a sighting of him on a CCTV camera at the junction of West Street and Kings Parade at five to eight.'

Grace stared at her in shock, for a moment thinking he had misheard. 'Bishop headed away from the Lansdowne Place Hotel, back in the direction of the Hotel du Vin? A completely different direction from the one he would have had to take to get to Sophie Harrington's home?' he grilled her.

'Yes, sir,' she replied.

Duigan then stood up and switched on the video monitor. 'I think everyone should see these,' he said.

The first showed a colour image of Brian Bishop in

Kings Parade, with several people behind him and a bus passing. There was no mistaking his face. He was wearing the clothes Grace remembered from when he interviewed him later that same night – a black blouson jacket over a white shirt and blue trousers. And the sticking plaster on his right hand.

'What time did your witness reckon she saw Bishop outside Sophie Harrington's house?' Grace asked.

Duigan replied, 'Eight o'clock almost exactly. She knew because a television programme she wanted to watch was just starting.'

'And she's now formally identified him?'

'Yes, this afternoon she came in and carried out an identification procedure. She is absolutely certain it was him.'

'What clothes does she say Bishop was wearing?' Grace asked.

'She says he was in a dark tracksuit – a shell suit of some kind.'

Grace stared at the image of Bishop on the screen. 'What does anyone think? Could that black blouson jacket and those dark blue chinos be mistaken for a tracksuit?'

Alfonso Zafferone said, 'It was eight o'clock when she saw Bishop. Old people don't see dark colours so well, in poor light. I think that blouson jacket could easily be mistaken for a tracksuit top, at that time of day.'

'Or,' Guy Batchelor said, 'Bishop could have pulled on a tracksuit over his clothes, to protect them.'

'Both good points,' Grace said. Then he turned his mind back to the time-line. 'He could have got from Kings Parade to Ms Harrington's address in ten minutes by taxi.'

Duigan pressed the remote and a second image of Bishop appeared. Now he was down on the seafront itself, with part of the Arches clearly visible in the background, several kayaks on trestles outside the front of one.

Reading on, DC Corbin said, 'Bishop was sighted again at eight fourteen by a CCTV camera in front of the Arches. The phone mast log indicates Bishop remained static in this area during the next forty-five minutes, and then headed back, west, to his hotel. Two staff members at a seafront bar, Pebbles, have confirmed that he was in their bar from approximately eight twenty to about eight fifty. They said he drank a beer and an espresso and seemed deeply distracted. On several occasions he got up and paced around, then returned and sat down again. They had been concerned he was going to walk off without paying.'

Bella Moy cut in when the DC paused. 'Roy,' she said, 'it almost seems as if he was deliberately trying to get himself noticed.'

'Yes,' Grace said. 'Could be. But equally it's typical behaviour of someone in a highly agitated state.'

Duigan clicked the remote again. It was darker on the screen now. The image was a rear view of a man who strongly resembled Bishop, in the same place as the earlier photograph, passing along the Arches.

'At eight fifty-four,' DC Corbin read on, 'Bishop was again recorded on the same CCTV camera as at eight fourteen, this time walking in the opposite direction. From the phone mast log we have the information that he headed west again, in the direction of the Lansdowne Place Hotel. A member of the hotel reception staff recalls that Bishop returned to the hotel at approximately nine twenty-five, when she gave him the message that Detective Superintendent Grace had left for him.' She looked up at Grace. 'He then rang you at nine thirty.'

'Yes.'

'Then he drove up to Sussex House, where Detective Superintendent Grace and DS Branson interviewed him, the interview commencing at ten twenty-two. According to the phone mast plot, Bishop did not leave the hotel until nine forty-nine.'

'He'd have driven almost past Sophie Harrington's door on his way from the hotel to here,' Glenn Branson said.

'The drive here would have been at least fifteen minutes – I only live half a dozen streets along from the Lansdowne,' Grace replied. 'I do the drive every day, at all times of the day and night. It always takes fifteen to twenty minutes. So that would have left him eighteen minutes to kill Sophie Harrington. Impossible, not with what was done to her, all those holes drilled in her back. He couldn't have done that and cleaned himself up in that time frame.'

'I agree,' Duigan said.

'Which means we have a problem,' Grace said. 'Either Bishop didn't kill Sophie Harrington or he had an accomplice. Or . . .'

He fell silent.

106

Grace went straight from the briefing meeting, past his office, past the mostly empty desks and offices of the detectives' room and put his head around the door of Brian Cook's office. He was relieved to see the Scientific Support Branch Manager was still at work.

Cook was on the phone, making what sounded like a private call, but waved him in, cheerily told the person at the other end that he would hold him to that drink and hung up. 'Roy, has John Pringle contacted you yet about Cleo Morey's car?' he asked.

'No.'

'I put him on it today – told him to report to you.'

'Thanks, Brian.' Changing the subject, Grace said, 'Tell me something, what do you know about the DNA of twins?'

'What do you want to know?'

'How close would the DNA of identical twins be?'

'It would be identical.'

'Completely?'

'One hundred percent. The fingerprints would be different, interestingly. But the DNA would be an exact match.'

Grace thanked him and walked along to his own office. He went in and closed the door, then sat quietly at his desk for some moments, planning what he was going to say very carefully before he rang the mobile number in front of him.

'Leighton Lloyd,' the man answered, his voice crisp and ready for a fight, as if he already knew who his caller was.

'It's Detective Superintendent Grace, Mr Lloyd. Can we have this conversation off the record?'

There was some surprise in the solicitor's tone. 'Yes. OK. We're off the record. Do you have some new information?'

'We have some concerns,' Grace said, remaining guarded. He still didn't trust the man. 'Would you happen to know if your client has a twin?'

'He hasn't mentioned anything. Do you want to elaborate on this?' Lloyd asked.

'Not at this stage. It might be helpful to all of us if we could establish or eliminate this. Could you ask your client urgently?'

'It's after visiting hours. Can you authorize Lewes prison to let me speak to my client on the phone?'

'Yes, I'll get that done now.'

'Would you like me to call you back tonight?'

'I'd appreciate it.'

As Grace hung up, his phone rang again, almost immediately. 'Roy Grace,' he answered. The voice at the other end sounded very serious and pensive.

'Detective Superintendent, it's John Pringle. I'm with SOCO and I was asked to look at a fire-damaged MG motor car that was brought into the pound this morning. Brian Cook told me to report my findings to you.'

'Yes, thank you. He said you'd be calling.'

'I've just completed my examination of the vehicle, sir. Extensive fire damage to the interior has caused some of the wiring to melt, so I cannot give as complete a report as I would have liked.'

'Understood.'

'What I can say, sir, is that the fire wasn't caused by anyone trying to steal the vehicle or by vandalism.' There was a long silence.

Grace clamped the phone tighter to his ear and hunched over his desk. 'I'm listening. What did cause it?'

'The vehicle had been tampered with. Deliberate sabotage without any question. An extra set of fuel injectors had been added and positioned to spray petrol directly into the driver footwell when the ignition was switched on. A wiring loop had been connected from the starter motor so as to send out sparks into the footwell when it activated. Combined with that, although it is hard to be certain, because so much of the wiring has melted, it looks to me as if the wiring of the central door locking had been altered, so that once locked the doors could not be unlocked.'

Grace felt a cold prickle crawl down his spine.

'This has been done by someone very clever, someone who knew exactly what they were doing. It wasn't about harming the car, Detective Superintendent. In my view, they were intending to kill the driver.'

*

Grace sat on one of the two large red sofas in the downstairs room of Cleo's house, with Cleo snuggled up beside him, the empty fish tank sitting on the table still filled with water. He had one arm draped around her and he was holding a large glass of Glenfiddich and ice with his free hand. Her hair smelled freshly washed and fragrant. She felt warm, alive, so intensely, beautifully alive. And so vulnerable.

He was scared as hell for her.

Bizet's *The Pearl Fishers* was playing on the hi-fi. It was exquisite music, but it was too poignant, too sad for this moment. He needed silence, or something cheerful, but he didn't know what. He suddenly felt that he didn't know anything. Except for this. That he loved this beautiful, warm, funny creature he was holding. He loved her truly and deeply, more than he had ever imagined he could love anyone after Sandy. And that somehow he had to let Sandy go. He did not want her shadow destroying this relationship.

And he could not stop thinking what would have happened if that sad little villain, who was still fighting for his life, had not beaten her to her car.

If there had been no police stakeout. Nobody around to pull her out.

The thought was almost unbearable. Some psycho had planned to kill her and had gone to great trouble.

Who?

Why?

And if that person had tried once and failed, then was he – or she – going to try again?

His mind went back to Sunday, when someone had sliced open the soft-top of the MG. Was that just a coincidence or was there a connection?

Tomorrow a detective would sit down with her and go through a list of all the people she might have upset during her work. There were plenty of relatives of victims who got angry about their loved ones having post-mortems – and invariably they took their anger out on Cleo rather than on the coroner, who was actually the person responsible for that decision.

Cleo had initially greeted the news with disbelief, but during the past hour, since he had arrived, it was starting to sink in, and the shock was now hitting her.

She leaned down, picked up her wine glass and drained it. 'What I don't understand is—' She stopped in mid-sentence, as if a thought had struck her. 'If someone was going to wire my car to blow up, wouldn't they do it to make it look like an accident? They'd know that forensics would be crawling all over it afterwards. It sounds like what this person did made it look very obvious.'

'You're right. Whoever it was, they did, they made it very obvious. Although I doubt they could have easily disguised what was done. I'm not a mechanic, but it was a lot more elaborate than just crossing a couple of wires.' It was vicious, sadistic, he thought but did not say. He hadn't yet told her that her car was now being treated as a crime scene, the event categorized as a major incident, with a senior investigating officer being appointed and a full inquiry team.

She turned and looked at him with round, worried eyes. 'I just can't think of anyone who could have done this, Roy.'

'What about your ex?'

'Richard?'

'Yes.'

She shook her head. 'No, he wouldn't go this far.'

'He stalked you for months. You had to threaten him with a court order at one point – that was when he backed off, you said. But some stalkers don't go away.'

'I just cannot imagine him doing this.'

'Didn't you say he raced cars?'

'He did, until God started occupying his weekends.'

Grace's mobile rang. He put his glass down and disentangled himself from Cleo, to retrieve it from his jacket pocket. Glancing at the caller display, he saw it was Lloyd.

'Roy Grace,' he answered.

'OK, I've spoken to my client,' the solicitor said. 'He was adopted. He doesn't know anything about his birth parents.'

'Does he know anything about his background at all?'

'He only found out he was adopted after the death of his parents. After his mother died he was going through her papers and found his original birth certificate. It was a big shock – he didn't know.'

'Has he made any attempt to find his birth parents?'

'He says he had been planning to quite recently, but hadn't yet done anything about it.'

Grace thought for a moment. 'Did he by any chance tell you where his birth certificate is?'

'Yes. It's in a filing cabinet in his office at Dyke Road Avenue. It's in a folder marked *Personal*. Would you like to tell me any more?'

'Not at this stage,' Grace replied. 'But thank you. I'll let you know what I find.'

He ended the call, then immediately dialled the number of the Operation Chameleon incident room.

107

Despite being desperately tired, Grace slept fitfully, woken by the slightest noise and not settling again each time until he was certain that it had come from outside Cleo's house, not from inside.

His mind was a jumble of dark thoughts. A burning MG. A tattoo. A gas mask. A body with crabs falling off it, rolling through the surf on a Brighton beach, Janet McWhirter's smiling, cheerful face in her PNC office.

Clear the ground under your feet.

The words of his own mentor, the recently retired Chief Superintendent Dave Gaylor, were rolling around like surf inside his head. Gaylor had been a detective inspector when Grace had first met him. The youngest ever DI in Sussex. Twelve years his senior, Gaylor had taught him much that he knew today. In a sense, his own attempts at helping Glenn Branson were his way of passing that knowledge on.

Clear the ground under your feet. It was an old CID expression. Gaylor had always impressed on him the importance of looking at what was immediately around you when you were at a crime scene. Of not ignoring anything, however irrelevant it might seem at the time. He had also told Grace that if something *felt* wrong, then it probably *was* wrong.

Janet McWhirter's death felt wrong to him.

The words of one of his own personal mantras, *cause*

and effect, were also tumbling around in his mind. *Cause and effect. Cause and effect.*

After fifteen years in the police PNC department, Janet McWhirter falls in love. She goes for a career change, a lifestyle change, plans to move to Australia. Was the *cause* of her lifestyle change the man she met? And the *effect* for her to end up dead?

It was really troubling him.

Dawn was breaking outside. Grace had never been afraid of the dark, even as a child, perhaps because he knew his policeman dad was there, in the next room, to protect him. But he had been worried during these past hours of darkness now. Concerned who might be out there wanting to harm Cleo. Her insanely jealous ex-fiancé, Richard?

Richard Northrop-Turner.

The man who had stalked Cleo relentlessly and increasingly nastily, until she had threatened to go to court. Then he had gone away, or so it seemed. Richard Northrop-Turner, who raced cars and did the mechanics himself. Despite all Cleo's protestations that she did not believe her ex would go as far as trying to kill her, the first call he would make this morning, when he left here, would be to the SIO on the investigation into her attempted murder, a competent DI called Roger Pole, and suggest they concentrate on Richard Northrop-Turner as the prime suspect.

Cleo stirred and he kissed her lightly on the forehead, feeling her warm, sour breath on his face. He wanted to move her out of here and into his own house for the next few days, which would, ideally, mean getting rid of his lodger. For some moments, as he lay awake, he wondered whether he could do a swap with Cleo. Let Glenn Branson come and stay here – and act as a guard – while she stayed with him.

But when he suggested it to her as he was getting dressed a while later, she was less than enthusiastic.

'It's safe here,' she said. 'There's only one way in and out, through the front gates. I feel secure here.'

'You're not secure when you leave here. How many more nights are you on call-out?'

'All this week.'

'If you have to go out again in the middle of the night, I'm coming with you.'

'You're sweet. Thank you.'

'How secure are you at the mortuary?'

'The doors are always locked. I have Darren there all the time, and Walter Hordern most of the time, as well.'

'I'm going to get extra patrols around here, at night, and also have patrols keep an extra vigilant eye around the mortuary. Do you have a reasonably recent photograph of Richard?'

'Loads,' Cleo said. 'On my computer.'

'Email me one this morning – something that's a good likeness. I'm going to get it circulated to the local police – in case they see him anywhere.'

'OK.'

'How will you get to work today?'

'Darren's picking me up.'

'Good.'

Grace told Cleo he would bring round a Chinese take-away tonight, as soon as he could get away, and a bottle of wine. She kissed him goodbye, telling him she thought that was a very good plan.

It was a quarter to six when he left the house and he just about had time to dash back to his home to shower, shave and change. He entered as quietly as possible so as not to wake up Glenn Branson – more to avoid having to endure another round of early-morning soul-searching from his friend than from any concern for the Detective Sergeant getting his requisite hours of beauty sleep.

As usual, Glenn had left the living room looking like a tip. CDs and DVDs, pulled from their sleeves, were spread around everywhere, and the detritus of some reheated ready meal in a foil box – fish pie, it smelled like – was lying on and around a tray on the carpet, along with two empty cans of Coke and an ice-cream carton.

Grace got himself ready and fled, pausing only to slip a CD, from a rapper he had never heard of, into the living room hi-fi and switch it on, turning the volume up high enough to shake a man's fillings out five miles away.

It was far too loud for him to hear Glenn Branson's shouts and curses as he drove away.

108

There was a brown envelope lying on Roy Grace's desk when he walked in, just before seven, with an explanatory note from Bella Moy taped on top, stating these were the certificates for Brian Bishop he had requested. She had also written down the name and contact details of a post-adoption counsellor who, she said, had previously helped the local police through the obstacle course of finding out information on adopted people.

Inside were two creased, oblong documents, about six inches high and a foot wide. They were on yellowing paper with red printing, and handwritten details inserted in black fountain-pen ink. He unfolded the first one. It was headed: **Certified Copy of an Entry of Birth.** Under that were a series of columns.

When and Where Born: Seventh September, 1964 at 3.47 a.m.
Royal Sussex County Hospital, Brighton
Name, if any: Desmond William
Sex: Boy
Name and Surname of Father:
Name and Maiden Surname of Mother: Eleanor Jones

Then, in a space at the extreme right, was written *Adopted*. It was signed *Albert Hole, Superintendent Registrar*.

Grace then unfolded the second document. It was headed: **Certified Copy of an Entry in the Records of the General Register Office**. At the very bottom of the document were the words, **Certified Copy of an Entry in the Adopted Children Register**.

Then he read along the columns.

Date of Entry: Nineteenth September, 1964
Name of Adopted Child: Brian Desmond
Sex of Adopted Child: Male
Name and Surname, Address and Occupation of Adopter or
   Adopters: Mr Rodney and Mrs Irene Bishop, 43 Brangwyn
   Road, Brighton. Company director.
Date of Birth of Child: Seventh September, 1964
Date of Adoption Order and Description of Court by which Made:
   Brighton County Court
Signature of Officer Deputed by Registrar General to attest the
   entry: Albert Hole.

He read both documents through again carefully, absorbing the details. Then he looked at his watch. It was too early to call the post-adoption counsellor, so he decided he would do it straight after the eight-thirty briefing.

*

'Loretta Leberknight,' she answered in a warm, gravelly voice.

Grace introduced himself and explained briefly what he was looking for.

'You want to try to find out if this Brian Bishop has a twin?'

'Exactly,' he replied.

'OK, what information do you have on him?'

'I have his birth certificate and what appears to be an adoption certificate.'

'Is it a long birth certificate or a short one?'

Grace described it to her.

'Good,' she said. 'It's the long one – more information on it. Now, there's usually one sure way to tell – if the birth is in England and Wales. Is it?'

'Yes, he was born in Brighton.'

'Can you read out to me what it says under *When and Where Born*?'

Grace obliged.

'It says, *Seventh September, 1964 at 3.47 a.m.*?' she checked.

'Yes.'

'And the place of birth is given as where?' she asked, checking again.

'Brighton. The Royal Sussex County Hospital.'

'You have the information right there!' She sounded pleased.

'I do.'

'In England and Wales the time of birth in addition to the date of birth is only put down for multiple births. From that information, Detective Superintendent, you can be 100 percent certain that Brian Bishop has a twin.'

109

Minutes after its ten a.m. opening time, Nick Nicholl
walked through the entrance scanner poles and into the
handsome, pastel-blue room of the Brighton Reference
Library. The smells of paper, leather and wood reminded
him of school, but he was so exhausted from yet another
virtually sleepless night, courtesy of his son, Ben, that
he barely took in his surroundings. He walked over to
the inquiry desk and showed his warrant card to one
of the librarians, explaining what he needed.

Five minutes later the young detective was seated,
beneath the domed and stuccoed ceiling, in front of one of
a bank of microfiche units, holding a rectangle of film with
a red band along the top which contained the register of
births in the whole of the UK for the third quarter of 1964.
He inserted it the wrong way around three times, before
finally getting the hang of the reader. Then he fiddled with
the jerky controls, trying to scroll through the lists of first
names beneath surname headers, in print that was almost
too small and blurry to read – for his tired eyes at any rate.

As directed by the helpful post-adoption counsellor,
Loretta Leberknight, he was looking for unmarried mothers
with the surname *Jones*. The clear indicators would be a
child with the same surname as the mother's maiden name.
Although, with one as common as Jones, the librarian had
warned him, there would be some instances of two persons
marrying who had the same surname.

Despite the words SILENCE PLEASE written in large,

clear gold letters on a wooden board, a father somewhere behind him was explaining something to a very loud-mouthed, inquisitive boy. Nick made a mental note never to let his son speak that loudly in a library. He was fast losing track of all the mental notes he had made about irritating things he was not going to let his son do when he was older. He totally doted on him, but the whole business of being a parent was starting to seem daunting. And no one had ever really, properly warned him that you had to do it all while suffering sleep deprivation. Had he and Jen really had a sex life once? Most of their former life together now seemed a distant memory.

Near him, a fan hummed, swivelling on a stand, momentarily fluttering a sheaf of papers before it turned away again. Names in white letters on the dark screen in front of him sped past. Finally, he found *Jones*.

Belinda. Bernard. Beverley. Brett. Carl. Caroline.

Jiggling the flat metal handle awkwardly, he lost the Jones list altogether for a moment. Then, more by seren-dipity than skill, he found it again.

Daniella. Daphne. David. Davies. Dean. Delia. Denise. Dennis. Then he came to a *Desmond* and stopped. *Desmond* was Bishop's first name on his birth certificate.

Desmond. Mother's maiden name Trevors. Born in Romford.

Not the right one.

Desmond. Mother's maiden name *Jones*. Born in Brighton.

Desmond Jones. Mother's maiden name *Jones*.

Bingo!

And there was no other *Desmond Jones* on the list.

Now he just had to find another match of the mother's first and maiden name. But that was a bigger problem than he had anticipated. There were twenty-seven matches. He wrote each one down, then hurried from the library to his next port of call, phoning Roy Grace the moment he was out of the door.

Deciding it would be quicker to leave his car in the NCP, he walked, heading past the Royal Pavilion and the Theatre Royal, cutting through the narrow streets of the Lanes, which were lined mostly with second-hand jewellery shops, and emerged opposite the imposing grey building of the town hall.

Five minutes later he was in a small waiting room in the registrar's offices with hard grey chairs, parquet flooring and a large tank of tropical fish. Grace joined him a few minutes later – the post-adoption counsellor had advised them they would probably need to pull rank in order to get the information they required.

A tall, urbane but rather harassed-looking man of fifty, smartly dressed in a suit and tie, and perspiring from both the heat and clearly being in a rush, came in. 'Yes, gentlemen?' he said. 'I'm Clive Ravensbourne, the Superintendent Registrar. You wanted to see me rather than one of my colleagues?'

'Thank you,' Grace said. 'I appreciate your seeing us at such short notice.'

'You'll have to excuse me making this brief, but I'm doing a wedding in ten minutes' time.' He glanced at his watch. 'Actually, nine minutes.'

'I explained to your assistant why we needed to see you – did she brief you?'

'Yes, yes, a murder inquiry.'

Nicholl handed him the list of twenty-seven Jones births. 'We are looking for a twin,' he said. 'What we need is for you to tell us if any one of these boys is a twin of –' he pointed at the name – 'Desmond William Jones.'

The registrar looked panic-stricken for a moment. 'How many names do you have on this list?'

'Twenty-seven. We need you to look at the records and see if you can get a match from any of them. We are pretty sure one of them is a twin – and we need to find him urgently.'

He glanced at his watch again. 'I don't have the – I – hang on, though – we could short-circuit this.' He nodded to himself. 'Do you have a birth certificate for this Desmond William Jones?'

'We have copies of the original and the adoption certificate,' Nicholl replied.

'Just give me the birth certificate. There'll be an index number on it.'

Nicholl pulled it out of the envelope and handed it to him.

He unfolded it and scanned it quickly. 'There, you see,' he said, pointing at the left-hand edge of the document. 'Just wait here. I'll be right back.'

He disappeared through the doorway and re-emerged after a couple of minutes, holding a large, dark red, leather-bound registry book. Still standing, he opened it approximately halfway through and quickly turned over several pages. Then he appeared to relax a little.

'Here we are!' he said. 'Desmond William Jones, mother Eleanor Jones, born at the Royal Sussex County Hospital, 7 September 1964 at three forty-seven a.m. And it says *Adopted*, right? Got the right chap?'

Grace and Nicholl both nodded.

'Good. So, right underneath it, bottom of the page, we have Frederick Roger Jones, mother Eleanor Jones, born at the Royal Sussex County Hospital, 7 September 1964 at three fifty-two a.m. Also subsequently adopted.' He looked up with a smile. 'He sounds the ticket to me. Born two minutes later. That's your twin. Frederick Roger Jones.'

Grace felt a real surge of excitement. 'Thank you. That's enormously helpful. Can you give us any further information?'

The registrar shut the book very firmly. 'I'm afraid that's as much as I can do for you. Adoption records are more tightly protected than the crown jewels. You'll now have to do battle with Social Services. And good luck to you!'

Ten minutes later – most of them spent on his mobile phone, in the hallway of the town hall, being shunted from extension to extension within Social Services, Grace was beginning to understand what the man had meant. And after a further five minutes on hold, listening to a perpetual loop of 'Greensleeves', he was ready to kill.

110

Twenty minutes later, still standing in the grand entrance of the town hall, Grace finally got put through to the Director of Social Services. Managing – just – to keep his temper under control, he explained the circumstances and his reasons for needing access to an adoption file.

The man listened sympathetically. 'Of course, Detective Superintendent, you understand that to do this would be a very big exception to our policy,' he said pedantically. 'I would need to be able to justify releasing this information to you. And I would need assurances that it would only be for the purposes you have outlined. Some adopted people do not know they are adopted. The effects on them, from hearing the news, can be very traumatic.'

'Probably not as traumatic as it was for the two women who have been murdered in this city in the past week,' Grace responded. 'Or for the next woman on this maniac's list.'

There was a brief silence. 'And you really think this twin might be the killer?'

'As I've just told you, it's possible he could be responsible – and if he is, he could kill again. I think the public's safety is more important at this stage than hurting the feelings of one middle-aged man.'

'If we did release information that would enable you to find him, what would your intentions be?'

'My intentions? I don't have any interest or agenda for this information other than finding the man as quickly as possible, with a view to questioning him and eliminating him from our inquiries.'

'Or arresting him?'

'I can't speculate. But if we have reason to believe, after interviewing him, that he is involved in the very savage murders of two innocent young women, then that is almost certain, yes.'

There was another long silence. Grace felt his temper straining again, pulling like a tattooed pit-bull terrier on a leash. And the leash was fraying.

'It's a difficult decision for us.'

'I appreciate that. But if a third person is murdered, and it turns out that this twin was the killer, or could have led us to the killer – and you could have prevented it – how would you feel about that?'

'I'll have to make a phone call and check something with our legal department. Can you give me five minutes?'

'I need to make a decision whether to go back to my office or hang around downtown,' Grace replied. 'Will it be just five minutes or longer?'

'I will be very quick, Detective Superintendent, I assure you.'

Grace used the time to make a quick call to Roger Pole, the SIO on the investigation into the attempted murder of Cleo Morey, to get a progress update. Two officers had gone this morning to interview her former fiancé, Richard Northrop-Turner, at his chambers in Chichester, Pole told him. And it looked like the barrister had an alibi. Before they had finished speaking, Grace's phone started beeping with an incoming call. He thanked Pole and switched to the new call. It was the Director of Social Services again.

'All right, Detective Superintendent. You won't need to explain all of this to the post-adoption social worker – I will get her to bring you the file and let you have the information you require. Is it the names of the people who adopted Frederick Roger Jones that would suffice for your purposes?'

'That would be a good starting point,' Grace responded. 'Thank you.'

*

A bus rumbled past the first-floor window of the small, sparsely furnished conference room in the Council office building. Grace glanced out, through the venetian blinds, at the pink banner advertising the television series *Sugar Rush* below its top deck. He had been sitting in this damn room with Nick Nicholl for over a quarter of an hour, with no offer of a coffee or even a glass of water. The morning was slipping by, but they were at least making some progress. His nerves were badly on edge. He was trying to concentrate on his own cases, but he could not stop thinking and worrying about Cleo, almost every second.

'How's your lad?' he asked the young DC, who was yawning and pallid-faced despite the glorious summer weather.

'Wonderful!' he said. 'Ben's just amazing. But he doesn't sleep very well.'

'Good at changing nappies, are you?'

'I'm becoming world class.'

A leaflet on the table was headed *Brighton & Hove City Council Directorate of Children, Families and Schools.* On the walls were posters of smiling, cute-looking children of different races.

Finally the door opened and a young woman entered, managing to put Grace's back up even before she opened her mouth, just from the way she looked, combined with her scowl.

She was in her mid-thirties, thin as a rake, with a pointed nose, a hoop-shaped mouth ringed with red lipstick, and her hair was dyed a vivid fuchsia, gelled into small, aggressive-looking spikes. She was wearing an almost full-length printed muslin dress and what Grace thought might be vegan sandals, and was carrying a buff file folder with a Post-it note stuck to it.

'You're the two from the police?' she asked coldly, in a south London accent, her eyes, behind emerald-framed glasses, finding a gap between the two detectives.

Grace, followed by Nicholl, stood up. 'Detective Superintendent Grace and Detective Constable Nicholl from Sussex CID,' Grace said.

Without giving her name, she said, 'The director has told me that you want to know the adoptive parents of Frederick Jones, who was born on 7 September 1964.' Now she looked straight at Grace, still intensely hostile.

'Yes, that's right. Thank you,' he said.

She pulled the Post-it note off the folder and handed it to him. On it was written, in neat handwriting, the name *Tripwell, Derek and Joan*.

He showed it to Nick Nicholl, then looked at the folder. 'Is there anything else in there that could give us any help?'

'I'm sorry, I'm not authorized,' she said, avoiding eye contact again.

'Did your director not explain that this is a murder inquiry?'

'It's also someone's private life,' she retorted.

'All I need is an address for the adoptive parents – Derek and Joan Tripwell,' he said, reading from the yellow note. Then he nodded at the folder. 'You must have that in there.'

'I've been told to give you their names,' she said. 'I haven't been told to give you any more.'

Grace looked at her, exasperated. 'I can't seem to get it across – there may be other women in this city whose lives are in danger.'

'Detective Superintendent, you and your colleague have your job to do, protecting the citizens of Brighton and Hove. I have my job to do, protecting adopted children. Is that clear?'

'Let me make something clear to you then,' Grace said, glancing at Nicholl and clenching up with anger. 'If anyone else is murdered in this city, and you are withholding information that could have enabled us to prevent it, I'm going to personally hang you out to dry.'

'I'll look forward to it,' she said, and left the room.

111

Grace was driving his Alfa up the hill, past ASDA and British Bookstores, about to turn in through the gates of Sussex House, when DC Pamela Buckley rang him. He stopped.

'I'm not sure if it's good news or bad, Detective Superintendent,' she said. 'I've checked the phone directory and the electoral register. There are no Tripwells in Brighton and Hove. I've done a broader sweep. There is one in Horsham, there are two in Southampton, one in Dover and one in Guildford. The one in Guildford matches your names, Derek and Joan.'

'Let me have their address.'

He wrote it down. *18 Spencer Avenue.* 'Can you get me directions?'

*

The traffic system in the centre of Guildford, Grace decided, had been designed by an ape, out of its mind on hallucinogenic mushrooms, who had tried to copy the Hampton Court maze in tarmac. He had got lost every time he had ever come to Guildford previously, and he got lost again now, stopping to check his street map twice and vowing to buy himself a SatNav system at the next opportunity. After several frustrating minutes, his temper worsening along with his driving, he finally found Spencer Avenue, a cul-de-sac near the cathedral, and turned into it.

It was a narrow road on a steep hill, with cars parked on both sides. There were small houses above him to the right and below him to the left. He saw the number 18 on a low fence to his left, pulled his car into a gap a little further on, parked and walked back.

He went down the steps to the front door of a tiny, semi-detached house, with a trim front garden, nearly tripping over a black and white cat which shot across his path, and rang the doorbell.

After some moments the door was opened by a small, grey-haired woman in a strap-top vest, baggy jeans and gumboots, wearing gardening gloves. 'Hello?' she said cheerily.

He showed her his warrant card. 'Detective Super-intendent Grace of Sussex CID.'

Her face dropped. 'Oh dear, is it Laura again?'

'Laura?'

'Is she in trouble again?' She had a tiny mouth that reminded him of the spout of a teapot.

'Forgive me if I've come to the wrong address,' he said. 'I'm looking for a Mr Derek and Mrs Joan Tripwell, who adopted a boy called Frederick Jones in September 1964.'

She looked very distressed suddenly, her eyes all over the place. After a few moments she said, 'No, you haven't – haven't come to the wrong address. Would you like to come in?' She raised her arms. 'Excuse my appearance – wasn't expecting visitors.'

He followed her into a tiny, narrow hallway, which had a musty smell of old people and cats, then through into a small living and dining room. The living area was domin-ated by a three-piece suite and a large television set on which a cricket match was playing. An elderly man, with a tartan blanket over his thighs, a sparse thatch of white hair and a hearing aid, was slumped in one of the armchairs in front of it, asleep, although from the colour of his face he could have been dead.

'Derek,' she said, 'we've got a visitor. A police officer.'

The man opened one eye, said, 'Ah,' then closed it again.

'Would you like a cup of tea?' she asked Grace.

'If it's no trouble, that would be very nice, thank you.'

She indicated the sofa. Grace stepped over the slumbering man's legs and sat down as she went out of the room. Ignoring the cricket, he concentrated on looking around the room, searching for photographs. There were several. One showed a much younger Joan and Derek with three children, two boys and a rather sullen-looking girl. Another, on top of a display cabinet filled with Capo Di Monte porcelain figures, was in a silver frame. It contained a picture of a teenage boy with long, dark hair in a suit and tie, posing for the camera with what appeared to be some reluctance. But he saw in the boy's looks what resembled, very definitely, a young Brian Bishop.

There was a cheer on the television, followed by clapping. He glanced at the screen and saw a helmeted batsman walking away from the crease, the middle stump behind him bent sharply back.

'Should have just blocked it,' the man who appeared to be asleep beside him said. 'Silly idiot tried to hit it through the covers. You a cricketing man?'

'Not really. Rugger's my game.'

The man grunted and fell silent.

The woman came back into the room with a tray containing a china teapot, milk jug, sugar bowl, cups and saucers and a plate of biscuits. She had removed her gardening gloves and replaced her gumboots with pompom slippers. 'Would you like tea, Derek?' she asked, raising her voice.

'Got a bloody rugger bugger in the house,' he grumbled, then appeared to fall asleep again.

'Milk and sugar?' she asked Grace, setting the tray down. He eyed the plate of biscuits on the tray hungrily, realizing it was lunch time and he'd barely had any breakfast.

'Milk, no sugar, please.'

She handed the plate over to him. It was laden with digestives, Penguins and marshmallows. He took a Penguin gratefully and unwrapped it.

She poured his tea and passed it to him, then pointed at the silver-framed photograph. 'We didn't like the name Frederick, did we, Derek?'

A small, negative-sounding moan came from the man's mouth.

'So we renamed him Richard,' she said.

'Richard,' the old man echoed, with a grunt.

'After Richard Chamberlain, the actor. *Dr Kildare.* Did you ever see Dr Kildare?'

'Before his bloody time,' her husband mumbled.

'I remember it vaguely,' Grace confessed. 'My mum was a fan.' He stirred his tea, anxious to get to the point of this visit.

'We adopted two children,' Joan Tripwell said. 'Then our own came along. Geoffrey. He's doing well – he does research for a pharmaceutical company, Pfizer. Working on cancer drugs for them.'

Grace smiled. 'Good.'

'Laura's the problem one. That's what I thought you had come about. She's always been in trouble. Drugs. It's a bit ironic, isn't it, our Geoffrey doing so well with a drugs company and Laura in and out of homes, always in trouble with the police.'

'And Richard – how is he doing?' Grace asked.

Her little mouth closed, her eyes all over the place again suddenly, and Grace realized he had touched a nerve. She poured her own tea and added two lumps of sugar, using silver tongs. 'What exactly is your interest in talking about Richard?' she asked, her voice suddenly full of suspicion.

'I was hoping you could tell me where I can find him. I need to speak to him.'

'To speak to him?' She sounded astonished.

'Plot 437, row 12,' the old man said.

'Derek!' she admonished.

'Well, that's where he bloody well is. What's the matter with you, woman?'

'Excuse my husband,' she said, picking her cup up daintily by the handle. 'He's never really got over it. I suppose neither of us has.'

'Got over what?' Grace probed, as gently as he could.

'He was a premature baby, like his brother, poor little soul. He was born with a congenital weakness – malformed lungs. They never developed properly. He had a weak chest, you know? Always getting infections as a child. And really bad asthma.'

'What do you know about his brother?' Grace asked, too interested now to take a bite of his Penguin.

'That he passed away in the incubator, poor little mite. That's what they told us.'

'What about their mother?'

The woman shook her head. 'The Social Services were terrible on giving out information.'

'Tell me about it,' Grace said bitterly.

'It took us a long time to find out that she was a single parent – of course that was a bad thing in those days. She was killed in a car crash, but we never really knew the details.'

'Are you sure that Frederick – I'm sorry, Richard,' he corrected himself, 'that Richard's brother died?'

'You can't be certain of anything the Social Services say. But that's what they told us at the time.'

Grace nodded sympathetically. There was another roar on the television. Grace glanced at it and saw a replay of a silly-mid-on fielder making a catch. 'Can you tell me where I can find your son, Richard?'

'Already bloody told yer,' the old man grumbled. 'Plot 437, row 12. She goes there every year.'

'I'm sorry,' Grace said. 'I don't understand.'

'What my husband is trying to tell you is that you are twenty years too late,' she said.

'Too late?' Grace was getting all kinds of bad, confused signals.

'When he was twenty-one,' Joan Tripwell said. 'Richard went to a party and forgot to take his Ventolin inhaler – he always had to carry it with him. He had a particularly bad asthma attack.' Her voice was faltering. She sniffed and dabbed her eyes. 'His heart gave out.'

Grace stared at her in astonishment.

As if reading some uncertainty in his face, Joan Tripwell said emphatically, 'Poor soul, he died. He never really had his life.'

112

After an hour's drive back, a very despondent Roy Grace reported his findings to the Operation Chameleon team in MIR One, then he sat down and began reviewing all the evidence that they had for Brian Bishop.

Convinced that Joan Tripwell had been telling the truth, he was left with a number of anomalies that did not quite fit together. It was like trying to hammer pieces into a jigsaw that looked sort of right but were not the exact shape.

He was bothered by the details of the twin that the Superintendent Registrar had read out to him. Grace re-read the notes he had written down in the town hall, then rechecked Bishop's birth certificate and his adoption certificate. He had been born on 7 September at three forty-seven – five minutes earlier than his brother, Frederick Roger Jones, who was renamed Richard, and died at the age of twenty-one.

So why had Social Services told Joan Tripwell that the other twin had died?

He rang the post-adoption counsellor, Loretta Leberknight. She responded cheerily that in those days it was exactly the kind of thing that Social Services might do. They didn't like to split up twins, but there was, even back then, a long list of people waiting to adopt. If one had been sickly, in an incubator for a period of time, they might have made the decision to put the healthy one out for adoption, then, if the other survived, tell a white lie in order to satisfy another couple desperate for a child.

It had happened to her, she added. She had a twin yet her adoptive parents were never informed of that.

From his experiences with the hag earlier, he could well believe they were capable of anything.

Grace put the CCTV footage up on the monitor in the room and stared at it, checking it against the detailed mobile phone log that DC Corbin had prepared. That man up on the screen was Brian Bishop. He was absolutely certain, unless the man had an exact double. But the fact that the log showed him leaving the immediate vicinity of the Lansdowne Place Hotel and then returning to it made the chance of an accidental double, in exactly the right place at the right time, too big a coincidence to accept.

On his pad he wrote down the word *complicity*, followed by a big question mark.

Had someone gone to the trouble of having surgery to make himself look like Brian Bishop? Then somehow obtained fresh semen from the man?

His thoughts were interrupted by the sound of his name being called, and he turned his head. He saw the heavily bearded figure of George Erridge, from the Photographic Unit. Erridge, who always looked like an explorer just returned from an expedition, was walking towards him excitedly, holding a sheaf of what looked like photographic paper in his hand.

'This CCTV footage you gave me yesterday, Roy, from the Royal Sussex County Hospital? The bearded guy in sunglasses and long hair who was in there, creating a scene on Sunday?'

Grace had almost forgotten about it. 'Yes?'

'Well, we've got something! I've been running it through some software they've developed at the Missing Persons Helpline. Yep? To detect changes of identity in people – how they might look in five, ten, twenty years' time? Yep? With hair, without hair, with beards, without beards, all that stuff. I've been trying to persuade Tony Case we need to invest in it for here.'

'Tell me?' Grace said.

Erridge put the first photograph down. Grace saw a man with a heavy beard and moustache, long, straggly hair that hung low over his forehead and large, tinted glasses, dressed in a baggy shirt over a string vest, slacks and sandals.

'We've had the computer remove the long hair, the beard, the sunglasses, yep?'

'OK,' Grace replied.

Erridge slapped down a second photograph on Grace's desk. 'Recognize him?'

Grace was staring at Brian Bishop.

For some moments he said nothing. Then he said, 'Bloody hell. Well done, George. How the hell did you get the eyes behind the glasses?'

Erridge grinned. 'We got lucky. There's also a CCTV camera in the men's room. Your guy took his glasses off in there to wipe them. We got footage of his eyes!'

'Thank you,' Grace said. 'This is ace work!'

'Tell that tight bastard Tony Case, will you? We need this kit here. Could have got this back to you yesterday if we had it in-house.'

'I'll tell him,' Grace said, standing up and looking around for Adrienne Corbin, the young detective constable who had been working on the phone log. Addressing no one in particular, he asked, 'Anyone know where DC Corbin is?'

'Taking a break, Roy,' Bella Moy said.

'Can you get hold of her – ask her to come back here quickly?'

He sat down, staring at each of the photographs in turn, thinking. The transformation was extraordinary. A total metamorphosis, from a suave, good-looking man into someone you'd want to cross the road to avoid.

Sunday, he was thinking. Bishop was at the hospital late on Sunday morning. So he was out and about.

It was Sunday morning when Cleo had the roof of her car ripped open.

He leafed through the time-line report until he reached Sunday morning. According to Bishop's own statement, in his first interview, he had spent the morning in his hotel room, catching up on his emails and then had gone to some friends for Sunday lunch. There was a note that the friends, Robin and Sue Brown, had been contacted and confirmed that Bishop had arrived at half past one and stayed with them until just after four. They lived in the village of Glynde, a fifteen- to twenty-minute drive from the Royal Sussex County Hospital, Grace estimated.

The time showing on the CCTV footage on the first photograph was twelve fifty-eight. Tight, but possible. Very possible.

He looked back at the time-line for earlier that morning. The duty FLO, Linda Buckley, reported that Bishop had remained in his hotel room until noon, then had left in his Bentley, telling her that he was going to the lunch and would be back later. She had logged his return at four forty-five.

The concern inside him was growing. Bishop could easily have diverted on his route to the hospital and gone via the mortuary. But why? What on earth would have been the point? His motive?

But then again he had no motive yet for the death of Sophie Harrington.

Adrienne Corbin came hurrying into the room, puffing from exertion and perspiring, her dumpy frame clearly not suited to this hot weather. 'Sir, you wanted to see me?'

Grace apologized for cutting short her break and told her what he needed from the phone mast records and from the CCTV records. He wanted to plot Bishop's movements from midday on Sunday, when he left the hotel, to the time he arrived at the Browns' home in Glynde.

'Old-timer?' Branson, who had been sitting quietly at his workstation, suddenly spoke.

'What?'

'If Bishop was treated in A&E at the hospital, he'd have had to sign the register, right?'

And suddenly Grace realized just how tired he was and what an addling effect it was having on his mind. How on earth could he have overlooked that? 'You know what?' he replied.

'I'm all ears.'

'Sometimes I actually think you do have a brain.'

113

Finding a route through the red tape of Social Services had been a doddle compared to the phone marathon that now ensued with the Brighton Health Care Trust, Grace rapidly discovered. It took Glenn Branson over an hour and a half of being shunted from official to official, and waiting for people to come out of meetings, before he finally got through to the one manager who was in a position to sanction the release of confidential patient information. And then only after Grace had been put on the line and pleaded his case.

The next problem was that no one by the name of Bishop had been seen at the A&E department on Sunday, and seventeen people had been treated for hand injuries during that day. Fortunately Dr Raj Singh was on duty, and Grace dispatched Branson to the hospital with the photograph from the CCTV in the hope that Singh would recognize him.

Just after four thirty, he stepped out of MIR One and phoned Cleo, to see how she was.

'Quiet day,' she said, sounding tired but reasonably cheerful. 'I've had two detectives here all the time, going through the register. I'm just tidying up with Darren, then he's driving me home. How's you?'

Grace relayed the conversation with DI Pole he'd had earlier.

'I didn't think it was Richard,' she said, sounding strangely relieved, which annoyed him. He was being irrational, he knew, but there was a warmth in her voice whenever she mentioned her ex, which concerned him. As if it was over, but not really over completely. 'Are you going to be working late?' she asked.

'I don't know yet. I have the six-thirty briefing and will have to see what that throws up.'

'What do you fancy for supper?'

'You.'

'How would you like me garnished?'

'Naked, with just a lettuce leaf.'

'Then get yourself over here as early as you can. I need your body.'

'Love you,' he said.

'I quite like you too!' she said.

*

Deciding to take advantage of the first free moment he'd had all day, Grace walked across to the PNC unit, at the far end of the building, where poor Janet McWhirter had spent so much of her working life.

Normally the large office area, with many of its team civilian computer staff, had a lively buzz of activity. But this afternoon there was a subdued atmosphere. He knocked on the door of one of the few enclosed offices. It had been Janet McWhirter's room and now, according to the label on the wall, housed Lorna Baxter, PNC and Disclosure Unit Manager. He had known her, like Janet, for a long time and liked her a lot.

Without waiting for a reply, he opened the door. Lorna, who was in her mid-thirties, was heavily pregnant. Her brown hair, normally long, was cropped short into a clumsy monk's fringe, which accentuated the weight that had gone on to her face, and although she was dressed lightly, in a loose floral-patterned dress, she was clearly suffering in the heat.

She was talking on the phone, but signalled at him cheerily to come in, pointing to a chair in front of her desk. He closed the door and sat down.

It was a small, square room, her desk and chair, two visitor's chairs, a tall metal filing cabinet and a stack of box files just about filling it. There was a Bart Simpson cartoon pinned to the wall on his right with coloured drawing pins, and a sheet of paper on which was crayoned a large heart and the words, I Love You Mummy!

She ended the call. 'Hey, Roy!' she said. 'Good to see you.' Then she shrugged. 'Bummer, isn't it?' She had a strong South African accent, despite having lived over twelve years in England.

'Janet?'

She grimaced. 'We were good friends.'

'So what happened exactly? I heard that she fell in love with someone and was moving to Australia with him to get married.'

'Yes. She was so happy. You know, she was thirty-six and had never really had a serious boyfriend before. I think she'd almost resigned herself to being single for the rest of her life. Then she met this fellow and he clearly shot the lights out for her. She was a changed person in weeks.'

'In what way?'

'She had a total makeover. Hair, clothes, everything. And she looked so happy.'

'And then she wound up murdered?'

'That's what it sounds like.'

'What do you – or anyone here – know about this man, her fiancé?'

'Not much. She was a very private person. I probably

knew her as well as anyone – but she was a real closed book. It was a long while before she even admitted to me that she was dating. She didn't say much about him, although she did let on that he was very wealthy. Big house in Brighton and a flat in London. The big *but* was that he was married. Planning to leave his wife.'

'For Janet?'

'That's what he'd told her.'

'And she believed him?'

'Totally.'

'Any idea what he did?'

'He was in software,' she said. 'Something to do with rostering. A very successful company, apparently. He was opening up in Australia and decided he wanted to make a new life there – with Janet.'

Rostering. Grace was thinking hard. *Rostering.* That was the business Bishop was in. 'Did she ever tell you his name?'

'No, she wouldn't tell me. She kept telling me she couldn't give me his name because he was married, and she'd sworn to keep their affair secret.'

'She was hardly the type to blackmail someone,' Grace said. 'And I wouldn't have thought she had a lot of money.'

'No, she didn't. She used to travel to work on an old Vespa.'

'So what could have been his motive for killing her – assuming he did?'

'Or maybe they were both killed?' she replied. 'And only her body has turned up?'

'That's possible. Someone after him and she just happened to be in the wrong place at the wrong time? Wouldn't be the first time. Have you heard anything from the investigating team?'

'Not much progress so far. There's just one small thing that's interesting.'

'What's that?'

'I saw Ray Packham earlier – from the High Tech Crime Unit?'

'Yes, I know him. He's smart.'

'He's been running forensic software on the computer Janet used here, and he's recovered the electronic diary that she deleted when she left.'

Someone knocked on the door and entered. Grace looked up and saw a young man he recognized from this department standing there. Lorna looked up at him. 'Sorry, Dermot, is it anything urgent?'

'No – no problem – see you tomorrow.'

He went out and closed the door.

Her face blanked. 'Where was I?'

'Janet's diary,' he prompted.

'Yes, right. There was one name on it, about nine months back, that none of us here know. It was an entry for an evening in December last year. She had written down, *Drink, Brian.*'

'Brian?'

'Yes.'

Grace felt a sudden frisson. *Brian. Rostering. Big house in Brighton. Flat in London. A murdered woman.*

Now his brain was really engaging, all his tiredness gone. Was that why he had woken in the middle of the night, thinking about Janet McWhirter? His brain telling him that there was a connection?

'It looks like this means something to you, Roy.'

'Possibly,' he said. 'Who's running the inquiry on Janet?'

'DI Winter, in MIR Two.'

Grace thanked Lorna and headed straight to the

incident room that had been set up in MIR Two. There he explained the possible connection to his own double-inquiry that he had just learned.

Then he returned to MIR One, almost colliding with a triumphant-looking Glenn Branson, who came round the corner at a speed close to a run. 'Got him!' Branson said, pulling a piece of paper from his pocket and unfolding it. 'I've got a name and an address!'

Grace followed him into the room.

'His name is Norman Jecks.'

Grace looked down at the crumpled sheet of lined paper, with a jagged edge where it had been torn from a ring-pad. On it was written *262B, Sackville Road, Hove.*

He looked up at Branson. 'That's not Bishop's address.'

'No, it's not. But that's the one the man wrote down on the A&E registration form on Sunday morning. The disguised Brian Bishop. Maybe he has two lives?'

Grace stared at it, with a bad feeling. As if a dark cloud was swirling around his insides. Did Brian Bishop have a second home? A secret home? A secret life? 'Is it a real address?'

'Bella's checked the electoral register. There's a Norman Jecks at that address.'

He looked at his watch, adrenaline pumping into his veins. It was ten past six. 'Forget the briefing meeting,' he said. 'Find out who the duty magistrate is and get a search warrant. Then get on to the Local Support Team. We're going to pay Norman Jecks a visit. Just as fast as we possibly can.'

He sprinted back along the labyrinth of corridors to the PNC suite.

Lorna Baxter was halfway out of the door when he arrived.

'Lorna,' he said breathlessly, 'have you got a moment?'

'I've got to pick my eldest up from a swimming lesson.' She looked at her watch. 'Is it something quick?'

'Just a few minutes – it's really important – sorry to do this to you. I'm right, aren't I, that Janet McWhirter would have had signatory authority to make entries on the PNC?'

'Yes. She was the only person here who could.'

'On her own, unsupervised?'

'Yes.'

'Would you mind looking up something for me on the PNC?'

She smiled. 'I can see you need me for more than just a few minutes. I'll get someone to pick Claire up,' she said, pulling her mobile from her handbag.

They went and sat down in her office, and she tapped her keyboard, logging on. 'OK,' she said. 'Shoot!'

'I need you to look up someone's criminal record. What information do I have to give you?'

'Just his name, age, address.'

Grace gave her Brian Bishop's details. He listened to the click of the keys as she entered the information.

'Brian Desmond Bishop, born 7 September 1964?'

'That's him.'

She leaned forward, closer to her screen. 'In 1979, at Brighton Juvenile Court, he was sentenced to two years in a young offenders' institute for raping a fourteen-year-old girl,' she read. 'In 1985, at Lewes Crown Court, he received two years' probation for GBH on a woman. Nice guy!' she commented.

'Is there any anomaly with the entry?' he asked.

'Anomaly? In what sense?'

'Could it have been tampered with?'

'Well, there is just one thing – although it's not that

unusual.' She looked up at him. 'Normally records as old as these are never touched – they just sit on the file forever. The only time they are touched is when amendments are made – sometimes because of new evidence – old convictions getting quashed or a mistake that needs rectifying, that kind of thing.'

'Can you tell when they've been touched?'

'Absolutely!' She nodded emphatically. 'There's an electronic footprint left any time they are altered. Actually there's one here.'

Grace sat bolt upright. 'There is?'

'Each of us with signatory authority has an individual access code. If we amend a record, the footprint we leave is our access code, and the date.'

'So can you find out whose access code that is?'

She smiled at him. 'I know that access code without having to look it up. It's Janet's. She amended this record on –' she peered closer – '7 April this year.'

Now Grace's adrenaline was really surging. 'She did?'

'Uh huh.' She frowned, tapped her keyboard, then peered at the screen again. 'This is interesting,' she said. 'That was her last day in the office.'

114

An hour and a half later, shortly before eight o'clock, Nick Nicholl drove a marked police Vauxhall Vectra slowly up Sackville Road. Grace was in the front seat, wearing a bullet-proof vest beneath his jacket, and Glenn Branson, also in a bullet-proof vest, sat behind him. Both men were counting down the house numbers on the grimy Edwardian terraced buildings. Following right behind them were two marked police Ford Transit vans, each containing a team of uniformed officers from the Local Support Team.

'Two-five-four!' Glenn Branson read out. 'Two-five-eight. Two-six-zero. Two-six-two! We're here!'

Nicholl double-parked alongside a dusty Ford Fiesta, the other vehicles pulling up behind him.

Grace radioed the second LST van to drive round and cover the back entrance, and to let him know when they were in position.

Two minutes later he got the call back that they were ready.

They climbed out of the car. Grace instructed the SOCO to stay in his vehicle for the moment, then led the way down the concrete steps, past two dustbins, then a grimy bay window with net curtains drawn. It was still daylight, although fading fast now, so the absence of any interior light did not necessarily mean the flat was empty.

The tatty grey front door, with two opaque glass panes in it, was in bad need of a lick of paint, and the plastic bell-push had seen better times. Nonetheless, he pressed it. There was no sound. He pressed it again. Silence.

He rapped sharply on the panes. Then he called out, 'Police! Open up!'

There was no response.

He rapped again, even more loudly. 'Police! Open up!' Then he turned to Nicholl and told him to get the LST team to bring the battering ram.

Moments later two burly LST officers appeared, one of them holding the long, yellow, cylindrical door-busting ram.

'OK, Chief?' he said to Grace.

Grace nodded.

He swung the ram at one of the glass panes. To everyone's amazement, it bounced off. He swung it again, harder, and again it bounced off.

Both Branson and Nicholl frowned at him. 'Didn't eat enough spinach when you were a kid?' the LST officer's colleague joked.

'Fuck this!'

His colleague, who was even more heavily built, took the implement and swung it. Moments later he was looking sheepish too, as it bounced back from the glass again.

'Shit!' the constable said. 'He's got armour-plated glass!' He swung it at the door lock. The door barely moved. He swung it again, then again, breaking out into a sweat. Then he looked at Grace. 'I don't think he likes burglars.'

'Obviously been taking advice from his local crime prevention officer,' Nick Nicholl quipped, in a rare display of humour.

The constable signalled them to move out of the way, then took an almighty swing at the centre of the door, low down. It buckled, with wood splinters flying off.

'Reinforced,' he said grimly. He swung again, then again, until the wood was sheared away and he could see the steel plate behind it. It took another four swings of the ram before the plate had been bent back enough for someone to crawl through.

Six LST officers went in first, to establish if anyone was in the flat. After a couple of minutes one of them unlocked the damaged door from the inside and came back out. 'The flat's empty, sir.'

Grace thanked the LST team, then asked them to leave, explaining that he wanted to limit the number of officers on the premises in order to conduct a forensic search.

As Grace went in, pulling on a pair of latex gloves, he found himself in a small, gloomy basement room, almost every inch of the shabbily carpeted floor covered in partially dismembered computer equipment, piles of motoring magazines and car manuals. It smelled damp.

At the far end of the room was a workstation, with a computer and keyboard. The entire wall in front of it was covered in newspaper cuttings and what looked like flow charts of family trees. To the right was an open door, with a dark passageway beyond.

He crossed the room, threading a careful path through the stuff on the floor, until he reached the ancient swivel chair at the workstation. Then he saw what was pinned up on the wall.

And he froze in his tracks.

'Shit!' Glenn Branson, now standing right beside him, said.

It was a gallery of news cuttings. Most of the pages, cut or torn from the *Argus* and from national newspapers, appeared to track Brian Bishop's career. There were several photographs of him, including a wedding photograph of his marriage to Katie. Alongside was an article, on a pink page from the *Financial Times*, on the meteoric rise of his company, International Rostering Solutions PLC, talking about its entry, last year, into the *Sunday Times* list of the UK's hundred fastest-growing companies.

Grace was vaguely aware of Branson, and other people, moving past him, pulling on rubber gloves, doors and drawers opening and closing, but his attention was riveted by another article Sellotaped to the wall. It was the front page of a late edition of Monday's *Argus* newspaper, carrying a large photograph of Brian Bishop and his wife, and a smaller, inset photograph of himself. In one of the columns beneath was a red ink ring around his words: *Evil creature.*

He read the whole passage:

'*This is a particularly nasty crime,*' Detective Super-intendent Grace, the SIO, said. '*. . . we will work around the clock to bring the evil creature who did this to justice.*'

Nick Nicholl suddenly waved a flimsy, legal-looking document in front of him. 'Just found this lease. He's got a lock-up! Two in fact – in Westbourne Villas.'

'Phone the incident room,' Grace said. 'Get someone to type up a new warrant and get it down to the same magistrate, then bring it here. And tell them to shift!'

Then, as he was staring, again, at the red ring around the words *Evil creature* he heard Glenn Branson call out, in a very worried voice, 'Boss man, I think you'd better take a look in here.'

Grace walked down a short passageway into a dank, windowless bedroom, with a narrow borrowed light high up. The room was lit by a solitary, naked, low-wattage bulb hanging from a cord above a bed, neatly made, with a cream candlewick counterpane.

Lying on the counterpane was a long, brown-haired

wig, a moustache, a beard, a black baseball cap, and a pair of dark sunglasses.

'Jesus!' he said.

Glenn Branson's response was simply to point with his finger past him. Grace turned. And what he saw chilled every cell in his body.

Taped to the wall were three blown-up photographs, each taken, he reckoned, from his limited knowledge of the craft, through a long lens.

The first was of Katie Bishop. She was wearing a bikini swimsuit, leaning back against what looked like the cockpit rail of a yacht. A large red-ink cross was scrawled over her. The second was of Sophie Harrington. It was of her face, in close-up, with what looked like a blurred London street behind her. There was also a red-ink cross scrawled over her.

The third was a picture of Cleo Morey, turning away from the front entrance door of the Brighton and Hove Mortuary.

There was no cross.

Grace pulled his mobile phone from his pocket and dialled her home number. She answered on the third ring.

'Cleo, are you OK?' he asked.

'I'm fine,' she said. 'Never better.'

'Listen to me,' he said. 'I'm being serious.'

'I'm listening to you, Detective Superintendent Roy Grace,' she slurred. 'I'm hanging on to every word.'

'I want you to lock your front door and put the safety chain on.'

'Lock the front door,' she echoed. 'And put the safety chain on.'

'I want you to do it now, OK? While I'm on the phone.'

'You're so bossy shometimes, Detective Shuperinten-dent! OK, I'm getting up from the sofa and now I'm walking over to the front door.'

'Please put the safety chain on.'

'S'ham doing it now!'

Grace heard the clank of a chain. 'Do not open the door to anybody, OK? Nobody at all until I get to you. OK?'

'Do not open the door to anybody, until you get to me. I've got that.'

'What about your roof terrace door?' he asked.

'That's always locked.'

'Will you check it?'

'Right away.' Then, jokingly repeating the instruction back to him, she said, 'Go up to roof terrace. Check door is locked.'

'There's no outside door, is there?'

'Not last time I looked.'

'I'll be there as quickly as I can.'

'You'd better!' she slurred, and hung up.

'That's very good advice you've been given,' a voice behind her said.

115

Cleo felt as if her veins had filled with freezing water. She turned, in terror.

A tall figure was standing inches behind her, brandishing a large claw hammer. He was garbed head to foot in an olive-green protective suit that reeked of plastic, latex gloves and a gas mask. She could see nothing of his face at all. She was staring at two round, darkened lenses set into loose-fitting grey material, with a black metal filter at the bottom in the shape of a snout. He looked like a mutant, malevolent insect.

Through those lenses, she could just make out the eyes. They weren't Richard's eyes. They were not any eyes she recognized.

Barefoot and feeling utterly defenceless, she took a step back, stone-cold sober now, quaking, a scream jammed somewhere deep inside her gullet. She took another step back, trying desperately to think straight, but her brain was shorting out. Her back was against the door, pressing hard against it, wondering if she had time to yank it open and scream for help.

Except hadn't she just put the damn safety chain on?

'Don't move and I won't hurt you,' he said, his voice sounding like a muffled Dalek.

Sure, of course not, she thought. *You're standing in my house, holding a hammer, and you're not planning to hurt me.*

'Who – who – who?' The words jetted out of her mouth

in high-pitched spurts. Her eyes were swinging wildly from the maniac in front of her to the floor, to the walls, looking for a weapon. Then she realized she was still holding her cordless phone. There was an intercom button on it that she'd hit a few times in the past in error that would set the extension in her bedroom shrieking. Trying desperately to remember where on the keypad the button was located, she surreptitiously pressed a key with her finger. Nothing happened.

'You had a lucky escape with the car, didn't you, bitch?' The deep, baffled voice was venomous.

'Who – who—' She was shaking too much, her nerves twisting around in knots inside her, jerking her throat closed like a ligature each time she tried to speak.

She pressed another button. Instantly there was a shrill sound up above them. He tilted his face towards the ceiling for one distracted instant. And in that moment, Cleo leapt forward and hit him on the side of the head as hard as she could with the phone. She heard a *crack*. Heard him grunt in shock and pain and saw him sag sideways, thinking for an instant that he was going to go down. The hammer fell from his hand and clattered on to the oak floor.

*

It was difficult to see inside this thing, the Time Billionaire realized, recoiling dizzily. It had been a mistake. He could not get any real peripheral vision. Couldn't see the fucking hammer. Could just see the bitch, hand raised, holding her shattered phone. Then she was lunging on to the floor – and then he saw the gleam of the steel hammer right in front of her.

Oh no, you don't!

He dived down on to her right leg, caught her bare

ankle, which was sticking out of her jeans, and jerked it back, feeling her wriggling, strong, wiry, fighting like a big fish. He saw the hammer, lost sight of it again. Then, suddenly, a quick gleam of steel in front of his face and he felt a fierce pain in his left shoulder.

She'd bloody hit him.

He let go of her leg, rolled forward, seized a handful of her long, blonde hair and pulled sharply towards him. The bitch howled, stumbled then turned, trying to pull free. He pulled harder, jerking her head back so sharply for a moment he thought he'd snapped her neck. She howled again, in pain and anger, twisting round to face him. He head-butted her hard in her temple. Saw the hammer spinning like a top across the floor. He tried to scramble over her, still missing too much of his vision, then felt an excruciating pain in his left wrist. The bitch was biting him.

He swung his right wrist, hit her body somewhere, swung it again, trying desperately to wrench his arm free from her teeth. Hit her again. Then again, crying out in pain himself.

*

Roy! she thought desperately, biting harder, harder still, trying to bite his bloody arm off. *Please come, Roy! Oh, God, you were on the phone. If you'd just stayed on one second longer. One second—*

She felt the blow on her left breast. Then on the side of her face. Now he had her ear, was twisting it, twisting, twisting. God, the pain was agonizing. He was going to wrench it off!

She cried out, released his arm, rolling away from him as fast as she could, scrambling for the hammer.

Suddenly she felt a grip like a vice around her ankle. She

was jerked sharply back, her face scraping along the floor. As she turned to resist, she saw a shadow hurtle at her face, then felt a jarring, blinding, agonizing crunch, and she was falling on to her back, giddily watching down-lighters in the ceiling hurtle past above her, out of focus.

And now she could see he had the hammer again, was on one knee, crouching, levering himself to his feet. And she was not going to let this creep get the better of her, was not going to die, here in her home, was not going to let herself get killed by a madman with a hammer. Not now, especially not now, just at this moment when her life was coming together, when she was so in love—

A weapon.

There had to be a weapon in the room.

The wine bottle on the floor by the sofa.

He was on his feet now.

She was by the bookshelves. She pulled a hardback out and flung it at him. Missed. She pulled out another, a thick, heavy Conan Doyle compendium, getting on to her knees and launching it at him in one movement. It hit him in the chest, making him stagger back a couple of steps, but he was still holding the hammer. Moving towards her.

Now through her pain and anger she suddenly felt scared again. Looking desperately around, she saw Fish's empty tank on the table. Lunging forward, she seized it, lifted it up, water sloshing. It was so damn heavy she could barely hold it. She swung it at him, hurtling the entire contents – several gallons of water and the pieces of miniature Greek architecture – at him. The weight of the water took him by surprise, knocking him back several steps. Then, with all her strength, she threw the tank at him. It struck him in the knees, bowling him over backwards like a skittle, with a muffled, angry howl of pain, then shattered on the floor.

Still holding the hammer, somehow, he was already starting to get back on to his feet. Cleo stared around frantically again, trying to work out her options. There were knives in the kitchen. But she would have to pass him to get in there.

Upstairs, she thought. She had a few moments on him. If she could get upstairs, into her bedroom, lock the door. She had the phone in there!

*

Staggering to his feet, ignoring the excruciating pain, the sound of his breathing echoing all around him as if he were in a diving chamber, he watched, with pure, utter hatred, tinged with a degree of satisfaction, as her bare ankles and feet disappeared up the stairwell.

And a deep stab of lust.

Nothing up there, sweetheart!

He knew every inch of this house. Jangling in his trouser pocket, inside his protective suit, were the keys to the roof door and to the locks of all the triple-glazed windows. Her mobile phone was lying on the sofa next to an open folder containing some project she appeared to be working on.

He was aroused now. She had put up a spirited fight, just like Sophie Harrington, and that had been a very big turn-on. He smiled at the thought of the nights he had slept with Sophie Harrington, when all the time she had thought he was Brian Bishop.

But the biggest turn-on of all was now. The knowledge that in a few minutes he would be making love to Detective Superintendent Grace's woman.

Evil creature.

You'll think twice before you ever call anyone an EVIL CREATURE again, Detective Superintendent Grace.

He limped forward, his left shin in particular hurting like hell, knelt and unplugged the phone jack from the cordless base station. As he stood up again, he saw a jagged rip in his left leg, just below his knee, with blood leaking out. Too bad, nothing he could do about that now. Carefully, he placed his foot on the first tread of the stairs. It wasn't so easy in this gas mask, as he could not see directly down in front of him very well.

In addition his balance didn't seem to have been too good these past couple of days. He was still feeling feverish, and in spite of the medication he was taking, his hand did not seem to be healing up. It had been a big decision, wearing this. He liked the thought that it would frighten the bitch. But most of all, he liked the idea that a third victim found with a gas mask would make Detective Superintendent Grace look a fool, because it would show he had the wrong man locked up.

He liked that a lot.

In fact, the gas mask had been a masterstroke! He had Brian to thank for that – he had found it by chance in a cupboard beside the Bishops' bed when he had been looking for toys to entertain Katie with.

It was the only thing in his entire life that he had to thank his brother for.

*

Cleo slammed her bedroom door shut, hyperventilating. In near blind panic, she grabbed the Victorian wooden chest at the end of her bed, and dragged that over, jamming it against the door. Then she threw herself at her large bed, grabbed it by one leg and tried to pull it. But it would not budge. She tried again. It wasn't moving. 'Shit, you bastard, come on!' Her eyes jumped around the room, looking at what else she could use for a barricade. She dragged across her small, black lacquered wood dressing table, then the chair, which she wiggled into the remaining space between the dressing table and her bed. Not brilliant, but at least it should hold long enough for her to dial Roy, or maybe 999. Yes, 999 first, then Roy.

But as she pressed the button to activate the phone, she let out a whimper of terror. The line was dead.

And the stainless-steel door handle was turning. Slowly. Incredibly slowly. As if she was watching a freeze-frame video inching forward.

Then a loud *BLAM-BLAM-BLAM* as if he was kicking the door, or hitting it with his hammer. Her stomach curdled in terror. The door was moving, just a fraction. She heard wood splintering, and realized to her horror it was the wooden trunk and the chair from her dressing table that were both, slowly, disintegrating.

In desperation she ran over to the window. She was two storeys up, but it might be possible to jump. Better than being in here. At least out in the courtyard, even injured, she would be safe, she reasoned. Then a shiver rocked her.

The window was locked and the key was missing.

Frantic, she looked for something heavy, ran her eyes over make-up bottles, hairspray, shoes. What? What? Oh, please God, what?

There was a metal reading lamp on her bedside table. Gripping it by the top, she swung the flat, round base at the window. It bounced off.

Down below she saw one of her neighbours, a young man with whom she occasionally exchanged pleasantries, wheeling his bike across the courtyard, engrossed in a call on his mobile. He was looking up, as if trying to see where the banging had come from. She waved at him frantically. He waved back cheerily, then, continuing his conversation, headed with his bike towards the front gates.

Behind her she heard another *BLAM-BLAM-BLAM*.
And more splintering wood.

116

Branson found a small silver, pay-as-you-go Nokia phone hidden beneath Norman Jecks's mattress and took it over to Grace, who was looking at his watch, fretting. It was now nearly nine p.m. and he was growing increasingly worried about Cleo being alone in her house, despite the relative safety of a gated development.

'Bag it,' he said distractedly, thinking he should send a patrol car up to check Cleo was OK.

It was over three-quarters of an hour since Nick Nicholl had phoned the incident room, asking for a search warrant for Norman Jecks's lock-ups to be typed out and taken to the same magistrate who had signed the one for here. It should have taken a maximum of ten minutes to complete the damn thing, fifteen minutes' drive to the magistrate's home, and the signing should have been a ten-second formality. Add a further fifteen minutes to get here. OK, he knew in his impatience he wasn't allowing for any delays, traffic hold-ups, whatever, but he didn't care. He was scared for Cleo. There was someone out there. A man he had thought was securely banged up in Lewes prison.

A man who had done one of the most chilling things to a woman he had ever seen.

BECAUSE YOU LOVE HER.

Just as Branson was sealing the bag, he suddenly remembered the speculation about a pay-as-you-go mobile phone. 'Actually, hang on, Glenn. Let me see it.'

Under current guidelines, all phones seized should be

handed straight to the Telecoms Unit at Sussex House, untouched. But there wasn't time for that at this moment, any more than he had time for half the new policies that got dreamed up by idiot policy-makers who had never been out in the real world in their lives.

Taking it in his gloved hands, he switched the machine on, and was relieved when it didn't ask him for a pin code. Then he tried to figure out how to navigate the controls, before giving up and handing it to Branson. 'You're the tekkie,' he said. 'Can you find the list of recently dialled numbers?'

Branson tapped the keys, and within a few seconds showed Grace the display. 'He's only made three calls on it.'

'Just *three*?'

'Uh huh. I recognize one of the numbers.'

'And?'

'It's Hove Streamline Taxis – 202020.'

Grace wrote the other two down, then dialled Directory Inquiries. One was for the Hotel du Vin. The second was the Lansdowne Place Hotel.

Pensively, he said, 'Seems like Bishop might have been telling us the truth.'

Then a SOCO who had accompanied them into the flat suddenly called out, 'Detective Superintendent, I think you should see this.'

It was a walk-in broom closet just off the entrance to the kitchen. But it had clearly been a long time since any brooms were kept in here. Grace stared around in amazement. It was a miniature control centre. There were ten small television monitors on the walls, all switched off, a console with a small swivel chair in front of it, and what looked like a stack of recording equipment.

'What the hell is this? Part of his security system?' Grace asked.

'He's got three entrances – can't see why he'd need ten monitors, sir,' the officer said. 'And there aren't any cameras inside or outside – I've checked.'

At that moment Alfonso Zafferone came into the room, holding the signed search warrant for Norman Jecks's lock-ups.

*

Ten minutes later, having left Nick Nicholl and the SOCO officer continuing their search of the flat, Grace and Branson stood in the small mews that was tucked behind a wide, leafy residential street of substantial detached and semi-detached Victorian villas. There were a few small businesses in the mews – a couple of car-repair outfits, a design studio and a software company – all closed for the night – and then a row of lock-up garages. According to the document they had found, Norman Jecks leased numbers 11 and 12. The blue-painted wooden doors of both were secured by hefty padlocks.

The Local Support Team gorilla who had bashed in the door of the flat, and four further members of his team, stood in readiness. It was almost dark now, the mews eerily silent. Grace briefed them all that once the door was open, no one was to go in if the place appeared empty, which seemly likely, to preserve it forensically.

Moments later the yellow battering ram smashed into the centre of the door, splintering the wood around the padlock's hasp, sending the entire lock, along with a jagged chunk of wood, on to the floor. Several flashlight beams shone in simultaneously, one of them Grace's.

The interior, mostly taken up by a car beneath a fitted

dust cover, was silent and empty. It smelled of engine oil and old leather. On the floor at the far end, two pinpricks of red light gleamed and then were gone. Probably a mouse or a rat, Grace thought, signalling everyone to wait, then stepping in himself and looking for the light switch. He found it, and two startlingly bright ceiling bulbs came on.

At the far end was a workbench on which was a machine resembling the kind he had seen in shops that offered key-cutting services. A variety of blank keys were fixed to the wall behind it, in a carefully arranged pattern. Tools were hung on all the other walls, very neatly again, all in patterned clusters. The whole place was spotlessly clean. Too clean. It felt more like an exhibition stand for tools than a garage.

On the floor was a small, very ancient suitcase. Grace popped open the catches. It was full of old buff file folders, corporate documents, letters, and near the bottom he found a blue Letts schoolboy's diary for the year 1976. He closed the case – the team would go through the contents carefully later.

Then, with Branson's help, he removed the car's cover, to reveal a gleaming, moonstone-white 1962 3.8 Jaguar Mk II saloon. It was in such immaculate condition that it looked brand new, despite its age. As if it had come straight from the factory to here, without ever being soiled by a road.

'Nice!' Branson said admiringly. 'You ought to get one of these, old man. Then you'd look like that detective geezer on the box, Inspector Morse.'

'Thanks,' Grace said, opening the boot. It was empty, and just as brand new-looking as the exterior. He closed it again, then walked towards the rear of the garage and stared at the key-cutting machine. 'Why would someone have one of these?'

'To cut keys?' Branson suggested, less than helpfully.

'Whose keys?'

'The keys of anything you want to get into.'

Grace then asked the LST officers to turn their attention to the next-door unit.

As the door splintered open, the first thing his torch beam struck was a pair of licence plates, propped against the wall. He went straight over to them and knelt down. They each read: LJ 04 NWS.

It was the number of Brian Bishop's Bentley.

Possibly the number that had been photographed by the ANPR camera at Gatwick on Thursday night.

He switched on the interior lights. This garage was every bit as immaculate as the one next door. In the centre of the floor was a hydraulic hoist jack capable of lifting an entire car. Other tools were tidily arranged around the walls. And when he walked down to the far end and saw what was lying on the workbench, he stopped in his tracks. It was the workshop manual for an MG TF 160. Cleo's car.

'I think we just hit the jackpot,' he said grimly to Branson. Then he pulled out his mobile phone and dialled Cleo's home number. He expected she would answer within a couple of rings, as she normally did. But instead it rang on, four rings, six, eight. Ten.

Which was strange, because her answering machine was set to kick in after six. Why hadn't it? He dialled her mobile. That rang eight times, then he got her voicemail message.

Something did not feel right. He would give it a couple of minutes, in case she was in the loo or bath, he decided, then try again. He turned his attention back to the MG manual.

Several pages were marked with yellow Post-it tags. One

was the start of the section on the central locking. Another, the section on the fuel injection. He dialled Cleo's home number again. It rang on endlessly. Then he tried her mobile again. Eight rings followed by her voicemail. He left a message, asking her to call him straight back, his concern rising every second.

'You thinking what I'm thinking?' Branson said.

'What?'

'That we might have the wrong man in jail?'

'It's starting to look that way.'

'But I don't get it. You saw the parents of Bishop's twin. Genuine people, you said, right?'

'Sad little old couple, they seemed genuine enough, yes.'

'And their adopted son – Bishop's twin – they said he was dead, yeah?'

'Yes.'

'They gave you the number of his plot in a cemetery?'

Grace nodded.

'So how come if he's dead, he's still around? Are we dealing with a ghost or something? I mean, that's your terrain, isn't it, the supernatural? You think we're dealing with a spirit? An unrested soul?'

'I never heard of a ghost ejaculating,' Grace said. 'Or driving cars. Or tattooing people with power drills. Or turning up in the A&E department of hospital with a hand injury.'

'Dead men don't do any of those things either,' Branson said. 'Do they?'

'Not in my experience, no.'

'So how come we have one who does?'

After some moments Grace replied, 'Because he's not dead enough.'

117

Somehow the barricade was still holding, but it wouldn't for much longer. With every jarring thump on the door it opened a fraction more. The chair had already collapsed and she had taken its place with her own body, her back jammed against the foot of her bed, the frame digging into her spine agonizingly, her legs wedged against the drawers each side of her dressing table.

The dressing table was not sturdily built. It was cracking, its joints slowly giving out. At any moment it was going to shatter like the chair had done. And when that happened, the maniac would be able to push the door a good eighteen inches open.

Roy! Where the hell are you? Roy! Roy! Roy!

She could hear the faint ringing of her mobile, downstairs. Eight rings, then it stopped.

BLAM-BLAM-BLAM on the door.

Then a faint *beep-beep* from downstairs, her mobile telling her, uselessly, that she had a message.

BLAM-BLAM-BLAM.

A splinter of wood flew off the door and a new, deep coil of terror spiralled through her.

BLAM-BLAM-BLAM.

More wood splinters and this time the head of the hammer came right through.

She tried to control her panic-breathing, to stop herself hyperventilating again. *WhatcanIdo?PleaseGodwhatcanIdo?*

If she moved, she would have just a few seconds before

he shoved the door open. If she stayed put, it would only be a few minutes before he had smashed a hole in the door big enough to get his arms through. Or even climb through.

Roy!PleaseRoywhereareyouohGodpleaseRoy!

Another loud bang, more wood splintered away and now there was a hole three or four inches across. And she could see one glass lens pressed up against it. The faint shadow of an eye flickering behind it.

She thought for an instant she was going to vomit. Images of people flashed through her mind. Her sister, Charlie, her mother, her father, Roy, people she might never see again.

I am not going to die here.

There was a sharp crack, like a gunshot. For a moment she thought the man had fired a weapon at her. Then she realized, horrified, what it was. The wood on the right-hand bottom drawer of her dressing table had split and her bare foot had gone through. She withdrew it, then jammed it against the next drawer up. That seemed firm, for a moment. Then the whole thing began collapsing.

*

He was really enjoying himself! It was like opening a particularly challenging tin of sardines. One where you got the lid to lift up just a tiny fraction, so you could see the sardines lying there beneath you, tantalizing you, but you couldn't yet touch or taste them. Though you knew in a few minutes that you would!

She was feisty! He was staring at her now, her face flushed, eyes bulging, hair all tangled and matted with perspiration. She was going to be great to make love to! Although clearly he was going to have to quieten her down or restrain her first. But not too much.

He took a couple of steps back, then slammed the sole of his shoe, his solid, metal-tipped and heeled workman's shoe, against the door three times. It yielded a good inch! The most by far for one attempt! Now he was cooking with gas! The lid was peeling! A few more minutes and she would be in his arms!

He licked his lips. He could taste her already.

Not bothering with the hammer any more, he stepped back again and kicked out.

Then he heard the shrill ring of the front-door bell. He saw the change in the bitch's expression.

Don't worry, I'm not going to answer it! We don't want anybody to disturb our little love nest, do we?

He blew her a kiss. Although, of course, she couldn't see it.

118

There were windows on either side of Cleo's front door, but she had vertical venetian blinds carefully adjusted so that she could see out, while it was impossible for anyone to see in. Grace, standing anxiously outside her front door, rang the doorbell for the third time. Then he rapped on a window pane for good measure.

Why wasn't she answering?

He dialled her mobile phone again. After a few seconds he heard it ringing from somewhere on the far side of the door. Downstairs.

Had she gone out and left her phone behind? Gone to get some food or to an off-licence? He checked his watch. It was nine thirty. Then he stepped back, trying to see if he could spot any movement in one of the upstairs windows. Perhaps she was up on the roof terrace, preparing a barbecue, and couldn't hear the bell? He took another couple of steps back and collided with a young, shaven-headed man in Lycra shorts and a top, pushing his mountain bike.

'I'm so sorry!' Grace said.

'No problem!'

He looked vaguely familiar. 'You live here, don't you?' Grace asked.

'Yep!' He pointed at a house a few along. 'Seen you around a few times, too – you're a friend of Cleo's, right?'

'Yes. Have you seen her this evening by any chance? She's expecting me, but she doesn't seem to be in.'

The young man nodded. 'Actually, yeah, I did see her – earlier. She waved at me from an upstairs window.'

'Waved at you?'

'Yeah – I heard a noise and looked up, wondering where it had come from. And I saw her in the window. Just a neighbourly wave thing.'

'What kind of a noise?'

'Sort of a bang. Like a gunshot.'

Grace stiffened. '*Gunshot?*'

'That's what I thought for a moment. But obviously it wasn't.'

Every alarm bell in his body was ringing. 'You don't have a key, do you?'

He shook his head. 'No. Got one for Unit 9, but not Cleo's, I'm afraid.' Then he glanced at his watch. 'I gotta rush.'

Grace thanked him. Then, as the young man walked away, the bicycle ticking, the detective heard several very distinct, muffled bangs coming from right above him. Instantly his anxiety turned to blind panic.

He looked around for something heavy and saw a pile of bricks beneath a loose blue tarpaulin, outside the house directly opposite, on the other side of the courtyard.

He sprinted across and grabbed one, then removed his jacket as he ran back, wound it around the brick in his hand, then punched Cleo's left window, shattering it. Too bad if everything was fine and she had just popped out to the shops. Better this than take a risk, he thought, bashing away more glass. Then, with his free hand, he pushed apart some of the slats of the blind.

And saw to his cold, stark terror the mess of water, smashed fish tank, the upturned coffee table, books strewn around.

'CLEO!' he yelled at the top of his voice. 'CLEEEEEE-OOOOO!' He turned his head and saw the young man with the bicycle, who had stopped in the middle of opening his front door and was staring at him, with a startled look. 'Call the police!' he yelled.

Then, ignoring the jagged shards sticking out of the frame all around, Grace hauled himself up on to the ledge and dived head first into the room, hitting the floor with his hands, rolling, then scrambling to his feet as fast as he could, looking wildly around him.

Then he saw the trail of blood across the floor leading to the stairs.

Sick with fear for Cleo, he sprinted up them. When he reached the first-floor landing and peered through the open door to her empty office, he shouted out her name again.

From directly above him he heard her voice, muffled and tight, call out, 'ROY, BE CAREFUL! HE'S IN HERE!'

His eyes shot up the stairs to the second-floor landing. Cleo's bedroom to the right, guest bedroom to the left. And the narrow staircase up to the roof terrace. At least she was alive, thank God! He held his breath.

No sign of any movement. No sound except the *boomf-boomf-boomf* of his own heart.

He should call for back-up assistance, but he wanted to listen, to hear every sound in the house. Slowly, tread by tread, as silently as he could in his rubber-soled shoes, he made his way up the staircase towards the second floor. Just before he reached the landing, he stopped, pulled out his mobile phone again and called 999. 'This is Detective Superintendent Grace, I need immediate assistance at—'

All he saw was a shadow. Then it felt as if he had been hit by a truck.

The next moment he was falling through air. Crashing head over heels backwards down the stairs. Then, after what seemed an eternity, he was on his back on the landing floor, with his legs up above him on the stairs, and a sharp pain in his chest – a busted or cracked rib, he thought dimly, staring up, straight into Brian Bishop's face.

Bishop was coming down the stairs, dressed in a green all-in-one suit, holding a claw hammer in one hand and a gas mask in the other. Except that it wasn't Bishop. Couldn't be, his dazed mind thought. He was in jail. In Lewes prison.

It was Brian Bishop's face. His haircut. But the expression on his face was unlike any he had seen on Brian Bishop's. It was twisted, almost lopsided, with hatred. Norman Jecks, he thought. It had to be Jecks. The two of them were absolutely identical.

Jecks came down another step, raising the hammer, his eyes blazing. 'You called me an *evil creature*,' he said. 'You don't have any right to call me an *evil creature*. You need to be careful what you say about people, Detective Superintendent Grace. You can't just go around calling people names.'

Grace stared at the man, wondering whether his phone was still switched on and connected to the emergency operator. In the hope that it was, he shouted as loudly as he could, 'Unit 5, Gardener's Yard, Brighton!'

He saw the nervous dart of the man's eyes.

Then upstairs there was a sudden screech of wood on wood.

Norman Jecks turned his head for an instant, looking anxiously back over his shoulder.

Grace seized the moment. He launched himself up on his elbows, then kicked his right foot as hard as he could, straight up between the man's legs.

Jecks expelled a winded gasp, doubling up in pain, the hammer falling from his hand, clattering down the stairs and thudding past Grace's head. The detective swung his leg up again, aiming another kick, but somehow Jecks, despite his pain, grabbed hold of it and wrenched it sharply round in fury. Grace rolled over, his ankle hurting like hell, going with the direction of the twist to stop the man breaking it, and lashing out with his other foot, striking something hard and hearing a cry of pain.

He saw the hammer! Lunged after it. But before he could get up, Jecks crashed down on top of him, pinning his wrist to the floor. Using every ounce of strength in his body, Grace jabbed back with his elbows and broke free, rolling over again. The man rolled with him, slamming a punch into his cheek, then another into the back of his neck. And Grace was on his face on the floor, breathing in the smell of wood varnish, a dead weight pinning him down, his throat clamped in a grip that was tightening every second.

He rammed his elbow back, but the grip tightened further, choking him. He was struggling to breathe.

Suddenly the grip slackened. A fraction of a second later, the crushing weight on his body lifted. Then he saw why.

Two police officers were clambering through the window.

He heard footsteps running up the stairs.

'Are you all right, sir?' the constable called out.

Grace nodded, clambered to his feet, his right leg and his chest agony, and launched himself up the stairs. He reached the landing, stepping over the gas mask. There was no sign of Jecks. He carried on up to the second floor and saw Cleo's face, badly bruised and bleeding from a gash in her forehead, peering nervously out of her smashed, partially open bedroom door.

'Are you OK?' he gasped.

She nodded, looking in total shock.

There was a bang above them. Oblivious to his pain, Grace ran on up and saw the roof terrace door swinging back against the wall. Then he limped out on to the wooden decking of the terrace. And just caught a flash of olive green disappearing, in the failing light, down the fire escape at the far end.

Breaking into a run, he dodged around the kettle barbecue, the tables and chairs and plants, and hurtled down the steep metal steps. Jecks was already halfway across the courtyard, heading to the gate.

It banged shut in Grace's face as he reached it. He hit the red release button, oblivious to everything else, jerked the heavy gate open, not waiting for the two constables behind him to catch up, and stumbled, breathlessly, out into the street. Jecks was a good hundred yards ahead, sprinting and hobbling at the same time down past a row of closed antiques shops and a pub with jazz music blaring and drinkers outside, crowding the pavement and part of the road.

Grace ran after him, determined to get this fucker. Utterly, utterly determined, everything else in the whole world blocked out of his mind.

Jecks turned left along York Place. The bastard was fast. Christ, he was fast. Grace was sprinting flat out, his chest on fire, his lungs feeling like they were being crushed between rocks. He wasn't gaining on the man but at least he was keeping pace. He passed St Peter's Church on his right. A Chinese takeaway, followed by endless shops on his left, everything except the fast-food places closed, just window display lights on. Buses, vans, cars, taxis passed by. He dodged around a gaggle of youths, all the time his eyes locked on to that olive-green suit that was increasingly blending into the closing darkness as York Place became the London Road.

Jecks reached the Preston Circus junction. He had a red traffic light against him and a line of cars crossing in front of him. But he sprinted straight through and on up the London Road. Grace had to stop for a moment, as a lorry thundered past, followed by an interminable line of traffic. *Come on, come on, come on!* He glanced over his shoulder and saw the two constables some way behind. Then, recklessly, almost blinded by the stinging perspiration in his eyes, he raced across the road in front of the flashing headlights and angry blaring horn of a bus.

He was fit from his regular running, but he didn't know how much longer he could go on.

Jecks, now about two hundred yards in front of him, slowed, turned his head, saw Grace and picked up speed again.

Where the hell was he going?

There was a park on the right side of the road now. On his left were houses that had been converted into offices, and blocks of flats. The irony did not escape him that he was at this moment running past the Brighton & Hove City Council Directorate of Children, Families and Schools, where he had been earlier today.

You have to start tiring soon, Jecks. You are not getting away. You don't hurt my darling Cleo and get away.

Jecks ran on, past a garage, over another junction, past another parade of shops.

Then, finally, Grace heard the thrashing wail of a siren coming up behind him. *About sodding time,* he thought.

Moments later a patrol car slowed alongside him, the passenger window going down, and he heard a burst of static, followed by a controller's voice coming from the radio inside.

Barely able to speak, Grace gasped to the young constable, 'In front of me. That guy in the green suit. Do a hard stop on him!'

The car roared off, blue light showering from its roof, and pulled into the kerb just past Jecks, the passenger door opening before it had come to a halt.

Jecks turned and bolted straight back towards Grace for a few yards, then darted right, towards Preston Park railway station.

Grace heard the sound of another siren approaching. More back-up. Good.

He followed Jecks doggedly up a steep hill lined on both sides with houses. Ahead was a high brick wall, with an access tunnel to the platforms and the street on the far side. Two taxis were parked up.

There was a pick-up area in front of the station, with a couple more taxis waiting, and an unmade-up residential road to the right, which ran along the side of the railway line for several hundred yards.

Jecks turned into it.

The first police car shot past Grace, following Jecks. Suddenly the man doubled back on his tracks, then dashed into the tunnel and up the steps to the south-bound platform, barging past a young woman with a suitcase and a man in a business suit.

Grace followed, dodging through more passengers, then he saw Jecks running down the platform. The last door of the train was open, with the guard hanging out, signalling with his torch. It began to move.

Jecks leapt off the platform, disappearing from Grace's view. Was he on the track?

Then as the guard slipped past him, the train accelerating, Grace saw its red tail light. And Jecks, clinging to a handrail on the rear of the last carriage, his feet perched precariously on a buffer.

Grace yelled at the guard, 'Police, stop the train! You've got a man hanging on the back!'

For a moment the guard, a spindly young man in an ill-fitting uniform, just looked at him in astonishment as the train continued gathering speed.

'Police! I'm a police officer! Stoppppp!' he yelled again. The guard, now several yards ahead of him, was only just in earshot.

The guard ducked inside. Grace heard a shrill bell, then suddenly the train was slowing, the brakes screeching. There was a hiss of air pressure and it came to a jerky halt fifty yards beyond the end of the platform.

Grace ran down the slope and on to the track, keeping clear of the raised live conductor rail, stumbling through loose, weed-strewn ballast and over the sleepers.

The guard jumped down and ran back towards Grace, flashing his torch beam. 'Where is he?'

Grace pointed. Jecks, looking fearfully down at the live rail below him, edged over to the right-hand buffer, then leapt, but not far enough, and his right foot brushed the top of the second conductor rail. There was blue flash, a crackle, a puff of smoke, and a scream from Jecks. He landed on the ballast in the centre of the north-bound track with a sharp crack, then fell over, his head striking the far rail with a dull thud, and lay still.

In the beam of the guard's flashlight, Grace saw his left leg sticking out at an odd angle, and for a moment he thought the man was dead. There was an acrid, burning smell in the air.

'Hey!' the guard yelled in panic. 'There's a train coming! The nine fifty!'

Grace could hear the rails singing like the whine of a tuning fork.

'It's the fast one! Victoria! Express! Oh, Jesus!' The guard was trembling so much he could barely keep the beam on Jecks, who was gripping the rail with his hands, trying to drag himself forward.

Grace put a foot over the conductor rail, on to the loose ballast beyond. He wanted this bastard alive.

Suddenly Jecks tried to get up, but he instantly fell forward with another howl of pain, blood trickling down his face.

'No!' the guard shouted at Grace. 'You can't cross – not there!'

Grace could hear the sound of the approaching train. Ignoring the guard, he swung his other leg over and stopped in the space between the two sets of tracks, looking left. At the lights of the express train that was tearing out of the darkness, straight at him. Seconds away.

There was a space on the other side before the next track. Enough room, he decided, making a snap decision and vaulting the second live rail. He grabbed the partially melted, heavy-soled shoe on the broken leg, which was the nearest part of Jecks to him, and pulled with all his strength. The lights bore down. He heard Jecks's scream of agony above the train's klaxon. He could feel the ground vibrating, the rails singing at a deafening pitch now. The rush of wind. He pulled the man again, oblivious to the howl of pain, the shouting of the guard, the roar and blare of the train, and staggered back, hauling the deadweight over the far rail and on to the rough ground as hard and fast as he could.

Then, losing his footing, he fell sideways on to the track, his face inches from the rail. And heard a terrible human screech.

The train was thundering past, a vortex of air ripping at his clothes, his hair, the clang of the wheels deafening him.

A final whoosh of air. Then silence.

Something warm and sticky was spurting into his face.

119

The silence seemed to go on for an eternity. Grace, gulping down air, was momentarily dazzled by a flashlight beam. More warm, sticky fluid struck his face. The beam moved away from his eyes and now he could see what looked like a narrow, round length of grey hosepipe jetting red paint at him.

Then he realized it was not red paint. It was blood. And it wasn't a pipe, it was Norman Jecks's right arm. The man's hand had been severed.

Grace scrambled on to his knees. Jecks was lying, shaking, moaning, in shock. He had to stop the bleeding, he knew, had to staunch it immediately or the man would bleed to death in minutes.

The guard was alongside him. 'Jesus,' he said. 'Jesus. Oh, Jesus.' Two police officers joined him.

'Call an ambulance!' Grace said. He saw faces pressed up against the windows of the stopped train. 'Maybe see if anyone on the train is a doctor!'

The guard was staring down at Jecks, unable to take his eyes off him.

'SOMEONE RADIO FOR AN AMBULANCE!' Grace yelled at the police officers.

The guard ran off towards a phone on a signal post.

'Already done,' one of the constables said. 'Are you all right, sir?'

Grace nodded, still breathing hard, concentrating on finding something for a tourniquet. 'Make sure someone's gone to help Cleo Morey, at Unit 5, Gardener's Yard,' he said. His hands went to his jacket, but then he realized it was on the floor somewhere in Cleo's house. 'Gimme your jacket!' he yelled to the guard.

Too surprised to query him, the guard ran back over and let Grace pull the jacket from him, then ran off again. Grace stood up and, holding both sleeves, tore it apart. One sleeve he wound as tightly as he could around Jecks's arm, a short distance above where it was severed. The other he balled and jammed against the end as a plug.

Then the guard ran back, panting. 'I've asked them to switch off the power. It should only take a few seconds,' he said.

Then suddenly the night erupted into a cacophony of wails. It sounded as if every emergency vehicle's siren in the whole of the city of Brighton and Hove had been switched on together.

*

Five minutes later, Grace was travelling, at his absolute insistence, in the back of the ambulance with Jecks, determined to see the bastard securely into a hospital room, with no chance of escaping.

Not that there seemed much danger of that at this moment. Jecks was strapped down, cannulated and barely conscious. The paramedic, who was monitoring him carefully, told Grace that although the man had suffered heavy blood loss, his life was not in immediate danger. But the ambulance was travelling urgently fast, siren wailing, the ride rocky and uncomfortable. And Grace was not taking any chances: there was a police car escort in front and behind them.

Borrowing the paramedic's mobile phone, Grace called

both Cleo's numbers but got no answer. Then the paramedic radioed for him, putting him on to the controller. An ambulance was on site at Gardener's Yard, the woman told Grace. Two paramedics were attending superficial wounds to Cleo Morey, who was reluctant to go to hospital, wanting to remain at home.

Grace then got himself patched through to a patrol car that was also outside Cleo's house and told the two constables to remain there until he returned, and also to get hold of a glazier to secure the window as quickly as possible.

By the time he had finished giving instructions, the ambulance was already turning sharply left, up the hill to the Accident and Emergency entrance to the hospital.

As Grace climbed out of the back, not taking his eye off Jecks for an instant, even though the man now seemed completely unconscious, a second police car wailed up behind them and stopped. A young constable climbed out, green-faced and looking very close to vomiting, and hurried over towards them, holding something inside a heavily bloodstained handkerchief. 'Sir!' he said to Grace.

'What have you got?'

'The man's hand, sir. They may be able to sew it back on. But some of the fingers are missing. It must have gone under the wheels a couple of times. We couldn't find the fingers.'

Grace had to struggle to restrain himself from telling him that by time he had finished with Norman Jecks, he probably wouldn't have much use for it again. Instead, he said grimly, 'Good thinking.'

*

It was shortly after midnight when Jecks came out of the operating theatre. The hospital had not been able to contact the one local orthopaedic surgeon who had had some success in reattaching severed limbs, and the general surgeon who was in the hospital, and had just finished patching up a motorcycle rider, decided the hand looked too badly damaged.

It was the hand with the hospital dressing on, Grace noticed, and requested it be kept in a refrigerator, to preserve it forensically if nothing else. Then he ensured that Jecks was in a private room, on the fourth floor, with a tiny window and no fire escape, and organized a rota of two police constables to guard him around the clock.

Finally, no longer exhausted but wide awake, wired, relieved and exhilarated, he drove back to Cleo's house, his ankle hurting like hell every time he depressed the clutch. He was pleased to see the empty police car in the street outside and that the window had already been repaired. As he limped up to the front door, he heard the roar of a vacuum cleaner. Then he rang the bell.

Cleo answered. She had a sticking plaster on the side of her forehead and the surround of one eye was black and swollen. The two constables were sitting on a sofa, drinking coffee, and the Hoover lay on its side on the floor.

She gave him a wan smile, then looked shocked. 'Roy, darling, you're injured.'

He realized he was still covered in Jecks's blood. 'It's OK – I'm not injured, I just need to get my clothes off.'

Behind her, the two officers grinned. But for the next moments he was oblivious of them. He stared back at her, so desperately grateful that she was OK. Then he took her in his arms and kissed her on the lips, then hugged her, holding her tightly, so tightly, never, ever wanting to let go.

'God, I love you,' he whispered. 'I love you so much.'

'I love you too.' Her voice was hoarse and small; she sounded like a child.

'I was so scared,' he said. 'So scared that something had—'

'Did you get him?'

'Most of him.'

120

Norman Jecks stared up sullenly at Grace. He lay in the bed, in the small room, his right arm bandaged from the elbow down to the covered stump where his hand should have been. An orange hospital ID tag was clipped around his left wrist. His pallid face was covered in bruises and grazes.

Glenn Branson was standing behind Grace, and two constables sat in the corridor outside the door.

'Norman Jecks?' Grace asked. He was finding it bizarre talking to this man who was such a complete clone of Brian Bishop, even down to his hairstyle. It was as if Bishop was playing some prank on him, and really was in two places at the same time.

'Yes,' he replied.

'Is that your full name?'

'It's Norman *John* Jecks.'

Grace wrote it down on his pad. 'Norman John Jecks, I'm Detective Superintendent Grace and this is Detective Sergeant Branson. Evidence has come to light, as a result of which I'm arresting you on suspicion of the murders of Ms Sophie Harrington and Mrs Katherine Bishop. You do not have to say anything. But it may harm your defence if you do not mention when questioned something which you later rely on in court. Anything you do say may be given in evidence. Is that clear?'

Jecks raised his left arm a few inches and, with a humourless smile, said, 'You're going to have a problem handcuffing me, aren't you, Detective Superintendent Grace?'

Taken aback by his defiance, Grace retorted, 'Good point. But at least we'll now be able to distinguish you from your brother.'

'The whole world's always been able to distinguish me from my brother,' Norman Jecks said bitterly. 'What's your particular problem?'

'Are you prepared to talk to us, or do you wish to have a solicitor present?' Grace asked.

He smiled. 'I'll talk to you. Why not? I've got all the time in the world. How much of it would you like?'

'As much as you can spare.'

Jecks shook his head. 'No, Detective Superintendent Grace, I don't think you want that. You don't want the kind of time I've got banked away, believe me, you really don't.'

Grace limped over towards the empty chair beside the bed and sat down. 'What did you mean just now when you said the whole world's always been able to distinguish you from your brother?'

Jecks gave him the same, chilling, lopsided grin that he had given him last night, coming down the stairs in Cleo's house, after him. 'Because he was the one born with a silver spoon in his mouth, and me – you know what I was born with? A plastic breathing tube down my throat.'

'How does that make you physically distinguishable from each other?'

'Brian had everything, didn't he, right from the start. Good health, well-off parents, a private-school education. Me? I had under-developed lungs and spent the first months of my life in an incubator, here in this hospital! That's ironic, isn't it? I had chest problems for years. And I had pretty crap parents. You know what I'm saying?'

'Actually no, I don't,' Grace said. 'They seemed pleasant enough people to me.'

Jecks stared at him hard. 'Oh yes? Just what do you know about them?'

'I saw them yesterday.'

Jecks grinned again. 'I don't think so, Detective Superintendent. Is this some kind of a trick question? My father died in 1998, God rot his soul, and my mother died two years later.'

Grace was silent for a moment. 'I'm sorry, there's something I don't understand.'

'What's not to understand?' Jecks shot back. 'Bishop got a beautiful home, a good education, every possible start in life you could have, and last year his company – *the idea he stole from me* – made the *Sunday Times* list of the hundred fastest-growing companies in the UK. He's a big man! A rich man! You're a detective, and you can't spot the difference?'

'What idea did he steal from you?'

Jecks shook his head. 'Forget it. It's not important.'

'Really? Why do I get the sense that it is?'

Jecks lay back against his pillows suddenly and closed his eyes. 'I don't think I want to say any more, not now, not without my solicitor. See, there's another difference. Brian's got himself a fancy brief, the best that money can buy! All I'm going to end up with is some second-rate tosser courtesy of Legal Aid. Right?'

'There are some very good solicitors available at no cost to you,' Grace assured him.

'Yeah, yeah, yadda yadda yadda,' Jecks responded, without opening his eyes. 'Don't worry about me, Detective Superintendent, no one ever has. Not even God. He pretended He loved me, but it's Brian He loved all along. You go off and cherish your Cleo Morey.' Then, his voice suddenly icy, he opened his eyes and gave Grace a broad wink. *'Because you love her.'*

*

There was an air of expectancy in the packed conference room for the Friday morning briefing meeting.

Reading from his notes, Roy Grace said, 'I will now summarize the principal events that occurred during the course of yesterday, prior to the arrest of Norman John Jecks.' He glanced down at his notes. 'One major item in our investigation into the murder of Katie Bishop is conclusive evidence provided this morning by the forensic odontologist, Christopher Ghent, that the human bite mark found on Norman Jecks's severed right hand was made by Katie.'

He paused to let the significance sink in, then continued. 'DS Batchelor has discovered that for two years, until March of this year, a Norman Jecks, matching our man's description, worked in the software engineering department of the Southern Star Assurance Company as a computer programmer. That timing is significant, in that he left approximately four weeks after Bishop allegedly took out a three-million-pound life insurance policy on his wife with this company. We have now requisitioned all Bishop's bank records to see if any premium was in fact ever paid. I suspect we may find he did genuinely have no knowledge of this.' He sipped some coffee.

'Pamela and Alfonso have been checking further into the criminal record of Bishop. They have been unable to find any mention of either crimes in the local or national press around the times they allegedly occurred, or around the dates of the convictions.'

He turned another page. 'Yesterday evening in a raid on garage premises rented by Jecks, we discovered a duplicate set of licence plates identical to those on Brian Bishop's Bentley. In a raid on his flat in Sackville Road, Hove, at the same time, we discovered evidence of an unhealthy obsession Jecks had – or rather, would appear to *have* – with his twin brother, Brian Bishop. This included the discovery of video monitoring equipment linked, via an internet connection, to concealed surveillance cameras in the Bishops' Brighton home and in their London flat. Jecks further admitted his hatred of his brother in a conversation Glenn Branson and I held with Jecks under caution this morning.'

Grace continued, listing what had been found at Jecks's flat, although he held back the information about the three dialled numbers that he and Branson had found on the man's pay-as-you-go phone, as they were not really supposed to have examined it, and it had now been passed to the Telecoms Unit.

When he had finished going through his notes, Norman Potting raised a hand. 'Roy,' he said, 'I know it's not strictly our case, but I did a ring around the Brighton and Hove travel agents yesterday afternoon, asking if they had any record of a Janet McWhirter asking about flights to Australia back in April of this year. There's a company called Aossa Travel. A lady there by the name of Lena found an inquiry form with the name of Janet McWhirter on it. She had put down her travelling companion as Norman Jecks.'

*

When the briefing meeting was complete, Grace went to his office. First he called the SIO on the Janet McWhirter inquiry and told him about Potting's findings. Then he dialled Chris Binns, the Crown Prosecution Service solicitor for the Katie Bishop case, and brought him up to date on their findings.

Although the evidence seemed to be pointing increasingly away from Brian Bishop and towards his brother, it was still early days, and it would be reckless to move too quickly in freeing a suspect. Bishop was due to appear in court on Monday for his next remand hearing. The two men agreed on a strategy. Chris Binns would speak to Bishop's solicitor and inform him that the Crown might be experiencing some difficulties with the prosecution as a result of new evidence coming to light. Provided Bishop would agree to keeping the police informed of his whereabouts, and to surrendering his passport, the bail application on Monday would not be contested by the CPS.

When Roy Grace finished the call, he sat in silence for a long time. There was one part of the puzzle still missing. One very big part. From one of the files on the pile on his desk, he removed Brian Bishop's birth and adoption certificates, and those of his brother.

His door opened and Glenn Branson's head appeared round it. 'I'm just off, old-timer,' he said.

'What you looking so happy about?' Grace asked.

'She's letting me put the kids to bed tonight!'

'Wow. Progress! Does that mean I get my house back soon?'

'I dunno. One swallow doesn't make a summer.'

Grace looked back down at the adoption certificates. Branson was right. One swallow did not indeed make a summer. Nor, it seemed, did two men under arrest make a solution to a puzzle.

Norman Jecks just said this morning that he spent the first months of his life in an incubator. And that his parents were dead. And according to his parents, he was dead.

Why were they lying about each other?

121

For the first time in what seemed a long, long week Grace was in bed before midnight. But he slept only fitfully, trying to move as little as possible as he lay awake in order not to disturb Cleo, who was naked and warm and sleeping like a baby in his arms.

Maybe when Norman Jecks was behind bars, he would start to relax. All the time he was at the Royal Sussex County Hospital, it was too easy for a man of his cunning to escape, despite the police guard. And every unfamiliar noise in the night was potentially a Norman Jecks footfall.

It was the Black & Decker power drill that Cleo had found in her broom cupboard that upset him – and her – the most. She had never owned an electric drill in her life and had had no workmen in the house recently. It was as if Jecks had left behind a souvenir of his visit, a little token, a reminder.

BECAUSE YOU LOVE HER.

The drill was now in an evidence bag, safely locked up in the crime scene evidence store at the Major Incident Suite. But the image of what it represented, and those words breathed at him earlier today by Jecks, from his hospital bed, would shadow him for a long time to come.

His mind returned to Sandy. To Dick Pope's utter conviction that he and Leslie had seen her in Munich.

If it was true, and she had run away from them, what did that say? That she had started over again and wanted no connection with their previous life? But that made no sense.

They had been so happy together – or so he had thought. Perhaps she had had a breakdown of some kind? In which case Kullen's suggestion of trawling all the doctors, hospitals and clinics in the Munich area might produce a result. But then what?

Would he try to rebuild a life with her knowing she had left him once and might do it again? And destroy all he had with Cleo in the process?

There was of course the possibility that the Popes were mistaken. That it had been just another woman who resembled Sandy, like the one he had chased across the Englischer Garten. It was nine years now. People changed. Sometimes even he had difficulty remembering Sandy's face.

And the truth was, in his heart, it was Cleo who now mattered most in his life.

Just that one day in Munich had nearly caused a rift in his relationship with her. To engage in a full-scale search of the city and all the time that involved would be a major undertaking and who knew what repercussions that might have? He'd had nine years of chasing shadows on wild-goose chases. Perhaps it was time to stop now. Time to leave the past behind him.

He fell asleep resolved to try, at any rate.

And awoke two hours later, shaking and shivering from the recurring nightmare that visited him every few months or so. Sandy's voice screaming out of the darkness. Screaming for help.

It was nearly an hour before he fell asleep again.

*

At six in the morning he drove home, changed into his jogging kit and went down to the seafront. Almost every muscle in his body was hurting and his ankle was too painful to run, so he hobbled down to the promenade and then back, the fresh morning air helping to clear his head.

As he stepped out of the shower afterwards and began drying himself, he heard Branson's bedroom door open, then the toilet seat being lifted. Moments later, as he began lathering his face, he heard his friend urinating with a sound like a supertanker emptying its bilges.

Finally the cistern clanked and flushed. Then Branson called out, 'Tea or coffee?'

'Am I hearing right?' Grace asked.

'Yeah, I've decided I would make you a lovely wife.'

'Just make me tea. Hold the nuptials, OK?'

'Tea coming up!'

Branson was humming cheerily as he clumped down the stairs and Grace wondered what pills he was on this morning. Then he turned his mind back to the business of shaving, and the problem he had still not been able to solve. Although at some time during the small hours, he had realized what his starting point should be.

*

Shortly after ten he was back in the small, cubicle-like waiting room in the registrar's offices at Brighton town hall, holding a file folder.

After only a couple of minutes, the tall, urbane figure of Clive Ravensbourne, the Superintendent Registrar, entered. He shook Grace's hand, looking very much more at ease than on the previous occasion they had met, a couple of days ago – if a little curious.

'Detective Superintendent, very nice to see you again. How can I help you?'

'Thank you for coming in on a Saturday, I appreciate it.'

'No problem. It's a working day for me.'

'It's in connection with the same murder inquiry I came to see you about on Thursday,' Grace said. 'You kindly gave me some information about a twin. I need you to verify it for me – it's very urgent and important to my inquiry. Certain things are just not adding up.'

'Of course,' Ravensbourne said. 'Whatever I can do – I will try.'

Grace opened the folder and pointed at Brian Bishop's birth certificate. 'I gave you the name of this chap, Desmond Jones, and asked if you could establish if he had a twin, and the twin's birth name. There were twenty-seven possible babies all with the same surname. You suggested you could bypass having to go through each one simply by looking up the records from the index number on the birth certificate.'

Ravensbourne nodded emphatically. 'Yes, correct.'

'Could I ask you to double-check for me?'

'Of course.'

Ravensbourne took the birth certificate and went out of the room. A couple of minutes later he returned with the large dark red, leather-bound registry book, put it down with the birth certificate next to it and leafed through it anxiously. Then he stopped and checked the birth certificate again. 'Desmond William Jones, mother Eleanor Jones, born at the Royal Sussex County Hospital, 7 September 1964 at three forty-seven a.m. And it says *Adopted*, right? This is the right chap?'

'Yes, he checks out. It's the one you gave me as his twin brother who doesn't.'

The registrar returned to the tome and looked down the page. 'Frederick Roger Jones?' he read out. 'Mother Eleanor Jones, born at the Royal Sussex County Hospital,

7 September 1964 at three fifty-two a.m. Also subsequently adopted.' He looked up. 'That's your twin. Frederick Roger Jones.'

'Are you sure? You couldn't be mistaken?'

The registrar turned the book around, so that Grace could see for himself. There were five entries.

'That birth certificate you have, it's actually a copy of the original – the original is this entry in here, in this book. Do you understand that?' the registrar asked.

'Yes,' Grace replied.

'It's an exact copy. This is the original entry. Five entries to a page – see – the bottom two are your chaps, Desmond William Jones and Frederick Roger Jones.'

As if to demonstrate his veracity, Ravensbourne turned over the page. 'You see, there are another five on this—'

He stopped in mid-sentence and turned back a page, then turned it forward again. And then he said, 'Oh. Oh dear. Oh, my God, it never occurred to me! I was in a hurry when you came to see me, I remember. I saw the twin – you were looking for a twin. It never occurred to me—'

There on the next page, the top entry, in neat, slanted black handwriting, was: *Norman John Jones, mother Eleanor Jones, born at the Royal Sussex County Hospital, 7 September 1964 at three fifty-seven a.m.*

Grace looked at the man. 'Does this mean what I think it means?'

The registrar was nodding furiously, half out of embarrassment, half from excitement. 'Yes. Born two minutes later. The same mother. Absolutely!'

122

Back-issue after back-issue of the *Argus* newspaper sped past Roy Grace's eyes. He sat hunched in front of the microfiche unit in the Brighton and Hove Reference Library, scrolling through the film containing the 1964 editions, slowing down occasionally to check the dates. April . . . June . . . July . . . August . . . September.

He stopped the machine halfway through the 4 September 1964 pages, then slowly cranked forwards. Then he stopped again when he reached the front page of the 7 September edition. But there was nothing of significance. He read through each of the following news pages carefully, but still could find nothing.

The splash of 8 September was a local planning scandal. But then, two pages on, a photograph leapt out at him.

It was of three tiny babies, lying asleep in a row inside the glass casing of an incubator. Inset next to this was a photograph of a small, mangled car. Above was the caption: *Miracle Babies Survive Horror Death Crash.* And there was another photograph, of an attractive, dark-haired woman in her mid-twenties. Grace read every word of the article straight through, twice. His eyes went back to the picture of the babies in the incubator, to the woman's face, to the car, then he read the words again, cutting through the sensational adjectives, just picking up the facts.

Police were investigating why the Ford Anglia veered across the A23, in heavy rain early on the evening of

6 September into the path of a lorry . . . Eleanor Jones, single mother, science teacher . . . thought she was carrying twins . . . had been undergoing treatment for depression . . . Eight and a half months pregnant . . . kept on life support in intensive care after they were delivered prematurely by Caesarean section . . . mother died during the operation . . .

He stopped the machine, removed the microfiche, replaced it in its container and handed it to the librarian. Then he almost ran to the exit.

*

Grace could barely contain his excitement as he drove back to Sussex House. He was longing to see everyone's faces in the briefing meeting this evening, but most of all he was looking forward to telling Cleo. Telling her that they had got the right man, for sure.

But first he wanted speak to the helpful post-adoption counsellor, Loretta Leberknight, and ask her one question, just as a double-check. He was dialling her number on the hands free when his phone rang.

It was Roger Pole, the SIO for the attempted murder of Cleo, thanking him for the information about the discovery of the MG TF workshop manual in Norman Jecks's garage and informing him they were now making Jecks the prime suspect.

'You won't be needing to look any further,' Grace told him, pulling over and stopping. 'Out of interest, how's the poor scumbag who tried to steal the car?'

'He's still in intensive care at East Grinstead, with 55 percent burns, but they are expecting him to live.'

'Maybe I should send him some flowers for saving Cleo's life,' he said.

'From what I hear, a bag or two of heroin would be more appreciated.'

Grace grinned. 'How's the officer from the Car Crime Unit?'

'PC Packer? OK. He's been released from hospital, but he has quite severe burns on his face and hands.'

Grace thanked him for the information, then called Loretta Leberknight. When he told her what had happened she laughed sympathetically. 'I've known that before,' she said.

'There's one thing that's bothering me, though,' Grace said. 'His first two names, *Norman John*. When we spoke originally, you told me that adoptive parents change their names, or perhaps move the birth name to a middle name. In this instance he has both names. Is there any significance?'

'None,' she said. 'Most parents change but some don't. Sometimes if a child isn't adopted for a while they go to a care home – foster parents – and then they'll probably end up keeping their birth Christian names.'

*

Grace bumped straight into Glenn Branson as he headed across to his office.

'What you looking so pleased about, old-timer?' Branson asked.

'I've got some good news. And hey, you're in a pretty sunny mood yourself today,' Grace said.

'Yeah, well, I've got some good news too.'

'Tell me.'

'You first.'

Grace shrugged. 'You remember that nasty social worker in the adoption services?'

'The one with the pink hair and bright green glasses? Face like roadkill?'

'The very one.'

'Got a date with her, have you? She'd be well fit. So long as you take a paper bag to put over her head.'

'Yes, I have got a date with her. And her boss. At three o'clock this afternoon. Remember I told her that if she was withholding information that could be helpful to us, I would hang her out to dry?'

Branson nodded. 'Yes.'

'Well, that's what I'm going to do. I'm going to hang the bitch out to dry.'

'Not that you're a vengeful sort of person.'

'Me? Vengeful? Nah!' Grace looked at his watch. 'I've just had an interesting time down at the town hall and the reference library. You're going to like this a lot. I think we are game, set and match on Norman Jecks. Fancy a lunchtime jar, and I'll tell you about it?'

'I would – but I have to dash out.'

'So what's your good news?'

The DS beamed. 'Actually, you know what, it's probably good news for you too.'

'The suspense is killing me.'

His beam broadening into the happiest smile Grace had seen on his friend's face in many months, Glenn Branson said, 'I've gotta go see a man about a horse.'

DEAD MAN'S FOOTSTEPS

Read on for an exclusive extract from the

new Detective Superintendent Roy Grace novel,

to be published by Macmillan in June 2008.

1

If Ronnie Wilson had known, as he woke up, that in just a couple of hours he would be dead, he would have planned his day somewhat differently.

For a start he might not have bothered to shave. Or wasted so many of those last precious minutes gelling his hair then messing around with it until he was satisfied. Nor would he have spent quite so long polishing his shoes or getting the knot of his expensive silk tie absolutely right. And he sure as hell would not have paid an exorbitant eighteen dollars – which he really could not afford – for the one-hour service to have his suit pressed.

To say that he was blissfully unaware of the fate awaiting him would be an exaggeration. All forms of joy had been absent from his canon of experiences for so long that he no longer had any idea what *bliss* was. He didn't even experience bliss any more in those fleeting final seconds of orgasm on the rare occasions when he and Lorraine still made love. It was as if his balls had become as numb as the rest of him.

In fact, recently – and somewhat to Lorraine's embarrassment – when people asked him how he was, he had taken to replying with a brief shrug of his shoulders and the words, 'My life is shit.'

The hotel room was shit too. It was so small that if you fell over you wouldn't even hit the floor. It was the cheapest room the W had, but at least the address helped him maintain appearances. If you stayed at the W in mid-town Manhattan, you were a *somebody*. Even if you were sleeping in the broom closet.

Ronnie knew he needed to get himself into a more positive mode – and mood. People responded to the vibes you gave out, particularly when you were asking for money. Nobody would give money to a loser. Not even an old friend – at least, not the kind of money he needed at this moment. And certainly not this particular old friend.

Checking out the weather, he peered through the window, craning his neck up the sheer grey cliff face of the building facing him across 39th Street until he could see the narrow slit of cobalt sky. The realization that it was a fine morning did nothing to lift his spirits. It merely felt as if all the clouds had drained out of that blue void and were now in his heart.

His fake TAG Heuer watch told him it was 7.43 a.m. He had bought it on the internet for forty pounds, but hey – who could tell it wasn't real? It looked like it cost ten thousand. He had learned a long time ago that expensive watches gave off an important message to people you were trying to impress: if you cared enough about a detail like time to buy one of the best watches in the world, then you would probably care just as much about the money they were going to entrust you with. Appearances weren't everything, but they mattered a lot.

7.43. Time to rock and roll.

He picked up his Louis Vuitton briefcase – also fake – placed it on top of his packed overnight bag and left his room, wheeling them behind him. Emerging from the elevator on the ground floor, he skulked past the front desk. His credit cards were so maxed out he probably didn't even have enough to settle the hotel bill, but he would have to worry about that later. His BMW – the swanky blue convertible that Lorraine like to drive around in, posing to her friends, was about to be repossessed, and the mortgage company was about to foreclose on his home. Today's meeting, he knew, grimly, was the last-chance saloon. A favour he was calling in. A ten-year-old favour.

A favour he hoped had not been forgotten.

*

Sitting on the subway, cradling his bags between his knees, Ronnie was aware something had gone wrong in his life, but he couldn't really put a finger on what exactly it was. All his contemporaries from school had gone on to become some kind of a success, leaving him floundering in their wake, getting increasingly desperate. Financial advisers, property developers, accountants, lawyers. They had their big-swinging-dick houses, their trophy wives, their kids to die for. What did he have? A neurotic bitch queen of a wife who spent the money he never had on endless beauty treatments she seriously did not need, on designer clothes they seriously could not afford, and picking up the tabs of absurdly expensive lunches of lettuce leaves and mineral water with her anorexic friends – who were all far richer than they were – in whatever happened to be the latest hip restaurant of the week.

But of course Ronnie was too proud to admit to Lorraine the mess he was in. And, ever the optimist, he always believed there was a solution just around the corner. A chameleon, he blended perfectly into his environments. As an estate agent he used to look pin-sharp, with a gift of the gab that was unfortunately better than his financial acumen. As that business went down the toilet, he had rapidly segued into property developing, where he used to look convincing in jeans and a blazer. Then, as the banks foreclosed on his twenty-home development which ran aground on planning issues, he reinvented himself yet again as a financial adviser to the rich. That business hit the buffers too.

Now he was here in the hope of convincing his old friend Joe Hatcook that he knew the secret of making money out of the new future golden goose, biodiesel. Joe was rumoured to have made north of a billion in derivatives – whatever they were – and had lost only a paltry couple of hundred thousand investing in Ronnie's failed estate agency business ten years ago – and, claiming to accept all Ronnie's reasons for the failed enterprise, assured Ronnie he would back him again one day.

Sure, Bill Gates and every other entrepreneur on the planet were looking for the way forward in the new, environmentally friendly biofuel market – and had the money to throw at it to make it happen – but Ronnie reckoned he had identified a niche. All he had to do this morning was convince Joe. And Joe was sharp, he'd see it. He'd get it. It ought to be – in New York parlance – a slam dunk.

In fact, the further the train headed downtown, while he mentally rehearsed his pitch to Joe, the more confident he became. He felt himself turning into the character Michael Douglas played in *Wall Street*. Gordon Gekko. And he sure looked the part. In his Brooks Brothers shirt, chalk-striped suit and tasselled loafers, he passed muster as an Ivy League New Yorker. Just like the dozen other sharply dressed Wall Street players sitting in this swaying carriage with him. If any of them had just half his troubles, they kept them well hidden. They all looked so damned confident. And if they bothered to glance at him, they would have seen a tall guy with lean good looks and slicked-back hair who looked equally confident, quietly beaming to himself, and flipping through a fifty-page business plan with coloured flow charts and all kinds of convincing looking graphs.

He had read somewhere that if you hadn't made it by the time you were forty, then you were never going to make it. And he was coming up to thirty-eight in just three weeks time.

And he was coming up to his station. Chambers Street.

He emerged into the fine Manhattan morning, and checked his bearings on the map the hotel concierge had given him last night. Then he looked at his watch. 8.10 a.m. From past experience at navigating New York office blocks, he reckoned he should allow himself a good fifteen minutes to get to Joe's office once he reached the man's building. It was also a good five-minute walk to get there from here the concierge had told him – and that was assuming he did not get lost.

Passing a sign informing him he was now on Wall Street, he walked past a Jamba Juice shop on his right, then a shop bearing the sign Expert Tailoring and Alterations, followed by the New York Dolls Gentleman's Club, then entered the packed Downtown Deli.

The place smelled of stewed coffee and frying eggs. He sat on a red-leather bar stool, and ordered freshly squeezed orange juice, a latte, scrambled eggs with a side order of bacon, and wheat toast. As he waited for his food, he flipped through the business plan once more. Then he looked at his watch, and mentally calculated the time difference between New York and Brighton, England.

England was five hours ahead. Lorraine would be having lunch. He gave her a quick call on her cell phone, told her he loved her. She wished him good luck in the meeting. He told her he loved her again, then hung up.

Twenty minutes later he paid the bill, stepped out into the street, and continued his journey towards Joe Hatcook's office, which, according to the information that had been emailed to him, was on the eighty-seventh floor of the South Tower of the World Trade Center.

It was 8.35 a.m. on the morning of Tuesday, 11 September 2001.

2

October 2006

Abby Dawson had chosen this flat because it felt secure. At least, inasmuch as she was ever going to feel secure *anywhere*.

Apart from the fire escape at the back, which could only be opened from inside, there was just one entrance. It was eight floors directly below her, and the windows gave her a clear view up and down the street.

Inside she had turned it into a fortress. There were panic buttons in each room. Unbreakable glass with locks on every window. Reinforced hinges, steel plating, three sets of deadlocks and safety chains on the front door and on the fire-escape door at the back of the tiny utility room. Any burglar trying to break in here was going to go home empty-handed. No one who wasn't driving a tank was going to get in unless she invited them.

But, just in case, as back-up she had canisters of pepper spray in easy reach in each room, a hunting knife and a baseball bat.

It was ironic, she thought, that, the first time in her life she was able to afford a home large and luxurious enough to entertain guests, she had to live here on her own in secrecy. For however long it took to be free of him.

And there was so much to like about this place. The dark teak floors, the huge sofas, home-cinema television, the high-tech kitchen, the massive, deliciously comfortable

Dux beds, and the even bigger bathroom with the shower which turned into an aroma-therapy steam room, and the sharp, modern art on the walls. It was like living in one of the designer pads she used to covet on the pages of glossy magazines. On fine days the afternoon sun streamed in and on blustery days, like today, when she opened a window she could lick salt off the air and hear the cries of gulls. Just a couple of hundred yards beyond the end of the street and the junction with Kemp Town's busy Marine Parade was the beach. She could walk along it for miles to the east or west.

She liked the neighbourhood too. Small shops close by: safer than going into a large supermarket because she could always check who was in there first. All it needed was for one person to recognize her.

Just one.

The only negative was the lift. Extremely claustro-phobic at the best of times, and recently more prone than ever to panic attacks, she never liked to ride in any lift alone unless she absolutely had to. And the tiny, jerky capsule the size of a vertical two-seater coffin, which serviced her flat and had got stuck a couple of times in the past month – fortunately with someone else in it – was one of the worst she had ever experienced.

So, up until the past couple of weeks, when the work-men renovating the flat below hers had turned the staircase into an obstacle course, she normally walked up and down, which was fine – it was good exercise, and if she had some heavy shopping bags, well, that was easy, she would send them up in the lift on their own, and climb the stairs – except on the very rare occasions she encountered one of her neighbours and had to ride shoulder to shoulder with them. But most of them were so old they never went out much. Some seemed as old as this mansion block itself.

The few younger residents, like Hassan the smiling Iranian banker who lived two floors below her and sometimes threw all-night parties – the invites to which she always politely declined – seemed to be away, somewhere else, most of the time. And at weekends, unless Hassan was in residence, this whole west wing of the block was so silent it seemed it was inhabited only by ghosts.

And in a way she was a ghost too, she knew. Only leaving the safety of her lair after dark, her once long blonde hair cropped short and dyed black, sunglasses on her face, jacket collar turned up, a stranger in this city where she had once been a business studies student, where she had once worked in bars, done temporary secretarial jobs, had boyfriends, and, before the travel bug hit her, even fantasized she would raise a family.

And now she was back. In hiding. A stranger in her own life. Desperate not to be recognized by anyone. Turning her face away on the rare occasions when she passed someone she knew. Or saw an old friend in a bar and immediately had to leave. Goddammit, she was lonely!

And scared.

And not even her parents, brother or sister knew she was back in England.

Just turned twenty-nine three days ago – and that was some birthday party, she thought ironically. Getting smashed up here on her own, with a bottle of Moet and Chandon, an erotic movie on Sky and a vibrator with a dead battery.

She used to pride herself on her natural good looks. Brimful of confidence she could go out to any bar, any party, and have the pick of the crop. She was good at chatting, good at laying on the charm, good at playing vulnerable, which long back she had understood was what guys liked. But now she was vulnerable for real and she was really not enjoying that. Not enjoying having to stick on false nails to cover her own, which were bitten down to the quick.

Not enjoying being a fugitive.

The shelves, tables and floors of the flat were piled high with books, CDs and DVDs, ordered from Amazon and from Play.com. During the past two months she had read more books, seen more films, watched more television than ever before in her life.

She had come back because she thought she would be safe here. That this was the one place where he would not dare show his face. The only place on the planet. But she could not be sure.

She closed *Sussex Life* magazine, in which she had been browsing dream country houses, crushed out her cigarette, drained her glass of Sauvignon and began her pre-exit checks.

An old flame some years back, Phil Homan, used to take her places in a helicopter. She remembered sitting beside him in the cockpit of the blue four-seater Robinson as he went through his pre-flight checks from a printed list he held in his hand. And that's what she was doing now in a way, her pre-flight checks. Except after four months she didn't need to look at her list, she knew them by heart.

First she walked to the window and peered down through the blinds at the wide street of Regency terraced houses. The sodium glow of the street lights bled orange into every shadow. It was dark enough, with a howling autumn equinox gale blasting rain as hard as buckshot against the window panes; tomorrow night the clocks would go back, making the evenings even darker still. As a child she used to be scared of the dark. Now, ironically, it made her feel safe.

She knew all the cars that were regularly parked on both sides, with their residents' parking stickers. Ran her eyes over each of them. She used not to be able to tell one make from another, but now she knew them all. The grimy, bird-shit-spattered black Golf GTI. The Ford Galaxy people carrier belonging to a couple in a flat across the street who had grizzly twins and seemed to spend their lives lugging shopping and collapsible strollers up and down their front steps. The odd little Toyota Yaris. An elderly Porsche Boxster belonging to a young man she had decided was a doctor – who probably worked at the nearby Royal Sussex County Hospital. And another dozen or so cars, all of whose owners she knew by sight. Nothing new down there, nothing to be concerned about. And no one lurking in the shadows.

A couple, arms linked, were hurrying by with a bloated umbrella threatening, at any moment, to turn inside out.

Window locks in bedroom, spare bedroom, bathroom, living/dining room. Activate timers on lights, television and radio in each room in turn. Check CCTV cameras activated in each room and tape running. Blu-Tack single cotton thread, knee high, across the hallway just inside the front door.

Paranoid? Moi? You'd better believe it!

She'd learned how to take care of herself from watching *CSI*, reading crime novels, surfing websites. And plain common sense.

She tugged her long mackintosh and umbrella from the hooks in the narrow hallway, stepped over the thread and peered through the spyhole. The dull yellow fish-eye glow of the empty landing greeted her. And the scratched grey metal door of the lift.

She unhooked the safety chain, opened the door cautiously, then stepped out, and smelled the boiled vegetable smell of old people's cooking. Then she closed it behind her and turned the keys in turn in each of the three deadlocks.

Then she stood, listening. Somewhere downstairs, in one of the other flats, a phone was ringing unanswered. Friday night. She shivered, pulling her fleece-lined mac around her, still not used to the damp cold after years of living in the sunshine. Still not used to spending a Friday night alone. But she couldn't be a recluse forever. Approaching thirty, single, and uncomfortably aware of her biological clock ticking away, she knew she had to try to get her life back. Step by step.

Her plan tonight was to catch a movie at the multiplex in the Marina, *Notes on a Scandal* with Cate Blanchett and Judi Dench, and grab a bite to eat – a quick bowl of pasta – then, if she had the courage, go to a bar for a couple of glasses of wine and at least feel the comfort of mingling with other humans. Maybe the Karma bar, which she had walked past and liked the look of. Although she knew that when she got there she probably would not feel brave enough to go in.

Dressed discreetly, in designer jeans, ankle-length boots, and a black, knitted polo neck beneath the coat, wanting to look nice if she did go into a bar but not to draw attention to herself, she opened the fire door to the stair-well, and saw to her dismay that, despite her call to the bolshy caretaker – who lived in another block nearby – the workmen had left the stairwell blocked for the weekend with lengths of plasterboard and a whole pile of timber.

Cursing them, she debated whether to try to stumble her way through it all, then, thinking better of it, she pressed the button for the lift. And seconds later heard it clanking, jerking, bumping obediently upwards, reaching her floor with a jarring clang, before the door slid open with a sound like a shovel smoothing gravel.

She stepped in and the door closed again with the same sound, enclosing her. She breathed in the smell of someone else's perfume and lemon-scented cleaning fluid. The lift jerked upwards a few inches, so sharply she almost fell over.

And now, too late to change her mind and get out, with the metal walls pressing in around her and a small, almost opaque mirror reflecting her mostly invisible face, they lunged sharply downwards.

She was about to realize she had just made the worst mistake of her life.

extracts reading groups
competitions books new
discounts extracts
competitions
new
events books
new
interviews
discounts
new books events
events new
discounts extracts discounts
www.panmacmillan.com
extracts events reading groups
competitions books extracts new